BOYS
CAN'T BE
WITCHES

Published by Clockwork Dragon Books
www.clockworkdragon.net

First printing, March 2018

Boys Can't Be Witches is a work of fiction sited in a fictional version of the Pacific Northwest. People, places, and incidents are either products of the author's mind or used fictitiously. No endorsement of any kind should be inferred by existing locations or organizations within it.

No horses, dogs, teenagers, dragons, displaced gods, or witches were harmed in the making of this books. The ghosts, on the other hand, were curb-stomped.

ISBN: 978-1-944334-24-6

BOYS
CAN'T BE
WITCHES

LEE FRENCH

Spirit Knights book 5

Clockwork
Dragon
Books

Acknowledgments

Special thanks Stefan and Gabrielle for their incredible performances in bringing the characters to life for the audio versions of this entire series. I met them by pure chance and have never regretted entrusting Spirit Knights to them.

PROLOGUE

Iulia

Dwight hovered an inch above brown grass inside a secluded pocket created by evergreen trees. Rain passed through him to turn the already muddy ground into spongy soup. The standing headstones sheltered in this area of a vast Portland cemetery all bore his family name, Evans. The death dates ran as early as 1893.

"He didn't even get me a proper burial," Dwight grumbled. Tiny bursts of color flickered over the surface of his ghostly mist as he gained power from a fresh memory. One swirl revealed the plaid of his red and black flannel shirt, another the dried blood staining his faded jeans.

Iulia wished she could slap him. Her form remained bound inside his, and she had to humor him if she wanted to keep him from trying to dominate her again. Their psychic stalemate—his brute force matched against her wits—meant she could still accomplish her goals.

First, she wanted her body back. Claire and her little witch boy had ruined everything. Twice. She'd knock Claire out of her body and take control of the boy. Dwight would deal with Justin, then he could handle whatever other Knights still lurked in the area, if any. Then no one would know anything about her and she could do as she pleased.

She needed more power. So far, they'd spent time drifting through the local cemeteries, devouring a ghost here or there. In those early few days after Claire took Iulia's body, they'd found plenty. They'd lurked near a few hospitals and elder care facilities. The result had given them enough to gain control over one person. Iulia had yet to select and dominate that person.

Somehow, Iulia needed to cause a great deal of death. The more people she could kill in one fell swoop, the better. She'd gorge on the power and take back her body.

If she dominated a witch, everything got easier. To find a witch, she knew she could follow the local Knight bloodlines. Some of the women had to have the gift. She recalled someone in Justin's family meddling with her efforts, which had destroyed all her plans after Claire died. Best to avoid his family. She didn't think she should look into Claire's side either, because the infuriating girl would probably notice. That left one clear option.

"I have a new idea. How would we find Drew's extended family? Specifically, his mother or aunts?"

Dwight rubbed his chin. "The internet, I guess."

"I fail to see how fishing will help us locate people."

"What? No, not a net, a computer. We gotta find someone who can use one for us. Maybe at the library. That was where Justin always did stuff for school. At least, that's what the brat told me." Dwight growled. "Probably was really out running with that girl he married. I'm gonna enjoy dealing with her after I take his body."

Shying away from the idea of Dwight's repugnant plans for Justin's wife, Iulia chose to assume libraries had a different function than the ones in her time. They'd never included ancestries that she'd seen. "To a library then." He'd proven more receptive when she acted deferential to him, so she added, "Please."

"Sure." He drifted through the trees, startling a pair of joggers on the nearby path. The woman screamed, and the man fell to the ground. Laughing at them, Dwight kept going.

At this point, Iulia had given up trying to convince Dwight to avoid being seen. He enjoyed violence too much to care. As soon as she regained her body, she planned to leave Portland to him. The world had plenty of space, and she wanted to see Antium again. If her home still existed, she would take it by whatever means necessary.

They flowed down a street lined with skeletal trees. People rushed past with hoods covering their heads, not paying attention to their surroundings. Day by day, Iulia grew accustomed to this time. Everything about it had overwhelmed her at first. Fierce determination had won her what she'd accomplished so far.

The building where they stopped looked like all the other buildings to Iulia. Dwight passed through a white wall and into a bright room full of books on shelves with some sort of vomit-colored floor covering. Modern people had odd ideas about aesthetic beauty.

"Those are computers," Dwight said, pointing to a cluster of gleaming boxes and other alien things.

"Fine, just get someone to look up Drew Sanders and find women related to him. Pretend he's your nephew, or something of the sort." She waited while he approached a desk covered with more boxes and books and brightly colored papers strewn with English words.

A poster on the wall showed a volcanic eruption with more text at the bottom. Once, Iulia had prevented Mount Vesuvius from erupting. Another time, she'd forced open and directed an unnamed vent in the ocean floor to kill a giant squid. The people of Syracuse had praised her vainglory of a husband for it.

"Excuse me," Dwight said.

A woman in a maroon sweater smiled without looking away from her box. "How can I help you?"

"I need some help finding some people on the computers."

The woman flicked her gaze to him. She blinked. Her mouth fell open. "Oh my God. You're a...a..."

"A ghost, yes, ma'am." Dwight smiled. "I can't use the keyboard, you know? I'd like to find some of my family, but I can only remember one name. Can you give me a hand with that?"

Iulia had to admit Dwight could be charming when he wanted. He acted like he wanted to sweep the woman off her feet and hand-feed her roast dormice with the finest olives and wine.

The woman blinked at him. "Were you there when that cop fought those giant bugs downtown?"

"Don't say yes," Iulia said, sure his ego would try to claim any glory he could. "She'll want to hear all about it, and that takes time."

"No, ma'am. I'm just trying to reunite with family."

Her movements stiff and disjointed, the woman nodded. She cleared her throat and tapped on her keyboard. "You have a name you wanted to look up?"

"Drew Sanders. He's a teenager. Looking for his mom or aunt. They're my cousins."

While Dwight and the woman discussed finding Drew's relatives, Iulia thought of Antium. She wanted to walk on the beach again. She wanted to claim the glory her wretched, arrogant, egotistical, pig-headed husband had always stolen from her and his men. She wanted to find statues of that ass and destroy them.

"Thank you, ma'am," Dwight said. "I appreciate your time and effort. Wish me luck talking to her."

"Good luck," the woman said.

Iulia didn't need luck. Luck was for fools. She only needed power.

And her body. She needed her body back.

CHAPTER 1

CLAIRE

Claire opened her eyes in the gloom of her chilly bedroom, not sure what had awakened her. Muted gray light seeped around the edges of thin, brown curtains covering her closed window. The subtle red-gold glow of the locket face in her right hand, replacing the flesh, blood, and bone of her palm in a heart shape made of whorls and dots, did nothing to pierce a murky morning in Vancouver, Washington.

She didn't want to think about how the locket face wound up like that. Dying hadn't been fun, and neither had taking Iulia's body. If she avoided thinking about it, she could pretend she didn't have a demesne, which let her pretend she was normal. Sort of.

On the wooden nightstand, Enion, her tiny silver dragon, slept silently on a fluffy pillow inside a doorless, decorated bird cage. Drew lay beside her, his breathing slow and quiet. His possessed dog, Mutt, snored softly at their feet, proving a blazing inferno of heat.

"C'mon, Claire," Justin said, his voice muffled by the door. He knocked, his knuckles rapping three times on the hollow wood. "And

Drew. Let's go. Time to get up."

Drew groaned and rolled over. Mutt raised his head and smacked his jaws together, licking the edges of his mouth. Enion huffed.

"It's the first day of Christmas vacation," Claire said. She whined and knew it and didn't care.

"Yes it is," Justin said, sounding more like a stern dad than usual. "And everyone else is up already. You've slacked off on your Knight duties enough since Thanksgiving. It's time to get back to work now that you don't have to worry about school for a few weeks. And Drew needs to get up and come with us."

Drew rubbed his eyes. "We shouldn't have to worry about school at all," he grumbled, too soft for Justin to overhear.

"Go away," Claire snapped at the door. She draped an arm over her eyes, the soft cotton of her long-sleeved nightshirt brushing her cheek.

"You have ten minutes to get moving," Justin said. "Then I'm coming in with a bucket of ice water."

She heard his footsteps recede. "Jerk."

Drew sat up and raked a hand through his unruly mop of red curls. "He'll do it," he said through a yawn. "I believe him." His hand collected a layer of blue ice. He grimaced and shook it out, the ice disappearing. Little lapses like that kept happening with his power, especially when he was tired. Neither of them knew what to do about it.

Mutt jumped to the floor. "It's cold! Master, I need to go outside."

"That's even colder," Claire mumbled.

"Just a minute, Mutt." Drew leaned over Claire and planted a soft kiss on her lips. "Get up."

Lifting her arm, Claire saw Drew reaching over her for his glasses on the nightstand. He smiled at her.

Enion stepped out of his cage to shove the glasses at Drew's hand. "Boy go. Take dog."

Claire snorted and grinned at her dragon. No one else could understand Enion, or any of the other dragons in his flight. Enion in particular took advantage of that fact to say uncharitable things about the boy he considered a rival for Claire's affection.

She watched Drew rub under Enion's chin and wanted to lie around for the next two weeks. Listening to Drew read a book aloud sounded like a good way to pass time. Add hot cocoa and blankets, and it would be a perfect day.

She yawned. "Coming back for breakfast, or are you going to hide?"

"Hide my ghost-possessed butt from a trained, experienced ghost hunter? Sure. How could that possibly go wrong?"

"Master, I really need to go outside."

Drew sighed. "Yeah, yeah." He climbed over Claire to stand up and slide his feet into his fluffy slippers. His dark green T-shirt had " $\sqrt{-1}$ 8 Σ Π and it was delicious" printed on the front, and it matched his pajama pants. "See you over breakfast."

"Yeah," Claire said. "Gimme about half an hour."

Mist issued from Drew's body to spin around him and Mutt. The fog concealed them, then dispersed with both Drew and Mutt gone. He'd used the mist to teleport them elsewhere, a trick he'd gotten good at over the past few weeks. The fog left a frigid, damp chill behind, making Claire wish she could roll over and snuggle in the blankets for a while longer.

Enion flew to the door and sat beside it. "Claire get up now. Hungry."

"Working on it." She flipped the covers aside and forced herself up.

Her feet touched the floor, and she hissed at the chill settled on the bare wood. "This room needs a rug," she muttered. "Or better heating." At least she got to sleep in her own room in the cottage these days. Fixing the roof after an explosion caused by her death had been a major project, and they'd only finished it a week ago.

She stood and opened the door for Enion. The dragon darted out. Justin's young daughters would coo over him like they always did and feed him fruit and oatmeal. How that dragon survived on tiny amounts of food when he could shift his body to the size of a horse, she didn't understand. Maybe he ate trees when she wasn't paying attention.

Shutting the door again, she looked for her slippers and didn't see them. She gave up and rummaged through the drawers of her new dresser for clothes. Justin had applied his carpentry skills to building it for her, and it worked fine. With everything he did to make her feel welcome in his home and family, she did owe him at least the decency of trying to help him handle the repercussions of their shared actions in destroying the only thing keeping ghosts from roaming the Earth en masse.

Since that had happened, she'd seen a total two ghosts, and one of them had been herself. As for the second, she thought Dwight's ghost had been destroyed when she took Iulia's body. Giant mutant ants and cockroaches had proved a much bigger problem than an unrealized, overblown threat of ghostpocalypse. Those things had smashed buildings and spat concrete-eating acid.

She trudged to the cottage's one bathroom and commandeered it for a shower. Over the past few weeks, she'd gotten used to the idea of having someone else's body with her own face still staring back at her in the mirror. The strange scars still tripped her up, though. Iulia had been through a lot for someone in her early twenties.

In her sixteen years, Claire had only acquired a few random marks.

Iulia's body had stretchmarks, three thin white lines from blade wounds, two round, ragged messes from an arrow through her leg, and a collection of burn scars. Normal clothes concealed all of it, so she hadn't had to explain anything to her teachers. Except the loss of muscle mass. Her gym teacher had thankfully bought Claire's lie about the flu over Thanksgiving vacation. He'd been helping her with strength training since then.

The locket hand had been a special problem, of course. She'd gotten through school so far by wearing stretch gloves with the fingers snipped open. When the weather turned warm again, she'd have to come up with some other solution. Everyone at school talked about the cop who'd looked straight in the camera and told everyone magic is real. They chattered about glimpses of ghosts, a car driving itself, men with swords, and dragons.

For one brief, shining moment, Claire had considered revealing her locket and Enion. People would fawn over her. They would pay her to ride a dragon. She imagined having a pile of money, her own house, and...no privacy, ever again. In stories, regular people always wanted the ones with magic to solve their problems for them.

She didn't want to solve everyone else's problems. She had enough of her own.

Claire showered and dressed. By the time she entered the large, open space serving as kitchen, living room, and dining room, Justin's wife, Marie, had already left for her part-time job. Justin sat on the couch with their two girls, reading aloud a simple story about unicorns. Lisa, the five-year-old, glanced at Claire and gave her a tiny wave. Her little sister, Missy, didn't notice her.

They'd both heard the story five thousand times but still hung on every word when Daddy rumbled them.

Drew sipped orange juice at the kitchen table. Claire saw neither Mutt nor Enion. That wasn't strange for breakfast.

She sat across from Drew, who pushed a bowl of cereal at her. He poured milk into her bowl, as well as his own. He'd waited for her.

They sat, crunching and slurping without speaking. The silence felt comfortable and companionable, like it always did with Drew. Since they'd started sleeping in the same bed, everything felt right with Drew. Claire still changed her clothes without letting him watch, though. She didn't feel ready to cross that line with him. Justin had asked them to wait until she finished high school, and she had no problem with the request.

"Daddy." Lisa poked Justin in the arm. "Are you going out again today?"

"Yes, Pumpkin."

"Is Claire going to watch us?"

"No, you'll stay with Grandma and Grandpa. Claire is coming with me. So is Drew. You two should go get dressed."

Lisa heaved a melodramatic sigh. "That's not fair! I want to play with Claire."

"Claire!" Missy jumped up and down on her father's thigh. Her platinum blonde hair, the same color as her mother's, fluffed and flounced. "I want Claire!"

Claire grinned, pleased to be wanted. Only three months ago, no one had wanted her except Drew. Now she had two little sisters, a mom and dad, two grandparents, an aunt, and a flight of dragons, all eager to spend time with her.

"We'll play later," she told the girls. "First, we have to go work.

Dad's a bigtime slavedriver, right?" She still felt weird calling him Dad, especially with him only eight years older than her, but she kept trying. He and Marie had adopted her, after all.

Justin chuckled.

Lisa crossed her arms in a remarkable echo of her mother, complete with their shared platinum blonde hair wisping around her head. "You promise we'll play later?"

"I promise," Claire said, raising her hand in a solemn oath. "Not sure exactly when, but definitely before bedtime."

"Okay." Lisa climbed off her dad and dragged Missy with her to their bedroom.

Justin rose to his full six feet of brawny, broad-shouldered height and watched them go. He tucked the girls' worn, battered book into a bookshelf beside their white toy chest. "I'll meet you outside when you're done."

Claire nodded. "Are we driving?" She hadn't been able to practice driving much while in foster care, and only had her permit. Any opportunity to take out a vehicle sounded good to her.

"Ride dragons if you want," Justin said. "It's cold enough that you can bundle up so no one recognizes you. The other option is walking because Marie took the truck."

Riding dragons around the city sounded even better than driving and a great way to start the day. Claire devoured her cereal as fast as she could, eager to get outside.

CHAPTER 2

DREW

Riding a dragon sounded a thousand times more incredible than the reality of it. Drew leaned low over the neck of a dragon named Rhubark with his eyes screwed shut, trusting the horse-sized creature to follow Enion and Claire as they soared over Portland. He'd never before seen the city from above. Not that he saw it on this flight. Wind buffeted him. He wore his hat low, with his scarf covering his face to protect his skin from random debris. Below them, Justin rode Tariel, his white horse, through the city streets.

At least he had winter clothes. He wore a sweater under his coat and wool socks under his jeans and hiking boots. When Grandpa Jack and Grandma Tammy had taken him in two months ago, they'd let him have spending money for the first time in his life. He'd blown it all on new clothes and shoes. Finally, after all the years in foster care, everything fit, nothing had holes or patches, and he felt warm in the winter.

Except now. None of his clothes had been intended for flying one hundred miles per hour at two hundred feet up with snow threatening to fall any moment. As a bonus, his power seemed to make everything a thousand times worse. He tried to use it to warm himself and made his teeth chatter instead.

Rhubark angled into a dive. Drew clung to the dragon's neck, cursing the choice to ride one. He could've used mist to get wherever Justin wanted to go, but he thought this way would be fun. For once, being recognized with a dragon didn't matter. Unfortunately, taking off had left behind his stomach, the air wanted to rip off his flesh, and he couldn't feel his legs.

Kay, the spirit possessing Drew, said, "I'm pretty sure this is the opposite of fun." No one else heard the voice in his head.

Though he could communicate with Kay by thinking at him, Drew preferred to stick to talking out loud. Keeping it internal made him squeamish about the whole idea of sharing his body with another being. They had an agreement, but Drew knew the terms had come mostly from Kay's fear of Claire. If Claire ever died again, there would be another negotiation.

He meant to do everything in his power to keep her alive this time.

Rhubark landed. Drew groaned with the jarring impact and fell off the dragon's back. He landed on solid ground with a grunt.

"Are you okay?" Claire asked.

Drew opened his eyes to see her crouching beside him. Her green hat and scarf kept her dark hair from falling forward.

"No?" He pushed up his glasses and rubbed his eyes with gloved hands. Ice crystals fell from his eyelashes. "Am I dead? I feel dead."

Claire raised an eyebrow at him and smirked. "I doubt that."

"Smooth," Kay said. "Really smooth."

Drew coughed. "I meant I'm cold. Freezing. Like a cor—" He

sighed as the image of Claire's dead body came to mind. "Sorry. Never mind. It's just, this would probably be more fun in the summer."

"I guess so. For you, anyway. The sprite bond protects Justin and me." Claire twitched her mouth with annoyance. "Should've thought of that."

"It's okay. No big deal." Drew took her hand and let her help him sit up. Headstones, grass, and leafless trees surrounded them. Tiny, glowing worms of green magic writhed on the lawn, all wriggling in slow motion toward the nearest ley line. Justin sat astride Tariel nearby in his chain armor and jeans, keeping watch over the group. Enion sat beside Rhubark, the dragon pair rumbling at each other in deep, resonant chirps.

"Why are we in a cemetery?" Drew asked.

"I can't imagine why anyone looking for ghosts would check places where corpses are collected," Justin said.

Claire grinned and helped him stagger to his feet.

"This one is clear," Justin said. "Charlie said he's up to his eyeballs in ghosts in the Olympia area, but we're still in Portland city limits. Avery probably has time to patrol here. I'm willing to bet he spends most of his time on the east side of the city, though. Let's hit Mount Calvary next, and the smaller ones near there."

Drew nodded. Then he remembered which other cemeteries they'd find and liked this outing even less. "Maybe we should split up. More efficient."

"As the one with actual experience doing the less exciting parts of this job, I think that's a terrible idea." Justin offered his gauntleted hand to Drew. "You can ride with me instead of on that dragon."

Claire flashed concern at Drew. "What's wrong?" she murmured.

He waved Justin off and shook his head. "I'm fine. I'll meet you at

Mount Calvary."

"Suit yourself." Justin patted Tariel's neck and they lurched into a gallop.

Claire draped her arm over Drew's shoulders. "What's bothering you?"

The words refused to blurt out of Drew's mouth. "Nothing."

"Sure." She didn't believe him. He could tell by the way she quirked her eyebrow.

"Ever since I got bound as your guardian, I'm not wild about cemeteries." Lying to her made his chest tighten, but he did it anyway. Seeing his parents' graves today sounded worse than the dragon ride.

"I have no idea why you don't just give her the goods," Kay said. "Something something relationships and mutual trust."

"Shut up, Kay."

"Yeah," Claire said. "Shut up, Kay." She set a hand on Drew's shoulder and met his gaze. "If you really want to go home, you should. We don't need your help to do this, and you don't have to learn about it. I do, but you don't. You're not a Knight."

She made him feel like a coward. Claire faced danger without flinching. Drew couldn't do that. Not even when he'd crushed ants with his mind had he been confident enough to tackle things on his own. Having Claire by his side had made all the difference in the world.

Maybe he needed to stop avoiding the training he'd promised himself he'd get. Confidence came from competence, or so people said. Even if it didn't, he'd learn to control his still-new witch power.

Claire had control over her stuff. Drew didn't.

He rubbed his glove over his forehead, wishing he could massage his power into obedience. "You're right. I'm going to go see if Anne is around. That's a lot more important if I'm ever going to be useful to you."

She kissed the tip of his nose. "You're useful to me, just not necessary for this. Big difference."

"You know what I mean."

"Yep." She smiled at him. It reached her eyes and made him reconsider leaving.

No, he had to get this started. The sooner he begged Anne to help him, the sooner he'd be a full witch. The stupid slip-ups with his power would stop happening. "I'll see you later, at home."

"Take Rhubark." She gestured for the dragon to come closer. "Rhubark, go small and stick with Drew. Keep him safe."

The dragon flashed silver and became the size of a small cat. He flapped to Drew's shoulder and sat, his tail swishing across Drew's back.

Protests sat in Drew's throat, unwilling to spill free. He didn't want to argue with her over something this dumb. Instead of trying to remove the dragon, he flashed her a smile he hoped didn't reveal how defeated he felt and spun out mist.

CHAPTER 3

CLAIRE

Riding a dragon around the city proved far less enjoyable than Claire expected. Brief bursts of euphoric flight punctuated long rambles through dead, empty graveyards. Handfuls of people pointed at her and Enion along the way. She followed Justin's example and waved to them like some kind of hero.

Had any of them come to mourn people killed by the giant mutant bugs she'd accidentally unleashed on the city? She hoped not.

Enion loped around yet another cemetery with no roaming ghosts. Claire waved to Justin from across a field dotted with death, then the dragon leaped into the air again. Ten seconds later, they landed in the next one. She kept looking for Leeloo too, because Enion had reported the other dragon missing this morning.

Over and over, they found nothing. Magic seemed thin, but that sounded good, not bad.

They circled to the east side of Portland, flying over clusters of cookie cutter houses separated by frosted green spaces, and wound up in

Troutdale while light snow fell. Claire patted Enion to make him stop in front of a cluster of standing stones carved with her parents' and brother's names. Tariel paused beside him.

Snowflakes perched on blades of green grass. Gray, leafless tree branches reached for the sky like claws. Silence pressed on Claire's shoulders, urging her to feel something.

"Do you need a few minutes?" Justin asked.

Claire stared at the names. She remembered nothing about these people. Her father's corrupted ghost had taken the place of the dad she couldn't recall. Mom and Tyler existed as vague shapes. She felt nothing for them. At some point, she must have loved them and cared about them, but now...empty.

"No. I'm kind of curious who they were, I suppose." She noticed the other stones. One grave beside her parents and brother had the same last name as her, Terdan, while the rest in the cluster had a different one, Marius. "I guess I'm part Italian, or whatever that name is. Is ancestry hard to look up?"

"I don't know." His words came out clipped and forced. "I've never been all that curious about my family. My parents never kept in touch with them."

She frowned, not sure if she should pry. He didn't sound like he wanted to talk about it. Tracing the names on the stones with her gaze, she fretted about putting him in a bad mood for the girls. But if his memories still held enough anger and pain to make him close off like this, maybe he needed to be poked. The social workers always said to let feelings out and not bottle them.

He'd done so much for her that she thought she ought to give back when she could. Even if he didn't like the gifts she gave.

"You know, I never told you about what we saw when we faced your dad's ghost."

"Tariel, let's move on." Justin turned toward the road.

The horse grumbled and stood firm.

Justin scowled at her. "I do not."

"It was one memory," Claire said, hoping that might convince him to hear her out. "Just one. I don't think he recalled a second before we blew him up."

He grunted in the back of his throat. "Fine. What was it?"

"He was in a kitchen with floral print wallpaper and a cheap, plastic table. Breakfast included some kind of alcohol."

"Whiskey, and you'll have to get more specific than that." Justin crossed his arms and glared at the trees in the distance. "Because that sounds like every morning."

"There was blood on the floor."

"Still not specific enough."

Claire recoiled from the idea that he had multiple memories with blood on the floor in his own kitchen. He'd turned out pretty well for a guy with that in his past. Still, she didn't want to ruin his day.

"Never mind. It's not a big deal."

"No. You started this. Finish it."

She'd never seen him so hard and cold. Even when he'd been possessed for a day before Thanksgiving, he'd still tried to do the right thing, and he'd thought his actions would save her. He'd just been confused about what "the right thing" meant.

Knowing he wouldn't hurt her on purpose kept her from fearing him, but she didn't know how he'd react to being pushed too hard. Would adding more detail push him, though, or would refusing to?

"Bad thing," Enion murmured. His muscles tensed.

Claire patted her dragon's neck and decided to picture the fight with Iulia and Dwight. "It was spatter. Blood spatter on the floor. Beer in the fridge. He wore jeans and a T-shirt. Said his 'lousy, good-for-nothing wife' cooked for him there. Called you a brat. An ungrateful brat."

Justin snorted without amusement. "That probably would've been the time he beat my mother to death in front of me. No arrest because that Dwight is a stand-up guy. She must've provoked him, you know. A one-hundred-pound, five-foot-three babysitter made him hit her. Besides, she would've been fine if she'd just called for an ambulance. Never mind that the phone had been smashed to pieces. She must've dropped it, the silly girl."

Horrified, Claire could see why Justin didn't like cops much. "A stand-up guy?"

"He ran the bar at a bowling alley where a bunch of cops played in a league. Bought them a pizza every week. I went to work with him sometimes, and he wouldn't let me have even a handful of pretzels."

"So, it's kind of good he's dead."

"You could say that. I'm thankful my daughters never met him. All three of them."

In a way, Claire had met Dwight, but she chose not to mention it. Justin had called her his daughter. Every time he did that, she wanted to hug him, forgive anything, and spare him whatever she could.

"Maybe we should go home."

Tariel whickered.

Justin nodded. "Go ahead. I'm going to take a ride."

Claire didn't know if she'd pushed too hard or not. He didn't seem mad at her, but he looked like he wanted to punch something. She didn't blame him. Some of her foster parents had acted like they could murder someone they loved. Having that kind of person for his father must've been a thousand times worse than living with one for a few months.

"I'm sorry."

He sighed and shook his head. "It's fine. Let's go, Tariel. Take the long way home. Don't stay out too late."

Tariel carried him away, her hooves chiming once they reached the pavement. Claire watched until they disappeared from sight. Marie would know what to do. She'd mention it to her adoptive mom and let her sort out Justin.

She returned her attention to the headstones, wondering what it meant that they generated nothing more than curiosity in her. Did that make her a bad person? Had her time as a ghost permanently erased those memories?

Why did she have such a stark line between things she remembered and things she didn't? Her memories began with the funeral as if she'd been born as a ten-year-old that day. Gaps and blurry spots remained, but she felt the reality of time having passed through them. The empty space before the funeral didn't exist.

The things she remembered saying to her father's Phasm didn't make sense to her anymore. They spoke of a shared history. Claire no longer had one with anybody but Drew.

"Go home?" Enion asked.

"Yeah. Let's go."

CHAPTER 4

DREW

Anne wasn't home. Drew waited for five minutes, then shifted into her living room. He saw no signs of foul play, leading him to believe she'd probably stepped out to the store or her part-time job. She had a life, and he had no right to get annoyed with her about it.

"Time to go see Sophie?" Kay asked.

"I guess so." Drew pictured her golden hair and soft smile. She'd been nice to him.

The dragon chirped. Drew needed to get rid of Rhubark so he didn't tell Claire about Sophie. Claire would get all kinds of wrong ideas. She'd punch him in the face before he had a chance to explain.

Kay made a noise of mild discomfort. "I'm just going to point out Claire's a real bearcat. Doublecrossing her for some doll with pouty lips wouldn't be the smartest thing you ever did."

Some of the words Kay used sounded funny in Drew's head, but he got the idea. "Rhubark, why don't you go home? There's nothing dangerous here."

Rhubark dug his tiny claws into Drew's shoulder and shook his head. He chirped a storm of scolding at Drew.

"I'm going to guess that means you won't leave because Claire told you to stay."

The dragon nodded.

"Great. Hunker down, then, because we're about to do some boring stuff." Drew patted the dragon's head.

"You sure you want to see Sophie?" Kay asked.

"I have no intention of seeing her."

"You're going to look at her with your eyes. And probably drool or say something dumb. Maybe both."

Drew scowled. "I'm allowed to think a girl is pretty without wanting to date her."

"I'm sure none of this has anything to do with the fact you haven't mentioned her to Claire."

Guilt tightened Drew's chest. "She's not a witch, and I kind of needed to do the school thing, so it never came up. I don't just randomly spew everything at her."

"Sure. Keep telling yourself that."

"Shut up, Kay." He spun out mist and shifted to the front porch of Sophie's house.

Strings of unlit, multicolored Christmas lights hugged the house frame and shrubs, and a smiling, orange and black witch with a Santa hat hung from a hook on the door. Raising his fist to knock, Drew imagined Sophie's mom answering the door.

She'd beat him with a broom. It would hurt, because he'd try to explain that he didn't sleep with her daughter, he just accidentally stole her power. Which was worse, of course. He didn't think she'd try to kill him, at least. Probably.

Kay huffed. "Either knock or let's go wait for Anne."

Drew stepped back from the door. He'd grown up in this house. From his one brief glimpse inside, he knew they hadn't changed the floor plan. They'd repainted and replaced some of the flooring, but the walls remained.

"I see what you're thinking," Kay said. "Before you do it, let's take a moment to appreciate how stupid this plan is."

Ignoring Kay, he pictured the upstairs hallway and used mist to move himself there. All five doors stood open. Knowing Sophie had two younger brothers, and having seen her in a pink sweater, he guessed the room with the pink stuff belonged to her.

Downstairs, people laughed. Drew picked out at least three distinct voices. He wondered if Sophie's mom would notice his presence without seeing him.

He shivered for no reason and moved to the head of the stairs, attracted by the voices. They reminded him of his parents. They'd have friends over for dinner, and he'd get a special dessert.

As his foot hovered over the top stair, Rhubark chirped a question.

Kay said, "What are you doing? If you're going to carry out this idiocy, at least hide."

Drew recoiled from the stairs. His parents were dead, not downstairs. He slipped inside the pink bedroom, the same room he'd used as a child. Stuffed animals lounged on the shell pink comforter over the tidy bed. She had a white desk with a matching bookcase, chair, and dresser. The mirror on her wall, framed in white, reminded Drew he needed to take off his scarf and hat or she might attack him as a stranger in her house.

He sat in the chair and noticed a thin book on her desk. It fit in its place, but reminded him of Iulia's notebook. For some reason, he'd never gone back to Iulia's hideout, even though he'd intended to. Claire and school had occupied his mind so much he'd forgotten to do too many things. Or avoided them.

The bedroom door shut. Drew snapped his head around to see Sophie in black leggings and a sky blue blouse. Her golden hair hung free and loose past her shoulders, and her blue aura remained as weak as he remembered. He wanted to touch her. He wanted to take the focus stone he knew she wore under her shirt.

"What are you doing here?" she whispered with a scowl as she crossed the room. The moment she reached him, she slapped him.

Drew's cheekbone exploded with sharp pain, his glasses hit the wall, and his eyes watered. He slumped against the desk and cowered away from her. At least his glasses hadn't been damaged. Somehow. He scrambled to shove them back onto his face.

"Oh, I get it," Kay said. "There's an affinity here, of a sort. I mean, lusting for the focus stone is me. But the rest of it, this attraction thing you've got going on, is like thinking pigs are pretty because bacon tastes good. You stole her power, you want more, so you also want her."

Drew groaned. "Bacon?"

Sophie shoved his shoulder and crossed her arms in a huff. "I'm not bacon," she growled. "Keep your voice down or Mom will hear you. She already thinks I slept with you. Finding you in my bedroom would just make everything worse."

"Sorry." He covered his face. The throbbing in his cheek faded as Kay healed it. Focus. He needed to focus. "Um, I came here because I need help." If he couldn't look at her without wanting to steal her power, maybe he'd made a mistake.

"And you can't pick up the phone like a normal person?"

He deserved her anger, he knew. "I don't have your number," he mumbled. "Or a phone."

Sophie huffed. "Fine. What do you want?"

"I remember you being more...friendly. More interested in helping."

"That was before my mom grounded me. Because of you." She jabbed a finger into his back. "And then nothing. Not even a peep to say hi, or helping me escape for a day. Nothing. Poof. Gone. I helped you, and you disappeared. You used me."

He winced. "I didn't mean to get you into trouble." A dozen excuses formed, but he swallowed them all.

"Too late for that." Sophie crossed her arms. "Either tell me what you want or get out."

"I like her."

"Shut up, Kay."

Rhubark jumped off Drew's shoulder and poked the book on the desk.

Sophie sucked in a breath. "Is that...is it a real dragon?"

Thankful for the distraction, Drew nodded. "His name is Rhubark."

The dragon dug his snout under the book's cover and flipped it open. Drew smirked as Sophie watched, her eyes wide with wonder. Then he noticed the handwriting on the open page. This book didn't belong to Sophie, it belonged to Iulia.

Brushing the dragon aside, Drew picked up the book and flipped through the pages. "Where did you get this?" By force of will, he kept himself from either leaning toward or cringing away from Sophie.

She shrugged and bent to take a closer look at Rhubark. "I don't know. It was in a stack of journals my mom gave me to read. This was the only one not in English. Took me a while to figure out it's not just lousy handwriting."

Drew doubted Sophie's mom had taken the notebook. "You said you belong to a coven, right?"

"Yeah. The same one as my mom. And Anne." She held her finger out for the dragon. Rhubark sniffed her, then rubbed along her hand like a cat. "Aw, he's adorable."

At least the dragon had done some good in defusing Sophie.

"At that size, sure." Someone in the coven had visited Iulia's hideout. Anne might have, but she would've come to him with the notebook, not given it to the coven. He thought so, anyway. Maybe she'd offered it for general reading. Maybe Sophie's mom could read Latin. "Can I take this?"

"No." Sophie snatched away the journal and held it out of his reach. "Not unless you tell me why."

He met her gaze and had to restrain himself from reaching out to touch her skin. Now that he knew why he felt this weird attraction, it felt like a food thing. If he touched her, he'd siphon her power, and if he wasn't careful, he might kill her. The thought of that turned his stomach and made him want to lick his lips at the same time.

"Settle down, Vlad the Aura Impaler," Kay said.

"It's Iulia's."

Sophie gave him a blank stare. She hadn't been there and didn't know anything about Iulia. No one had told the coven.

Drew sighed and decided to break his word to Justin. Sophie

needed to know. "Let me explain some things that happened over Thanksgiving."

CHAPTER 5

CLAIRE

Marie sat at a computer terminal in the bright, airy Cascade Park library, her platinum blonde hair in a loose ponytail at the nape of her neck. As she'd been since starting her part-time holiday job, she seemed tired and strained. Despite that, she smiled enough to crinkle the corners of her eyes.

Claire had no idea how Marie, only six years older than her, managed to be so competent and adult. Where Justin seemed like a big kid who ran off to do crazy things like save the world, Marie kept the family together and fed. No matter how hard she tried, Claire couldn't picture Marie as anything other than a grown-up.

Brown carpet and light wood shelves gave the library building a warm, friendly feel. A handful of people sat with books in their laps or tapping on other computers. The room smelled like the fresh coffee with the donation box beside it on a front table.

Sitting beside Marie, Claire spelled out the next name on her list from the headstones. The first few had been too common to wade through the results. Enion hung around Claire's neck, silent and still.

"Here's an obit for Angelo Marius, and it has the right dates and the right wife's name." Marie pointed to the screen. The newspaper had been scanned and uploaded, offering the full obituary page from a twenty-year-old copy of the Portland Tribune. Her finger tracked over the words, showing Marie could read faster than Claire.

"Your mother was named Isabella, right? There's her name as one of his great-grandchildren. We can probably find one of her siblings or cousins." Marie took the notebook and wrote names. "I wonder why your parents never took you to visit family," she mused.

Claire kept her mouth shut. No one had told Marie that Claire had been dead. Justin thought they should, that enough time had passed, but Claire had, so far, resisted. She didn't see how it helped anything.

More importantly, she didn't want to talk about it. Talking about it meant admitting all of it had happened. She just wanted to feel normal. As normal as possible with dragons, a talking dog, and a possessed boyfriend, anyway.

That left Claire with a need to lie if she wanted to explain her strange lack of memories.

Worse, she'd forgotten her mother's name until she'd seen it on the headstone this afternoon.

"Maybe I just don't remember it," she said, trying not to feel guilty for the lie as she spun it. "I mean, none of them took me in. I might've blocked them all out or something. Convinced myself they don't really exist."

Marie patted Claire's hand. "Let's look up your father."

Fluttering in Claire's stomach made her clamp her mouth shut again. She didn't want to see pictures of him. She desperately wanted to see pictures of him.

The first result on the search engine punched Claire in the gut. *Local Park Ranger and Family Killed in House Fire.* Marie clicked on the link. The first picture with the article showed their charred house, jagged fingers of dark ruin jabbing into the sky, flanked by fire engines. She scrolled past the image, filling the screen with text and ads. Another, smaller picture, showed her father.

Claire stared at the smiling image. He looked exactly like his Phasm, except with color and a ranger hat. This man had become a stranger to her. Had she ever really known him? Mark Terdan, the enigma, gazed at her.

She tore her attention away from him to read the article, tripping over the dates and her own name. Six years ago, someone had recorded the dispassionate facts about the worst day of her life and spat them out for people to read. Those people had probably read it and felt sorry for her. Pity. She'd been a brief object of pity for hundreds, maybe thousands of strangers.

Marie scribbled on the notebook page. Mesmerized by the article, Claire blinked when the page changed to a new list of search results. She checked the notebook and read what Marie had written.

"Who's Virginia Terdan?"

"Your grandmother. She was quoted in the fire article." Marie glanced at Claire. "You've been through a lot."

Rather than agree or disagree, Claire stayed quiet while Marie scrolled and clicked. She moved from page to page while Claire rubbed Enion's head. He wrapped a claw around her finger and held on. His solid warmth and weight provided comfort she didn't realize she needed.

"That can't be right," Marie muttered.

Claire looked up to see Marie tapping her fingernail on the screen with a frown. "What?"

"Virginia's husband was named Adam. He died when your father was nineteen. According to his obit, his father was Matthew, who also died fairly young. Matthew had a sister Abigail. I looked up Abigail Terdan and found Abigail Kessler. Kessler was my mother's maiden name. Which isn't that strange, except I just looked her up. Abigail was my great-grandmother. You and I are related. Not close, but related."

Squinting at the text, Claire tried to grasp the information. Marie sketched it for her with boxes. Their grandparents had been cousins.

"Okay. So all of this means...?" Claire tried to fill in the blank with a useful word. Why did she write down the headstone names in the first place? What difference did it make?

"It means we were already family when we took you in."

In Claire's head, static crackled and buzzed. She didn't know what to think or feel.

Marie clicked more. She covered her mouth with a hand. "That's even—" She wrote another two names. *Corwin & Jacqueline Evans.* "I mean, it's such a distant relation, it hardly matters. Right?"

Claire stared at the names. "Evans is Justin's last name. And yours."

"Yes. This is a common ancestor for all three of us. A common *local* ancestor. Your father had plenty of relatives in the area. If he'd taken you to see them, we might've all met years ago."

The idea of several people around Portland who'd refused to take her in bothered Claire. She didn't know if she wanted to meet any of them. Had they been the people she barely knew at the funeral? All of them had looked at her and walked away. At this point, she knew all the local Knights had showed up, including Justin. The women she thought had been her mother's book group might've included relatives. Relatives who'd left her there.

She wanted to hunt down Virginia Terdan and scream at her.

Marie closed the browser. "We should go. I need to make dinner. If we leave Justin in charge of that, it'll be delicious, but he'll screw up the grocery budget."

Still fuming at her grandmother, Claire let herself be herded out of the library and up the street. They walked with Marie's hand on Claire's shoulder, and Enion still holding her finger. Claire simmered.

Somewhere in Portland, her grandmother sat in a rocking chair with a bag of yarn, knowing she'd left her granddaughter to the system and not caring. This horrible old woman cackled and made cookies to eat in front of neighborhood children without sharing. And she kicked cats. For fun. She knitted severed heads with blood-red Xs for eyes.

The image tumbled out of control with lawn gnomes coming alive in her garden and gnashing their teeth. Claire stopped. This woman must've had a good reason to leave Claire to foster care. Right? Maybe she had a medical problem.

She still wanted to scream at Virginia. Even if her grandmother couldn't take care of her, she still should've kept in touch. Birthday cards would've been nice. Random visits would've shown Claire she wasn't alone in the world. For six long, horrible years, she'd thought she had no one. The fire had taken everyone from her.

"I'll see if I can find Virginia's address," Marie said as they neared home. "My mom might be able to go through family to find her."

Jealousy stabbed through Claire's belly. Marie had living parents, a sister, and cousins. She remembered her life. She had Justin and their daughters. No one had ever told her to shut up and go cry in the dark so nobody had to listen to her blubbering while trying to watch the news on TV.

"Why didn't we see any of them for Thanksgiving?"

Marie's brow raised. She looked Claire over for long enough to make Claire self-conscious about her tone. Maybe she'd snapped. She might've growled once.

Claire stuffed her hands in her pockets, kicked a rock, and watched it tumble ahead of them, unable to look Marie in the eye.

"My mother's family does a big gathering for Christmas Eve instead. My father's family isn't around here, so we only trade cards and phone calls with them. Grandpa Jack grew up in Nebraska. Ask him why he came out here if you want to know. He'll tell you."

People moving to Portland didn't interest Claire.

Enion perked up as they reached the driveway. "Look for Rhubark. Check on boy." Claire thought she caught an underlying message of Enion thinking Drew must have gotten himself into trouble while unsupervised. He scrambled to her shoulder and leaped into the air.

"Don't harass him," she called after Enion.

Marie squeezed Claire's shoulder. "Do you want to ask Grandma Tammy about finding Virginia? If you want me to do it, it'll have to wait until after dinner."

Claire shrugged, not sure if she wanted to meet Virginia or not. So long as she never met the woman, she could make up excuses on her behalf and rage at an imaginary person.

"I'll take care of it."

CHAPTER 6

DREW

Though he wanted to spend hours with Iulia's journal, now tucked into his coat pocket, Drew sat on a rock with Sophie in the snow. He kept his hands to himself, grateful that the last of her anger had drained when he told her about Iulia.

Trees surrounded the secluded spot in Forest Park. He'd brought them both to the trailhead his mother had preferred. As a small boy, he'd raced along the paths while Mom struggled to keep up.

They'd plunged off the trail to find privacy. Frost rimed the carpet of dead leaves and fallen branches while tiny flakes drifted from the gray sky.

Weeks of practice shaping the mist and selecting his targets had paid off, because Drew had *accidentally* left Rhubark behind on Sophie's desk. The dragon might tell Claire about witches, but he couldn't remember saying Sophie's name.

"Controlling magic is mostly about understanding it and knowing your limits," Sophie said. She wore a white jacket and gloves she'd picked up on her way out the front door. Drew had met her outside. This way, her parents knew she'd gone someplace without knowing where or with whom.

Drew recoiled from an urge to drain her to a shriveled bacon husk. He felt like a creepy vampire stalker. A bacon vampire stalker. "Understanding it how?"

"What it is. What it can and can't do." She held her hand over a patch of moss and bit her lip. The moss rippled in slow motion, shifting in color from a faded gray-green to a more vibrant green. "At its core, magic is about life. It's a byproduct of living things. Because it's created by life, it can't cause death."

"That's not true. I crushed ants with it." Drew held up his hand and mimed the action.

"What?" Sophie grimaced with disgust, making Drew cringe away from her.

"Those giant ants. The ones shooting acid at everything. I picked them up with magic and crushed them. Like this." He reached with his will for a stick, lifting it into the air. Kay assisted him, managing the power as he always did. When it reached eye level, Drew snapped his fingers into a fist. The stick exploded in a shower of splinters.

Sophie shrieked and dove off the rock. Kay kept the splinters from hitting either of them.

"That's not right," Sophie gasped. Peering over the rock with her eyes wide, she seemed terrified of Drew. "It's not what magic is for!"

He recoiled from her fear. "I didn't know! They wanted to kill me."

"Great," Kay said with a grumble. "She's useless. Take her home and go back to Claire."

"She's not useless." To Sophie, Drew said, "Maybe what they told you wasn't the whole truth." He held up his hands in surrender. If he tried to ask Claire or Justin anything about magic, they'd tell him to talk to Anne. One way or another, he needed a witch's help, and he preferred the girl who he already owed something. He couldn't pay her back if he never talked to her again.

"Maybe..." He cast about for some way to explain that might soothe Sophie's conscience.

"The ants were already magical?" Kay suggested. "That doesn't really explain the stick, but that's a dead piece of wood. I can explode dead pieces of wood without trying."

"Yes." Sometimes, having a second mind in his head helped. "There's a difference between magical creatures and non-magical ones, right? I mean, that was no ordinary bug. It was magically enhanced. It's possible I was able to tap into that without realizing that's what I was doing."

Sophie frowned and furrowed her brow, looking at the rock instead of Drew. "I suppose so. You're really powerful."

She feared him. Great. Drew pressed his palms together and refused to think about bacon. "I really appreciate whatever help you're willing to give, Sophie. This is about defending the area from things like that. The better I can do it, the fewer people get hurt."

"Right." She sat on a different rock, leaving several feet of space between them. "Life. It's about life." Her gaze settled on the ground. "Magic comes from plants and animals. It's dispersed and repelled by water. I don't know why, but it'll always be harder to use in the rain and impossible underwater. Witches have a personal reservoir, and that determines what your aura looks like. Yours is a pretty strong blue-tinted silver. The silver is the ghost stuff. Blue means you have an affinity for water."

"You just said—"

Sophie held up a hand. "I know. It doesn't mean actual water. It's a metaphor."

"Sure. A metaphor." Drew smirked. "Because when you want to teach new witches how to do stuff, a metaphor is the best plan."

"Yeah." One corner of Sophie's mouth quirked up. "That's kind of what I said when they told me."

"Excellent," Kay said. "Keep doing that. We could use a pet witch girl."

"Shut up, Kay." Drew sighed. Two minutes ago, Kay wanted to dump her, now he wanted to keep her as a toy. He had the attention span of a toddler sometimes. The morals of one, too. "What's the metaphor mean?"

Sophie glanced at him, then at the ground again. "Your power works like water. It flows, sloshes, and sprays. When you're trying to direct it, you have to treat it like a pool or stream. Allegedly, you can control ley lines easier than other affinities, but I think they just said that to make me feel more confident about doing it."

"Witches are weird," Kay said.

Drew agreed, but he didn't say so. "Aside from the crystal color, does that have any real impact on how I use magic?"

"It's harder for us to do things with crackling, snapping, or flickering. Things that fire does. I've never tried to do anything like crushing an ant, so I don't know how that works. Probably, what you did is create a pool of power around it and then compress or contract it."

Kay gave the impression of nodding. "Sounds about right."

"I'm sure the ghost part affects things, but I don't know how. I don't think anyone would. Knights usually kill people who get possessed."

Drew rubbed his neck, thinking that he should avoid Knights other than Claire, Justin, and Avery. He doubted any others would understand. From what Claire had told him about her first time at the Palace, he also doubted they'd give him more than half a second to explain himself. Even after the Palace's destruction, Justin had proven he remained dedicated to the cause. Other Knights probably felt the same.

Sophie met his gaze, fear still in her eyes, warring with curiosity. "What's it like?"

"Being possessed?" When she nodded, Drew furrowed his brow and tried to decide how to explain.

"Please," Kay said. "Do tell. I'd love to hear this."

Knowing he had to live with Kay for the rest of his life, Drew chose to err on the side of enigmatic. "I dunno. What's it like to be a girl witch?" He shrugged. "There's someone else in my head with me. We get along most of the time."

Kay chuckled. "How diplomatic. And appropriately vague. I'm impressed. You'll do, kid. You'll do."

Sophie grimaced. "That sounds awful."

Drew chuckled at both of them. "I'm used to it. Can we go back to witchcraft?"

"Oh. Right. Sorry." Sophie seemed more at ease again. "Like I said, magic is life. I was taught it can't take a life, but I guess they either lied or meant human life. It can do just about anything else. What it's best for, though, is manipulating plants and insects. That's why so many witches are gardeners." Her mouth fell open. "Oh. You fought ants. Insects. I'll bet it wasn't that hard to affect them. Or the cockroaches."

"Interesting," Kay murmured.

"I wouldn't say it was easy, but I handled several." Drew saw no reason to elaborate on the experience. Sophie didn't need to know about his cowardice or how useless he'd been for most of it. Mentioning Claire likewise seemed dumb, though he couldn't say why. He'd told Sophie about Iulia and the Palace being destroyed but hadn't given details about the Knights involved.

Sophie shifted one rock closer and leaned toward him. "How big were they? I saw some news footage, but the video didn't show the scale."

He held his hands about two feet apart. "About this big, not counting legs and antennae. A little bigger than a cat, a little smaller than a medium-sized dog." Thinking he saw a tinge of hero worship in her eyes, Drew coughed and returned to the subject. "Can we change plants fundamentally, or just make them grow, or what?"

"Stace says if you're really powerful—"

"Stace? Anastasia? Your mom's cousin?" Drew had no idea why it never occurred to him that Sophie would know Aunt Stace. Had he thought of it, he might've found time to visit much sooner.

"Yes. She's part of the coven. I thought you knew that."

"No, I didn't realize she was a witch." Drew frowned and had a new question. "Can we manipulate people with our power? Like making them do things or modifying their memories?"

Sophie bit her lip and looked away. "They all say no, but..."

"But?" Drew had a sinking feeling he knew what had happened to his missing memory of Aunt Stace.

"But we can do things like that to animals, and humans are animals, so it must be possible." Sophie shook her head. "I don't think I'm powerful enough, which explains why they say no instead of launching into an ethics discussion." She met his gaze with fear creeping back into her eyes.

"I'm powerful enough."

She nodded. "You shouldn't do it."

"No, I can't think of a reason why I would."

"Liar," Kay said. "You've got five situations on the tip of your tongue where you'd do it in a heartbeat. We both know you'd feel guilty afterward, but you'd do it."

Drew ignored Kay. "Maybe I should talk to Aunt Stace about that."

Sophie seemed relieved as she nodded. "That's a good idea. I can give you her phone number."

"How about her address?"

CHAPTER 7

CLAIRE

Claire spent an hour playing with the girls. They had stuffed unicorns, princess tiaras, magic wands, and wooden swords. After letting Missy and Lisa rescue her from Enion several times, then defeat her to rescue Enion several times, she brought them inside and helped them wash up for dinner.

She'd expected Drew to return home by dinnertime. They sat around the rickety dinner table in the cottage kitchen with Drew's seat beside Claire remaining empty. Enion usurped his plate, sitting on it with a pile of carrot sticks, cherry tomatoes, and lettuce leaves. He knew whose spot he'd taken.

"You're a snot," she murmured at her dragon.

Claire wanted to pile spaghetti and salad on Drew's plate. He wouldn't let it go to waste. No respectable foster care kid ever let good food get cold. Two months in this household hadn't changed that for either of them.

Lisa chattered about everything and nothing. Justin made random noises like he heard her, though he seemed preoccupied. Marie kept Missy from flinging noodles and sauce all over the place. Claire imagined horrible things happening to Drew.

Something tapped on the kitchen window. Everyone stopped and looked. A large dragon pressed its snout against the glass. Justin jumped out of his seat to open the front door for it. Claire saw the silver flash as it turned into a tiny dragon who sailed through the door to land beside Enion.

"Boy gone," Rhubark told Claire.

Claire clamped down a surge of panic. "More details, please."

"Anne gone. Boy go to house. Meet girl. Take girl. Not take Rhubark."

The report didn't sound like he'd been abducted or attacked. Claire had no idea why Drew would abandon Rhubark on purpose, though. "Girl? What girl?"

Rhubark seemed frustrated for several seconds. "Pink."

Having a feeling she wouldn't get much more, Claire picked up a tomato and offered it to Rhubark. "Good job. Wait. If he left you behind, then you flew here from the house, right?" When the dragon nodded with a mouthful of tomato, she grinned. "Then you can find it again."

Pleased with herself, Claire looked up to see the whole family watching her. None of them understood his side of the conversation, of course. "Drew's off with someone Rhubark doesn't know. I'll go check it out."

Justin glanced at his wife while he finished chewing a bite. Claire looked from him to Marie and back. Though she saw nothing specific pass between them, she knew they managed to communicate without words. Adults.

"Do you want backup?" Justin asked.

"Nah. I'll have two dragons along. I should be fine. Besides, Drew isn't dumb."

"There's no school for two weeks," Marie said to Justin.

He nodded his agreement. "I'd like to see you both home by dawn. Enion," he pointed his fork at the dragon, "I expect you to watch over Claire. And if you need help, don't worry about what time it is."

The lenient terms didn't surprise Claire. She'd lived with them long enough to expect this. "Yes, Dad." She shoveled one last bite into her mouth, then grabbed both dragons. On her way out, she tousled Missy's hair and patted Lisa on the head. Thank goodness she'd been able to play with them before dinner.

Rhubark led them into the air and to the south. They circled a neighborhood before landing behind an elementary school building. From there, Rhubark sat on her shoulder with Enion and directed her to a two-story house. For the flight down to Portland, Claire had imagined all kinds of horrible things. This tidy home didn't strike her as menacing.

"Are you sure?" she asked Rhubark.

The dragon nodded. "Mist into room with bed."

"He shifted himself into a bedroom?"

"Pink."

Claire frowned at the house, not sure she got the intended message. Because it sounded like Drew had used his mist to break into a girl's bedroom, then left Rhubark and took the girl someplace else. That didn't sound like Drew.

"I guess we should find out who lives there." She approached the door and rang the bell. Both dragons dove into her scarf to hide.

A woman answered the door. She looked like any of a dozen PTA moms Claire had met over the years. Her blonde ponytail swished, and an extra-long white sweater hung over dark leggings.

"Are you one of Sophie's friends?"

The mystery of the girl's name had been solved. "No, ma'am. I'm looking for a boy I think she's out with. His name is Drew. Red hair, glasses, about this tall."

The woman raised her brow and seemed unamused. "Drew Sanders?"

"Yes, ma'am. That's his name. Have you seen him today?"

She crossed her arms and leaned against the doorframe. The pose reminded Claire of a casual interrogation. "And how do you know him?"

"He's my boyfriend."

"Is that so? Do you know Sophie at all?"

"No, ma'am."

The woman, who seemed likely to be Sophie's mother, stared at Claire as if she had x-ray vision and could see through skin and bones to judge souls. "What are you?"

Taken aback by such a rude question, Claire crossed her arms. "Excuse me? What are you?"

"The witch asking the questions. What are you, and why did you come here to find him?"

Enion popped his head out of the scarf. "Mean lady!"

Claire covered his head with her hand, trying to shush him. She decided she didn't want to deal with the whole girl Knight thing for once. "The Dragonkeeper. I came because my dragon tracked Drew here. Have you seen him or not?"

Her brow raised in skeptic dismissal, Sophie's mother said, "There's no such thing as a dragonkeeper. Those little disasters belong to

Anne. Why do you have one?"

Stifling a growl in the back of her throat, Claire worked to restrain herself from punching this lady in the face. "Look, I just want to find Drew. I'm worried something happened to him."

The woman leaned closer and bared her teeth. "He defiled my daughter. I hope something does happen to him and it's worse than your little head can imagine. No, Dragonkeeper, he's not here. Because if he was, you'd be able to hear him screaming."

Claire stopped. Her breath, her heart, and her brain all ground to a halt. She stared in mute shock at Sophie's mother, unable to believe the words she'd just heard. "Excuse me?"

"You heard me. When you find him, feel free to bring him here to submit to my mercy." Sophie's mother shut the door before Claire could think to stop her.

He'd said he meant to visit Anne. Instead, he came to *defile* a girl named Sophie.

Claire's feet moved of their own free will, carrying her away from the house. She considered visiting all the places he'd ever mentioned or shared with her to see if he'd taken Sophie there. To think she'd worried about him. She'd thought him in danger.

Lifting her hand, she tugged off her glove. The locket face pulsed with her heartbeat. With it, she could find him. Why hadn't she thought of that before? They could've flown straight to him.

Because she wanted to know what house Rhubark saw.

Because...she wanted to feel normal.

For the past month, she'd ignored the locket aside from covering it when she left home. Touching it to the brand on the inside of Drew's elbow let her hear Kay, tugging on its line let her call Enion to her side, and holding it over her heart while sitting on the couch let her enter her demesne. None of these things felt normal.

For some reason, riding a dragon didn't infringe on the veneer of normalcy. Neither did wearing an enchanted dagger under her coat.

She pressed her hands to her eyes, hating herself for wishing she could go back to a time when things sucked but made sense. Some half-remembered fairy tale had a girl faced with that choice. A group-home foster mom had read it to her and a few other kids. In the story, going back had been a real choice, and when the girl picked it, everything went wrong.

In this case, she had no real choice, just a weird, wistful nostalgia for lying in the dark, knowing no one cared and nothing would ever go right.

"Why weren't there any ghosts to destroy today? That would've made everything better." The words made no sense. Neither did anything else.

The school loomed in the darkening evening with a crust of frost on the roof and nascent icicles clinging to the eaves. She jogged into the campus and shook her head. Spirit Knights didn't retire. This job was a life sentence. In her case, two life sentences stacked together.

Enough whining. Time to girl up and get going.

"Rhubark, stay in the scarf. Enion, let's get into the air. We're going to find Drew, and I'm going to..." How they found Drew would make a big difference to how she chose to finish the sentence.

Enion flashed silver. She climbed onto his back.

"Hunt boy?"

Claire narrowed her eyes as she focused on her link to Drew. "Yes. Hunt boy." A shimmering, silvery line appeared in her vision. She pointed in that direction with a chop of her hand. "Full speed ahead."

CHAPTER 8

DREW

Drew had never been to the west side of Hillsboro before. He shifted himself and Sophie as far as he could, then they caught a bus. Past the DMV, Sophie led the way on foot as the sun set. The ground here had no snow or frost, and nothing fell from the gray sky.

The road seemed familiar to Drew, as if he'd been someplace with the same low shrubs, clusters of trees, and empty farm fields. Maybe he had. Maybe he'd been here before, visiting Aunt Stace for ice cream. As they walked down a narrow side road, he tried to glean every detail he could from that memory snippet.

Aunt Stace had bought him an ice cream cone. He remembered her handing him a red-dyed cake cone with a scoop of strawberry ice cream. Ruby red chunks of real fruit studded the rounded, pink mass. Cold radiated from it.

His memory ended there. No, he recalled one more thing. The ice cream hadn't been framed. No glasses, yet he remembered everything in focus. That revelation placed it before fourth grade. Sometime during that year, he'd noticed creeping blurriness in the distance.

They reached a forested grove with a narrow gravel road plunging inside. To one side of the path, a bright red mailbox with a hand-painted, gold number on the side rested on a post. Sophie led him up the path to a log-cabin-style cottage nested among the trees. The brown trim and leafy-green accents had whimsical whorls and curves, as if Aunt Stace wanted people to mistake her home for undecorated gingerbread.

"That's it?" Drew asked

"Yeah. The first time Mom brought me out here, I expected a farm, then we pulled into this. It's like the house from Hansel and Gretel." She stepped to the front door and rang the bell.

"Does anyone else hear creepy music?" Kay asked.

"Shut up, Kay," Drew muttered.

"Tell me you're not even a tiny bit worried about what we'll find inside."

The door opened. Aunt Stace appeared. Her coppery aura glowed so bright Drew wanted to shield his eyes. Kay had to filter it down for him to see the woman underneath.

Streaks of gray lightened Stace's brown hair and lines crinkled the corners of her eyes. She wore the same kind of busy-patterned, multi-colored, loose dress she had every other time Drew had seen her.

He remembered his mom calling her a hippie as a joke at a family picnic, and then they both laughed. That picnic had been at Multnomah Falls. At the time, he hadn't understood why they laughed about her hips. Why did he remember that day and not the ice cream thing?

Aunt Stace smiled at Sophie, then she saw Drew. The corners of her mouth slipped. She scanned the small clearing in front of her house. "Your mother didn't bring you?"

"My mother is dead," Drew spat.

Sophie coughed. "Um, no. We took the bus."

Aunt Stace sighed and stood aside so they could enter the house. "Well, come in. I'm not going to turn you aside."

She hadn't been talking to him. Drew knew it when he answered, but he wanted her to know how he felt. He wanted her to remember how she'd abandoned him.

Sophie waved for Drew to come with her as she stepped inside the house. Drew watched her and didn't know if he wanted to follow.

"Drew, honey, it's cold out here. Come on. I'll make you some hot cocoa."

"Go in," Kay said. "It's rude to make her hold the door open. We can always escape if we need to."

Kay expressing concern about rudeness made Drew want to snort. He hustled into the small house anyway, agreeing with the point about escape.

Unlike Anne's house, Stace had no doilies or crystals sitting out. Natural wood with glowing green streaks of life dominated the decor of the first small room. Sophie sat on a bench made from a log, but it was alive. All the furniture, the floor, and the walls shone with life.

Stace had grown the house out of a living tree.

"This is amazing," Kay murmured. "Imagine having a place of your own in the woods. Justin would have to trudge through the forest to threaten us with impolite waking methods."

Drew gaped like an idiot. He touched the wall, feeling the vibrant, strong pulse of the young plant. With a flick of his will, he could siphon away all this power, leaving a dull, dry husk behind.

Stace settled a warm, bony hand on his shoulder. "The last time you were here, I still had the old shack. That was some time ago."

Her words startled Drew out of his daze. He snatched his hand back. "Was that before or after you refused to take me in? I can't remember."

"Have a seat," Stace said. She nudged him toward Sophie. "I'll be right back."

Drew shuffled to the bench and glowered as he sat as far from Sophie as possible.

"I didn't bring you here to shove your hate at her."

"You didn't have to bring me here."

Sophie jumped to her feet. "You're right. I didn't have to do anything for you. Don't worry, I won't make that mistake again." She turned her back on him and stormed to the front door.

"Smooth," Kay said.

Drew covered his face and wanted to hit something. Sophie yanked the door open.

"Who're you?" Sophie said.

"I'm looking for a boy named Drew," Claire said from outside the house. "Red hair, glasses, about this tall." She sounded annoyed.

Kay gulped. "Oh boy."

Drew looked up and blinked, his brain no longer working.

"In there," Sophie snapped.

Claire stomped into the room. While he stared, dumbstruck, she rushed him. Her arm moved, then he blinked at the ceiling. Pain flooded his jaw and flared out to encompass his head.

"Damn," Kay said. "She's fast."

"Are you Sophie?" Claire asked.

"If I say yes, are you going to hit me too?"

"No."

"Then yes." Sophie cleared her throat. "Is he okay?"

"He'll be fine. Kay can heal it." Claire growled, low and dangerous. "Then I'll hit him again."

"What's going on?" Aunt Stace asked, breathless. "Who are you? Dear Mother Earth, *what* are you?"

"I can't wait to see how you handle this."

"Shut up, Kay," Drew gasped as he tried to sit up. Holding a hand in front of his face, he shrank away from Claire. "Why are you hitting me?"

Claire lunged, grabbed him by his jacket, and thumped him against the wall. Fiery rage twisted her face into a dark snarl. She'd recovered more strength than he realized—his feet didn't touch the floor.

As if that wasn't enough, two dragons popped out of her scarf and growled at him. Their tiny mouths flickered with barely contained fire.

"I thought you were in trouble," Claire snapped. "Instead, you're running around with this girl you've never once bothered to mention, whose mom knows your name and hates you, after ditching Rhubarb on purpose. Don't even try to tell me it was accident he got left behind."

"Good thing you kept this a secret from her. That worked swell."

Drew needed Kay to shut up. Face to face with a furious Claire, he needed not to say those words out loud. She'd probably hit him before he clarified who he wanted to stop talking.

Claire yanked him off the wall and slammed him into it again.

Knowing she might break him hurt worse than the impact.

"Young lady, that boy is my nephew, and I'd appreciate if you didn't get his blood on my wall."

"Can we talk this out?" Sophie asked.

"I don't know," Claire growled. "Can we?"

Drew's heart beat so fast he thought his chest might explode. He closed his eyes and took as deep a shaky breath as he could. Even without seeing it, her anger still battered him as a palpable, burning heat. "Um. Can...uh, can we maybe do that privately?"

"Drew, honey, who is this girl?"

Cracking one eye open, Drew saw Aunt Stace's concerned face over Claire's shoulder. "My girlfriend."

"Nice to know you remember that," Claire snapped. She shoved him again, this time letting go so his feet hit the ground.

His legs refused to hold him up. Drew crumpled to the floor in a heap. He knew he could use magic to defend himself, but not against Claire. Not when this all had to be a misunderstanding.

"You have a girlfriend?" Sophie asked.

Kay giggled.

Claire pointed at Sophie. "What did you do to her?"

Aunt Stace raised her brow. "What does she mean?"

"This just gets better and better," Kay said.

Shifting to his hands and knees, Drew couldn't take the commentary anymore. "Dammit, Kay, shut up! Can I have five minutes without you butting in?"

"Get over it," Kay snapped. "You did something stupid, and now Claire is here to make you pay. That's how the world works. Pull yourself together, sort this out, and grovel to whoever you have to. I hate healing our body. It's taxing."

"Who's Kay?" Aunt Stace asked.

"Drew is that possessed boy Anne told the coven about," Sophie said. "Kay is the spirit."

"She told the coven?" The shock of betrayal stung Drew, surging over everything else. "Why would she do that?"

Claire stepped on his back and held him down as he tried to sit up. "No. Don't you change the subject. What did you do? Did you sleep with Sophie or not?"

"What? No. I swear." Drew cranked his body to meet Claire's angry gaze. "I barely touched her, and what I did was an accident."

Sophie stepped closer and laid a tentative hand on Claire's arm. "He stole my power. We kind of flirted a little bit, but then he did that and disappeared, and I had no idea he was already seeing someone."

"That sounds worse," Claire said.

"It is and isn't," Aunt Stace said, her voice grave and solemn. She stayed behind Claire, not physically interfering. "Can I interest anyone in hot cocoa while we sort all this out?"

CHAPTER 9

CLAIRE

Her anger tamped down, Claire sat on the bench with Drew. Enion and Rhubark sat between them. Sophie took a separate chair. The woman who'd introduced herself as Stace handed each of them a steaming mug of cocoa before taking a different chair.

Claire hadn't realized how much she'd riled herself up during the flight from Sophie's house. Meeting the pretty blonde he hadn't told her about had shoved her off a cliff, and hitting him had felt so good. However innocent he turned out to be, she wouldn't apologize. He deserved that fist. For lying to her.

Probably. Maybe. They'd talk about it later. She probably shouldn't have hit him. No, he deserved that, and he could heal it fast enough that it didn't matter much. The stuff after, though... With the heat of the moment past, it seemed excessive. She shouldn't have banged him against the wall. Or held him down with her foot. At the time, it hadn't seemed wrong.

Stace sat with her legs crossed and her fingers laced on her knee. She reminded Claire of an earthier version of Anne. Witches seemed to have that new age feel about them, though Sophie and her mom looked like aerobics instructors.

Heaped in a lump on the other end of the bench, Drew sipped his cocoa in silence. Claire could see him gathering himself, figuring out how to start. She also noticed that Sophie didn't seem to want to say anything else at this point. Whatever had happened, guilt wrapped around both.

Enion, Claire noticed, kept checking one of the shelves. Claire took a look but saw only old books. Nothing worth seeing there.

"Drew," Aunt Stace said, "what were you doing when you stole Sophie's power?"

Claire watched him. He glanced at Sophie. She met Drew's gaze and looked away.

"It was my fault," Sophie mumbled.

Drew sighed and stared into his mug. "We awakened my latent witch power. I siphoned off hers to save myself without realizing it."

Sophie's cheeks turned pink. "You're not going to tell Mom, are you?"

He'd never told her how he got that sudden power boost he used on Thanksgiving vacation. "Wait." Claire held up her hands. "Why does your mom think he 'defiled' you?"

Rolling her eyes and huffing at the ceiling, Sophie made a grumbly noise in the back of her throat. "She read my aura signature in his and assumed we'd had sex."

Apparently, Mrs. Harris had some mad aura-reading skills. "Why didn't you just tell her what really happened?"

"Because," Stace said, not quite hiding a smirk, "using a ritual you barely understand and aren't trained with on a possessed boy to create an abomination is worse. From the perspective of a witch, anyway."

"Abomination is a little melodramatic," Claire said.

"He's a male witch. Even without the ghost, that's not supposed to exist."

Claire barked a laugh. "Girls can't be knights and boys can't be witches." Her lingering anger evaporated. She grinned at Drew. "Welcome to the club."

She saw tension ease from Drew's shoulders. "We should get jackets or something."

Sophie cleared her throat. "This is serious."

"It is," Stace agreed.

Shrugging, Claire looked to Drew. "Did you apologize for stealing her power?"

"Of course I did." Drew sighed. "More than once. I helped her get to a ley line, too. And took her home."

"And then never showed up again!" Sophie jabbed her mug at Drew. Cocoa sloshed out and slid down the side. "I got in trouble, and he forgot about me until he needed something again."

"He's a boy," Claire said.

"He really is." Sophie nodded.

Out of the corner of her eye, Claire saw Drew frown and open his mouth. Without saying a word, he sipped from his mug.

"Poor Drew." Stace chuckled. "I'm glad this is all straightened out. Why did you come here, though?"

"I need help learning to use the witch power," Drew told his cocoa. "Sophie thought we could trust you."

"You can," Stace said. "I won't discuss this with Belinda. That's Sophie's mother," she added, looking at Claire. "Do you have time now?"

Claire had a feeling the subject would bore her. She stood. "Our curfew is dawn." Scooping up the dragons, she flashed a smile at Sophie. "I'm taking the dragons outside. Do you want to come with me? We won't go far."

"Sure."

Drew looked like he wanted to object, but he huddled on himself and kept his mouth shut.

Letting Sophie lead the way, Claire carried the two dragons outside. As soon as the door shut, she tossed them into the air.

"Stay close," she told Enion and Rhubark as they righted themselves and streaked into the woods.

For a while, the two girls stood and watched the dragons fly around the trees, root through the fallen needles and leaves on the ground, and peel bark.

"You didn't tell Stace what you are," Sophie said.

"I'm a Spirit Knight." Claire tugged off her glove and held up her locket hand. "It's a long story. Mostly, it's about how my dad made this to save my life, and if I ever lose it, I die." Not that keeping it had saved her from Caius.

Sophie leaned close to examine the locket face. "This is amazing," she gasped. She reached a finger toward the locket face without touching. "You can see right through the holes."

Claire moved her hand to close the distance. She watched Sophie's eyes flare wide and her mouth form an O shape.

"I can feel the pulse. Magic and blood at the same time. Amazing." Sophie traced a whorl with her fingertip. "Can you feel that?"

"Yeah. It's like regular flesh. Not sure what would happen if someone stabs me there. Not interested in finding out."

Sophie grimaced and pulled her finger away. "I can understand that." As Claire replaced her glove, Sophie said, "You know, that design is familiar."

Claire shrugged. "One of my ancestors was kind of obsessed with it. Not sure why my dad made this with it, but I figure it has something to do with how he did it. Which no one knows."

"Ancestor?" Sophie scrunched up her face. Claire could see why Drew might think of Sophie as cute. The lines of her face reminded Claire of a cat, in a way. Then Sophie's expression cleared and she snapped her fingers. "Wait, I know. I saw it in a journal. My mom gave me a bunch of journals from our family. One of them had it. That one wasn't as hard to read as Iulia's because at least it was in English, but she had tiny, cramped —"

"Wait. Back up. You have Iulia's journal? And you know who Iulia is? Because that's the ancestor."

"Drew has it." Sophie pointed at the house. "He told me about Iulia because he wanted to take the journal. But this was a different one. I think it was the one by Jackie Evans."

Claire gave her a long, slow blink. "You mean Jacqueline Evans? The wife of Corwin Evans?"

"That sounds right. I think he died pretty young, though."

She goggled at Sophie. "Jackie is my ancestor too. On my dad's side. Iulia is on my mom's side. What's your last name? Mine's Terdan."

"Oh my gosh!" Sophie covered her mouth. "Are you serious? That's Stace's last name. And Stace is related to my mom. That means you and I are some kind of cousins. Actually, you're related to about half of our coven, one way or another."

How had Claire stumbled onto a pile of relations all in one day?

She didn't know how to react to this any better than she had earlier with Marie. "Okay. If Stace is a Terdan, then..." Then why had Stace acted like she'd never seen Claire before?

"You know what else?" Sophie sounded more hesitant as she asked this. She bit her lip. "Drew calls Stace his aunt, which means you're also related to him somehow. I don't know how close. Maybe your parents can clear this up. I mean, they must not have any magic, or—"

"My parents are dead."

"Oh. I'm sorry. I didn't realize. That's awful."

"It happened a while ago." Claire waved off her sympathy. "I met Drew in foster care. My dad was a Knight. I don't think my mom was a witch, but maybe some other relations were." She didn't know why none of them had claimed her either. None of their names had stuck in her mind like Virginia's.

The front door of the house opened, and Drew stepped outside. He seemed dazed as he wrapped his scarf around his neck. Maybe he'd had too much information shoved into his brain at once.

"Stace?" Claire said, approaching the door. She saw Stace standing behind Drew with a pleasant smile. "Anastasia Terdan?"

Stace's smile faltered. "Yes?"

Drew's eyes popped wide open, as did his mouth, but he made no noise.

Claire resisted the urge to gulp. Stace could turn out to be a warm-up for Virginia. "My father was Mark Terdan. Was he your brother?"

"No." Stace frowned and shook her head. "My cousin. His father and my mother were brother and sister. I'm sorry about your family. I didn't realize that's who you are."

"I don't remember seeing you at the funeral." She recalled the crowd feeling large and oppressive. Faces had blurred together. Most of them had been nothing more than skirts and slacks to her.

Stace nodded. "I wasn't there." Claire noticed her gaze flicking to Drew and back to her. "I didn't live here at the time, and didn't get the news until much too late. The same is true for your parents, Drew. I moved back when my sister finally told me that our mother had Alzheimer's, which was why I wasn't getting news soon enough to deal with it. That was only a few years ago. She's since passed."

"So Drew and I are related."

"Yes, of course. My Aunt Patty is his grandmother. Mark, Lynn, and I were cousins. You two are, I think, second cousins. You're fine to be dating, because that's not very close."

Claire tried not to give Drew a funny look. Like Stace said, no one cared about anything past first cousins. "And Sophie?"

"More cousins." One corner of Stace's mouth quirked up. "I have all this in a book. Would you like to see it? I've drawn all the lines. It's much easier to understand visually."

Drew bobbed his head. "I would."

"Me too," Sophie said.

Claire had no reason to argue.

CHAPTER 10

DREW

The book blew Drew away. He sat on the bench, crowded between Sophie and Claire. All three held a thick, leather-bound book filled with yellowed pages. Elegant script in black ink listed names and dates, and showed the connections between hundreds of people. Many had pictures, and the sepia-toned ones captured his attention.

Corwin Evans had carried a sword in 1890, the year he married Jaqueline Whidby.

All this time, he'd had family all over the Portland area and never known it. He and Claire had both been victims of missed messages and confusion. Then he flipped a page and it blew his mind. Again.

"Wait, you're related to Kurt?" Kay said.

Drew tapped a black and white photograph of a young couple. Emmeline Terdan had married Kurt Marsh in 1930. Emmeline's date of death put her at ninety-six years old when she passed. "This man died in September."

"One more death I missed," Stace said with a sigh.

"It happened in the Palace," Claire said. "So there was no body for anyone to find. Justin probably didn't know who to notify."

"This whole book is amazing," Sophie said. "I notice it doesn't have anyone our age, though. Except for your sister's kids."

"No. I lost track of people and put things off. I guess I have some work to do updating it." Stace yawned. "I don't mean to chase you all away, but I don't normally stay up too late."

Drew joined Claire and Sophie in apologizing and handing over the book. "Would it be okay to come back and look through this more?"

"Of course. I don't go out much. Stop by anytime." Stace set the book aside and escorted them out.

Night had fallen. Through the trees above, Drew could see a zillion stars. It seemed colder than before. At the same time, Drew carried a queer, fuzzy feeling in his belly.

Claire said, "I think we should all chat. Drew, take us someplace."

"Like where?"

"I should probably go home," Sophie said. "Another time? We can go to a coffee shop and have cupcakes or something."

"Sounds great," Claire said. She smiled at Sophie.

Something about that smile worried Drew. He decided not to comment as he spun mist around them. Sophie waved goodbye across the street from her house and Drew took himself, Claire, and the two dragons home. They landed in Claire's bedroom.

She slapped him across the face. His glasses remained in place. His eye felt like it exploded.

"Ow!" He rubbed his cheek. "Will you please stop hitting me? What is *wrong* with you?"

Claire frowned at her hand as if it had lashed out on its own. "I don't know. I'm sorry. But you shouldn't have left Rhubark behind."

Enion and Rhubark both squawked at him. They chattered competing streams of what sounded like harsh scolding.

To Drew's surprise, Kay didn't chime in to pile on. "Sorry, Rhubark. It won't happen again." He didn't know whether to worry or not about her reaction.

She shook her head, then kissed his cheek. "I'm going to let Rhubark out and make sure the folks know we're home. When I get back, we should look over Iulia's journal."

"Right." He removed the journal from his coat and set it on the nightstand. Over the next few minutes, he shifted to his own bedroom, changed into pajamas, collected Mutt, and let Grandma and Grandpa know he'd come back. Then he returned to find Claire sitting on the edge of her bed, wearing her nightshirt. She flipped through the journal.

"It's still in Latin," she said.

"Yeah. It'll take some work to translate." He sat beside her and pet Mutt's head. "My Latin isn't as good as Iulia's. Is Justin mad at me?"

"No. Disappointed. He expects you to work with me as a partner. Hey, this is a map." She held up the book, open to a page with labeled lines in a grid.

Drew took the book and read the labels. Justin's disappointment bothered him. He hadn't realized he cared what the guy thought. "This is in English," Drew said. "She just used the Latin letter forms. This is the intersection of— Oh. That's where Ki's bar is. We already know what's near there."

"The node."

He checked the next few pages and found Skidmore Fountain, the cemetery with Claire's family, and one unfamiliar location. "I don't know what's at the corner of Southeast Twelfth and Oak."

Claire squinted at the map, then shrugged. "Yeah, I know where that is, but I can't picture it either. I guess we should take a look. She might've started something there we need to make sure doesn't get finished."

"Field trip tomorrow." Drew gave back the book.

"Master, is it time for sleeping yet? I'm sleepy. I chased five squirrels while you were gone. Grandpa Jack threw a stick for me three and a lot times. The ley line in the woods is weak, so I want to sleep now."

"Is it?" Drew glanced at Claire. "It seemed fine when I tapped it a few days ago."

"Don't look at me," Claire said. "I don't pay attention to that."

He thought over everything he'd seen during the day. Nothing had seemed drained or stressed, though he'd been in several places he'd never seen through Kay's eyes before. Speaking of his co-pilot, Drew worried something had spooked him.

"Kay?"

"Hm?"

"You've been awfully quiet for a while."

"You keep telling me to shut up. I listened for once. Try not to have a heart attack."

Drew smirked. "I'll mark it on the calendar."

Claire set the book aside and nudged Drew. He stood. Watching her tuck her feet under the covers brought up the memory of Justin telling him not to do anything stupid. Any other day, he slipped under the covers, kissed her goodnight, and curled up with her to sleep in blessed warmth.

Stace's book loomed at the forefront of his mind.

"What's wrong?" Claire propped herself up on an elbow and held out her locket hand.

"We're related," he blurted.

"Are you joking?" Kay asked.

She snorted. "I thought you were the smart one between us."

Kay laughed. "What she said."

"What?"

Claire leaned out of bed and grabbed his hand. "Aside from the fact you and I are second cousins at best, this body is over two thousand years old, remember? You're so far removed from Iulia as an ancestor that there's no issue here."

Drew blushed and let her tug him close. He'd gotten so wrapped up in the idea, he'd forgotten about reality. "Oh. Right. That makes this weird in a really different way."

"Agreed," Kay said.

Rubbing his eyes with a finger and thumb, Drew considered trying to prod Kay again. On one hand, he hated thinking about Kay at times like this. True privacy with Claire needed treasuring. Besides, talking to him with other people in the room, especially Claire, bothered Drew. At the same time, he didn't think he'd get to sleep without knowing what had made him go quiet.

"What's wrong now?" Claire still held his hand, and he still stood next to her.

"Nothing. Just thinking."

"Amazing," Kay said. "There's no smoke coming out of your ears."

Claire said, "Think under the covers. Right, Mutt?"

"Please get into bed now, Master," Mutt whined.

"Sorry." Drew squeezed Claire's hand. "I need to do something. I won't be long."

She let go. "Is this like when you said you were going to visit Anne and went to see Sophie instead?"

He sighed. "I did visit Anne. She wasn't home. I picked the next witch on my list."

"Who happens to be a pretty, blonde teenage girl you never mentioned before."

For some reason, he'd thought the subject had been dealt with.

"Before you open your mouth," Kay said, "I'd like to make a suggestion. Do not admit you find Sophie attractive. Tell her instead about the power drain phenomenon."

"You mean the bacon thing?"

Claire squinted at him. "Bacon?"

"Déjà vu," Kay said.

"Yeah." Drew spun mist, not wanting to get into this again. "I'll be back in a few minutes, I promise."

Claire's confused annoyance disappeared, replaced by the bare walls and floor of his tidy bedroom in Grandpa Jack and Grandma Tammy's house. He sat on the edge of his bed. The dresser and closet held all his clothes, the fabric hamper held all his laundry, and the desk held all his school things.

He hadn't slept here since the night he got Claire back in Iulia's body.

"Never mind that," he told the room. "Kay, what's bothering you?"

"Me? Nothing."

"Liar."

Kay sighed. "I've been considering the potential impact of bloodlines on the way we're integrated, and if there's a possibility we might be separated through the manipulation of that knowledge. It keeps coming down to the part where I need a body of some sort no matter what, making it a futile mental exercise.

"For fun, I've also been wondering if Kurt knew about your distant relation to Emmy, and whether your father might've actually been one of his descendants. He did call you his grandson, and even though we're sure that's not the case, it might've been technically true, or truth-adjacent. You shut the book and handed it over before reaching his pages, after all."

Drew thought of the safety deposit box his first social worker had set up for him along with the trust fund holding the proceeds from the sale of his parents' house and their life insurance policies. Into it, she'd put a stack of documents and pictures taken from his home.

He'd never asked for the key.

When he turned eighteen, he'd get his file, and the key would be inside it. Maybe it had a picture of his family, including Kurt.

"By the way, you sat with Stace for at least half an hour and didn't bring up the ice cream thing."

Stace had spent the whole time explaining how to use crystals and bind a focus stone in minute detail. He'd asked her for one and she'd told him to find his own because she didn't have extras. He felt like the explanation had taken about fifteen minutes, but that didn't matter.

"She distracted me. The next time I see her, don't let me leave without asking."

"Sure. Now go back to Claire, tell her she's pretty, and get some sleep, because ice is forming on your hand."

CHAPTER 11

CLAIRE

The next morning, the sky glowed blue as if it had been cleansed by the minor snowfall. Claire and Drew hopped off a bus in front of a silent construction site on the east side of Portland. Enion sat on Claire's shoulders, his head peeking out of her scarf below her left ear. Sunshine reflected off puddles of melted slush and ice. Mutt, who'd run alongside the bus from Holladay Park, where Drew had shifted them by mist, panted as he rejoined them.

"Bacon is a weird direction to go with that," Claire said as they walked past a chain-link fence, "but I have to admit it makes sense when you explain it that way."

"That's how I feel about it," Drew said.

Now that she knew the whole story, Claire considered the subject of Sophie closed. She had no reason to doubt Drew because everything he said sounded exactly like him. Besides, if she'd done something she felt that guilty about, she had a feeling she might keep the whole thing a secret too. Like she'd kept dying a secret from Marie.

They turned the corner onto Twelfth Street and kept going. Cars lined both sides of the street, though few people walked around. Like the construction site, the nearby stores and warehouse-like buildings all seemed closed. The flouncy name of one reminded Claire about the focus stone issue.

"Where do you want to go to find a crystal?"

"I dunno. New age store? I can probably find one for ten bucks or less. I thought about asking Anne, but Iulia gave me one that blew up when I tried to use it. I don't know if she set it up to do that on purpose, or if there's something about using someone else's crystals." He paused. "Right. Or it could just be me. Because I'm an abomination."

Claire rolled her eyes. As much as she liked Anne, she could see why the Knights had issues with witches. Theirs had spawned mostly from how Caius had depicted Iulia, but she had a feeling witches in the world had reinforced the schism. Justin didn't even like witches much, and he had one for a sister-in-law.

"Anyone else calls you that, let me know. I'll punch them in the face for you."

He squeezed her hand. "Thanks." A moment later, he pointed up the street. "The ten bucks in my wallet says we found the spot."

They'd passed the construction site and strolled by a long building that looked like apartments. Ahead, Claire saw a reddish sign that read *St. Francis of Assisi* in gold letters.

"A church? Yeah, probably. Justin said churches attract ghosts and allow them to find rest. And before you ask, he doesn't know what that actually means either. Other than they go away and don't get corrupted."

"What could Iulia have wanted to do here?"

The sign, Claire noted, reported that all were welcome, and if they went inside, they'd find Sunday morning mass in progress. Steps led to the front door of a brown building with white trim. Tall evergreens dusted with frost flanked the entry and lined the building.

Claire heard faint music, probably from the church service inside. The melody wrapped gentle arms around her and breathed whispers of welcome into her ears. Its warm embrace promised comfort and an end to pain.

"What are you doing?" Drew clutched her arm from two steps below her.

She hadn't realized she'd climbed two steps. What was she doing? Not sure why she'd moved closer to the church, Claire scanned the greenery. She saw a flicker of fog through the branches.

"Aah!" Mutt dove behind Drew.

"Did you see that?" Claire asked. The oddness of the sight freed her from whatever had urged her forward.

Drew peered in that direction and frowned. "The building has a magical signature. Kay says that's normal for churches. He also says we should stay outside it, and he's kind of panicky about that fact."

"Fog isn't normal for churches." Claire reached under the hem of her coat and gripped the hilt of the dagger clipped to her waistband at the small of her back. She approached the thirty-foot tall tree and batted at the branches with the blade.

A thick, ill-defined arm of mist swiped through the air, missing her face by an inch. Claire jumped back.

Mutt barked his terror again.

Drew squeaked. "What was that?"

"It looks like a ghost. Why is it here?"

"You're asking me?" Drew hurried close, but stayed behind her.

"Kay says it shouldn't be out like this during the day. If it's going to wander, it should be in a cemetery until dusk. And if it gets this far, it should either go to the doors or keep moving. And it shouldn't care about us."

"That's a lot of 'shoulds' it's ignoring." Seeing no further activity, Claire took a tentative step closer again. She poked the tree with her dagger.

High-pitched, screechy wailing blasted her ears. As she cringed, she saw Drew covering his ears. Mutt howled. Enion growled.

Claire backed off again, taking Drew with her. The sound died.

"Master, that thing is awful."

"I'm with Mutt on that one," Claire muttered.

"Maybe we should get Justin."

She shook her head. "I don't think we need him. He'll say to stab it. I can stab something. Stabbing things is easy."

"So stab it," Drew said. "Don't leave it there."

Claire glared at the tree. "I feel like we should collect some information or something. I mean, if this is such bizarre behavior, why is it doing that? It can't be a coincidence that Iulia's journal led us to a screwed-up ghost."

"Sure. Okay." Drew gulped. "You do that. Gather some information. I'll be over here."

As he started to take another step away, Claire snagged his coat. "Not so fast. I want Kay's input."

"He says to kill it a lot."

Not amused, Claire tugged him closer. "Try again, Kay." She tapped the end of a branch with the tip of her dagger.

The ghostly arm lashed out again and its shrill scream seemed harsher than the first time. Claire held Drew's arm, keeping him from bolting. Drew covered his ears and leaned to the side. More mist surged toward him. They backed off.

When the noise faded, Drew lowered his arms. Two men opened the church door and peered outside. Claire tucked her dagger away and smiled at them as if an otherworldly screech hadn't come from the tree.

"Are you okay?" one man called out.

Claire tried to act confused why they'd ask. "Yes, we're fine."

Both men scanned the area, shrugged, and closed the door again.

"Kay says there's something wrong with it."

"Thanks for the tip."

"No," Drew said with a huff. "Actually wrong with it. It has a weird aura. It's like...like when you trip over a wire and pull it out of the wall, and you get tangled up in it." He frowned. "No, Kay, that can't be right. There must be some other explanation. She can't be the only one."

"What's up?" Claire couldn't think of any reason why someone would do that to a ghost instead of either destroying it or running from it.

Drew held up a finger for her to wait. "How could that even be a possibility? We all saw what happened."

Claire shook her head and stared at the tree. A witch angry at the church might've done this, she supposed. From what she knew of history, that didn't seem far-fetched.

"Only if you're sure," Drew said.

"Does he need to see it again?"

"No."

Nodding, Claire grabbed her dagger again. This time when she teased it, she didn't back away. She sliced her dagger through the white arm. Enion belched a tiny ball of fire at it. Smoke puffed from the thick needles. The screaming softened, but didn't end. Claire swiped her dagger through the branches, not sure why the ghost still existed to make noise.

Enion jumped off her shoulder and into the tree. He bounced on the branches with defiant chirps, shaking out dirt, twigs, and loose needles.

Not sure what to look for, Claire focused and shifted her vision so she and Enion could see magic. The switch brought into focus vivid streamers of color. She saw a thick, clear cord of pure power winding through the branches, but no sign of the ghost.

"Should I cut this magicky thing or leave it?" She had to shout over the half-muted shrieking.

"Cut it!"

Claire shoved her dagger at the ropy power and met resistance. She sawed back and forth over it. Enion, also able to see it, hopped into range and blew fire at it.

"What are you kids doing?" a man shouted.

Claire ignored him. She kept sawing. Bands of power sprang apart, like cutting through a braided, high-tension cable.

Enion's fire weakened the cord, making it easier to cut through.

"She thought she saw something," Drew said.

Mutt barked his alarm. "Go away, stranger!"

Someone in a suit wrapped thick arms around Claire's waist and tried to haul her aside. "Stop screaming!" he shouted.

"I'm not," Claire said. She grabbed a thick branch and held on. "Let go!" Her dagger no longer reached the cord.

"The tree is burning," the man said. "Get away from there."

"Get off me." Claire jabbed him in the side with her elbow. Her dagger flashed in the light of Enion's small fire.

The man let go and stepped away. "I'm calling the cops."

"I can explain," Drew said.

Free to ignore them again, Claire attacked the cord. Between her efforts and Enion's fire, the cord snapped and flung itself at the building. As it flew through the air, it dissolved. Sparks reached the wall and bounced off it. The noise stopped.

Claire swiped Enion and lunged for Drew's blazing silver-blue aura. "Time to go!"

As she plowed into him, she almost laughed at the distressed surprise on his face. Mist enveloped them. When it cleared, they landed in a patch of woods. Sunshine lit up the evergreens mixed with bare sticks. Drew hit the ground with a grunt. Claire fell on top of him. Her hand popped open, releasing Enion. Mutt sat on the ground beside them.

Enion flapped until he gained enough altitude to land on Mutt's head.

"Sorry." Claire sheathed her dagger and sat up, straddling his hips. "Things were getting weird."

"Getting?" He gasped for breath.

Claire smirked and looked around. The trees seemed familiar. She thought she'd leaped over that rock a bunch of times while running with Justin. "Are we home?"

"Yeah."

"Are you going to tell me what Kay said?" She stood and offered him a hand.

Drew took the help and shook his head. "I think he's nuts."

"Tell me anyway and we'll laugh at him together."

When he turned toward the house, Claire walked with him. Mutt followed, carrying Enion on his head without complaint.

"He thinks Iulia did it."

Claire didn't think that was funny.

CHAPTER 12

DREW

"You're acting like we didn't come right here to tell you about it first thing," Drew said. He and Claire sat together on the old stump Justin used to chop firewood. The clearing around it connected to a path between the Brady house and the Evans cottage. Firewood stacked under a lean-to dominated one edge, and the woods extended into the distance opposite it.

Justin stood in front of them, his arms crossed and mouth drawn into a deep frown. "You should've come to get me right away instead of—"

"Instead of what?" Claire snapped. "Handling it? You keep telling me this is my job, then when I do it, you get mad. Kind of a mixed message here."

"That's fine for normal things."

Claire snorted. "Exactly what about this job is ever normal?"

"Routine," Justin said. "This is anything but routine."

Drew cleared his throat. "No one got hurt and the ghost is destroyed. Can we maybe not worry so much about this, and worry more about Iulia somehow binding ghosts despite being dead?"

Justin sighed. "Fine. I'm just worried about you two getting into things you can't handle."

Claire turned her back on Justin to say to Drew, "What makes you think it was Iulia?"

"The signature on the cord matched her aura. I haven't met a lot of witches, but she's the only one with a clear aura I've seen. Maybe we'll come across another one—"

"No," Kay said, forcing Drew to pause to listen. "We won't. I promise. My knowledge of magic may not be encyclopedic, but I know enough to be firm about this. Clear is not a normal aura form."

Drew nodded. "But I doubt it."

"What if Iulia set up whatever magic that was before she died?"

"Possible. But doubtful," Kay said.

Drew nodded again. "She wasn't around very long. She can't have had much time to do all the things we know she did—set up her lair, write that journal, and experiment. Adding complex magical workings to that seems a bit much."

"And she was obsessed," Kay said. "Don't forget that part."

"Even if she did have enough time," Drew continued, "why would she do it? Nothing about that had anything to do with setting up the seal she wanted."

"The cord you described sounds like what Anne did to the dragons," Justin said. "They were trapped when I found them. She told me it took a huge amount of power and over a day of work, and she was only able to do it because Kurt supported her. Even if Iulia only needed half that time, she didn't have it between when the Palace was destroyed and when she died."

"I've noticed," Kay said, "that neither of them say we killed Iulia.

They always make it sound like she tripped and fell onto a sword."

Drew coughed to hide a wildly inappropriate bark of laughter from the metal picture. "That being the case, what does it mean? Did she make a Phasm? We don't know the rules for how ghosts work now, and we just saw one in broad daylight."

"Did she make the journal?" Claire asked. "I mean, after she died. Did her ghost somehow write it?"

Drew frowned and pulled out the journal to show Justin. "No, we found it in her lair. I didn't pick it up then, but when I saw it there, it was full of writing. I don't know how much, though."

Flipping through the small book, Justin nodded along. He stopped at the section with the maps. "If she wrote this before her death, why did she make maps of these places? Actually, where did you get this?"

"Sophie said her mom gave it to her in a stack of old family journals." Drew shrugged.

"Who's Sophie?" Justin asked.

Drew struggled with what to tell Justin. He didn't understand a lot of magic stuff, and the whole bacon thing sounded awful without context. It sounded awful with context too. "A member of Anne's coven. Our age. She's nice to us."

Claire asked, "Where did her mom get it?"

"I don't know. They're witches." Drew crossed his arms, not sure why this line of questioning bothered him.

"You're a witch," Justin said.

Kay snorted. "Walked into that one."

Drew scowled. "Yeah? And?"

"This isn't about you," Claire said. "The point is, there's something fishy about Sophie having that journal. And now maybe Iulia isn't as dead as we thought."

"You're right," Justin said. He tapped the open page of the journal in Drew's hands. "I'm not sure we should trust anyone in that coven, including Anne, until we learn how they got this journal. In the meantime, I'd like to check all the places she made maps for. How many are there?"

Drew flipped through the pages. "Five, counting the church."

"Given what you found at the first location, let's assume we'll encounter trouble at all of them. That means I'd like to go as a group and not split up to handle them. Pick one and we'll go now, then we'll plan to check the rest after lunch." Justin headed toward Tariel's small stable behind the farmhouse.

Justin wanted to go once more unto the breach. Drew wanted to sit and read the journal.

Claire nudged his shoulder with hers. "You don't have to go."

He sighed. She had every reason to say that. Again.

"She's right. We should stay here. The last thing I need is more ghost encounters. It's bad for my sanity."

"Thanks for proving the point, Kay."

To his surprise, Claire reached over and unzipped his coat. She yanked it off one arm and gripped his wrist.

"Oh." Kay coughed. "Ah. Hm."

As she shoved his sleeve up, Drew realized her intent. Claire wrapped her hand around the brand inside his elbow. Her heartbeat filled his ears as a soft, soothing rhythm. Sometimes, when he couldn't sleep, he took her hand and settled it there to get this effect.

"Claire," Kay said, a nervous edge to his voice.

"Kay. Tell me what happened at the church."

"We met a ghost?"

She met Drew's gaze while talking to Kay. "And you panicked, which made Drew panic. Otherwise, he would've been scared, but not like that. Drew is capable of acting while he's scared."

Drew kissed her. She understood what had happened there. Without him having to explain.

"Yes, do that. I'll be over here."

Justin cleared his throat. Terrified Justin would smack him, Drew froze and jerked away.

Though she smiled at Drew, Claire kept her grip on his arm. "Answer me, Kay."

"Well. Ah. Er. We, well, we haven't had a lot of good experiences dealing with ghosts. None, in fact. I'm...*concerned* we'll be defeated by some other entity. Which would mean that we die, which is bad. The other option, that we get controlled, isn't exactly stellar either."

Claire raised her brow. "Is there some reason you think I'd just stand by and let that happen?"

"No," Drew said. The idea of Claire thinking he didn't trust her to step in if he needed help hurt him. Because he knew it hurt her. "Never."

Kay made a throat-clearing noise. "In my defense, I didn't panic about this before we failed a few times against Dwight. And also, panic is bad for critical thinking skills." When Claire said nothing else, Kay added. "It won't happen again."

"Glad to hear it." She let go, kissed Drew on the cheek, and nodded to Justin.

"Are we ready to go?" Justin asked. He sounded amused.

Tariel whinnied. She laughed at him. No, at all three of them.

Drew didn't know why he'd worried about Justin hitting him. More than once, Justin had made clear his opinion on the subject of Drew and Claire having a relationship and doing relationship things. Every time, he said to keep a clear head about it. Don't be a statistic. Take their time. Make conscious decisions. Talk things over.

Even more importantly, he'd never lifted a hand against either of them, not even when he'd been under Kurt's control. Justin, Marie, Grandpa Jack, and Grandma Tammy had the least volatile tempers in the universe. Claire would hit him. Justin would not.

He and Claire probably needed to talk about the hitting thing. In his head, the conversation consisted of him asking her not to hit him and her asking him not to do anything stupid.

The matter could wait. They had some sites to investigate and maybe some ghosts to dispatch.

"Oh boy," Kay said as Drew spun the mist to carry them to the first site. "This is gonna be more fun than a whoopie blow."

Drew had no idea what that meant, but he got the idea and agreed.

CHAPTER 13

CLAIRE

The mist cleared with them standing in front of the main green-roofed, brick building of Evergreen High School in Vancouver. Since moving in with the Brady and Evans families, Claire and Drew had been attending this school. For once, it had no cars in the parking lot. Nothing seemed out of place compared to last Friday. A few giant trees towered over the buildings. The rest of the trees had lost their last few leaves. Stubby icicles clung to the corners of the roofs. Except in the shady corners, the snow had turned to slush.

Unlike other schools she'd suffered at, Evergreen had been good to Claire. No one picked on her, and she never noticed anyone doing anything like bullying. At every other school over the past six years, someone had always picked her as their target.

"No cutting through doors," she told Justin with a smirk.

"I wasn't planning to." Justin climbed onto Tariel's back. "I'll take a ride around the perimeter. You two check the roof."

"Do you even know this school?" Drew asked.

Justin snorted. "I went here my senior year. It wasn't that long ago."

Tariel jumped into a trot across the parking lot.

"Do you have as hard a time picturing him as a teenager as I do?" Drew asked.

"I doubt it." She'd seen him at that age. "C'mon. Roof."

He spun mist around them, and they landed on the flat roof of the main building. Metal housings with exhaust vents stuck from the white, sectioned surface. Peaked hatches peppered the sections, and several parts rose higher than the main part of the building.

"Go big?" Enion asked.

"I don't know if the roof can support you. Better not chance it." Claire scanned for cameras, worried the principal would see them later on security footage.

"There's nothing up here," Drew said. "No magic at all. Barren. Just like inside the school."

"Okay. Let's think." Claire walked toward the gap in the center, where trees and shrubs grew in a concrete courtyard open to the weather. "If there was anything inside the school, you would've noticed it, right?"

"That ghost at the church was visible. You saw it without enhancing your vision. That means if there's something here, it must be in a dark spot no one goes into, like an unassigned locker." He pointed to boxy metal housing. "Or the ductwork."

"Enion, you're small. Go fly through that and see if you find anything." She tossed Enion at the nearest housing.

Enion chirped his agreement and darted inside.

"I wish we knew the point of that ghost and its containment," Drew said. "It doesn't make sense. Nothing about that spell would've helped set up a new seal."

Claire thought back to her conversations with her father's Phasm. He'd been obsessed, but still himself with less memory. His ghost had forgotten what Dad stood for and why he fought. She thought about shifting her sight to see magical auras, but Enion needed to see to fly through the ductwork, and it would affect him too.

"Maybe she's forgotten about the seal. Now that the Palace has been destroyed, maybe there's some other purpose consuming her."

Drew shrugged. "Like what? There's nothing to be gained from chaining and torturing ghosts."

"No idea." Claire peered over the edge to the courtyard. Nothing seemed out of place around the giant lowercase "e" painted green on the concrete. "I'm just saying there must be a reason. If it's Iulia's ghost, even if she went nuts, she'd still have a reason."

"Being nuts could be the reason." Drew spun out mist and shifted them into the courtyard. He glanced at her like he had something else to say, but kept his mouth shut and stalked around the trees. He passed the one gate to the outside and kept his hands shoved in his pockets.

She narrowed her eyes at his back and followed him. "What?"

"What what?"

"You looked at me like, I don't know. Like I might be responsible or something."

"No," he threw over his shoulder. "You're not."

She jogged to catch up and slapped a hand on his shoulder. "What crap is Kay whispering in your ear now?"

"Nothing." Drew sighed and tucked his fingers under his glasses to rub his eyes. "He's using a lot of words to say he doesn't know very much. Honestly, this slang he's leaning on is getting old. I have no idea what onions have to do with anything."

"Onions? What?"

"Kay! You aren't from the twenties. Use modern words. They're in my head, and I know you can see all that if you want to."

"The twenties." Claire furrowed her brow, not sure what to think about this situation. "He's using twenties slang."

"Now you're on the trolley. He's a swell fella," Drew grumbled. "A cake eater who really knows his onions."

Claire stared at him for a moment, then turned away to shake a tree and see if anything lunged at her. If Kay wanted to use old-timey slang, she had nothing to say to him.

"If you're not going to be helpful, Kay, then shut up." Drew huffed in frustration. He jumped into a planter.

The moment his boots hit the bare earth, he screamed. His body jerked and spasmed as if he touched a live electrical wire.

Shouting his name accomplished nothing. Claire rushed to him, stopping short of the dirt. She had no idea what he ran into or why it affected him. His screams stabbed her in the chest.

"What happened? What do I do?"

He fell to his hands and knees, every muscle in his body jerking. His screams grew hoarse.

"What's wrong?" Justin shouted from the other side of the gate. "I heard him from across the parking lot!"

"I don't know!" Claire reached for Drew. She wanted to touch him, but she didn't dare. "I can't see anything."

"Shift your sight," Justin called.

Feeling stupid for not thinking of that, Claire covered her ears and focused on her connection to Enion. Magic shifted into sight. Unlike the church, the surfaces outside the planters were, as Drew said, barren. The trees and dirt inside the planters glowed with tiny, writhing worms. A thick, clear rope wound around Drew's left leg, anchored in the ground. The pointed tip wriggled past his knee, growing with every passing second.

"It's like the ghost at the church." She didn't see why it hurt him so much, but knew what to do. At least, she thought she did. What if this one attacked her? Why did she even wonder that?

Drawing her dagger, she tried to decide if she could safely touch the earth or Drew. The question seemed stupid and dire at the same time. Clattering on the concrete behind her made her turn to see Tariel rising from a crouch after what must have been a jump from the roof, or maybe over the gate.

Justin jumped off the horse's back at a run, his sword already in hand, his cloak swirling. Where Claire hesitated with indecision, he acted. He rushed the planter and stabbed his sword into the ground while knocking Drew onto the concrete. The rope dissipated.

Drew lay on his side on the concrete. His spasms subsided. He gasped for rattling breaths.

Justin dropped to one knee and murmured to him.

Shocked by her incompetence, put into stark relief by Justin's gross competence, Claire stood and let her arms hang by her sides. Faced with something strange attacking Drew, she'd spent too much time weighing choices and not enough taking chances. How had that happened?

She'd punched through walls in more stressful situations. She'd fought Phasms and Knights. She'd sailed through the air to certain death to save everyone she cared about.

"I'm sorry," she breathed.

"Boy hurt?" Enion landed on her shoulder.

She stared, terrified Drew wouldn't recover. It would be her fault.

Justin nodded to Drew and stood. Sunshine glinted off his green-tinted chain shirt. His emerald cloak hung off one shoulder. He sheathed his sword like an epic hero. "Claire, ride Enion home. When you get there, ask Grandma Tammy to make something for Drew to eat. We'll meet you there."

Enion jumped off Claire's shoulder and flashed into his large form.

"I thought—"

"We'll discuss it later. Right now, Drew needs to get home, and he'll freeze to death on Enion's back." Justin bent again and scooped Drew into his arms.

Drew trembled, his body shivering so hard he couldn't speak. She saw a rime of ice covering his face. His lips looked blue.

Tariel bent her legs for Justin. He stepped onto her back, still holding Drew.

"Claire," Justin barked, "get home first!" He flipped his cloak over Drew.

"Get on back," Enion said.

"I don't understand." Claire stood still, confused by her own behavior.

Tariel lurched into a gallop around the courtyard, then leaped with impossible power and grace to the top of a decorative arch above a nearby door, then the higher building roof.

Enion nudged her with his shoulder. "Get on back now. Go home now."

"Yeah." She shook her head and had no explanation or excuse for herself. Climbing onto Enion's back, she sheathed her dagger and wondered how she'd face Drew later.

CHAPTER 14

JUSTIN

An hour later, John Avery's car rumbled in greeting as Tariel approached it in gloom of the downtown police station parking garage. She stepped into the parking space beside it. Justin climbed off her back. He patted the car's hood.

"I won't be long. Don't get comfy."

"You ask too much," Tariel said. "How could I possibly resist this dark, dank cave of concrete? It's so homey. I might want to move in and abandon my warm, plush wood stable forever."

Justin snorted as he walked away from her with a wave. He stepped through a door and entered a world of harsh, glaring light, bland industrial tile, and soul-crushing authority. Uniformed cops noticed him as he swaggered through the hall in his chain armor, jeans, work boots, and green cloak. They knew who he was.

The Knight of Portland had been a silly joke before the giant bugs. He'd used it to get away with riding around the city on a horse with armor and a sword. After the attack, people realized he did it for a reason besides eccentricity.

He climbed stairs two at a time to reach Avery's office on the third floor. The room he entered had desks arranged in the center of a wide space surrounded by offices. Fluorescent lights buzzed overhead. Detectives in suits toiled at computers yet still had stacks of folders with paper inside.

Avery's office door hung open. Justin walked in to find him eating a sandwich and staring at a glowing screen in the meager light of a desk lamp. Despite having an outside wall, he didn't get a window. Instead, filing cabinets lined the walls, making the space feel cramped and stagnant.

Justin shut the door and sat opposite the detective. The smells of mustard and mildew permeated the room.

"Afternoon," Avery said. He looked as crisp as ever in a tie and dress shirt. His navy suit jacket hung over the back of his cheap executive chair. His gun and badge lay on top of a pile of folders on his desk.

"I would've thought they'd move you to a better office."

Avery grinned and wiped his face with a paper towel. "I'm lucky they didn't fire me."

"And I have you to thank for not being arrested."

Nodding, Avery sat back. The springs and plastic of his chair creaked. "What brings you down here?"

"Haven't heard from you since that day." Justin laced his fingers in his lap, keeping the discussion casual. He hadn't come to interrogate or accuse and didn't want Avery to think otherwise.

"I've been spending all my free time trying to convince my family I'm not the asshole who terrorized them for five years." Avery shrugged. "Uphill battle. Especially with the boys. I think Brian might be a Knight, but I have no idea what that means anymore. And if he is, he's not going to listen to me about the job."

Justin made a mental note to offer Mutt as a way to help explain to Avery's older son. The younger one need it too. Later, though. "Have you done any patrolling?"

"I've been paying attention to the radio for reports of weird things going on and haven't heard anything."

Justin frowned at him. "None at all?"

"Did you come here to toss some guilt onto me for not pulling my weight?"

"No." Justin shook his head and didn't know what to think. "I took the kids out yesterday, touring cemeteries, and we found nothing."

Avery echoed Justin's frown and rubbed his chin. "If nothing is preventing ghosts from forming, it seems strange there aren't any in the area."

"It gets weirder, because I ran into Charlie the other day. Olympia is infested. It's all he can do to keep up with them. I rode around Saint Helens and Rainier for him two weeks ago, dealing with at least twenty ghosts haunting the trails and roads. That's why I took the kids on a patrol. Then today, the kids ran across a visible ghost chained to a tree at Saint Francis. Another chain seems to have been set as a trap for ghosts at the high school they go to. It caught Drew. He was still unconscious when I left him at home."

"Huh." Avery took a bite of his sandwich and chewed while staring at the wall. "Could be a helpful witch we don't know."

"That's possible, but I came because Kay thinks Iulia's ghost set the traps. Apparently, both had her signature."

Avery's brow flew up. "Is that even possible?"

"I'd like your help finding out. Hunting ghosts is what we do, after all."

Standing, Avery tugged his jacket off his chair. "Any thoughts on where to start?"

Justin also stood. "Drew picked up Iulia's journal. There are maps. Saint Francis, the school, Skidmore Fountain, Nine Cans, and Steel Bridge."

"Interesting list."

"That's what I thought." Skidmore Fountain had been the site of a piece of a seal Justin had destroyed. Nine Cans had been their entry into the Portland Underground, where the most powerful node in the city lay. On Steel, they'd all fought a giant mutant cockroach. Justin, Claire, Drew, and Marie had all gone to Evergreen.

"The only one I don't know why it's in the group is Saint Francis."

Avery clipped his gun and badge to his belt. "It's the oldest church in the city."

"Sure, but that doesn't make it connected to any of us, or any battles we've fought lately."

"My mother's family all go to that church and have since they moved here back in the nineteenth century. I haven't been since I married Caroline, though. She's not Catholic." On his way out of the office, Avery snagged his sheathed sword and tan trenchcoat from the floor behind his desk.

"Compared to the other links, that seems kind of thin." Justin followed him through the building, back to the parking garage. Along the way, other cops noticed Avery's sword and gave them both curious or knowing looks and nods.

Avery nodded to acknowledge some people along the way but ignored most. "If the rest of your families have been around for a while, they probably also attended that church."

"Which still seems weak."

"Maybe Iulia had grudge against Catholics. She lived in Rome, after all." Avery pushed through the door to the parking garage and saw Tariel. "Really? You parked your horse in a space?"

Justin chuckled. "I could've left her in the lobby."

"It would've been warmer," Tariel said with a sniff. "Where are we going?"

"Do you want to go have a look around Saint Francis?" Justin asked Avery.

"Did Claire or Drew go inside the building? Do a full perimeter check?"

"No. The trap and ghost were in a tree out front. They handled that, then they left to find me."

"Well-trained on that count, at least," Avery said. "Yes, we should take some time and make sure there isn't anything else to find."

Justin nodded toward Avery as the detective climbed into his car. "Like the man says."

"Since when do you listen to cops?" Tariel asked, her tail twitching.

"I listen to old Knights."

"Very funny," Avery said. The door shut and the car backed out of its space.

Laughing, Justin swung into the saddle.

Tariel followed the car out of the garage, then down the street and across Steel Bridge at the speed of traffic. They could've taken a different bridge to reach the church faster, but Justin suspected Avery wanted to check every place on that list as soon as possible. He shifted his vision and watched for ghosts, but saw nothing. The underside probably had something to see. With Enion's ability to fly, Claire would have more luck.

As they reached the other side of the bridge, he shifted his vision back to normal for Tariel's benefit. She needed to see the ground and traffic with clarity, even at thirty miles an hour.

They reached the front door of the church and its welcome sign. Avery stepped out of his car, and it drove off to find a parking space. Justin noticed him drop a fedora onto his head and pull the brim low over his eyes. After staring down a TV camera and becoming the go-to cop for anything weird, he'd lost all traces of anonymity in the city.

Justin sighed at the feel of an established church. He climbed down from Tariel's back and shifted his vision again. The church glowed with a solid, steady pulse of white light spilling over the grounds in a gentle, frothy wave. Nothing matched the gravity of this kind of site. The church had been rebuilt more than once, yet it still felt like it had stood for over a century.

"It's been too long," Avery murmured.

Churches reminded Justin of his father. No matter how comforting the grounds, he could never forget. He pointed to a tree next to the steps to the front door where the froth swirled. "I see where the ghost was."

"It must've been there for at least a few days."

"How did other people avoid setting it off?"

"Luck?" Shaking his head, Avery climbed the steps. "Let's take a look inside."

Justin set his boot on the bottom step, but frowned. "How could she have gone inside a church without being subsumed?" Something else occurred to him. "Do you think Drew needs to worry about that? Or, for that matter, Claire?"

"I don't know. I've never met a possessed person I didn't kill." Avery gripped the door handle. "I have no idea what Claire really is at this point."

Nodding, Justin joined him at the top of the steps. "Neither do I. She still has access to her demesne, and Rondy is still there. I'm worried about the fact she has control over an entire flight of dragons and might be nothing more than a powerful Phasm possessing an otherwise empty body that happens to look exactly like the one she was born with."

Avery opened the door and smirked. "Ah, the joys of raising teenagers."

Despite his concern, Justin laughed. He stepped inside the quiet church full of warm wood, lit by tall, thin windows near the ceiling of the two-story building. Golden haze suffused the entire room. Light yet earthy incense drifted in the air, mingling with an undercurrent of pine.

The place enticed Justin to sit. Avery set a hand on his shoulder, offering a reminder of their purpose.

A thirty-something man wearing a black shirt with a collar approached them and clasped his hands in front of himself. His gaze flicked to their swords and back to their faces. "Can I help you gentlemen?" He had a friendly, open face and a soft, smooth voice.

"Excuse us, Father," Avery said with a polite incline of his head. He flipped his trenchcoat and suit jacket aside to reveal the badge clipped on his belt. "Detective John Avery. We—"

"Pardon me for interrupting, but are you Melissa Avery's son? You have her eyes, and I seem to recall her mentioning her son was a police officer."

Avery sighed. "Yes."

His smile dimmed. "I don't remember seeing you at her funeral services last summer."

"No, I didn't attend, Father. That's a long story."

"It's Father Duncan. If you'd like to come talk about it, the door is always open. And is this your son?"

Justin blinked at the priest. "No. Not even close." He didn't want to get sidetracked like this. "Have you noticed anything unusual on the grounds in the past few weeks?"

"Unusual?" Father Duncan's smile faded to a blank line. "Two teenagers started a fire in a tree in front of the building during morning mass. That's unusual. But I didn't call the police. They seemed as upset by it as the two gentlemen who discovered them, then they disappeared in a strange swirl of mist. Besides, the fire only smoldered. It was easy to stop and caused no real damage."

"Anything else?" Avery asked. "Odd noises, other incidents with unexpected mist, strange women skulking around?"

"That's an interesting and oddly specific list. I do have two volunteers who claim they've seen Mary Magdalene's ghost in the dining hall kitchen. I think the first time that happened was a week or two after Thanksgiving. It's been three or four times, I believe."

Justin glanced at Avery. If a devout Catholic saw Iulia, he expected they'd assume she must be a saint. Otherwise, they might've seen a previous resident of the area. Either way, they needed to check on the sighting.

"May we take a look inside your dining hall, please?"

CHAPTER 15

DREW

Early fall sunshine filtered through trees in a park with a playground. Green, gold, and scarlet leaves fluttered in a warm breeze. Drew didn't know the name of the park, but his foster parents lived nearby. The mother stood at the park entrance with her arms crossed, leaning against a rock wall and watching him. He didn't like her. She hovered all the time and kept telling him to be careful.

Aunt Stace handed him a cone with a rounded scoop of fruit-studded strawberry ice cream from a street vendor.

He took the cone with his good arm and stared at it while Stace paid for it. On that day three months ago, his parents had been taking him to the beach for the day. They would've had ice cream there. Mom had promised.

"I'm sorry about your parents," Stace said as they moved away from the vendor. "I liked your mother quite a bit. Lynn was nice."

Drew kicked a rock. It tumbled down the asphalt path. He didn't want the ice cream. Stace had paid money for it, though, so he licked it.

Strawberry flavor, more potent than any real fruit could mimic, coated his tongue.

He paused and looked up at her. "When are you going to take me in?"

Aunt Stace smiled and patted his shoulder. "A month or two, maybe? I need to find space for you at my house. They have to do an inspection before they'll let me take you."

Drew could wait a month or two. Even if he didn't like this foster mother, she didn't do anything really mean.

They sat at a brown picnic bench. Rumbling filled the air. A big man on an old, beat-up motorcycle from World War II rolled into the parking lot. The big man parked his motorcycle and approached them. He wore tan pants with lots of pockets and a denim jacket with black leather gloves, and had a real sword buckled onto his belt.

Stace saw him and frowned. She shook her head as if to ward him off. When the man pulled off his helmet, Drew saw more white hair and wrinkles than he expected. An old man riding a motorcycle seemed weird.

"Stace, I've been looking for you everywhere."

"This isn't a good time, Kurt." She gestured to Drew.

"I didn't know you had a son." Kurt crouched beside Drew and smiled at him, creases in his face deep enough to drown in.

"He's not my son." Stace tried to shoo him away. "He's Lynn's kid. And you can just ignore him, because he's not going to be part of your world. There's nothing in him."

Crushed by her pronouncement, Drew hung his head and ate his ice cream in silence.

Kurt patted his shoulder with a large, heavy hand. "If he's got Emmy's blood, he could be a Knight in ten years. Would you like that, kid?

To ride around on a motorcycle and save the world with a sword?"

Drew stared at Kurt with his eyes wide. Saving the world sounded amazing. He cranked his head around to see the motorcycle and imagined himself riding it around the city. Something needed stabbing, and he rode with a rumble to go stab it.

Stace huffed at him and lowered her voice. "Knock it off. The only thing he has is witch potential he'll pass on to a daughter or granddaughter. Don't waste your time on him."

Her words punched the air out of Drew's fantasy.

"When did you get so hard and mean?" Kurt tousled Drew's hair and patted him on the back. "Don't listen to this hag, boy. Anybody can save the world if they want to." He nodded to Stace. "I need help with something. Let's go."

"You can't just ride up and grab me to go handle your Knight problems. I'm not your witch, or your wife. Deal with it yourself."

"Fine." Kurt stood with a grunt. "I won't expect you to be useful ever again."

"You shouldn't have expected it this time. Not after letting Charlie almost murder me."

Drew didn't understand any of the conversation, but he wanted to go with Kurt. The big man seemed nice, and he believed in Drew.

"That was your own damned fault. Good luck, boy. I'm sorry about your parents." Kurt stalked back to his motorcycle.

"What the hell was that?" Drew's foster mother stood with her fists on her hips, scowling at Stace. "You never said anything about meeting someone else." She grabbed Drew's arm, knocking his ice cream to the ground. "This visit is over."

Stace grimaced in annoyance. "I'm sorry, Drew. You're a sweet kid, and I would've liked to help you grow up, but I can't let you be part of that world." She pressed her hand to her chest and murmured something.

Drew stared at the ice cream on the grass. Numbness crept across him, radiating from his chest. He blinked and let darkness consume him.

Blazing heat flared across Drew's chest and stomach. Heated breath, thick with the smell of copper and earth, blasted his face. His left leg ached in a spiral from his ankle to his knee. Pressure held him down and made breathing difficult.

He groaned and opened his eyes. Mutt lay draped over his body, his open mouth close to Drew's face. The blank ceiling looked like his bedroom at the Brady farm. Pieces of the memory flickered and faded, difficult to recall over the throbbing pain.

"Master, I'm so happy you're awake."

"So am I," Claire murmured. She sat in a chair beside his bed, shoulders hunched. Her face seemed blotchy.

"Me too," Drew said. His throat felt raw and scratchy. "What happened?"

"Was hoping you could tell me," Claire said.

Craning his neck to get a better look at her, he noticed she seemed exhausted. The movement made his muscles ache and took too much effort. "No idea."

"I can explain." Kay's voice sounded thin and reedy. "We hit the same thing that ghost did. It caught you because it caught me."

"Ley line," Drew rasped.

Kay agreed.

"Grandma Tammy wants you to go to the hospital." Claire shook her head and raked her fingers through her hair. "Anne says you just need rest and food. Justin sided with Anne and told Mutt to make sure you stay in bed until you agree to eat something. Grandpa Jack and Marie decided to stay out of it. I trust Anne, at least about this."

Drew didn't want food. His stomach lurched and rolled, queasy and tight. "Water."

Claire picked up a cup with a straw and held it for him. The cool water soothed his throat, but only for a moment.

"How long?"

"A few hours. You missed lunch. Anne says your aura is scarred, whatever that means."

"It would mean bad things," Kay said, "but that's not what's wrong. I took the hit. You're fine."

"Not fine," Drew said.

"Yeah." Claire reached past him to flip the blanket off his leg. Mutt shifted without her telling him to. "Your leg is messed up."

Past the dog, Drew saw red cloth covering his calf from ankle to knee. He also realized someone had taken off his pants.

"That cord-thing cut into your flesh." Claire brushed her fingertips across his toes, their fiery heat almost painful. "It wasn't healing like it should, so we wrapped the bandages to add more pressure. Justin said you bled all over the place on the ride back here. Anne doesn't know what caused it, and everyone is worried. About you. You lost a lot of blood."

Drew closed his eyes and thought about how much he hated being part of the magical world. No matter how much power he collected, someone could still beat him down. Stace had been right. He didn't belong as part of it.

Maybe Kurt's Phasm had chosen him to host Kay because Kurt had always carried the idea of finding a way to bring Drew into it whether he had the spark or not. Then again, maybe Kurt left that meeting and forgot about him forever.

"How long to heal?"

"No idea," Claire said.

"I need some time to assess the damage in depth." Kay paused and gave Drew the sense of weighing possibilities. "Iulia might've found a way to cause damage to your body that I can't heal. Regardless, we both need a ley line. A strong one. A focus stone and the Portland node would be ideal."

Nothing about what Kay said was funny, but Drew laughed. It hurt. "Oh, is that all?" he rasped. "Sure you don't need a unicorn?"

Kay huffed, sounding too weak for a real laugh. "While that would work, it's probably not easier."

"Claire." Drew lifted his hand, finding the gesture more exhausting than he expected.

She took his hand. Her warmth made him shiver. "Yeah?"

"Need something."

"Anything."

He smiled, grateful to have her for his best friend, his girlfriend, his everything. Opening his eyes, he saw the red in hers. She had to have rubbed them a thousand times. Why had she been crying? They must've thought he might die.

Later. They'd talk about it when he could do things like sit up. "Blue stone with silver occlusions."

"If you tell me what an occlusion is, sure."

"Impurity. Silver."

Claire nodded and squeezed his hand. "Does it matter what kind of blue stone?"

Kay gave the feeling of a shrug. "The closer you match your aura, the better."

"Sky blue. Solid. Polished or rough. Any shape. At least as big as a quarter all around." The effort of talking left him breathless.

"Okay." She leaned forward and kissed his forehead. "But I'm not leaving until you eat something."

"Important. Get someone else while you hunt, and I'll eat. I promise."

She let go and stood. "You don't get your rock until you eat."

"Deal." Drew watched her leave. She waved from the door, then disappeared into the hallway.

Mutt slid his head under Drew's hand and stayed quiet. He seemed upset, and Drew couldn't blame him.

"What do you think of that memory?" Drew asked.

"The one Stace suppressed?" Kay asked. "I have no idea why it came up in your parade of horrors. Compared to all the death and despair in the other memories you've got locked up, it's not that bad. Kind of a big pile of nothing more than disappointment and squashed hope. I suspect she suppressed it more to keep that foster mom from doing anything than to screw you out of anything. And probably so you wouldn't remember she once intended to take you into her home."

"I meant Kurt."

"I liked Kurt," Mutt said in a soft whine. "He made me."

"Oh. That." Kay went quiet. By the time he spoke again, Drew heard someone approaching in the hall. "I suppose it's nice to have a memory of him from before he died. That few minutes tells us both a lot more about the man Kurt was than all the time we spent with his Phasm."

Grandma Tammy carried in a mug with a spoon. She bent to the task of fussing over Drew.

113

"Kurt was a good man," Kay said.

Drew agreed.

CHAPTER 16

CLAIRE

Claire stood outside the Brady farmhouse, bright sunshine not warming her through her coat. She hugged herself. As it had almost nonstop since it happened, Drew's scream echoed in her head. The agony on his face filled her vision.

She'd panicked. Sitting beside his bed for hours, she'd run over and over the moment. His skin remained pale blue, even after he woke, and icy cold. Her fault. Justin had charged in. She should have done that before he got there. But she'd hesitated.

Opening her hand, she stared at the locket face. "What am I?" she whispered. Claire the Knight wouldn't have feared something that affected ghosts. She shied away from the idea of herself still being a ghost.

She needed to talk to someone, but didn't know who. Justin would understand but have no answers or solutions. Visiting Rondy meant crossing into her demesne, which she still didn't want to do for reasons she had a hard time explaining to herself. Anne hadn't said anything yet, which Claire interpreted as not knowing anything.

Her problem needed someone with a lot of experience who didn't have a reason to lie to her. No one fit that description. On second thought, Rondy did, but she doubted he'd know anything about this. Until she found someone, she had Drew's request to focus on. He'd suggested a new age store before, but she didn't have much money. Stealing something for this seemed wrong, at least until she exhausted all other options.

This task needed someone who would let her barter for it. If anyone knew how to find that kind of someone, the bartender at Nine Cans would. Ki knew everyone.

Claire remembered Drew including Nine Cans in the list of places inside Iulia's journal, and that gave her pause. If each location had a ghost trap, and she tripped one, what would happen? Then again, Ki wouldn't let anyone set a trap in his bar. Whoever made those maps—Claire didn't believe for sure that Iulia's ghost could have done it—might have intended to set up a trap at each location and been foiled at Nine Cans.

With that thought, she summoned Enion through their link. She could trust Ki at least enough to believe his bar was safe. He had a reputation to maintain, after all. Though she knew nothing about who else he crafted that reputation for, she knew he put stock in it.

Enion darted to her side from the forest. He landed on her outstretched palm and sat on his haunches. "Boy wake?"

She smiled at her dragon. "Yes, he woke up. He's tired and hurt, but he'll be fine. I need you big. We're going back to Portland."

"Look for Leeloo?"

Claire frowned at him. "She's still missing?"

Enion nodded. "Worried."

"I'm not sure how to look for her. We'll have to think about that. For now, I need to help Drew. When he's better, we should be able to come up with something to find Leeloo."

Enion raised a foreclaw in a salute, then jumped off her hand. He flashed silver in midair and landed in his large form. Claire climbed onto his back and told him where to go. The dragon loped and leaped, his wings pumping to carry them into the air. They soared over Vancouver, then the Columbia River.

Without bothering to hide, Enion dove into a landing on Third Street, beside Nine Cans. Claire jumped off his back, he flashed small, and she snatched him out of the air. She knew people stared. If she cared, she could've taken the bus.

Inside the well-lit pub, customers sat at the polished wood tables scattered through the cozy room and at the bar across the back. They all looked like normal people to Claire. Three overweight men, not sitting together, drank beer from bottles and ate pretzels from wooden bowls. Two twenty-something women with piercings and decorative patches on their jeans hung on each other while playing darts with an old-fashioned, cork dartboard. One fit, trim man in a suit watched Claire with a glass of something amber and predatory glee.

"Minors aren't allowed in here," Ki said from behind the bar. The Native American man, his long black hair tied in a thin tail, dried a wine glass with a pristine, white towel.

"Yeah, I know." Claire pulled down her scarf so he could hear her. "I just need some advice, then I'll get out."

"Advice." Ki smirked. "She wants advice."

The nearest man with a beer belly chortled. "What's she gonna pay?"

"Depends on what it's worth," Claire said as she reached the bar and leaned against it. Sitting on a stool seemed like a step too far. "I'm looking for something and can't afford to just buy it from a regular store. Hoping you know someone who'll trade for what I need."

Ki slid the wine glass into a rack overhead and reached under the bar. Claire couldn't see what he did, and he straightened with his hand empty. A shiver ran up her spine for no reason. She ignored it. The room held too many unknowns to worry about a shiver.

"And what is the region's newest Knight looking for?"

Silence fell in the room. Claire felt the weight of everyone's stares on her back. Ki had outed her. The supernatural people in the room now knew one of the Sheriff's Deputies had shown up and wanted something.

She narrowed her eyes at him. "I'm looking for a particular kind of rock."

"A rock." Ki grinned. "The last time you needed a rock, we wound up in a hard place."

The downside of dealing with Ki presented itself in full bloom. "It's not for me this time. That problem doesn't have to be solved again." Claire considered removing her glove and showing him the locket, but decided against it. If these people only knew her by her jacket and the sound of her voice, she could still take them by surprise sometime.

"Tell me more about this rock, then."

"Can we step into the back?"

Ki's brown eyes glittered with amusement and gleamed gold. "What if one of my patrons has what you're looking for and I don't know about it? What a waste of time and energy that would be."

Certain he had some game in mind, Claire glared at him for a beat. She had no idea what he wanted, though. "Fine. I need a solid, sky blue stone at least this big—" She held up a finger and thumb to make a circle. "—and with at least one thread of silver running through it."

"What an opaque request." One corner of Ki's mouth curled up. "I can't begin to imagine what you might want with such a thing. Is it for something stupid?"

"No," Claire snapped. "That wasn't stupid, and neither is this. It's for Drew."

Ki leaned toward her and lowered his voice. "In that case, I can help you. For a price."

The shift in his demeanor left Claire confused. Mentioning Drew didn't seem like something that should entice people to help her. Maybe he'd gotten into more than she thought while she was dead. "Help me how, and what price?"

"It so happens that I have a box containing several stones that might meet your requirements. I'll let you paw through the box if you do something for me."

"Might?" Claire raised her brow. "I'm not doing you a favor for a maybe. Let me look through it first. If I see one that fits, I'll hear you out and decide if what you want is worth it."

Ki smiled at her with obvious delight. "And here I thought you were just another tiresome Knight." He pointed to the large man sitting at the bar. "Don't let him serve himself anything. I'll be right back."

When Ki disappeared into the back room, the man reached over the bar.

"I'll stop you," Claire said.

The man snorted. "You'll try."

She pulled her dagger and held it so the silver blade glinted in the light and caught his attention. "I'll just cut your hand off." Threatening a larger man with bodily harm didn't bother her. Much. If he persisted, she'd have to decide whether she was bluffing or not. "It'll make a mess, though."

He narrowed his eyes and stared at her. "Knights don't hurt people."

Since she met him in Ki's bar, Claire took a chance. Inside, she gulped and hoped he backed down or Ki returned before she had to prove anything. "Knights don't hurt human beings. Though, in fairness, we've been known to beat them up a time or two for causing problems."

Her pulse raced because the guy turned to face her. At least he'd stopped reaching behind the bar. "Silly chit like you couldn't beat up an eggplant. Better put away the knife before you cut yourself."

Claire smirked. She wanted to laugh, but feared it would sound hysterical. "Wanna bet a body part on that?"

The man sneered and turned away from her to reach behind the bar again.

Her hand shaking, Claire took a step toward him.

The back room door flew open and Ki returned with a wooden box. The man snatched back his hand and smiled like nothing had happened.

Keeping herself from gushing her relief took every ounce of will Claire possessed. She sheathed her dagger, hoping no one noticed how much she shook. Someday, she'd find out what kind of creature pretending to be a drunk she'd threatened with bodily harm. Not today.

Ki stuck out his tongue at the man and set the box on the bar. "Take a look." He popped off the lid for her.

Claire had to hop onto a stool to see inside the box. It held a number of rounded, polished stones with silver streaks across the faces. The stones came in all different colors, including black and white. She saw multiple shades of blue and flicked through the box to see if any matched what she thought Drew meant.

Through the fabric of her glove, she felt a tug on the locket face. Following its lead, she found a light blue stone with two silver lines cutting across it in smooth, flowing streams. The stone hummed just loud enough to hear.

Her connection to Drew had led her to the stone he needed. She wondered if he felt anything.

"Looks like we have a winner," Ki said. He replaced the cover on the box and held out his hand for the stone.

The piece of rock felt so natural in her hand, Claire hated to give it up. But she'd made a deal. Ki would keep up his end so long as she did her part. She let the stone fall into his open palm.

"What do you want for it?" She chose to be proud of the fact her voice didn't waver.

He rubbed his chin. "I suppose I could use a delivery girl."

Claire had no intention of agreeing to anything without knowing the details. Her dealings with Iulia had taught her that lesson the hard way. "Take what to where?"

"I like that you're not a silly chit." Combined with his word choice, his smile told her he knew exactly what had happened in his absence. "I have a certain object in my possession that requires delivery to a certain individual who can be found in a certain place. She's pleasant enough to those who bring her gifts. You only have to go to Toutle, a small town up in Washington. That shouldn't be a problem for you. It's what, sixty or seventy miles? Knights are all about having swift transportation."

"Sure. But what is it?"

"Something inside a box, and if you open it, she'll be cross with you."

Claire grimaced. "Is it a cross? Or a piece of *the* Cross?"

Ki laughed. "Very good." He produced a second, smaller box, about half the size of a paperback book, and gave her an address in Toledo. "Knock on the door. Tell the woman who answers that you're delivering something for Ki Oscar Teah. If she pretends not to know the name, tell her you don't care and to just take the box. Feel free to embroider."

"Great." Claire took the box and wondered if she'd guessed right. Ki wouldn't tell her. She had a feeling the intended recipient wouldn't either. "I don't suppose you could show me on a map?"

CHAPTER 17

JUSTIN

Despite occupying the same building as the church, the dining hall at St. Francis felt institutional and utilitarian. Simple and expansive, the tables and benches offered enough space to seat over a hundred people at once. Empty at this hour, silence hung thick under panels of fluorescent lights. White cabinets lined the white walls, punctuated by windows near their ceiling.

Avery stopped in the doorway with a deep frown. This end of the building commanded none of the gravity or reverence of the church, so Justin didn't know what stopped the detective. A memory, he supposed.

"Do you know where they saw the ghost?" Justin asked from behind Avery.

Father Duncan, standing with him, gestured inside the building. "It happened outside meal hours. They said she floated between the tables. The first time, she appeared where we're standing now, and drifted to the kitchen. The second time, she went in the opposite direction. As far as I could determine, they didn't see her in the kitchen."

"Based upon what they said, is there a chance the ghost's appearance changed from one visit to the next?"

Instead of answering, Father Duncan gave Justin a curious smile. "You sound as if you believe this really happened."

"You don't?"

"After the excitement of Thanksgiving weekend, I'm not so sure they didn't see what they wanted to see. We all want to experience the divine."

Avery sighed and shooed Father Duncan with one hand. "We'll take it from here, Father."

The priest blinked at him. "Excuse me?"

"You're excused." Avery strode into the building.

Justin stepped forward, crossing the threshold with one foot while still paying attention to the priest. Cold wind washed over him, coming from inside the building. He heard the swish of Avery drawing his sword. Breathy, maniacal cackling echoed from the walls.

Father Duncan's eyes widened, and he crossed himself. Turning and drawing his own sword, Justin saw mist seeping through the walls. Dark, wet liquid oozed from the windows, dribbling down the glass.

"You don't see that every day," Avery said.

"Not outside of a horror movie, anyway." Justin closed the door in Father Duncan's face and put his back to Avery's.

Mist streamed across the ceiling, meeting in the middle and creating a thick cloud that clung to the insulted tiles. As they watched, the fog rippled. Tendrils licked downward and retracted in a mesmerizing dance.

Justin flicked his gaze from the nearest windows to the ceiling and back. "Ideas?"

"I have a feeling the obvious answer isn't going to cut it. Pun intended."

Raising his sword, Justin scraped the cloud with the tip of his sword. The mist parted and recoiled. As soon as the blade stopped touching the fog, it rushed back as if he'd scooped water out of the ocean.

"No, probably not. You think something bad happens if it touches us?"

"Can you imagine anything good happening?"

A long, thin tendril of mist punched down, aiming for Justin's head. He ducked and swung his blade. The sword connected with the arm, producing a metallic clang. Stumbling from the unexpected contact, Justin hit a bench and grunted. His knees buckled against it and his back hit the table behind it.

Avery swore and kicked another table, sending it screeching across the floor and creating space for them to fight. He used his sword to bat aside another tendril.

Justin scrambled to his feet as another arm punched at him. The arm, leading with a fist shape, hit the table with a solid *wham!* and dented it. Whatever they'd encountered, it meant to kill them and had the ability to do the job.

With every passing moment, the mist thickened, its bottom edge inching closer to their heads. Justin shoved another table aside and dodged another arm. Avery pulled out his gun and fired at the ceiling. The fog swallowed the bullet with no sign he'd damaged anything, including the building.

"Worth a try," he grumbled as he holstered the gun again.

Another arm swung for Justin. He slapped it aside with his blade. Pain exploded through his back as another arm hit him from behind and sent him sprawling. Avery stepped close and chopped the next arm aside before it could slam into Justin where he lay on the floor.

Coughing and gasping to catch his breath, Justin scrabbled to his feet. "This isn't working."

"But *why* isn't it working?" Avery hacked another arm aside.

"Claire." Justin lunged aside and swatted another arm. He nodded toward the door.

Avery followed his lead and moved with him toward the exit. "Is she too far away?"

"Maybe our blades aren't made for this?" Justin hurried to the door and yanked it open. When Avery had darted through, he stumbled out and slammed the door shut.

Tariel charged into sight, leaping over shrubs to reach them.

Both men whirled to face the building, watching it.

Justin panted and rubbed his chest. The blow he took had felt like it shattered his spine and rammed the fragments through his lungs. With every passing moment, the pain receded, thanks to Tariel. Something inside still felt strange, though. Every breath sent an odd ache through his body. Like the healing failed to scrape away a layer of residue.

Father Duncan knelt on the sidewalk, praying in a quiet, steady voice.

"It's not leaving the building," Avery said.

Letting the tip of his sword lower to the ground, Justin took another step back. "Small blessings."

Avery nodded. "Father, that won't help. You can't let anyone inside this building. It's too dangerous."

The priest quieted and looked up. "You don't know it won't help."

"It never has before. I see no reason for that to change."

Justin kept watching the building. Maybe the walls contained the mess, and maybe Father Duncan's prayers had held it in. Nothing seeped out, though. "Did it seem like it targeted me more than you?"

"Now that you mention it, yes. Once you hit the floor, it could've one-two punched me, but it didn't." Avery sheathed his sword. "Which doesn't make sense. Unless you have a connection to this place that you don't know about."

"Maybe. I mean, I can't imagine why Iulia would hate me more than you. From her point of view, I'd expect her to see us as just two more Knights."

"She might have a plan for a new seal and this somehow helps fulfill it. Regardless, I'm ashamed to admit that I think we need your teenagers to help with this problem."

Huffing half a laugh that hurt, Justin sheathed his sword. The building seemed safe enough from the outside. "That's a good way to put it. I'll meet you at the house."

"I can't just close the dining hall," Father Duncan said. "People depend on us for meals."

Both Avery and Justin stared at him. "Would you like your volunteers and homeless people beaten to death by belligerent fog?" Avery asked.

"It might evaporate," Justin said. He offered Duncan a gloved hand to help him stand. "Even if it does, it might leave some lingering corruption behind. This is about their immortal souls, not their bellies. Do what you can to help them, but you're going to need to leave the dining hall closed until we can come back with more help to deal with this. It's the only responsible thing to do."

"How could this happen here?" Father Duncan asked as he stood, his voice breathy and his eyes begging for comfort.

Avery rolled his eyes. "Oh, please." He stalked to the sidewalk and walked away.

Justin gripped Father Duncan's shoulder and squeezed. "Someone decided to use your grounds for this, and there are no prayers that can stop such a person. You know that as well as I do." He let go, wishing he could offer the priest more solace than that. As he turned to leave, he thought to ask about something.

"Father Duncan, do you know if the Evans family ever attended this church? The last of us to show up would've probably been at least thirty years ago."

Father Duncan touched his forehead and stared at the ground, his eyes still too wide. Justin worried the priest might succumb to shock. He draped an arm around the priest's shoulders, fighting the building ache in his chest, and urged him to leave the haunted dining hall in favor of the church.

After a few steps, Father Duncan said, "I've only been here for a few years, but that name sounds familiar. I may have run across it while reading through the original records. Births, deaths, and marriages from the late nineteenth century. Not as many churches here when the first Saint Francis opened. Fewer options for that sort of thing."

"When the dining hall is sorted out, I'll come back to look into that. I don't know as much about my family as I'd like." Justin glanced back at the dining hall. Nothing seeped out, and the windows he saw appeared normal. "A few names and dates. That's about it."

"I hope we find something for you, then."

Justin nodded and thanked him. "We'll come back as soon as we can, with more firepower."

CHAPTER 18

CLAIRE

Cedars and leafless apple trees surrounded a small, one-story building facade in the middle of nowhere, near the western boundary of the Mount St. Helens National Volcanic Monument. Built into the side of a hill, it faced south into a pocket valley with the outer wall and roof covered in solar panels. Sunlight glared off one arc of glass in the center of the roof, but it had no other windows. A thin tendril of smoke drifted from a narrow pipe protruding from the hill beside the structure.

Claire and Enion had found the spot by following roads, including the narrow gravel one leading to the house.

They landed on a thick layer of snow covering the space outside the front door. Chickens clucked their disapproval as they darted from under the front porch to the dubious shelter of tangled, leafless bushes in a neat line. Muffled dog barking announced they'd roused the household.

Enion lifted one foreclaw and shook it. Slush flung in every direction. "Yuck. Cold."

"We just flew at four hundred feet up, and this is what makes you notice the cold?" Claire climbed off his back.

The moment her second boot touched the snow, Enion flashed silver and turned tiny. Gobs of sloppy snow fell to the ground and splattered on Claire's jeans. The dragon shook himself as he darted to Claire's shoulder.

"What d'you want?" A middle-aged woman with dark hair and dusky skin stood on the front porch. Claire hadn't heard the door open or shut. Over her jeans and brown slippers, she wore a knitted afghan draped across her shoulders. Blue and red triangles decorating the white blanket reminded Claire of Native American kitsch she'd seen in tacky gift shops.

"Hi. Sorry to bother you." Claire smiled at the woman, hoping to defuse any annoyance she might've already caused. She dug the box out of her coat pocket and held it up. "Ki Oscar Teah sent me to deliver this."

"Did he?" The woman crossed her arms and didn't answer Claire's smile.

Claire approached the woman, offering her the box. "I swear I didn't open it, and he wouldn't tell me what's inside. He just said to bring it here."

"So you brought it here." The woman didn't take the box.

"Yeah. It's a favor for a favor kind of thing."

The woman burst into a full-throated guffaw. Claire waited, figuring this woman considered her dumb for making a deal with Ki. She already knew that.

"Sorry, kid." The woman curbed her laughter and covered her mouth. "I'm sure it's a decent deal for you."

Claire stifled her annoyance. Knowing Ki made it likely this woman had some kind of unusual powers, just like Ki did. She and Drew hadn't figured out what Ki was, but they knew seals constrained his capabilities. That made him a magical creature of some kind.

She took another step to shove the box at the woman. "It will be when you take this."

Taking a step back, the woman waved Claire off. "No, I don't think so. Whatever Ki wants to give me, he can haul his flea-bitten butt up here and give it to me himself."

"Look. My boyfriend got hurt in a trap set for him by a witch, and I need something Ki has to help him recover. You take the box, I get the thing, my boyfriend gets better."

"What are you?"

Claire blinked at the woman. Twice now, women had asked her that altogether rude question. "A Spirit Knight. What are you?"

"A shadow of what I once was. Like Ki. And it's your fault. Well, not yours personally. Your order. But that's not what I asked. I want to know what you are, not what job you have."

Not knowing the answer, Claire shrugged. "A teenage girl?"

The woman raised her brow. "I see. And your boyfriend? What is he?"

Several smartass answers rattled through Claire's head. She decided to give the truth. "A possessed teenage boy with witch powers."

"That's interesting. My name is Lou. Would you like some tea?"

"Will having tea with you bind my soul or anything?"

Lou grinned. "No. But you're a clever girl for asking."

"If I come in and have tea with you, will you take the box?"

"Maybe. I definitely won't if you don't, though."

Faced with no choice, Claire sighed and nodded. "Then sure, let's have some tea." If she left the box in Lou's house, would that count as delivered? Probably not. She suspected Ki would know, somehow, that

Lou hadn't taken it.

Lou opened the door and led Claire inside a warm room made of honey-gold wood, with matching wood furniture. Bookshelves held wooden statuettes and creations made from crystals and other stones. The couch and chair upholstery featured a silver, gray, and white version of the pseudo-Native motif on Lou's afghan.

At Lou's prompting, Claire sat on the couch. She stayed still while Lou left the room through a door. Enion jumped down from her shoulder and poked at the cloth covering the couch.

"Real silver," he said.

"Not surprised. I think she's like Ki."

Lou returned with a tray holding a ceramic teapot and two cobalt blue mugs. Sunflowers decorated the pot, in a raised design Claire could believe might've been actual blooms somehow glazed into the porcelain. Once Lou poured tea for her, Claire took the mug and held it in her gloved hands.

"I haven't seen a dragon in a long time." Lou offered Enion a lettuce leaf.

Enion sniffed the leaf and prodded it with his snout. He looked up at Claire. "Safe?"

"It's quite safe, little dragon," Lou said. "Even a fool could see you're attached to your mistress. I have no need to try and remove you from her. I have a dog, which is quite enough for me. Mimi is afraid of you or she'd be in here, begging for a cookie."

As Enion took the lettuce, Claire asked, "You can understand him?"

"No." Lou smiled. "Given his mistress's hesitation outside, I made a guess."

"Ah." Claire raised the tea to her face and inhaled the aroma. The scent reminded her of Grandma Tammy's kitchen—warm and welcoming, with something sweet baking and someone willing to give hugs any time, day or night.

They sat in silence for long enough that Claire felt compelled to sip the tea. Her vision clouded over and she felt someone holding her from behind while they rode a black horse through a forest. She smelled horse, suede, earth, and a subtle musk. His large hand kept her safe. No matter what, he'd keep her on the horse's back and defend her from anything and everything.

He pushed a sycamore branch out of the way so it didn't hit her, and plucked a red-orange leaf from the tree for her. The huge leaf spread its spiky lobes wide enough to cover her whole face.

Claire blinked and gasped as the vision released her. "What is this stuff?"

"Tea." Lou blew steam from her mug. Stars danced in her dark eyes. "You saw something?"

"Yeah." Claire pressed a gloved hand to her forehead as the vision flickered and faded. "What does that mean?"

"That you lied to me. Which I already knew but find curious."

Blinking, Claire tried to figure out what she'd lied about. "I didn't."

"Ah." Lou sipped her tea.

"What do you mean by that? Am I supposed to think you're wise and ancient because you're cryptic?" She thought about throwing the cup at Lou's smug face.

"No. You should think that because it's true. But of course, no one will tell you anything, so you have no idea what to think or what you are.

As it always is with youth. We all stumble through that dark time before things make sense. Live through a century and you'll understand why trusting Ki is often the mistake that sets off a chain of disaster."

"A century." Claire frowned at her tea. She wanted to take another sip. She wanted to gulp down the whole thing. She wanted to set the cup aside and leave now.

"It's easier and harder than it sounds."

Tired of dealing with this lady, Claire huffed. "I had some of your tea, so how about you take the stupid box and I go back and save my boyfriend?"

Lou squinted at her, then nodded. "Very well. Take the box to the volcano and drop it into the caldera. I'll count it delivered then."

"What? You want me to throw—" Claire had no reason to object or care, but she didn't understand. Lou didn't want the box, and Claire wanted to know why. "How is that delivering it?"

Lou's shoulders slumped and she sighed. "You're so very young and know so very little."

"How am I supposed to learn anything if people like you just tell me how dumb I am?" Claire's frustration burst out of her in an exasperated burst. "It's always the simple version or a metaphor, or telling me I'm too young or stupid to get it. No one ever gives me a straight answer other than 'I don't know!' Everything about me is weird or unprecedented, or something nobody wants to talk about, and I'm so damned tired of it!"

She hadn't intended to shout at Lou. This strange woman owed her nothing.

"I can see why you wound up as a Knight." Lou set her tea aside. She clasped her hands and fixed Claire with a stern gaze. "Child, if you want information from me, you have to do something for me. A favor for a favor. Much like Ki, I'm not inclined to do something for nothing. Unlike Ki, I won't hide part of the deal from you."

Feeling chastised, Claire looked away. "Then why won't you just take the box? That's between you and Ki, isn't it?"

"It is. He should've told you to throw it in the volcano instead of sending you to me. Beware of dealing with him. The fact he sent you to me leads me to believe he had an ulterior motive for one or both of us, and his motives are never pure. He's a trickster, and his loyalty is to his people. You are not one of his people."

His people. Claire figured that meant beings also constrained by the seals. Knights had created those seals, which put them at odds. Even if she'd blown up the Knights, she still considered herself one. She did wonder why Lou didn't identify as one of Ki's people.

"Doesn't that mean you should check inside the box before I throw it away? Because we shouldn't trust Ki and he has ulterior motives?"

Lou shrugged. "I'd love to, but I can't. If I take it, the box will never be delivered, and your quest will never count as complete. Ki will know."

"Thanks." For being weird and insane, Claire thought. She stood and scooped Enion off the couch. He'd finished his lettuce leaf. "Maybe I'll come back sometime to trade that favor."

Lou spread her hands. "So long as you don't betray me or my location, you're welcome here. Remember that when it comes to betrayal, my wrath is swift and...unfocused."

Whatever that meant. Claire nodded and let herself out. She had a date with a volcano and a favor to collect.

CHAPTER 19

JUSTIN

The ride home proved an exercise in agony. Justin clenched his jaws as Tariel's every hoofbeat sent an aching jolt through his chest. By the time she turned up the driveway for the Brady farm, he had to bite back a constant stream of groaning. Whatever that mist had done to him, it lingered.

He dismounted and took Tariel to her stable, sure he wouldn't leave again for the day.

"You're limping."

Instead of answering, he grunted at Tariel and yanked off her saddle.

"Is the bond failing?"

"No. I don't think so, anyway." Justin set the saddle where it belonged and faced the brushes hanging on the wall. The normally pleasant tasks involved in taking care of her seemed like daunting, unpleasant chores. "I can still understand you, and everything healed."

"Except for whatever is bothering you."

"Yeah. Except that. Do you mind going without a brushing today?"

"No." She nudged him with her nose. "Get some rest."

He patted her neck and left her in the warm room. Avery's car rumbled up the driveway. Justin waved to both man and car. As Avery stepped out, Justin gripped his chest and grimaced. He needed to lie down for a while, not collect teenagers and fight more.

Avery raised his brow. "That punch did more than it seemed."

"Something like that."

"Would you like me to call Anne?" Avery retrieved his cellphone and held it up.

"Maybe later." Justin led him to the cottage, expecting to find Claire.

Marie and his girls sat in the living room, reading a book. Missy exploded to her feet, sending stuffed animals flying, and flew at him. He groaned when she hit his leg and felt a rush of fresh pain when he bent to pick her up. The agony clouded his vision.

He opened his eyes to see Avery crouched over him, frowning. One or both of the girls wailed nearby.

"Daddy's fine," Marie said. "He's just tired."

"You passed out," Avery said. "Can you stand?"

Justin struggled against sharp, stabbing aches to sit up. He gasped for breath. "Maybe. It wasn't this bad when we left the church."

"Then relax." Avery circled behind him and lifted him under his arms.

Not wanting to put his daughters in any more distress, Justin ground his teeth and held down the moan he otherwise would've let loose. The pain kept worsening. He watched his feet as Avery dragged him to the couch and did everything in his power to not make a sound as the detective heaved him into it.

With a wisp of a thought, they plunged through the couch and into Claire's demesne. Justin let out a strangled cry as he hit the ground. Avery stood.

The woods they landed in duplicated the woods behind the cottage as they appeared in the middle of fall. Brilliant orange, yellow, and red leaves hung on maples and sycamores. More leaves littered the ground. Cedars and firs filled in the gaps with mountains of green needles. Moss clung to trunks and rocks. A fresh, cool breeze carried the splash of burbling water from a nearby creek.

"Gentlemen." Rondy, a Jamaican-born Knight from Cleveland, stepped into view, clad from head to toe in colors matching the fall leaves. Though Justin had only ever known him as an old man, he appeared in the prime of his life, with no hint of gray in his dreadlocks and no lines on his face.

Avery shook hands with Rondy. "Nice to see you. It's been a while."

Rondy smiled, flashing bright white teeth. "It's been a while for everyone, even Claire, and she owns the place." He cocked his head to one side and scanned Justin from head to toe. "I see you came because you have a problem."

"You could say that." Justin stayed on the ground. If he didn't move and took only shallow breaths, he hurt much less.

"If you don't know what to do," Avery said, "we have witches to consult."

Crouching beside Justin, Rondy let his smile fade. "I doubt anyone *knows* what to do about this." He held his hand an inch above Justin's chest. "Interesting. It reminds me of something I encountered in my younger days. Think of it like a virus, except it's ghostly and infecting your soul, not your body."

"Great," Justin said. "Does that mean I'm stuck with it until my soul fights it off?"

Rondy grinned. "Maybe?" He looked up at Avery. "Stab him in the chest. The sword's enchantment might take care of it."

Avery flipped his trenchcoat aside and drew his sword. The corners of his mouth twitched with amusement.

Staring down the length of steel, Justin thought about how much being stabbed would hurt. He'd heal, of course. But it wouldn't be fun. "Is that really the best option?"

Still grinning, Rondy ran a hand up Justin's side and peeled his armor apart. "It's the only one I've got. That makes it the best by default."

"There was a time when part of me wanted to do this so very much," Avery said. He crouched and shoved Justin's shirt up, then prodded to find a spot between his ribs. Every poke jolted Justin with tiny sparks of pain. "It hit him in the back. Should we flip him over?"

Rondy shrugged. "So long as you stab all the way through, it doesn't matter."

"Yes, let's stab all the way through." Justin dug his fingers into the ground so he could hold onto something. "That sounds fantastic. Make sure you puncture as many internal organs as you can. We wouldn't want to leave anything to chance. Better get my blood all over everything too."

Avery chuckled at him as he positioned the tip of his sword. "I'll be swift."

Justin opened his mouth to say something else, but Avery shoved the blade through him. The shock of having so much warning and yet none at all kept him silent. His eyes snapped open. For a moment, he felt nothing but pressure. Then pain swamped him. He couldn't breathe. Copper filled his mouth. His legs went numb.

With a grunt, Avery yanked the blade out. Justin gasped and tried to lift his arms. They refused to budge.

Oily gray smoke streamed from the hole in Justin's chest, clinging to the tip of Avery's sword. Justin felt it ripping through him, tearing him apart. White sparks pricked his vision. He coughed blood, sending more agony shooting through his torso.

The cloud, stretched into a pulsing, bulging cord, tore flesh as it released Justin. The bloody end whipped at Avery's head. Justin gurgled as he tried to scream and breathe through the blood pooling in his mouth. Rondy heaved him onto his side. Blood drained from his mouth. His legs still refused to feel anything. The rest of him felt everything.

"No, you don't," Avery growled.

Raising his head, Justin saw Avery slashing his sword at the cloud. The cord hung between two tree branches and used them to dodge. Rondy left Justin to help Avery.

"Fascinating," Rondy said as he cut through a branch with his sword.

"Fighting now, insight later," Avery snapped.

"This would be easier with Claire here."

Healing soothed Justin's injuries, washing through him with less speed than he preferred. He spat another mouthful of blood and sighed as feeling returned to his legs. "I need a minute," he groaned.

He watched the dead leaves on the ground soak his blood and turn from brown to red. Avery and Rondy somehow missed the damned cord with every swing.

Justin rose to his hands and knees. He panted as the pain receded. Tariel could heal him faster than this.

"Rondy," Justin said, "you're a ghost. Can't you do something ghosty to it?"

"I don't have any experience with foreign entities intruding on the demesne."

"Here's your chance," Avery said.

Hoofbeats on the ground made Justin raise his head. He saw a huge stag charging them. The brown and white creature shimmered with green. Its impressive antlers flashed with green-tinted gold.

"Look out!" Justin threw himself behind a nearby tree.

Avery backed from the cord to face the deer. Rondy dove to the side. The stag ignored all three men to charge the cord. Its antlers swept across the cord. The cloud wrapped around the antlers. Glimmering motes of golden light swarmed the antlers, diving at the cloud.

Justin watched with his mouth hanging open. The stag's antlers blazed with light, forcing Justin to raise a hand and cringe away. Something sizzled and popped. He smelled sulfur.

The light faded. Justin lowered his hand and saw the stag standing in a beam of sunlight. Lines of soot marred its antlers.

Before he could gather his wits to say something, the stag approached him. It planted one hoof on his chest. He sensed the stag could shove its leg through him if it wanted. Instead, it applied only a subtle pressure, enough to feel it and to press him against the tree at his back.

He gulped and stared at the stag's brown eyes, noting they seemed alive with humanity. "Thank you," he whispered, unable to raise his voice louder.

The stag bleated with a goat-like sound. Though Justin didn't understand it, he got the feeling it chastised him. Maybe that was his imagination.

"What are you?" Rondy asked. He held out a hand to the stag. His head reached as high as the stag's shoulder. In life, Rondy had been near Justin's six feet of height.

Giving no answer, the stag shoved Justin, then let him go. It walked away, disappearing in the trees much faster than a creature of its size should.

All three men stayed quiet for several long moments. Justin rubbed his healed chest where the hoof had been. He had even less of an idea what to make of his adopted daughter than he had before.

"I think we need to have a chat with Claire," Avery said, still staring after the stag. "One she can't wriggle out of."

Justin shook off his awe and used the tree to stand. His chain shirt hung open, and blood stained his shirt and jeans. "I think I don't want to do that ever again."

Rondy nodded. "While I'd ordinarily advise seeking information wherever it can be found, I think it might be wise to keep all of this to ourselves."

Nodding, Justin held up the two side of his chain shirt, not sure what to do about it. "I'm not comfortable talking to Anne about what's in Claire's demesne anyway. You broke this," he said to Rondy, "can you fix it?"

Rondy stepped to his side and held the two halves together. He frowned at it, then let it fall, still split from the sleeve to the bottom edge. "No. Had I known, I wouldn't have torn it."

"All the more reason to see your teenager," Avery said with a smirk.

Justin sighed and nodded. "I'll change into clean clothes first."

CHAPTER 20

CLAIRE

Enion soared over the peak of Mount St. Helens, a huge snow-covered U-shape of jagged rock with the opening facing north. Glare from the sun in a clear sky kept Claire from staring at any of it. She didn't understand how throwing something at a mountaintop delivered it to anyone, especially not the lady living in a house several miles away.

More interested in getting that stone for Drew than solving the mystery, Claire pointed for Enion to dive into the caldera. She wanted to get it into that bowl, not sliding down the side.

Her dragon took her to the top edge. She dropped the box into a cleft, where it fell into the snow and out of sight. Enion worked to gain altitude and circled so she could make sure it didn't go the wrong way.

Steam blasted from the spot. Enion dodged a jet that seemed to aim for them. Claire heard deep rumbling below, like an enormous belly rolling with hunger. More steam billowed toward them. Dark specks rode the steam and burst from the top to fly in every direction. Sulfur and heat blasted her.

Claire covered her mouth, trying not to vomit. "Is it erupting?"

Enion crested the south ridge and darted toward Portland. Claire twisted to see the mountain. With every passing second, the column of steam grew larger and darker. She wanted nothing more than to get as far away from it as they could, as fast as they could.

Something on the ground flashed in the sunlight. Cars. People. Visiting the mountain. Snow covered the roads near the mountain, at least. No one could get too close. Maybe these people all had time to evacuate. If they knew.

She smacked Enion's neck. "Go back!"

"Loud. Stinky. Scary!"

"Go back to warn the people. Look." She pointed for him. "Only that close."

As he turned, she noted that Lou's cabin perched on a hill in the direct path if lava followed the path of least resistance from the caldera. Did she care? Ki had to have known this would happen. Even if he didn't, Lou must have. Unless she thought the box held something specific, and Ki had tricked them both.

Mount St. Helens pumped a billowing cloud of ash into the sky. Enion landed among picnic benches thick with families in snow suits.

Claire opened her mouth to shout. Enion squawked. The ground lurched with a deep, resonant grumble. Claire wrapped her arms around Enion's neck so she wouldn't fall. People shouted. Ash drifted from the sky. Someone pointed toward the mountain.

These people didn't need her to tell them about the danger. Claire shouted about the eruption anyway, then patted Enion's neck. He leaped into the sky.

"Take us back to Lou's cabin."

A few dozen feet off the ground, Claire noticed the air shimmering. Enion kept climbing. Something thick, heavy, and hot slapped them to the side. Roaring filled her ears. She tumbled. Everything spun. Her flesh burned. Enion disappeared.

She plummeted into trees. A branch hit her leg, snapping the bones in half. Her body flipped, and she gasped with the shock of impact. No longer falling, she hung, suspended somehow by her torso. The sensation from her chest made no sense. Her stomach churned, but she didn't throw up.

Dizzy and confused, she tried to understand why her arms dangled over her head. Her chest ached like someone had punched her. Blood spattered the wrong side of the nearest tree's needles.

The trees swayed and groaned. Wood cracked.

Claire lifted her head enough to see a branch, slick with blood, sticking out of her jacket. The sight made no sense.

She tried to lower her arms. No, she tried to lift them because her body hung upside-down. They waved in the air.

A loud crack popped in her ears. Her body jerked downward. Another crack rent the air. She fell. The snow didn't hold her. Bones crunched against the ground. Pain exploded in her chest and radiated outward. She screamed.

The ground rumbled.

"What have you done?"

Claire recognized Lou's voice, but couldn't move to see her. "You told me to," she gasped.

"You're a foolish child. Stay still. This will hurt."

Knives scraped her insides. Claire screamed again. Lou had pulled out the branch.

"You're lucky you're a Knight. Otherwise, you'd be dead."

Gasping for breath, Claire waited while the warming creep of healing trickled through her body. "Enion."

Hands lifted her leg and straightened it with a jerk. Claire's vision blurred with the agony. It hurt so much she made no noise.

"Ki tricked us both," Lou said with a growl. "He knows too much about the constraints placed on me. I'd like to punch him in the face."

Claire lay still on the trembling ground. "Dragon." She tried to say more but couldn't catch her breath.

"Ah. Of course. I don't see him." Lou scooped her off the ground and carried her through the woods. "There wasn't supposed to be another major eruption for a century or so. I want to know why Ki sparked one, and you're going to find out for me."

The healing kept Claire from hurting so much, but every step still sent tiny jolts of pain through her body. "Do it yourself."

"You have every right to be upset, but not at me. I didn't know what was in that box."

"Should've taken it. Opened it."

Lou rolled her eyes. "Think for a minute before you open your mouth, child."

Claire had no idea what she was supposed to think about. More adult vaguespeak didn't help. As her body recovered, she tried to imagine anything that made sense. Nothing. The healing accelerated, at least, which meant they'd found Enion, or would soon. "Give me a hint?"

The corners of Lou's mouth quirked up. "No. If you can't come up with the answer, you don't deserve to know it. And there's your dragon."

"I can walk now." Claire glowered at Lou, who'd helped and

annoyed her at the same time. The moment her boots hit the ground, she turned her back on the infuriating woman. Then she saw the big silver lump in the snow and forgot about adults who wouldn't answer questions.

She rushed to Enion, her chest and leg still aching, and checked him for injuries. The wing in sight had a break in the primary bone. Otherwise, he seemed fine. Her poor dragon must've whacked his head. Their bond, she'd noticed, kept him alive while she healed, then took care of him. As soon as the pain faded from her body, he'd wake up. She tugged off her glove and stroked his head. The bare skin and locket face seemed like they might help.

"How intriguing," Lou said. She approached and crouched beside Claire. "May I see your hand?"

Claire scowled at her. "No."

Lou burst into laughter. A low, explosive boom thrummed the air. "So be it. I think it's why Ki is using you, though. He wants one thing above all others, which is to have the seals broken. He'd do anything for that, so long as he believed the one making the promise could deliver. Your hand holds the symbol of our subjugation. Either he thinks he can manipulate you into breaking the seals, or he holds you responsible and wants to punish you."

Looking at her hand, Claire thought of Iulia. The whorls and dots had been her symbol, so she'd said. The heart shape came from someplace else, but the blood she passed to her descendants had something to do with this symbol. Claire had taken Iulia's body, which meant she now carried it in an undiluted form.

Not that Claire understood all of this. She shook her head and sighed. "I'd expect the punishment thing. I don't really see how making a volcano erupt punishes me, though. There are a lot of other people who'll get hurt or die because of it. I may have gotten hurt, but I'm fine."

Enion's wing snapped into alignment. He'd begun to heal.

Lou snorted. "He's a trickster. When he wants to punish someone, he does it in the abstract. After all, you caused the eruption. It's on your head. And those who will face the majority of the impact are white people, his usual favorite target since your kind arrived. The British ones, anyway."

"By the time white people came here, they were Americans," Claire said.

Lou patted her on the head. "You're sweet. A shame he hates you."

Enion opened his eyes and lifted his head. "Boom."

"Yeah." Claire kissed his head above his eyes. "Big boom."

"If I were you," Lou said, "I'd get moving. There's an avalanche headed this way." She started walking away.

The rumbling had never stopped, Claire had just ignored it in favor of her injured dragon. "What about you? Can we help you get clear of it?"

Lou stopped and turned to see Claire with her brow raised in surprise. "After that conversation, you want to help me?"

"You may be annoying, but you're still a person." Claire waved a hand in the air. "Or whatever you are. Alive and sentient, I guess. I'd save everyone if I could."

"Then Ki has chosen his enemies poorly. Tell him I said so." Lou nodded once in a show of polite respect. "Thank you for the consideration, but I'll be fine." She left, disappearing behind a thick fir.

"Weirdest—and worst—Christmas vacation ever." Claire stood aside to give Enion space to stand, then climbed on his back. "Let's go see what Ki has to say for himself."

CHAPTER 21

JUSTIN

Justin leaned against Drew's door frame, watching Tammy help Drew eat soup. Breathing seemed to exhaust the kid, and pain had etched lines across his face. Drew looked at least five years older and showed no signs of recovering yet. The dog laid on his bed with his head under Drew's hand, quieter than he'd ever been outside of sleeping.

He hated to interrupt when Drew needed to get food inside him, but Justin did it anyway. "Where's Claire?"

"She left maybe an hour ago," Tammy said.

The house rattled. Justin figured a heavy truck drove past. "Did she say where she was going?"

"Only the same thing you always say."

That meant she hadn't offered more than "out." Justin rubbed the spot on his chest where Avery had stabbed him. Before coming to look for Claire, he'd changed clothes and washed up, so at least he didn't have bloodstains all over. No matter how much danger he faced or how close he came to death, he tried to keep it from the family. Marie heard about the worst of it, but still in couched terms.

If anyone knew what Claire had gone to do, Justin figured it would be Drew. He fixed the kid with his best stern stare and waited.

Drew noticed him. The kid coughed and sputtered on the latest spoonful of soup.

Tammy wiped his face with a hand towel. "Have you had enough?'

"I think he has," Justin said. "At least for now."

Tammy huffed. "Drew, have you had enough for now?"

He closed his eyes and nodded. "Yeah."

"Fine. I'll come back later." Tammy took the bowl and gave Justin a dirty look on the way out. "You're not supposed to act like *her* father."

"Better than acting like mine," Justin said. He shut the door and took the seat next to Drew. "Where did she go?"

"I don't know."

"I don't believe you."

Drew cracked his eyes open and grimaced. "I really don't know. I didn't say anyplace, and neither did she."

Mutt whined without saying anything and buried his nose deeper in the covers.

The phrasing Drew had picked, even in exhaustion and pain, seemed curious to Justin. He leaned back and crossed his arms. Drew wouldn't cover for her unless he had a reason to think she'd get into trouble. Justin made a guess. "But you asked her do something."

"I don't know," Drew muttered. It sounded like he spoke to Kay.

Justin tamped down the urge to shake Drew until information fell out. "She's not in trouble."

"Sure."

"I need her to fix my armor."

Drew raised his brow. "What did you fight?"

Now that he had Drew's attention, Justin figured he might as well admit to ignorance. He'd always liked it when adults did that. "I'm not sure, but it wasn't pleasant." For good measure, he added, "Without the armor, I'd probably be dead."

"Fine," Drew said with a wheeze. "She went to find a stone I can use to channel enough power to heal. I'm wrecked until I can tap a line big enough to break through the damned block that stupid cord caused."

The house rattled again.

"I've never noticed trucks going past here before," Drew said.

Although Justin also wondered about the rattling, he needed to know about Drew's condition. "What do you mean about the cord and a block?"

"That cord...Kay says he's not sure how to explain what it did. It sort of bound stuff that isn't supposed to be bound? I dunno. The point is, we need a lot of juice to rip it free, and we're not recovering."

"Should I get Anne? Can someone on the outside help?"

To his surprise, Drew shifted with discomfort. "We're not sure who to trust. Kay doesn't know who or what made that trap, but it wasn't left at that school to catch random, wandering ghosts. Someone put it there to catch me."

Though he didn't know how he felt about it, Justin added, "Or Claire."

Drew frowned. "I don't know what it would've done to her. She's not..." He shook his head. "Claire is Claire. She's not an echo or memory. It's her soul in Iulia's body. But I don't know what that means. Maybe it was for her, I guess. Kay thinks Iulia made it, just like he thinks she made the other one, but I still don't see how that's possible. Even if her ghost is wandering around, it's a ghost. Ghosts can't do things like that."

"Maybe they can now." Justin shrugged. "We don't really know much about Iulia. Who she really was before Caius imprisoned her, I mean. She knew a lot about magic and ghosts."

Once again, the house rattled. Justin stood, ready to yell at whoever kept driving trucks down their street on a Sunday afternoon. "Do you have any idea where Claire might have gone?"

"No. None. I told her what I needed, and she left."

Justin nodded. "Get some rest," he said as he left the room. He stormed out of the farmhouse and stalked down the driveway.

Avery stood at the end, waiting for him. "I have no idea what's shaking—" He turned to see Justin and did a double-take back toward the property. "That's unexpected."

Twisting around, Justin saw trees, the house, puffs of smoke from the farmhouse chimney, and a giant, dark cloud spreading across the sky. "Why would a storm shake the windows when it's already north of us?" As he watched, it billowed toward them. "And why is weather coming from the north?"

"This reminds me of when Mount St. Helens erupted."

"I've never actually thought of you as old before."

Avery snorted. "Unlike you, I acquired my teenagers the usual way." He pointed at the sky. "If it's really an eruption, ash should start falling soon. I wonder if that has any effect on ghosts. Or, for that matter, witches."

Justin told him what Drew had said. "I guess we'll have to wait for Claire to come home. She knows better than to stay out all night, at least."

Avery crossed his arms, still watching the encroaching ash cloud. "Do you think she might've gone to Ki?"

"For a stone? That's about the last place I'd go."

"Have you shown her around the city yet? She could've gone to him as a source of information."

"Oh. Huh." Given the probable eruption, Justin wondered if he should go out and do things instead of staying home for his kids. If it was St. Helens, they lived about forty miles from the peak, a distance too short to dismiss danger from landslides and ash. This time of year, they also had avalanches to worry about.

Dark snow drifted from the sky. Justin held out his hand and collected a tiny clump of ash.

"It begins," Avery said. "The next few days will be a nightmare for the department. We'll all be pulling overtime dealing with traffic and people with breathing issues, probably through Christmas. I can't blow them off, so you're on your own for the rest of the week."

"Great," Justin grumbled. "I guess the church can wait."

"I suggest taking Claire and Drew whenever you can. At least have them check the building and try a few things." They crossed the street again and Avery waved to his car. "If they still can't deal with it, make yourself useful and help people conspicuously. Good PR never hurts."

"I'll keep that in mind."

Avery climbed into his car, the radio already busy with voices, and drove away.

Justin considered riding out to Nine Cans to check what Ki knew about Claire. If she'd never visited him, the ride would be a waste of time. Even if she had visited him, the ride might still waste his time. Maybe he ought to stay home and keep an eye on the news. If anything flowed in their direction, they'd have to evacuate the house, and they'd need him and Tariel to get that done. Besides, breathing ash helped no one.

He jogged to the cottage to help Marie move the girls to the farmhouse so they could watch TV.

Claire would have to use her head and get herself home.

CHAPTER 22

CLAIRE

By the time Enion reached Nine Cans, ash fell in Portland. Claire still didn't understand all the things Lou had said or why she'd refused Claire's help. She slid off Enion's back, noting how pedestrians hurried more than usual. They probably knew what this weather meant, or at least didn't want to breathe it.

Enion flashed silver and hung around her neck. She pushed open the bar's door. A dozen customers crowded the bar and stared at the TV, showing aerial footage of lava spraying from Mount St. Helens through a huge, dark cloud.

Ki's expression as he checked the door took Claire by surprise. She'd expected a mad, gleeful grin. Instead, he seemed pale and stunned.

"Claire," he said in a half-whisper, half-gasp.

Her anger stolen by his shock, she stepped to the end of the bar, where two men made space for her. "What was in the box, Ki?"

He shook his head. "I don't know."

She believed him. He seemed far too upset to lie. "Then why did you send me up there with it? You knew what I'd wind up doing with it."

Nodding, he lifted a glass mug already in his hand. The amber contents swirled with silver sparkles. Claire watched him drain half the mug, then he set it on the bar and offered it to her.

Claire's one experience with beer had taught her she didn't want another. One thing Lou had said popped into her head as she pushed away the mug. "Who asked you to have a Knight deliver that box?" When he shook his head and gripped the mug's handle, she touched his hand. "Who promised to break your seals?"

Ki raised the mug and chugged the rest of the drink.

Beer belly guy pointed at Ki. "Is this your fault?"

Ki flung his mug at the wall. The thick glass shattered. Half the customers flinched. The other half watched without reacting. Claire jumped. She'd never seen him do anything violent before.

"Out," Ki snarled. "Everyone out! Bar is closed until the ash stops falling."

"That could be days," the beer belly guy grumbled as he slid off his stool. He glanced at Ki, whose eyes had narrowed to slits and glowed with gold, and scuttled out of the bar with everyone else.

Claire stood her ground. She didn't know what Ki could do, but she had a dagger belted at her waist and knew how to use it.

The door clicked shut behind the last person, leaving them alone.

Ki slammed his hand on the bar. "Take it and go." He snatched his hand away to reveal the stone she'd picked out earlier. His body vibrated with pent up anger, and he bounced on his toes like he meant to hit things.

Worried he'd change his mind, Claire swiped the stone off the bar. She didn't like leaving him in this state, though. He could cause all kinds of damage, or get himself into trouble. Even with his terrible jokes and outing her earlier, she didn't want to see anything happen to him.

"Volcano, eh?"

"I said to leave."

"Yeah, I heard." Claire hopped onto a stool. "Gimme a soda, barkeep. Whatever kind you got that's clear. I don't do cola."

Ki gripped the edge of the bar with both hands and leaned forward until his nose quivered an inch from hers. "Get. Out."

She smirked and patted his cheek. "Get. A grip."

He recoiled with a growl to stand with his arms crossed over his chest. "You have no idea who you're dealing with."

"Oh, please." She snorted at him. Inside, she quivered with the fear he'd leap over the bar and attack her. Even if he had no magical ability, he still towered over her and had thighs as big as her waist. On the outside, though, she laced her fingers so he wouldn't see them shake and looked down her nose at him.

"Get over yourself. Yeah, you got played. Yeah, it sucks. I bet it doesn't happen to you very often, but boo hoo. It happens to the rest of us all the time. Tantrum's not gonna fix it. Where's my drink?"

"What do you want?" He scowled.

She shrugged. "I wanna know who played you."

"And why do you care?"

"I'm a Knight."

His jaw tightened and loosened, and shifted from side to side. He made a fist so tight his knuckles turned pale. "That reason doesn't make sense."

"Only because you don't want it to." Judging his mood to have softened, she leaned forward and plucked a glass from behind the bar. "You like having us all as the enemy because it means everything makes sense.

Nothing really changes, right?" She set the glass on the bar and pointed for him to fill it.

"I'm not your enemy, Ki. I'm the ghost police, not the whatever-you-are police."

His scowl faded to something more neutral and he used a hose to fill her glass with clear, bubbly liquid. "Knights have traditionally been nosy busybodies about all aspects of magic."

"Probably because the leader was an asshole."

One corner of his mouth twitched. "Perhaps."

Having talked him down from whatever cliff he'd teetered on the edge of, Claire took a deep breath and let it out. She gripped the glass with both hands, still wary of them shaking.

"A woman brought me the box. I didn't know her. She promised she'd break my seals if I got you, specifically, to deliver it to Loowit."

"And you believed her? Don't people promise you that all the time?"

He retrieved something from his pocket and laid it on the bar for Claire to see. The lump of blackened, cracked stone bore a partial imprint of the circular whorls and dots symbol marking all the seals around the world.

"Of course people try to make that promise at least three times a week. But she'd already broken one. There are only four more. Besides, I didn't expect you to walk through the door so soon. I figured I had months to investigate her and find out what she is and what her motives might be."

Claire prodded the stone with her finger. Nothing happened. "Where are the rest?"

"Split across the border between Massachusetts and Vermont. This one was on the Vermont side."

"Are you sure? It could be from any broken seal. This could've come from the ones Justin broke for the dragons."

Ki picked up the stone and rubbed his thumb over the partial design. "It's challenging to explain, but yes, I'm sure. This is real." He sighed and shook his head. "I should've opened that damned box right away. You'd think I could be patient about my seals after all this time, but you'd be wrong. The taste of freedom this gave me." He held up the stone and grunted in disgust, then tossed the rock to the floor behind the bar.

Someone with the ability to get to New England and back had made the trip to break one of Ki's seals so she could set up Claire to make Mount St. Helens erupt. For some reason.

"What can you tell me about this woman?"

He leaned against the bar, this time not projecting intimidation. His stance suggested conciliation and confidentiality. "If she doesn't break my seals by Christmas, I'll tell you anything you want to know about her. Otherwise, I'll handle her myself."

Claire doubted she'd get a better offer. "Deal." She sipped her soda and smiled at him. "Any thoughts on why me, or why that volcano?"

Straightening, Ki shrugged. "To answer a question like that, I'd ask what they've accomplished by doing so. In your case, I doubt they wanted you out of the way to perpetrate mischief on those you care about. If they wanted that, they would've targeted Justin or Avery. But remember that mischief comes in many forms, young Knight. It's not always obvious at the outset." He gestured over his shoulder to the TV. "Case in point."

"Thanks." Though it sounded general and useless, Claire appreciated the advice anyway. She took a swig of her soda and hopped off the stool. "We'll be messing with the node later. Just so you know."

Ki nodded. "Don't do anything stupid."

She grinned as she headed for the door, happy to hear his sense of humor returning. "Who? Me? Never."

Brakes squealed outside, then metal slammed into metal. Claire threw open the door and watched a pair of crumpled cars slide into a third.

"Call nine-one-one," she told Ki over her shoulder. She dashed to the wreck and saw unconscious, bloody people in the cars. Nothing weird seemed to have caused the crash but ash covered the road. This would happen all over the region. Worried paramedics might be already overloaded with similar crashes, she pulled Enion off her neck and tossed him into the air.

Going home would have to wait. "We need dragons. All the dragons. Now!"

Enion chirped his understanding and streaked into the distance. Claire ran to the nearest car and stabbed the door to get the driver free. In the distance, sirens wailed. Another punch of metal echoed off the buildings.

Ash blotted out the setting sun. Streetlights flickered on. Someone screamed.

Claire had a feeling she might miss her curfew.

CHAPTER 23

JUSTIN

The news showed helicopter footage of a car accident happening in real time, falling ash turning the picture gritty. One car, its brake lights glowing, plowed into another. Both bridges over the Columbia River had accidents blocking traffic. If anything happened to Vancouver, so many people would never escape.

Justin watched with a deepening frown while Tammy and Marie entertained the girls and made dinner. At this point, they'd all adjusted to feeling like a never-ending train rolled past the window.

"I should be out there helping," he muttered.

"If you want to go," Jack said, "then go. We'll be fine. The truck has a full tank of gas."

"To be honest, I'd feel better if you left when I did."

"This house has been here for a good, long time, and the last eruption didn't cause us any trouble."

"Spoken like a true cantankerous old man." Justin sighed and stood. He wouldn't get his wife's father to budge without a better reason than vague worry. Besides, the news kept showing how far they wouldn't get in the truck tonight. Heading north seemed worse than putting a river between them and the volcano.

"That shoe fits, so I wear it."

"I'll try not to be out too late." Justin ducked out the door without saying goodbye to avoid upsetting his daughters and headed for Tariel's stable.

Tariel sprang to her feet when he opened the door. "Do we have a plan?"

"We're going to see if we can help unblock some of the roads." He heaved her saddle onto her back and fastened the straps and buckles. "Rescue people from car crashes. That sort of thing."

"We're going to do heroic deeds."

"Yes."

"I like doing heroic deeds. It makes people more likely to give me food. Watch for damsels in distress who happen to have chocolate bars."

Justin snorted as he rechecked the buckles. "I'll get you some later. It's best if we don't leave people thinking regular horses should have chocolate."

"Justin!" Jack leaped into the doorway. "There's a huge avalanche and mudslide headed straight for us. Somehow. I wouldn't have believed it if I didn't see it with my own eyes. A helicopter caught it with their floodlight. Moving fast. We don't have much time, and somebody's gotta get Drew."

If a mudslide hit the house, it'd hit the whole valley. The truck would never outrun it. Even if it could, they'd hit traffic, and who knew how far the debris would reach. It could go all the way to the river.

He had no idea what to do. The Brady farm had been his home for long enough to feel permanent and sacred. But if Jack thought they needed to evacuate, they needed to evacuate. To where?

"Take them into Claire's demesne," Tariel said.

"What?"

"Everyone will be safe there. I can outrun this."

He stared at her. It would work. They'd avoid the roads, maybe making it easier for others to get clear. He patted her neck. "Wait for me. Jack, grab some food and water, and take it to the cottage. Bring whatever you can grab fast. Leave it by the couch. Get everyone else over there. I'll get Drew." When Jack stared at him like he'd never before heard anything so stupid, Justin barked at him, "Trust me! Do it."

The old man kept giving him that look. Justin growled and sprinted for the house. He crashed through the front door. With a thousand tons of rock and ice headed their way, damage to the front door meant nothing.

Marie already herded the girls. Tammy filled gallon jugs with water. They expected to leave in the truck.

"Tammy, Marie! Get the girls to the cottage and wait for me by the couch. You have maybe two minutes to grab food and water."

"The cottage?" Marie picked up Missy and settled the girl on her hip. "Are you crazy? It's not safer than this. We have to get out of the city!"

Justin didn't think he had time to explain things, but no one would listen if he didn't. He hurried into the kitchen and threw cabinet doors open. "We have access to..." To what? A magic happy funtime land? "I need you to trust me. I need everyone to trust me."

He grabbed canned soup and boxes of cereal out of the cabinet. Tammy produced a plastic bin for him to fill.

"Jay, the cottage isn't a haven. The roof blew up just a month ago."

He glanced at her and saw the worst kind of fear imaginable on her face. She must have thought he expected them all to die and put on a show so the girls would think they had a chance. Or something like that.

Leaving the food to Tammy, he rushed to his wife and wrapped his arms around her and Missy. Lisa hugged his leg. "I promise I can save all of us if we hurry and you let me do what I need to do."

"How?" Marie whispered. Tears slipped down her cheeks.

"Magic."

Marie touched his cheek with chilled fingers. "Jay—"

"I love you." He pulled away enough to meet her gaze and wiped her tears with his thumb. "I love Missy and Lisa. You know I would never ask you to trust me if I wasn't sure."

"I love you too, Daddy," Lisa said. "Mommy, can we get our blankets?"

Justin kissed his wife, wishing he could take the time to reassure her as much as she needed. "We have to hurry."

Marie pressed her lips together and nodded, fighting her fear for him. "Okay. Yes. We're going to run home and grab blankets."

He let go and swiped the filled bin off the counter. "C'mon, Tammy, you too."

She huffed and bustled to follow her daughter and the girls. "Don't forget about Drew."

"I won't." Justin brought up the rear, not sure how many times he'd have to move between home and the demesne.

Tariel watched them without a word as they jogged down the path between the two houses.

Justin had spent a year of his life clearing this path and transforming an oversized shed into a home for his family. He didn't expect any of it to survive. The people mattered more than the structures, of course, but he hated to lose it all.

They piled into the house. Lisa ran to the toy chest where he'd played silly games with both girls a thousand times. He's read them a hundred stories on the couch. He'd made love to his wife, changed diapers, given baths, washed dishes, and done so many other things inside these walls.

"Now what?" Jack said, skepticism etched across his craggy, weathered face.

Justin took Tammy by the arm and carried the plastic bin with her to the couch. This would work. He pulled her down to sit on the couch, flexed his will, and fell with Tammy into Claire's demesne.

He thanked everything, ever, that it worked.

"Rondy! Emergency! I'm bringing the family. I'll be right back."

He shouldered his way back home to find Jack staring slack-jawed at Justin while he stepped off the couch.

"Daddy!" Lisa clapped and jumped up and down. "Do the magic trick again!"

"Let's go, Jack." Without letting his father-in-law argue or demand answers, he grabbed Jack by the arm and dragged him through to the demesne.

When he returned home, Marie had another plastic bin with her in the kitchen, already half full of food. Both girls wrapped toys in their blankets. Justin scooped up Missy and Lisa and their bundles, and carried them across.

He wished he had time to savor the girls' joyful reactions.

Back at home, he didn't see Marie. She'd left the bin on the kitchen table. "Marie?"

"Getting clothes," she called from the back of the house. "How much time do I have?"

He paused for a moment and smiled. The amazing woman he leaned on so much had pulled herself together in no time. "A minute? I still have to get Drew."

"Then go get him."

"No. Not until you're safe."

"I'm not sure if that's gallant or dumb."

Chuckling, Justin picked up the plastic bin. "This is me we're talking about."

"So, it's both." She sprinted around the corner with a bulging laundry bag and a wild grin.

"Definitely." More than anything, he wanted to carry her across and stay with her forever. They jumped onto the couch, he took her across, and he planted a quick kiss on her lips.

"Go get Drew."

By the time he ran up the path between the two houses again to get Drew, he heard the rolling, continuous thunder of the approaching wall. The ground shook. He tossed open Drew's bedroom door, scooped the kid into his arms, and remembered to take the glasses sitting on the nightstand.

Mutt jumped to his feet. "Where are you taking Master?"

"Someplace safe," Justin snapped. "You can come." He ran outside, taking care to prop the door open long enough for Mutt to escape.

"You don't have much time left," Tariel shouted as he darted past her to the cottage.

"What's going on?" Drew mumbled.

Justin ran through the cottage door and flexed his will as he and Mutt reached the couch. In Claire's demesne, Rondy already entertained the girls. Jack and Tammy sat in two chairs while Marie tried to cobble together a new dinner from what they had.

"I'll be back later," he said as he set Drew on the ground, his head elevated by a flat stone.

Mutt's ears perked and his tail waved. "A demesne! We're in a demesne, Master!"

"Yeah," Drew mumbled. "Quiet."

"What do you mean?" Marie asked. "We're all safe now. You don't have to go back."

Justin knew the worry in her eyes. He'd put it there before, and he knew he'd put it there again in days to come. "I have to try to help people. You know I do. And Claire is still out there. Tariel can run like the wind. We'll be fine." After leaving Drew's glasses on the kid's chest, he took his wife's hand and kissed her cheek. "I'll be back."

Though he wanted to stay and hold her, to reassure her more, he didn't have time. He squeezed her hand, let go, and leaped through a tree to return to the cottage. On his way out the door, he picked up his cloak and swirled it over his shoulders.

Tariel waited outside the door, Justin's sword already hanging from a stirrup. He took the blade and climbed onto her back. The moment his butt hit the saddle, she dashed to the driveway and onto the street.

Cars zipped down the street toward the heart of Vancouver. Tariel raced on the sidewalk to avoid them. Ash streaked her coat and fell fast enough to block light half a mile ahead. The rolling thunder behind them grew louder. Justin knew people would die tonight. He hoped the number stayed low.

The house he'd put so much of his sweat into didn't stand a chance. Once the debris smashed into it, he didn't know how he'd reach

Claire's demesne anymore. They'd need food and water in a few days, so Claire would have to find a way soon. At least he didn't have to worry about his family tonight.

They reached the I-205 bridge, thick with stopped cars. Tariel galloped down the asphalt shoulder until they found a five-car accident on the southbound side. No emergency personnel had arrived yet. On the northbound side, cars sped by, headed into the disaster. Justin couldn't do anything about that.

He leaped off Tariel's back and sliced cars open, moving drivers and passengers to the pedestrian path while Tariel shoved broken cars to the shoulder. The moment she cleared a lane, cars rolled through.

As Justin lifted an unconscious woman from her demolished car, he chanced to see the lights shut off across Vancouver. A man took the woman in his car with a promise to drive her to the nearest hospital. He found others to take the rest of the injured, except one man who wouldn't survive long.

Justin left the scene on Tariel's back, carrying a man with a broken body. They streamed past cars and pounded into the city. Tariel followed signs for a hospital. She skidded to a stop outside the emergency room, her hooves scraping through a thin layer of ash. With her help, Justin dropped to the ground, still carrying his charge.

Chaos greeted him. People in scrubs rushed with clipboards. Shouting echoed off the walls. A nurse saw him and paused to press two fingers under the man's chin.

"I'm sorry, he's gone. You can take him over there." She pointed to a wall in the waiting area, as if Justin should dump his charge on the floor like a pile of garbage.

"Are you sure he's dead?" Failure punched him in the chest. He didn't even know the man's name.

The nurse gave him a soft, sad smile. "I'm sorry. Someone will help you, we're just shorthanded right now. He won't be left for long. Excuse me." She whisked away, swept back into the triage dance.

Justin trudged fifteen feet to the wall where she'd pointed and lowered the man's body to the floor. Crouching beside him, he closed the man's eyes and wondered how long his family would wait before deciding to consider him missing.

"I need to go," he told the man, not sure why he said it out loud.

White mist bubbled out of the body.

He'd never seen a ghost rise from a body before. Justin stood and took a step back, his hand on the hilt of his sword. Despite what he'd been taught, he didn't think he could give ghosts a chance tonight. There would be too many, and too many moments to corrupt them.

Someone screamed behind him. Justin drew his sword and slashed through the mist before it could form a coherent shape. The ghost fizzled and faded, its mist breaking apart and disappearing.

He turned to leave and saw four more globs of ghosts drifting through the emergency room. One engulfed the nurse he'd spoken with. She shrieked and spasmed. The mist constricted.

Independent ghosts weren't supposed to be able affect normal people with no magical signature. Animals, yes, but not human beings.

The other three ghosts hung in the air, their movements erratic.

Justin rushed the nurse. He had no idea what to do, but he had to do something.

CHAPTER 24

CLAIRE

Every time Claire had her dragons take off, they found another car crash. Brakes locked up in the ash and cars slid into each other, over and over. They handled victims in pairs, suspending a person between two dragons to transport them to hospitals. One pair of dragons returned with a blue sheet to carry people. After that, the rest sought similar hammocks.

Despite the dragons' good intentions, they couldn't handle the delicate work of extracting the injured from crumpled cars without hurting them more. Enion took Claire from accident to accident, where she cut open cars and pulled people out. Dragons ferried the injured to an emergency room she'd shown them. Once the ER staff stopped screaming at the first appearance of dragons, they handled the injured as swiftly as they could.

Enion flew over Skidmore Fountain with four dragons in tow. Scattered streetlights, spared from the Thanksgiving weekend destruction, offered weak yellow light over the plaza. Orange construction fencing covered the smashed fountain, and all the debris from the nearby destroyed walls had been cleared. A thick layer of ash covered the cobblestones, with dimples where the MAX tracks ran.

Streaks in the ash led to a white sedan buckled against a brick building. The dragons landed and converged. Claire saw a flicker of fire coming from the front of the car, but it hadn't caught on anything yet.

"People inside," Enion said.

"No moving the car," Claire said as two dragons reached for the trunk to drag it. She slid off Enion's back. "Stay back. Enion, break the window for me."

Her dragon punched a claw through the glass of the empty passenger seat. A little girl shrieked. Claire shooed the dragon and groped inside the car to open the door.

In the dim light, she saw a man in the driver's seat with a deflated airbag draped over his lap. Bricks had smashed through the window and crushed half his head. His one remaining unblinking, empty eye stared forward. Behind him, a little girl whimpered and clutched a teddy bear.

The kid reminded Claire of Lisa, with her dark hair in two thin braids and eyes too big for her face.

She also reminded Claire of Drew and his story about the crash that had killed his parents.

"Hi." She moved to the back door and opened it with a friendly smile. The door creaked. "I'm here to help. Are you okay? Does anything hurt?"

The girl sniffled and shook her head. "Are you a police lady?"

"No. I'm a Knight. The crash was pretty scary, huh?"

She nodded. "Daddy won't answer."

"Yeah." Claire didn't know how to say the words this kid needed to hear. "Can you undo your seatbelt?"

The girl squeezed her teddy bear harder, half-hiding behind it.

"Ghost," Enion hissed.

Claire whirled and drew her dagger. Shimmering in the yellow light, a cloud of mist drifted from the building toward the fountain. Not sure if she should attack it or not, Claire followed in its wake. If it wanted to go to a church, she knew she should escort it to make sure it arrived at one. Even if that meant ignoring other people in trouble, getting a ghost to its rest took priority. Or so she'd been told.

But the ghost didn't pass the fountain. When it reached the broken bowl, it hovered and flashed with silver. The flashes came in pulses, not quite matching Claire's heartbeat. She watched, not understanding what could have caught it.

The girl screamed again.

Claire spun to see Enion recoiling from the car. "Fire," he whined.

Another dragon stuck its head under the car. "Burning."

"What are they?" the girl shrieked.

"Dragons," Claire snapped as she sprinted back to the car. The ghost could wait. She reached the car and stuck her hand inside the back seat, offering to help the kid. "That's my noble steed. Sometimes knights slay dragons, but I tamed one and made him my mount. Which is way cooler than a horse. And I have five. If you come out of the car, I'll let you ride one."

The girl shrank from her.

"Please get out of the car." Claire sighed and remembered how she hadn't wanted to get out of the car that one time. "I promise I won't leave you alone. We'll go to a police station. Together. Okay?"

"What about Daddy?"

Claire glanced at the front seat. "I'll come back for him." She would, because she needed to deal with his ghost. "Let's get you safe first. That's what he'd want, because that's what all dads want. Even my dad."

With a start, she realized she hadn't left any word about Ki's errand. Then the volcano erupted, and she hadn't gone home yet. Justin was probably worried about her.

"C'mon. There's a lot of stuff going on tonight, and the sooner I get you someplace safe, the sooner I can take care of your dad and a lot of other people just like you who need help."

The girl gulped and finally clicked her seatbelt. She scooted toward Claire and took her hand. Claire whisked the girl into her arms and took care to keep her from seeing the driver. No one ever needed to see something like that, especially not the guy's daughter.

"What's that?" The girl pointed at the fountain.

"A ghost." Claire settled the girl onto a dragon's back. The teddy bear provided cushioning. "This is Tomako. He's going to fly alongside me and my dragon. We're going to the police station, and we're going to take it easy and slow." She patted Tomako's neck. "Hold on here," she told the girl. "The cold might sting your eyes."

With one last glance at the ghost, which hadn't left the fountain and kept pulsing, Claire climbed onto Enion's back. The small flight of dragons loped and leaped into the air, two flying below Tomako in case the girl fell. Claire only knew where to find one police station nearby. Avery had taken her there once. Justin had broken out of the place once.

They skimmed the roofs of downtown Portland, headed south. She saw flashing lights on the main roads. The first responders had kicked into high gear. Finally. Once she dropped off the girl and took care of the ghost, she could go home.

The dragons landed outside the downtown station. Claire helped the girl off Tomako's back and took her cold little hand. She considered taking the girl up to Avery's office but had no idea if he'd be there, or if anyone would stop her. Instead, she had the girl sit in the waiting area and approached the night duty clerk.

"Hi. I found this girl in a car about to blow up," she said, keeping her voice low. "It's on Ankeny Street, and the driver was dead when I got there. Car had plowed into a building. The driver was her dad. She doesn't know yet, and I don't know who she is."

The woman looked past Claire at the girl. "And you are?"

Part of Claire wanted to take responsibility and maybe grab some glory. Everyone knew a mysterious figure and dragons had helped during the bugpocalypse. But Avery had protected her identity for a reason. He and Justin took the glory. Claire and Drew got to stay anonymous.

Did she want to be anonymous? In the aftermath of Thanksgiving, she and Drew had kept their mouths shut. She couldn't say why. Because Justin asked them to, so it seemed. He'd said he worried about getting blamed for the destruction, even though giant mutant cockroaches had done it. Witches kept their power quiet for a reason, Anne had said.

Screw that. She wanted people to know about her. Both she and Drew deserved some credit for what they'd done.

"I'm the Dragon Rider." She flashed the woman a smile and turned her back on the desk. With a wave for the girl, she pulled her scarf into place to breathe through the ash and walked out of the building.

She climbed onto Enion's back and decided she'd done her duty to the city for tonight. "Let's go home," she told the dragons. "Get some sleep and snacks."

The dragons all chirped their eagerness and launched into the sky. They streaked north. As they crossed the river, Claire realized she couldn't see any lights in Vancouver, and it had nothing to do with the falling ash.

For the first time in her life, the I-5 bridge across the Columbia River had zero cars. Claire pointed for Enion to fly closer until she saw and heard the reason in the darkness. Massive mounds of debris blocked the north side in both directions. Mud, rocks, cars, snow, concrete, streetlights, smashed buildings, and more reached onto the bridge, then oozed through the girders to fall into the river. The deafening noise reminded her of movie tornadoes merged with thunder and car crashes at the same time.

The debris-strewn flow covered everything and hadn't yet stopped creeping to the river. As Enion carried her east, they saw the roofs of engulfed buildings all along the shore. Claire watched a building collapse in slow motion, succumbing to the pressure and joining the flow.

All of Vancouver had been buried.

"Get us home. Now. They're fine. They're all fine." If she said it enough times, she knew it would be true.

CHAPTER 25

JUSTIN

The nurse screamed. Justin shoved her. She hit the floor. High-pitched screeching filled the emergency room. Mist sank into the nurse's skin, disappearing from sight. Someone else screamed. Justin snapped his gaze to the new victim and saw a ghost enveloping a young man in the waiting area.

He sighted the other two ghosts. Leaping over the fallen nurse, he ran across the room. Before it could assault anyone, he slashed his sword through the third ghost. The fourth drifted through the wall.

As he rushed for the door, he pointed to a man in scrubs. "Get these two people onto gurneys. I'll be right back!" Justin chased the last ghost into the parking lot. His sword slashed through the ghost and lodged in a car's headlight.

With no other ghosts in sight, he sprinted back to the emergency room. Two men in scrubs tried to hold down the fallen nurse while her body spasmed.

"She's having a seizure," one man said.

Justin rushed to their side. He didn't have time to explain. "Get ready to stop bleeding," he snapped.

"What for?"

Before the man could protest further, Justin stabbed the woman. He shoved his blade straight through her shoulder, trying to cause as little harm as possible. It had worked for him, so he figured it would work for someone else.

The two men, both startled, leaned away from him. Justin drew out the sword with silvery mist spilling from the wound and dissipating in the air. Once the mist stopped, the woman's spasms ended, and blood seeped from the injury.

"That's what for. Get her some help. I need to do the same for that man." He pointed at an empty space where the injured man had been. "Where did he go?"

"What in the name of God," one of the men whispered.

The other man jerked into action, covering the nurse's wound and telling the first man what to do.

"Where is he?" Justin shouted at the people crowding the room.

One woman raised a shaking hand and pointed at an exit door.

Justin ran through the door and stopped outside the building. Tall lights in the parking lot showed the ash drifting from the sky. Cars gleamed. Trees in concrete planters shaded portions of the lot.

While he'd been distracted, a man possessed by a ghost had run into the night. Justin had no idea what it would do or where it would go. He didn't know what would happen to the victim. Would that man wind up like Drew? How many ghosts would rise tonight, and how many would attack living people?

"Tariel!"

The horse leaned her head around a corner. "Yes?"

"Did you see a man run from here?" Justin ran to her side and swung into the saddle.

"No, and it's challenging to pick up anything by smell in all this."

"Great. How the hell did he move that fast? I only turned my back on him for a few seconds."

"No idea. What do you want to do now?"

Scanning the parking lot, Justin had no idea what would happen to that man. Then he thought of Vancouver. How many had already died, and how many more would suffocate in the rubble? If every death created a ghost, what would happen? The river protected Portland from a swarm, unless they decided to use the bridges.

"Do you think it's possible to engineer a volcano eruption?"

Tariel turned her head enough to fix him with one big, blue eye. "Is this a serious question? Of course it's possible. Anything is possible. That's the whole point of magic. It violates the laws of physics. I certainly don't know *how* one would do that, or how much power it would take."

"Iulia." Everything kept going back to her. "Option one, the same thing that happened to Claire also happened to Iulia. In that case, we're looking at an entity that could be a full soul with all the knowledge of the witch who created the seals in the first place. Option two, it's Iulia's ghost, which makes no sense to me, but we're in a new world here. Option three, Iulia has possessed someone, and that someone is a witch."

"Why the eruption? Her goal is a new seal, not mass chaos and destruction."

"Chaos can be useful. It's distracting and causes a lot of small problems on top of the big problems." Justin patted Tariel's neck and pointed for her to leave the parking lot. He hoped people had stopped venturing outside or trying to go north of Portland.

Tariel clopped up the street. Justin watched the sidewalks for people in need of help.

Two blocks away, he spotted a figure lying on the sidewalk under the light of a streetlamp. The cut on his arm, oozing blood, matched Justin's memory of the possessed man. As Tariel closed the distance, Justin watched for any sign of a trick. He slid off Tariel's back when she stopped and circled the man.

"Help," the man rasped. His eyes didn't blink, and his chest didn't move. With a start, Justin recognized Brian Avery, Detective Avery's older son.

Had the ghosts only possessed people with magical signatures after all? The nurse could've had one. He didn't know all the witches in Portland. "What are you?"

Brian didn't answer.

Justin leaned closer, not sure what to think. He didn't know if a ghost could possess a dead body. After all, Claire had taken Iulia's. That might've been a special case, or it might've been the new normal.

"Broken." Brian's hoarse voice sounded forced.

"You can't use the body," Justin said, "so release it." The thought sparked another idea about Iulia, but he had a more pressing problem at the moment.

"Stuck."

Hoping he could still save Brian, Justin stabbed his blade into the existing cut on his arm. When he slid the steel free, white mist dribbled out of the wound. Justin slashed through the mist for good measure.

Brian sucked in a breath and groaned.

Relieved he hadn't failed Avery, Justin scooped up the kid and clambered onto Tariel's back. She lurched into motion, returning to the emergency room. They handed Brian to a nurse and left, expecting to find more trouble elsewhere.

As Tariel trotted through the city, Justin thought of his idea again. "What if Iulia wants her body back more than she wants a new seal? What if she believes she needs it?"

"Given that Claire took it, I can see how she'd believe it possible," Tariel said.

"If that's her priority, then she could be behind the church, the trap at the school, even the volcano. Somehow."

"It's worth mentioning that she knew where we live."

Justin tried to imagine the kind of person who'd destroy a city to get one house with one family. He couldn't fathom that level of depravity. On the heels of that thought, he considered that Iulia had tried to murder his family, and possibly also himself, with a volcano.

"Whatever her motives and methods, we have to find her and destroy her. I just have no idea where to look."

"Rondy might be helpful."

"I'm not sure how to get back to Claire's demesne either. I might need Claire for that."

"Then let's talk to Anne. Even if you don't want to trust her completely, she should be at home, and you should really make sure she knows her family is safe." Tariel picked up speed, heading west.

"Good thinking."

CHAPTER 26

CLAIRE

Nothing.

A vast sea of destruction and despair covered the whole valley as far as Claire could see. The massive lahar had swept away tall trees, buildings, and vehicles. People. Glass, rock, snow, branches, metal, woods, bricks, and so much more made a rocky, bumpy surface fifteen to twenty feet too high.

Claire wanted to believe she'd find living people under the mess. Specific living people. But Enion couldn't even find the Brady farm to start digging. They circled the area where it should've been and couldn't pick out nearby landmarks that should've pointed to its location. Even the freeways had been overrun.

She stared, stunned and in terrible awe of the power that had taken everything from her.

Power she'd unleashed.

Without understanding it.

Even when the eruption happened, she hadn't expected this. The caldera pointed north! How did so much rock and ice flow south? Why did it work like this? It shouldn't have.

Two dozen dragons, the full flight, tested the surface. Several flashed small and landed.

For two months, Claire had been part of a family again. After six long, horrible years, she'd found people who decided to care about her because they wanted to, not because someone paid them. Marie was so nice. Missy and Lisa didn't deserve this. None of them deserved this.

"This was my fault." Tears slid down her cheeks. "I should've told Ki to shove his box. Made Lou check inside it. Found another source for this stupid stone."

She covered her face and cried. The stone had been for Drew. He'd been so weak from that trap-thing, he never would've escaped this destruction on his own. Someplace under all this rubble, someone would eventually find his broken body. Or his skeleton. If they even bothered to try excavating Vancouver.

"Can't land," Enion said as he circled the spot the other dragons had chosen. "Too soft. Where to go?"

"I don't care," Claire gasped through sobs.

Drew had suffered through her death, and she had no idea how he'd managed. She'd only been dead for a short time, but he'd gotten a grip. She couldn't imagine ever surfacing from this agony.

The sun had set on everything.

Enion soared through the sky. Claire kept her hands over her face, not watching anything. Wherever she looked, she'd only see the world without Drew, without the girls, without Justin, without everyone who mattered. Alone again.

Forever. Because she never wanted to have people in her life again. People died. People hurt. Everything hurt. She and the dragons could fly into the woods and ignore the world.

Enion landed. In spite of herself, Claire lowered her hands. The dragons sat in Anne's backyard. In this place, Drew had been possessed by Kay. Too many terrible things had happened.

She slid off Enion's back and crumpled into a ball under the trees. Enion wrapped himself around her. For a long time, she stayed in that warm cocoon of comfort, unwilling to acknowledge the world.

"Claire?" Justin's voice reached her as her tears ran out. "What are you doing here?"

Overjoyed to hear him, Claire burst free and ran to him. He hopped off Tariel's back to hug her. His cloak swirled around her. She buried her face in his shirt. More tears sprang from her eyes.

"It's okay, Claire. You're going to be okay."

"They're all gone and it's my fault," she blubbered.

"What's your fault?" She heard his voice resonate through his chest.

"The volcano. I killed them all."

"Ah. Whatever you did, it's not your fault. Believe that. You were manipulated." He didn't sound upset, just tired.

Claire pulled away and wiped her face. "How can you be so..." She covered her mouth in horror. "You don't know." As with the little girl, she didn't have the words. Even if she did, she didn't want to say them out loud.

"Don't know what?" He frowned at her.

She wiped her face again. "Home. It's...it's..."

"Oh, that." He sighed like it wasn't the worst thing that had ever happened, like he didn't care. "I know about that already. It's kind of depressing, yeah."

"Who are you?" She recoiled from him. "How can you just—They're all dead, and it means nothing to you?"

"Dead?" Justin's brow raised. "They aren't dead. Everyone is in your demesne. It was the only place I could take the whole family in time to escape the lahar."

She stared at him.

"Aren't you linked to Drew? Can't you feel that he's not dead?"

How had she never thought of that? "I..." She had no idea how long she'd shed tears for living people in her demesne. She should've checked for Drew. Then she would've found everyone. And not felt stupid.

"C'mon, Claire." He offered an arm to drape over her shoulders. "Let's see Anne. She doesn't know yet and is probably worried. You can have some hot tea and figure out how to get me into your demesne without the couch."

She hugged him again, too confused to know what to think and feeling too much to bear.

He held her and patted her back like a dad should. "A lot of people did die tonight. We may never know how many. The important thing is to stop Iulia before she makes things worse."

"Iulia?"

With a squeeze, he tugged her toward Anne's front door. "Kay thinks she set the trap, and I think she wants her body back. Above all, we need to figure out how to find her."

"Oh." She frowned and rubbed her face while Justin knocked on Anne's door. "How did you get everyone into my demesne?"

"I ferried them through the couch."

"But that shouldn't work. Should it? I thought I had to give permission or something."

Justin shrugged. "I didn't stop to think about whether it was possible, I just did it."

"Oh."

Drew was alive. Marie, the girls, and Grandma and Grandpa were alive. Claire's chest filled to bursting with joy. She beamed at Anne when she opened the door.

"Oh, thank goodness you two are okay." Anne wrapped her arms around both and pulled them inside. The fuzzy ends of her shawl tickled Claire's nose.

"Everyone is fine," Justin said. "They all escaped just fine. Claire is shaken up, though. Could she have—"

"I'm not. I don't need anything." Claire giggled. "I just want to see them."

"Okay." Justin gave Anne a smile, then herded Claire toward the door again. "We just wanted to make sure you knew."

Anne nodded. "Where is everyone staying?"

"It's fine, we're all taken care of."

Claire noticed Justin not wanting to tell Anne anything. She approved. After what Ki had said, they had no way to know who worked for Iulia and who didn't.

They stepped outside.

"Are you sure you don't need anything?" Anne held the door open. "I heard power is out across the river."

"Sorry we barged in," Justin said. "Claire seemed like she needed something, but I guess she's fine. As soon as we have some kind of phone service, I'll let you know."

"Then I guess you should get some rest." Anne clutched her shawl and shut the door.

Justin set a hand on Claire's shoulders and steered her around the house. With him so close, she closed her eyes and focused on the thread between her locket and her demesne. Every time she'd tried this before, she'd needed the couch. But what did she need it for? Her demesne belonged to her. The connection between it and her couldn't be severed.

The chill in the air disappeared. She and Justin plunged into darkness. Without her presence in the demesne, the sun rose and set here as it did in Vancouver. With a grin, she raised the light to a dim glow.

Rondy saw her, but everyone else slept. Marie had curled around the girls on the ground, wrapped in pink and purple blankets. Grandpa Jack snored with his mouth hanging open in Rondy's chair. Grandma Tammy slept in Claire's chair. Mutt lay with his head on Drew's leg, both of them on the ground.

Claire wanted to hug everyone, but she didn't dare wake them. Instead, while Justin and Rondy watched, she shifted the chairs into cushioned easy chairs so Grandma and Grandpa would ache less when they woke. Under Marie and girls, she rippled the ground so they rested on a soft, springy surface. And for Drew, she changed his rock into a real pillow.

When they woke, she'd make them a better place to sleep. The girls could have their own little gingerbread house. Justin and Marie could have a cottage of their own. They could all have whatever they wanted.

Rondy waved for them to follow him. Claire nodded and called the light to her hand. They moved far enough to avoid disturbing anyone.

"They fretted for a while," Rondy said, "but I managed to calm them all. If you can, staying until morning would be best."

"We're not going back out tonight," Justin said. He stared into the darkness where his wife and daughters lay. "The biggest drawback here is a lack of real food and water."

Claire nodded. "I can't fix that. At least, I don't think I can."

Justin looked down at himself. "I guess that means no cleaning up tonight. We'll have to figure something out for that, and other things."

Things like showers and toilets came to mind. Claire grimaced. "I don't know what to do about that. We'll need a place on the other side to use."

Justin patted her shoulder. "We'll figure it out. Before you get some sleep, see if you can bring Tariel and the dragons across. I think we'd be better off knowing sooner than later. Tomorrow, we can test to figure out how to let everyone come and go on their own."

"Yeah. Sounds good." Claire looked forward to settling with Drew. And to waking in the morning.

CHAPTER 27

DREW

Sunshine on his face woke Drew. He still felt terrible. The spiral of pain kept its grip on his leg, worse than before. Trying to lift his hand proved more challenging than it had before sleep. If sucking down power through a stone didn't work, he didn't know how much longer he'd be able to breathe.

Claire slipped his glasses onto his face. "Morning."

"I'm so happy you woke up, Master."

Kay's voice rasped in his head. "I— Ooooh."

The sight of a sky blue stone shot through with silver, held by Claire, distracted both Drew and Kay.

"Found this," Claire said. She took Drew's hand and dropped the stone into his palm with all the gravity of passing him a blank piece of paper. "Thought you might appreciate it."

The stone warmed in his hand, pulsing in time with his sluggish heartbeat.

"I need a ley line." Drew had no idea why he whispered.

Claire nodded and leaned close. She kissed his cheek. "Can you eat?"

"No," Kay said at the same time as Drew.

Drew stared at the stone, unable to think about anything but breaking free of this wretched pain and malaise. "Let's go. Now."

Her brow raised. "Now? You don't even want to know about anything first?"

"No." In his hand, Drew held the key to shaking off the lingering effects of that trap, and she wanted to talk. "I'd like to go now."

"If you're sure."

He stared at her, sure she didn't understand. "Claire. I can't lift my hand by myself, and my leg is getting worse, not better. What other priority do you think I should have? Basketweaving?"

She sighed and stood. "Just a minute. I'll get Justin to help. I can't carry you."

His attention stayed on the stone. According to Stace, he had to make it his own before he'd get full use of it. Until then, he could use it on a line big enough break free. If he played this right, he could do both at once.

Stace had never made a focus stone, so she'd said. Her one attempt had ended in failure. The instructions she'd given him had all been theoretical, based upon what she'd been taught. He didn't know whether to trust her. Iulia had given him help once, and it had almost killed him. In fact, witches helping him hadn't turned out well on the whole. Even Sophie's help had been a disaster, in a way.

Justin dropped to one knee beside him without Drew noticing the man approaching. "Where do you need to go?"

"The Portland node."

Claire grimaced. "I don't want to see Ki right now."

"I don't think his jokes are *that* bad," Justin said.

"You wouldn't. You're a dad."

Drew wheezed because he couldn't muster a proper laugh.

"But that's not why," Claire said. "Mount St. Helens erupted because a woman promised Ki she'd break his seals if he convinced me to deliver a box to a woman near the mountain. Which I did to get that stone. For whatever crazy reason, the woman would only accept the delivery if I threw it into the volcano. None of us knew what it was. The point is, Ki is in kind of a bad mood because someone played him, and he knows it."

Drew stared at her.

"I don't like the parts between the lines of this story," Kay said.

"Did he tell you anything about this woman he made the deal with?" Justin asked.

Claire shook her head. "He wasn't in the mood for questioning."

"He's had a night to sleep on it. Let's go ask him now." Justin picked up Drew.

From his new vantage point, Drew noticed Tariel. Claire had figured out how to bring a horse across to her demesne. Then Justin climbed onto Tariel's back. Enion flashed large. The world shifted and turned dark.

Ash still fell. Sunlight even weaker than a normal cloudy day kept the streetlights glowing. Tariel clopped through the murky gloom of east Portland at high speed. Abandoned cars lined the roads, some intact and others not. Otherwise, they had the streets to themselves.

Drew didn't recognize anything until they reached Steel Bridge. In his condition, he didn't think they should court disaster by visiting a site on Iulia's list. He opened his mouth to suggest a different route.

The center span of the bridge clunked into motion, rising as Tariel crossed it. Though she ran too fast for him to get a good look at the river, he checked for boats and saw none. Tariel leaped off the end and stopped. She turned.

Drew saw a misty figure on the other side of the gap. They stood with their arms upraised, apparently lifting the bridge. Something seemed wrong about how it looked. Squinting didn't help.

"I have no idea," Kay said. "Don't even bother asking. Ghosts can't do what that ghost is doing."

"Let's not deal with this now," Drew said.

"You think we should leave it to wander freely?" Justin asked.

"I can't help." The words stuck in Drew's throat, bitter and sullen. "Worse, I'm a liability."

Enion swooped out of the sky and blasted fire at the figure. When the flames cleared, the figure was gone.

Justin shrugged. "I guess it doesn't matter. Dragon fire took care of it. Let's go, Tariel."

Tariel lurched into a gallop, taking them off the bridge and into the west side of Portland. They only had a few blocks to go.

"That's not right," Kay said. "Fire doesn't destroy ghosts. Powered by magic, fire can do some damage, but not dragon's breath, and not poof. If the fire could affect it, which it shouldn't, it should've acted like a person on fire. Screaming, flailing, panicking. Something weird is going on."

"Could just be the new rules," Drew said.

"I suppose."

Tariel stopped in front of Nine Cans. Drew cringed as Justin hopped off her back.

Enion landed beside them. Claire didn't climb off his back.

"There's something I want to check on while we're in this part of town," Claire said. "Do you need me for this?"

Drew didn't care if she came or not. Until the spiral knife burrowing into his leg released, he didn't care about anything but getting to the node. "No."

"Come back if you run into anything weird," Justin said. He carried Drew into the bar while Enion ran and leaped into the air.

Ki stood behind the bar as usual, stacking clean glasses. He glanced at them and returned his attention to his task.

"Good morning, Ki," Justin said.

"Is it?"

"No," Drew wheezed.

"Never mind, then. Can you help me get Drew into the basement?"

Ki flicked his gaze from Justin to Drew and back to his glasses. "Why would I want to do that?"

"So he can break free of the spell hobbling him and help me go beat the crap out of whatever woman caused Saint Helens to erupt."

Justin's answer sounded good to Drew. He hadn't expected something that coherent and well-aimed.

Ki set a glass on the stack in front of him and stared at the bar. "That matter is my business to tend."

"You want to punish her for wounding your pride. I want to punish her for destroying my home, threatening my family, and murdering thousands of people. Vancouver is gone, Ki. Gone."

Scowling, Ki crossed his arms and looked down his nose at them. "Then I want my seals broken."

"You find a way for me to get there and back, and I'll break them for you."

"I really wish he hadn't just said that," Kay whimpered. "He's being dumb. Make him stop being dumb."

"Can't," Drew said.

"Yes, I can," Justin said. "I just can't spare the time to travel that far. Get me there and back in two days, and I'll do it for you."

Kay groaned. "He's the dumbest person ever. You don't just unleash things without knowing what they are! We don't even know how many entities will be affected by those seals. It could be hundreds of things passing as human, suddenly flushed with power after two millennia without. And Ki could be a god, a demon, anything."

"Bad idea," Drew said.

Justin rolled his eyes. "Fine. Since Claire is busy, and Ki's not interested, I'll just handle it myself." He left Ki and pushed through the door to the back room before Drew could grasp what he meant.

Then he fell through the hatch to the floor of the basement in puff of dust. Pain lanced through every part of Drew's body. He cried out at the redoubled agony in his leg. The stone fell out of his hand. Everything seemed worse without it.

"We're going to get him back for that," Kay said. "I don't know how or when, but it'll happen."

Once he'd climbed down the ladder, Justin picked up Drew again, snagged the stone, and headed down the tunnel. "Sorry. Just trying to get this done. I can guess why Claire didn't get anything out of Ki about this woman."

"Cranky."

"Yes, he is."

The ley line bulged from the wall. "Stone."

"It's in my hand. Do you need it before we reach the node?"

Did he need it? No. He wanted it more than he'd ever wanted anything in his life. Almost. The stone wouldn't bring back his parents or return Claire to her own body.

"Yes."

Justin set the stone on Drew's hand.

Nothing changed, but the stone made success seem possible.

The walk seemed longer than forever.

Sooner than Drew expected, he felt power rippling against him, like approaching a bonfire. Justin kept going. Drew's flesh seared. How did the Knights feel nothing here? He tried to speak, to tell Justin to stop, but nothing came from his mouth.

They plunged into the node.

The stone burned. Drew screamed. Kay screamed. He fell.

Engulfed by molten lava, Drew saw darkness, then a light flickered into life. Cobblestones folded into existence, forming a plaza. Building facades flickered into life. He recognized nothing. Another light flickered on, emanating from a glass box on a post.

Skidmore Fountain rose from nothing to stand in the center of the plaza. Water sprayed from the bowl and splashed into the base. More water gurgled into the horse trough at the base. Drew had never seen it so clean and sharp.

"Traitor."

Drew whirled to see Caius facing Rondy atop a wooden platform, their swords crossed. Claire crouched beneath them, using her dagger to saw through one of the platform's legs.

Of all his memories, this ranked as one of the worst.

Except this didn't match that memory. Not quite. Caius and

Rondy both wore embroidered vests over white shirts with thin, dark ties. Each man had his hair slicked down and parted in the center. They wore dark slacks and polished shoes. Gold thread decorated Rondy's clothes.

Claire wore a green, ankle-length skirt with a matching jacket and white lace frothing at her collar and cuffs. Her hair had been gathered into a bun secured with more green cloth. Her pointed, buttoned shoes had fat heels.

On the other side of the plaza, Justin, Avery, and Khalid faced Djembe. Justin wore his usual jeans with suspenders, a coarse shirt, and a riding cap. Avery looked like an old-fashioned police officer, with a tall, rounded hat, a gold star and buttons on his navy coat, and black pants with polished shoes. Khalid would've fit into a movie about Persia, and Djembe wore loose clothing in a riot of colors. In the distance, Iulia raised her arms. She wore a fancy lavender dress with a bustle and a frilly, feathered hat.

The dragons seemed normal, but everyone else had been plunged into Portland's early years.

Drew looked down at himself and saw he wore denim pants, black boots, and a vest over a white shirt.

Somehow, he had to make sense of this. Before anything horrible happened.

CHAPTER 28

CLAIRE

Enion flew Claire to an ash-covered plaza, then circled Skidmore Fountain. Handling the ghost she'd left behind didn't seem like it would take much time or effort. Bringing Justin for this seemed like overkill. Besides, this way was more efficient. Drew would fix his problem, and she'd take care of this, and they'd meet afterward.

The ghost remained at the top of the fountain. To reach it with her dagger, Claire would have to drop into the empty bowl. She could, instead, climb from the base. Either way, she doubted she could avoid touching it. Throwing her dagger sounded stupid.

Of course, she had nothing to fear from a fresh, amorphous ghost. Touching it didn't matter because she could overpower it.

"Move closer," she told Enion.

"Not like ghost. Looks funny."

"That's why I'm going to stab it."

Enion huffed, but he moved close enough so she could avoid the construction barrier and reach the bowl with little effort. She drew her dagger and stuck it between her teeth. Standing on Enion's hind legs, she reached for the bowl.

Instead of the ghost lunging at her, a thin band of crystal clear power, visible as a shimmer in the air, whipped out and wrapped around her wrist. Sharp, violent agony tore through her body, ripping her apart. The line yanked her onto the fountain. She fell into the ghost and landed on her back inside the bowl. Her spine shattered.

"Claire!" Enion's voice sounded muffled and slow, like it had to pass through sludge to reach her.

The ghost drifted over her. Mist filled her vision. Her body lay broken, draped across the passenger seat of the sedan where she'd found the little girl and her dead father. Details filled in, probably from Claire's memory. The ghost couldn't have much to work with yet.

She smelled blood and ash. Bricks lay in the lap of the ill-defined man-shaped blob in the driver's seat. He wore his seatbelt. The girl whimpered in the back seat, but Claire couldn't turn to look.

One thing stood out as different. A white cord, similar to the one that had been tormenting the ghost at the church, looped around her wrist. The other end looped around the ghost's wrist, binding them together.

Claire tried to lift her hand. Pain shot up her arm, across her shoulder, and into her heart. She stopped. This fight would take a lot longer if she couldn't move.

"I'm not a ghost," she growled at the car. "Stop treating me like one."

The man-blob groaned. He sounded like a zombie.

"Shut up." She waited for healing to start.

Again, the ghost groaned. It raised its arm and their shared shackle, jerking Claire's arm to the side. The pain lanced through her once with the movement and a second time when her hand hit the center console.

"Stop it," she snapped.

The ghost screamed at her, its voice high-pitched and scratchy.

Claire cringed and thought her ears might explode. She'd never before encountered this kind of weapon or defense. Stuck like this, she had no way to attack or counter it. "Why am I not healing?" she shouted over the noise. When the ghost didn't quiet, she shrieked at it, "Shut up!"

They screamed at each other.

The ghost fell silent.

Claire stopped, her throat raw and breathing ragged. "I'm in charge here," she snapped. "You're just a blank ghost, and this is my car. I own you." Cringing in anticipation, she raised her arm and jerked the ghost closer. The agony made her want to cry. "No new ghost is going to own me!"

It cowered away from her. Though she'd been led to believe battles with ghosts always involved fighting, she counted that as a victory. If she'd dominated it, though, why hadn't they returned to the fountain? Her body still didn't heal, and they still sat in the car. This battle needed something more.

"Can you speak?"

The ghost moaned again.

It hadn't remembered enough to know anything yet. She knew from experience that the more the ghost interacted with, the more memories it would regain. "My name is Claire. I'm a Spirit Knight." The speech seemed like it would inspire more fear if she didn't sound so tired. "You bow to me. Swear obedience. If you don't, I'll destroy you."

For several long moments, the mist writhed. Then it boiled upward and outward to envelop her. The stupid ghost wanted to test her. She didn't bother trying to stifle her scream as she raised her tethered arm and punched the ghost. Her fist impacted with solid fog. The cord yanked her arm with it. Bright flashes of color flickered over the ghost's surface.

"That's right," she whimpered through clenched jaws. "Make a memory of pain. Pain caused by me. You're not going to win."

The ghost cowered from her. They fell through the bottom of the car. Healing rushed into Claire's body, repairing every bone and soothing every ache. Except her wrist. The cord, still connected to the ghost, cut into her flesh. She swung her dagger in a wide arc and stabbed the stupid magic tether.

Though the cord no longer bound them together, it remained wrapped around both, in two pieces. Claire growled at it and stabbed her own wrist to cut off the thing. She wound up sawing around her wrist. The stubborn, sticky cord refused to be destroyed all at once. Every part of the cord had to be cut. Even the part that fell off her arm needed slicing to dissipate.

If not for the healing provided by her bond with Enion, she would have had to cut off her hand.

"What is this crap?"

"Bad magic," Enion said.

Claire snorted as she wiped blood from the blade onto her jeans. "That's kind of a mild way to put it."

She looked up and saw the ghost lingering nearby with the other half of the cord tangled around its undefined form. Even without a face or detail, she could tell it drooped in defeat. The sad ghost made her sigh. It seemed confused more than pained, at least. Maybe the cord didn't hurt it as much as it had hurt her. Even if she wanted to remove it, though, she saw no way to do so without also cutting the ghost.

"I can't destroy that. It'd be like kicking a puppy."

"Take it to rest?"

"I don't know where to find the nearest church. Justin told me they don't necessarily go to the nearest church anyway. The building has to have gravity and peace. Churches aren't the only places they go, just the most obvious ones."

Heaving another sigh, she shook her head. "I guess we'll just take it with us for now. Maybe Drew can figure out what's up with the cord and do something about it."

Enion bared his teeth at the ghost. "Don't need another pet. One dog too many."

Too worn to laugh, Claire smirked. "Settle down, jealous dragon. We're not going to keep it. This is temporary." She climbed onto his back and hugged his neck. "C'mon. They're going to worry about us if we stay here too long. See if you can take the ghost by the cord. I can cut it off you."

Enion grimaced and reached for the ghost. His claws touched the cord. Nothing happened. He took the end of the cord and shrugged, bumping Claire up and down. When he loped across the plaza and leaped into the air, the ghost trailed behind him like a balloon.

"Here's hoping Justin doesn't freak out."

CHAPTER 29

DREW

Rondy snorted, still sounding like himself despite the Victorian suit and oiled hair. "You're an idiot, Caius. She has so much potential, and all you can see is her gender."

Nothing took hold of Drew and forced him to do something. When he faced memories, they always made him do the things he'd done at the time.

"I don't understand," he said.

"Neither do I," Kay said. "Stace didn't say anything about this. But then, we didn't talk about tapping the node. You know what, though, I get the feeling like something happened there that I don't remember, and that's just plain weird."

The platform holding Rondy and Caius swayed as Claire kept sawing at the leg.

"Not now, Kay. If I'm free to act..." Drew reached with one hand and tried to spin mist. Nothing happened. He saw the platform tottering, and Claire not moving out of the way.

Drew sprinted to her. He tackled her from behind, and they slid across the street. The platform crashed to the ground. Had he not acted, she would've been crushed. Just like last time.

Enion raced to her side and whined like he'd failed.

"Aren't you resourceful." Caius rose from the mess of the platform, holding an unconscious Rondy by his tie. Pieces of wood fell from his shoulders.

Drew needed to know what he'd fallen into. He jumped to his feet and jabbed his finger at Caius. "Let him go!"

Caius looked up with a snarl, meeting Drew's gaze. "You're not even a Knight," Caius said, disdain so thick Drew could taste it. "Go home, little boy. This isn't about you."

Claire scrambled to her feet. "That's right." She brandished her dagger. "This is about me."

He'd changed the memory. Neither Caius nor Claire had said either of those things.

As Drew realized he had a chance to save Claire, he noticed her readying to charge. "Together," he muttered out of the corner of his mouth.

She nodded. They watched Caius shift his attention to Rondy.

"I'm not going to stop this time, Claire." Caius raised his sword to kill Rondy.

"Now," Claire spat.

They charged with Enion. Drew threw his body at Caius. Claire swept her dagger at Caius's knees. Enion leaped at the sword. They knocked him to the ground. His sword fell with a clatter and skittered across the cobblestones. Iulia stopped its slide with her foot.

Claire slashed through Caius's knee. Enion dug his claws into

Caius's arm at the shoulder. Drew backed off, uncertain how else to help. He watched Iulia stride across the plaza, holding Caius's sword. She reached the man held helpless by a girl and a dragon.

"Golly," Kay said. "One little change made a really big difference."

"If only you could suffer the fate you truly deserved," Iulia spat in her crisp accent. She stabbed the sword into his chest.

Caius gurgled and died. Iulia ripped the sword out of his body and held Drew's new focus stone over Caius's body. Glimmering, golden lines of power drifted from his body to the stone. They grew thicker with every passing moment.

Mesmerized by the display of raw power, Drew missed everything else happening around him. Iulia's eyes widened with greed and glory. Caius's body dissipated into the lines.

When the last of Caius's body disappeared into the stone, Iulia smiled like a lazy, pampered cat. She looked over Drew's shoulder. "And now, we craft the new seal."

Her words snapped Drew out of his wonder. "Whoa, wait." He held up his arms, keeping himself between Iulia and Claire. "No, we're not going to do that."

Iulia raised her brow. "That was the point of killing him. That's why we did it. To remake the seal without him."

"But you want to make it with Claire at the center instead. Because you know she's descended from you on both sides of her family. And that doesn't solve anything."

"You foolish little boy." Iulia raised the stone, brandishing it like a weapon, and took a step toward him. Less than a foot from his face, the stone glowed with silver-streaked blue. "With this much power, you can't stop me."

Drew had no idea what to do. As far as he could tell, he had no access to magic here, except for Kay's voice in his head. Iulia, therefore, had an infinitely greater amount of power, plus the skill and knowledge to use it. He could throw a punch, but he didn't know how to fight. Besides, Iulia had endured centuries of torment and survived.

"Take it," Kay said.

Startled, Drew jerked his arm. He felt Kay take control of his hand for a moment, long enough to slap Iulia's hand. The stone flew through the air, shining like a tiny star.

"Get it!"

Drew dove for the stone. Iulia shoved him with her shoulder. Drew hit the cobblestones with a grunt, too far from the stone to reach it. He looked up to see Iulia raising Caius's sword.

For some reason, no one came to Drew's aid. The world seemed distorted beyond Iulia, as if they battled inside a glass bottle and the lights outside had gone dim.

Staring down a length of steel aiming for his heart, Drew kicked at Iulia's legs. She stumbled. He rolled to his feet and lunged for the stone. Iulia swatted him with the sword, hard enough to knock him sideways, though she didn't cut him.

Because Iulia had no skill with a blade. She knew how to hold one, but had never learned to fight with one. Had she ever learned even basic self-defense? Why bother when she had Caius, his soldiers, and witch power?

Drew didn't know how to fight either, and his usual approach to fighting included running to the nearest teacher. Facing Iulia, he saw Claire behind her, blurry and shifting. She pounded her fists on an invisible barrier. Maybe he only had to keep Iulia busy long enough for Claire to reach him. After all, this battle had been Claire's, not his.

Iulia growled as she heaved the sword at him.

Drew threw his body aside, evading her clumsy strike. "Is that the best you can do?" He swiped an arm across his face, trying to hide his fear. That blade could kill him even without its magical properties. "I know little girls who can swing better than that."

Scowling, Iulia raised her hand. White sparks crackled between her fingers. Drew didn't want to know what she planned to do. He kept his attention on the power, waiting for her to make her move.

She swung the sword at him. The blade sliced through his suspenders but failed to cut his flesh.

Kay huffed. "Can you please not fall for dumb things like that?"

"I'm doing the best I can!" Drew leaped at Iulia. They hit the invisible barrier.

Electricity jolted Drew's body, making his teeth chatter and burning a spiral down his leg. He grabbed the wrist of her sword hand and smacked it against the barrier.

Her hand around his neck, Iulia kept jolting him with a savage grin of glee. "You'll be part of the new seal," she snarled. "Just like Claire."

He smacked her hand again. The sword tumbled off the barrier to clang against the cobblestones. To his dismay, Iulia gained the use of her other hand and wrapped it around his neck to choke him.

As he gasped for breath and scrabbled to dislodge Iulia's hands, Drew hoped Claire broke through soon.

"I have an idea," Kay said. "Let's pretend this is all metaphorical. Iulia is the block on us. The barrier represents the fact that no one else can help us. Your job is to kill Iulia. Lurch forward and crack your skull against her nose, right between the eyes, then pick up the sword and stab her."

Kay's ideas usually turned out right, if more complicated and challenging than he made them sound. Drew let his arms fall, hoping Iulia would think he'd lost the will to fight. He let his eyes flutter shut. He gasped for breath.

Drew lurched forward with as much force as he could muster. The impact sent a sharp jolt through his head. He groaned. Iulia staggered and slumped against the barrier. She blinked and didn't seem to be able to focus.

"She'll recover soon. Get the damned sword and finish this, boy!"

Pressing the heel of his palm to his forehead, Drew bent and scooped up the sword. His brain throbbed. At least he no longer had to bear the spiral, and he could breathe.

He shoved the sword at Iulia. The amount of force he needed to drive it through her surprised him. The Knights all made stabbing things look easy. As Iulia twitched and gurgled, he had to lean his entire body against the blade.

Her body unraveled, disintegrating into tendrils of white light and streaking to the stone like Caius's had. Drew stumbled and yanked out the sword. With Kay goading him, he staggered to the stone and picked it up. Iulia disappeared, and the stone pulsed with a soft blue glow.

Claire stood before him, smiling, without the barrier between them. "You did it," she said. "You saved me. You saved us all."

"Why are we still here?" Kay asked. "You saved the girl and killed the witch. Mission accomplished."

Closing his fingers over the stone, Drew surveyed the scenery. He remained in old-time Skidmore. Everyone but Claire had disappeared.

"We broke free, but we didn't bind the focus stone yet."

"So, get to it."

Drew closed his fingers over the stone. Stace had said the process needed him to focus while channeling power through it to himself. The stone had to sync to his aura.

"I think the node has memories," Kay mused. "I wonder why it chose this time period."

"Who knows?" The stone warmed against Drew's skin.

"I know." Claire's mouth moved, but the words coming from her mouth sounded nothing like her. The voice echoed and rumbled, made of car horns, horses neighing, voices murmuring, women screaming, cats howling, dogs barking, crows shrieking, and concrete breaking. It sounded like a city.

Drew's mouth fell open. He had no idea what to say. Portland's node had a personality.

Claire's face shifted until her features formed a different woman, one with both white and Native ancestry. Her clothes remained the same, though the dagger disappeared. "I wake."

"I think Portland just got weirder," Kay whispered.

With no idea how to react or what to do, Drew gulped and did the natural thing. "Can I help you somehow?"

"Help me?" The woman held out her hands and looked at them as if she'd never seen such things before. "You're already pledged to an entity."

"Yeah, that wasn't the kind of help I meant. Look, you probably need to take some time and settle in, so if you could just release me, that'd be great."

She lowered her hands. One moment, she stood in front of Drew. The next, she stood behind him, her hands on his shoulders. "You're snared in my web. What will you grant me for the boon of releasing you?"

"Um."

"Service. Offer a service. Entities are into that."

"I accept." Portland's node kissed the back of his neck. Pain seared his skin and shot to his heart. The stone tore through the palm of his hand and punched into his chest. His heart exploded. Stars filled his vision.

Drew blinked and saw Justin crouched over him, worry crinkling the corners of his mouth and eyes. Drew lay on the ground in the room housing the node, the scent of dry, bare earth thick in the air. His heart kept beating, and he kept breathing.

"I'm alive. Right?" Healing rushed to his leg. Power vibrated in his flesh. He sighed with pure joy.

"I think we're good," Kay said. "Try something so we know for sure."

Justin offered him a hand to sit up. "I'm not sure I want to know what happened in there, but you look a lot less pale and strained."

Drew sat up and summoned mist. Fog swarmed them, swift and thick. He shifted them to Ki's bar with the ease of taking a single step.

Kay purred in his head.

"Yeah," he said. "We're gonna beat the crap out of Iulia." He'd worry about Kay's pledge to Portland's node later.

CHAPTER 30

JUSTIN

Justin opened the front door to discover the ash had stopped falling, though dark clouds remained overhead. Inches-thick layers of ash covered every surface, including two crashed cars in the middle of the street. The accident had obviously taken place some time ago, and no one had yet come to remove them. Justin suspected no one would until the city cleared the main arteries.

Enion dropped from the sky beside Tariel and backwinged into a landing, kicking up ash. The horse sneezed. Justin covered his face and stepped aside so Drew could leave the bar. In addition to carrying Claire, Enion held a glowing white cord with a ghost tangled in the other end.

The ghost seemed docile, but Justin touched his sword hilt. "Are we keeping that for some reason?" He nodded to the ghost.

Claire glanced at the misty figure as if she'd forgotten about it. "Temporarily, yeah. Drew?"

"Yes, we're keeping him too," Drew said. "Permanently, though, I hope."

Claire grinned at him. "Are you better?"

Drew nodded. "I'm fine. Maybe better than before. We'll see."

Justin climbed onto Tariel's back. "Now that we're all here and aren't suffering from anything dire, let's go check the Steel Bridge. I've thought about it, and I don't like the way that ghost just vanished earlier. It seems suspicious to me."

"I can move us there," Drew said.

"It's two blocks away." Justin leaned to offer Drew a hand onto the horse. "I think we can walk."

Drew rolled his eyes. "I'll meet you there."

Claire shrugged. "Suit yourself."

Enion walked beside Tariel as they headed up the street.

Justin glanced at the ghost again. "We usually destroy those."

"I thought we usually put them to rest. We would've taken it to a church, but came back to check in first."

Pleased by her answer, Justin reached over and patted her shoulder. "It's hard to do things like that in the middle of a crisis. I'm proud of you for making that effort. We can stop at one on the other side of the bridge."

Claire smiled at him. "Thanks."

Ahead, they saw the bridge still raised from before. Drew stood halfway up the on ramp, leaning against the low concrete wall serving as a railing. He held up a hand in greeting. Watching him not try to catch Claire's eye made Justin wonder what had happened in the node. That thought led him to wondering where that stone had gone. Drew had been attached to it before, but now, Justin saw no sign of it.

The bridge's motors whirred and clunked into life. He'd ask the kid later, when they didn't have a strange ghost and potentially animate bridge to investigate. The trio crested the rise to the bridge as the center span lowered into place. The bridge trembled, clunked, and clanged. Steel groaned.

Tariel stopped several feet from the center span. As Justin peered through to the other side, mist coalesced into a figure. He pulled his sword. With his gaze locked on the figure, he saw it gain more and more definition until it shimmered with color.

The ghost's body had broad shoulders, thick limbs, and a slight paunch around the middle. He—the ghost definitely seemed male—wore a red and black plaid flannel shirt, open over a black T-shirt. Spatters of dried blood stained the legs of his faded jeans. He held a metal baseball bat against his shoulder.

His face sharpened until Justin recognized his father. Dwight Evans, who had never been a Knight, had become a ghost. This echo of the worst man Justin had ever known couldn't have risen before the seal's destruction. That meant Dwight had regained enough memories to become defined in one month.

The blood on Dwight's jeans had come from one of two sources— Justin or his mother. Justin stared down the man who'd made his life hell for the first sixteen years of his life. With Kurt's help, he'd been able to escape, to leave Dwight behind, and to avoid making all the same mistakes with his own family.

Kurt had killed Dwight. Justin had known that since Dwight's ghost had showed up a month ago. Claire and Drew had said they took care of it. They'd been mistaken. Not caring what else might happen around him, he urged Tariel forward with his knees.

Tariel took one step and another, walking with a quickening pace until she reached the center span. At the edge, she launched into a gallop. Justin held his sword forward.

Dwight stepped onto the center span. The bridge shuddered and rose. Tariel raced across the bridge. Dwight hefted his bat. Justin expected to impale and destroy him.

The moment before the tip of Justin's sword reached Dwight's chest, dark, coppery metal shimmered over his body from head to toe. Dwight shifted, twisting his body to the side.

Justin's sword hit Dwight's chest and skittered across his armor. Dwight's bat connected with Justin's head and knocked him off Tariel's back.

Unable to stop before she reached the end of the center span, Tariel leaped off the edge and left Justin behind. He hit the road. The impact jarred his sword out of his hand and sent it sliding through the girders to fall into the river.

As Justin raised his throbbing, bleeding head, the bat connected with his gut and flung him over. Fire blasted Dwight. Enion yelped and the fire stopped. The bat smashed into Justin's chest from above.

Justin had no armor. Claire hadn't yet fixed it. The bat cracked ribs and knocked the wind out of him. Pain speared his lungs. He gasped for air. Healing soothed everything, but not fast enough. Dwight smashed his skull.

"I think that's enough," Drew said.

Dwight laughed and turned his back on Justin. Thunder crackled.

His brain bleeding and his eye oozing, Justin lay on the bridge, staring at the dark clouds and unable to do anything but feel agony. His father had always beaten him. The only way Justin had ever won against him was by leaving. He'd failed to protect his mother. He'd failed to protect his wife.

Kurt's intervention had spared Marie. Not Justin's.

He tasted blood. He'd always tasted blood. Kurt had given him a six-year respite and nothing more. Now that Dwight's ghost remembered, he would never stop.

Justin had never understood what Dwight wanted from him in life, and he had no idea what his echo would want in death. If the swords didn't work, he had no idea how to stop this ghost. He didn't even understand how Dwight hit him so hard with a baseball bat.

None of this made sense. He didn't know what to do.

CHAPTER 31

CLAIRE

Claire watched Justin ride onto the bridge, not sure if she should help or not. He seemed like he might need to face his dad's ghost alone. The bridge's center span lifted.

She glanced at Drew, caught his eye, and shrugged.

Something white fell from the other side of the center span. Tariel plummeted to the road. Silver glinted in the weak light as Justin's sword fell. Tariel landed on her hooves and screamed in defiance. The sword splashed into the river.

Justin's confrontation with his father had gone horribly wrong in no time at all.

"Okay, let's go help," Claire said.

Enion leaped into the air. Drew spun mist around them. They shifted to the space behind Dwight with Enion facing the wrong way. Claire twisted to see Justin lying on the bridge with a copper-coated version of Dwight beating the crap out of him. As Enion flapped through an arc, the ghost in the cord shrieked and lunged at Claire.

"What're you doing?" Claire shouted at it.

The world spun, and she sat in the car again. This time, she arrived intact. Her arm had become tangled in the cord, binding her to the stupid thing. Sitting in the driver's seat again, the ghost seemed as ill-defined as before, having remembered nothing more of itself.

With no time to think about the why or how of her situation, Claire reached with her dagger to stab the ghost. As her dagger neared it, copper rippled across the ghost's surface. Her dagger hit the metal and skittered across it with an ear-splitting screech. Her blade scored a shallow furrow across the new skin.

She blinked at it. The ghost punched her in the face with a thick arm of mist. It hit like a brick. Her head slammed into the car frame. While she reeled from the impact, the ghost punched her shoulder.

Scrabbling at the door, Claire couldn't remember how a handle worked. The ghost hit her again. Bones cracked in her arm. The noise bounced off the smashed windshield and echoed in her skull.

Her fingers found the handle and pulled. Another blow from the ghost sent her tumbling to the ground. Bricks lay scattered on the cobblestones and dust hung in the air. The murmurs faded from the back seat. Water splashed nearby.

"What the—"

The ghost surged at her, knocking her flat. It squealed its shrieky voice into her ear, setting her teeth on edge.

At least her body healed as fast as she expected. Claire rolled onto her back, then over again, trying to confuse the ghost. She popped up and jammed her dagger over her shoulder. Metal screeched against metal.

Pressure on her neck felt like a dog gnawing on her. Claire smacked the hilt of her dagger against the ghost. It stopped and wrapped mist arms around her neck. The arms squeezed. She raised her dagger and slashed at her own neck. Her blade squealed across the metal again. Gripping the dagger with both hands, she jabbed it at the ghost's arm.

Nothing mattered more to her in this moment than getting through that damned armor.

The tip of her dagger cracked the copper. Bits flaked off. She gasped for breath and heaved with waning strength to shove the dagger through the armor. The ghost shrieked at her again. Unable to muster enough strength to jam it in further, she used the only tool she could think of.

She lurched forward and hit the ground. The dagger hilt slammed against a cobblestone. Claire thought her head might explode from the ghost's horrifying wail.

Free from the ghost's grasp, Claire scooted to the side and turned. It writhed and wailed, fizzling and popping. The dagger remained wedged in its arm.

When Justin had destroyed her father's Phasm, it had faded without drama. This thing kept wriggling and hissing far longer than she wanted to watch.

Thick pieces of crumbly copper broke apart and fell to the ground in chunks with deep, dissonant clangs. The cobblestones fizzled into mist.

Claire thought she'd wake up on Enion's back, or maybe on the bridge.

She blinked and found herself in the car again. The ghost sat in the driver's seat, still as ill-defined as before, its metal armor renewed. The cord remained bound to her wrist.

"Seriously?" Claire flung the door open and leaped out, then ran to the intact fountain. The ghost streamed behind her.

She had to find a more efficient way to crack through the armor before the ghost recovered from her surprise movement. Why didn't her dagger break through in the first place, though? Caius had forged it with the purpose of cutting through ghosts and magic. Knights fought witches, after all. The dagger did crack the copper, she supposed.

That left her with a logical conclusion—the magic in the armor was stronger than the enchantment on the blade. Somehow, the ghost could conjure something so powerful it could defy her dagger.

One other type of magic thing had done that recently. The cords— all three of them—had been a hassle to cut, requiring all her effort. If Drew was right, Iulia had crafted the cords. Which meant Iulia bolstered the ghost somehow.

She jumped into the fountain to wrench her arm around and fling the ghost at the statues holding up the wide bowl. The water sizzled and burned against the armor on her legs. Whirling, she leaped out of the fountain's base and sprinted back to the car.

Knowing she faced Iulia didn't help her defeat this stupid ghost. Until someone else found Iulia's ghost and destroyed it, Claire had to find a way out of this damned ghost battle. Justin needed help. Even if Drew managed to do that, she didn't think either of them could get her out of this.

When she reached the car, Claire jerked to a stop, slamming the ghost into the vehicle, then bent and scraped it along the cobblestones. She scooped up a brick. The ghost shrieked. Claire punched down with her dagger hilt, knocking it against the ground. Before it could recover, she dropped the brick on it. Following that, she slammed the blade into it and drove it down with all her weight.

Chunks of copper fell to the cobblestones again. Her dagger hit mist. The street fizzled again.

She sat in the car again, the cord still wrapped around her wrist.

"I'm stuck," she growled. She'd dominated this stupid ghost in this stupid car three stupid times, and she still had to fight it.

This time, she pounced on the ghost, slamming her dagger into its chest. She leaned against it, ignoring its screeches and flailing until the dagger slid into the copper. The ghost and the car fizzled, replaced by the ghost in the car again.

Claire screamed her frustration at the ghost and ignored it in favor of sawing the cord. The ghost punched her arm. She rocked with the blow. Her dagger sliced off her thumb. Blood spurted from the stump, painting her jacket bright red.

She stared at her hand. The dagger wasn't supposed to be able to do that. It could cut her skin, but not deeper than a harsh papercut. The stump didn't hurt, either, but it kept spewing blood redder than reality. She'd seen more than enough of her own blood to know the difference.

The ghost hit her jaw, knocking her head into the car frame as it had the first time. She fumbled for the door handle. Another blow cracked bones in her shoulder. The door fell open, and she thumped to the cobblestones, spraying blood everywhere.

Screaming filled her head as she lay on the ground, trying to remember how to do things. The world fizzled.

She blinked in bright light, surrounded by trees blazing with fall colors. Drew knelt beside her, his hand touching her cheek. Bruises marred his face and neck with dark purple. As she watched, they faded to brown. Her own injuries healed the same way.

Beyond him, Rondy lifted his sword as if he'd just stabbed something. Enion stood nearby, his head lying next to hers. Farther away,

Justin lay on the grass, groaning. Marie screamed, her voice so normal and human that Claire wanted to cry.

"He's healing," Rondy said as Marie rushed to Justin. "Give it a few minutes."

"Hold still," Drew said. He lifted her arm. No ghost came with it, but the cord remained wrapped around her wrist like a fat slug. Her thumb had either regrown already, or had never been severed in reality. Drew's brow furrowed as he poked the cord with a finger.

"That sucked," she said. Her voice sounded hoarse. She had no idea why.

"Ssh." Drew glared at the cord. It unraveled, fraying into twelve individual threads. "Damn," he breathed. Each thread turned to vapor, one by one. When the last disappeared, Drew heaved a sigh.

"How is he doing that?" Marie whispered.

"Magic," Rondy said.

"Iulia is a nasty piece of work," Drew said.

"Yes," Claire said. "I want to kill her again."

"We need to prepare better." Drew offered her a hand. "Dwight beat the crap out of us. Since we found him in one of the locations in Iulia's journal, we have to assume she was responsible for that."

"We're gonna find her and kill her a lot," Claire said. Weariness flooded her, washing away the rush of battle. "Tomorrow."

CHAPTER 32

DREW

Kneeling beside Claire, he watched her eyes flutter shut. With a glance at Rondy then Enion, he confirmed she'd fallen asleep and not succumbed to another of Iulia's machinations.

Justin raised his arm and comforted his wife. Drew could imagine how horrifying the sight of him had been for Marie. The one eye hadn't healed yet before Dwight smashed Justin's skull again, then caved half his chest in and broke his arm. Drew had taken only one hit from that bat, and it'd nearly knocked his head off. He had nothing but respect for how much of a beating Justin could handle.

While Marie fussed over Justin, Drew leaned forward and kissed Claire's forehead. He couldn't lift her, so he waved Rondy closer.

"Can you carry her to a bed or something?"

Rondy smiled. "Of course. How about you?" He took Drew's chin in his hand. "You took a beating also?"

"I'm fine."

"Mmhmmm." Rondy scooped up Claire with a knowing look and

carried her to the bed she'd made for and shared with Drew.

Their bed. In her demesne. He sighed. Someday, he'd have time for simple things again. Not today. He patted Enion's head and followed Rondy. Near the bed, he'd left Iulia's journal, and this sounded like a good time to delve into it. He picked up the book and took it to Claire's chair.

"Can you read Latin?" he asked Kay.

"More or less. It was required when I went to school."

"You never went to school."

"You know what I mean," Kay grumbled.

Drew smirked and cracked open the book. "I can sort of read it too. Let's hope we have different gaps in vocabulary."

"That would be nice."

Taking his time, he ran his fingers across the page. The black ink had indented the page, so she'd used a ballpoint pen. He wondered where she'd picked up both a journal and a pen. The book itself had water damage and the cover showed signs of wear. He noticed pages had been removed on a straight line, as if she or someone else had used a ruler and a sharp knife.

When he'd seen it the first time, he didn't remember seeing that. Of course, he'd only seen the middle. Iulia had shown it to him in her effort to convince him and Claire to follow her directions.

Marie kissed Justin, distracting Drew from the journal. Adults so seldom displayed affection around him. Grandpa Jack and Grandma Tammy pecked each other on the cheek sometimes. Justin and Marie did the same. He'd gotten the impression the Bradys and Evanses considered anything more involved unsuitable for public behavior and had done his best to emulate that expectation.

Justin sat up with Marie in his arms and held her close. "I'm fine," he told her. "I'm sorry we came back like this."

"You big dope," she said. "You're lucky my parents took the girls for a hike."

He chuckled and held her tighter. "I love you too."

"That's how a normal married couple acts," Kay said. "I've seen the stuff in your head. You should ignore most of it and watch them. They love each other. A lot of those other people didn't. Not like these two. That's how it was between me and Emmy."

Drew chose not to question Kay's memories of Kurt. "Good to know." He returned his attention to the journal.

Kay murmured words in his head, reading what he could. Drew filled in some of the missing pieces. They both stumbled over enough words on the first page for Drew to decide they needed some books from the library.

"Drew?"

He looked up to see Justin standing over him, massive amounts of blood staining his clothes, with his arm around Marie's shoulders.

"Yes?"

"Thank you for getting us out of there."

Nodding, Drew smiled. He'd feared no one would agree with his decision. "It seemed like the best idea at the time. You know, while my jaw was reassembling."

Justin huffed in amusement. "Yeah. Get some rest. We'll have to figure out what to do, and that won't happen until we're all ready to do it."

Drew blinked at him. The man had been demolished five minutes ago, yet he sounded ready to go do it again. Knights were crazy. "Maybe you need a better sword before you go running back into the fray."

Marie snorted. "Maybe?"

Justin kissed his wife's head. "I'll talk that over with Claire when she's up to it. The old one went into the Willamette, and has definitely washed away by now. I need new armor too. If you're there when she wakes up, would you say something so she doesn't run off before doing anything about it this time?"

"Sure."

Justin thanked him again and escorted Marie into the trees and out of sight.

"He thanked us," Kay said.

"Yeah. Twice. That was cool." Drew stood and tucked the journal into his waistband at the small of his back. He looked around and saw Rondy leaning against a tree, pretending not to watch him or eavesdrop. Leaving now would probably make people panic if he didn't say something to someone.

He nodded to Rondy. "I'm just going to a library. I'll be back in an hour or two, maybe three at the most."

Rondy raised his brow. "Do you think that's wise?"

"I just proved I can fold mist to get straight here, so I think we'll be fine." He'd worried about getting here, but it had turned out to be no different than using the mist to get anywhere else. The connections between him and Claire did the job of bridging the gap between the real world and this one. "I'll run if anything attacks. I promise."

"Watch yourself," Rondy said.

He nodded and spun mist. It cleared with Drew standing in the reference section of the two-story Albina Library in Portland. He'd written at least a dozen school reports at the nearby computers. The institutional carpet and metal shelves filled with books struck him as a familiar note in strange times.

Voices and the aroma of fresh coffee filled the library today, which surprised him. He moved to the end of the row and leaned into the aisle. People sat in clumps, ash smeared across their faces and clothing. Some wore blankets draped across their shoulders or ate from paper plates. Many held paper cups.

The library had opened its doors to people who had nowhere else to go in a volcano eruption. He wondered how many had come from Vancouver and made it this far. Had the Kenton library, further north than Albina, been overrun with refugees?

Claire's demesne seemed like a gross luxury compared to camping in a library.

Drew spotted Sophie's mom helping someone with a blanket. He ducked behind books again and hoped she didn't notice his aura.

Someone thumped into him as he turned. Kay swore in his head. Drew raised a hand, gathering power to blast them.

Sophie jumped back, holding up her hands with a squeak.

Covering his mouth, Drew reeled the power in. Kay swore again.

"Sorry," he mumbled, pushing up his glasses for lack of a better way to occupy his hands. "Thought you were someone else."

"I'm sorry." She used a harsh whisper that sounded louder than her regular voice. "I should've said something instead of diving in for the surprise hug. I just didn't want to be loud enough for Mom to overhear."

"If you apologize to her again," Kay said. "I'm going to barf."

Since he'd been about to do that very thing, Drew snapped his mouth shut and paused. He lowered to a crouch, beckoning for Sophie to follow suit. "I'm glad you're okay."

For some reason, he didn't feel an overwhelming need to devour her. Maybe the Portland node had filled that hole for him. He still wanted to touch her, but not like before.

Sophie sat beside him on the floor, fluffing her ash-spotted pink skirt so it covered her legs. "I'm glad you're okay too. I was worried about you and Claire because I know where you live. What are you doing here, though? We're helping with the emergency shelter thing. Lots of homeless people are getting turned away at emergency rooms because they're hacking up ash."

That problem hadn't occurred to Drew. He hadn't had any trouble with breathing the ash, which he attributed to Kay. "I need a book."

"Now?"

"Yeah. I'm working on Iulia's journal. It's kind of time critical. Can you keep your mom busy for a few minutes? I need to slide a few aisles closer to where she's working."

"I suppose. But if you're fine, where are you staying? Is everyone else you live with okay? How about Claire?"

Kay coughed. "Let's not tell a witch things we don't want witches to know."

"We're all fine," Drew said. He considered taking Sophie into confidence. Iulia wouldn't have picked anyone of Sophie's power when she had other, more powerful options. She'd more likely corrupted someone in that Marius line. He leaned closer. "Can you keep a secret?"

"Yes, of course. I haven't told my mom what I did for you, though she'll probably hear about it from Anne or Stace at some point." Sophie held a hand over her ear so Drew could whisper.

"I don't know about this," Kay said.

"Shut up, Kay. We need more help."

"And you choose Sophie? Are we really that desperate?"

Drew ignored Kay. "We just tried to fight a ghost with Justin, and it handed us all our butts. I think Iulia's to blame."

Sophie sucked in a breath and covered her mouth. She turned to look at him with her eyes wide. "How can I help?"

Drew smiled. "Can you get away for a while?"

CHAPTER 33

CLAIRE

Drew's laughter woke Claire from a dream about dragons rescuing ghosts from lava. She found Mutt's head on her leg and Enion's tiny body on her chest. Both raised their heads and wagged their tails as she breathed in the fresh, clean air.

"You're the weirdest witch ever," a girl said.

Claire lifted her head and discovered Sophie and Drew sitting together on a nearby log. Ash spotted Sophie's pink dress and white cardigan. She held an open book. Another open book lay on the grass at Drew's feet. He held Iulia's journal.

"Probably true," Drew said with a grin. He glanced at Claire and his smile broadened. His face and hands seemed clean, though ash still smeared his jeans and sneakers. He beckoned for her to join them.

She sat up, dislodging both dragon and dog. Her body had repaired everything while she slept, so she felt fine. Stopping herself from pointing at Sophie and demanding to know why he'd brought a witch into her demesne, Claire stood and closed the distance.

"I think this journal is a fake." Drew held up the black book. "It's not blatant, but whoever wrote this wasn't fluent in Latin. Sophie's been helping me look up some of these words, and I can't imagine how Iulia, who spoke Latin as her native language, would've made some of these mistakes."

"I don't know why my mom gave me a fake journal," Sophie said. "I mean, that just doesn't make any sense. She wanted to me to read up about our ancestors. That's what she said. If she wanted to give *you* a fake journal, she would've found some other way, because she didn't want you anywhere near me again."

Claire opened her mouth, then shut it when she noticed she intended to say something mean. "So those maps were planted to make us go to those places."

"Yeah. Someone forged it, probably with instructions from Iulia. But I've been thinking about the maps. Kay also has some thoughts on the subject. That cord I got caught in? After talking it over with Sophie, we all think it might've been intended to trap you. It hit me because of Kay."

"It makes sense," Sophie said, bobbing her head. "And what Drew saw of the cord you hit sounds like it might've been meant for him. Hitting the wrong person didn't make them less unpleasant, so she may have considered the possibility and made them accordingly."

Knowing the technical explanations would mean nothing to her, Claire decided to accept their opinion. Even though it made no sense, Kay agreeing somehow gave her more confidence about trusting them.

"And the thing I ran into?" Justin asked as he approached the group.

Claire checked him over. She waved a hand and cleaned the dried blood off his jeans and boots. She'd made them, after all. The shirt,

236

though, she couldn't fix.

"Probably meant for you," Drew said.

Justin nodded and scratched a day of stubble on his cheek. "It did seem to aim for me more than Avery. That means Iulia set traps specifically for the three of us. Why? Other than Claire, I mean."

"Wait, what? Why other than me?"

"She's probably a little mad we killed her?" Drew shrugged.

"I had nothing to do with that." Justin sat on the ground and waved for Claire to do the same. He seemed to accept Sophie's presence, so they must have been introduced earlier. "Given she seems to be working with Dwight, though, I suppose it makes sense."

Claire sat and glared at him for ignoring her question. Of course, Iulia did have a compelling reason to hate her. Setting it aside for the moment, she thought about the ghost and the cord. If it had been meant for Drew, maybe the goal had been to separate Kay from Drew. That would kill both. Iulia wouldn't have had to deal with Drew anymore.

"About that," Drew said. "I've been talking over the fight with Sophie. We think Iulia was there, somehow sharing space with Dwight. I don't think either of you saw much of what happened to me on that bridge. Dwight was beating the crap out of you, so I zapped him with what's basically lighting. Instead of hitting that copper armor, something lanced out of his back and blocked it. Then he used my head for batting practice."

"From everything you've all explained," Sophie said, "I think you're right that Iulia either doesn't care about the seal anymore, or has shifted it lower in priority. But I don't think she wants to kill all of you. If she did, I'm pretty sure you'd be dead already. At least one of you would, for sure. She's using complex magic to harm but not kill you."

"Drew's trap might've killed him," Claire said.

"Maybe." Drew nodded. "You might be right. What that means is we can only be sure Iulia doesn't want to kill either you or Justin. She may or may not care about me."

Justin shook his head. "I'm sure Iulia wants her body back, so that explains not wanting to kill Claire, but me?"

Claire blinked at him. Such a simple idea made so much sense. How had she not thought of it herself?

Without pausing, Justin continued, "If Dwight is the reason she's including me in this, then I have no idea why they would be trying to keep me alive. My father, knowing he faces no consequences, would kill me."

Sophie recoiled. Claire agreed. A man who'd kill his own son because he could sounded worse than any foster parent she'd ever dealt with. Even the one who'd tiptoed to the edge of molesting her hadn't been that horrible.

Thinking about some of her past foster parents made Claire's skin crawl. She squirmed and tried to pass it off as shifting to get more comfortable. Drew caught her eye. He understood.

"Okay, that's messed up," Claire said with a grimace, "but go back to the part about Iulia wanting her body?"

Sophie squinted at him. "I didn't understand that either."

"Long story," Drew said to Sophie. "But Kay and I both agree it makes sense."

"If Iulia wants her body back," Justin said, sounding like the wheels turned in his head with clunks and stutters, "then maybe she's gotten Dwight to cooperate by promising mine to him?"

Shivers wriggled down Claire's spine. She imagined Justin's body carrying a monster who'd terrorize Marie and girls, kill Grandpa Jack and

Grandma Tammy, and use Justin's hard-won good-guy reputation to rampage across Portland.

"That..." Drew gulped. "Would, um, yeah. It makes a lot of sense."

"I don't really understand how a ghost can do all this," Sophie said, "but let's go ahead and skip that part. Because what you really need to do is destroy both before they can manage it, right?"

"And they kicked our asses," Claire grumbled. "We need more firepower. A lot more firepower."

"We do. We can get Avery. And, if we think we can trust her, Anne. It's a safe bet Iulia has at least one witch working for her, though. Sophie, if you want to come with us, you're welcome to." Justin frowned and stared at nothing. "You know, there's something we didn't consider as an outcome of the volcano. It took away our homes and caused chaos in Portland, but it also killed a large number of people. What if that was the real plan and destroying our home was a bonus for Iulia?"

Killing people didn't sound useful for any reason Claire could think of. Dead people didn't do anything useful, not even for Iulia. They couldn't get in the way, call the cops, or do anything for Iulia. They only made ghosts.

Her jaw fell open. Thousands of ghosts would've made their way to the surface of the debris over the past day or so. Iulia had already proven she had plenty of power. If she could control them all...

Drew met her gaze and seemed as unsettled as she. "What if she's raising an army? If she can give them all that copper armor, it makes reaching her impossible."

"It does," Justin said. "That means our job is even more important over the coming months and years. For right now, though, it means Iulia has a staggering number of ghosts at her command, possibly all protected from ghost-killing weapons. How do we counter that? Much as I hate to say so, we're going to need a better plan than rushing in and stabbing."

"Claire," Sophie said, "Can you make armor and weapons that can defeat magic as well as ghosts?"

"I don't know." Claire frowned and tried to think. "I infuse them with power through memories, and I don't have any of defeating witches or magic. I haven't fought any except Iulia, and Drew did all the work then."

"Can we infuse Drew's memories into it?" Sophie asked. "Can you do something like that? Or can Drew and I enchant them once you've done your part?"

Claire raised her hands in surrender. "I have no idea. We can try, right? Maybe if we all work on that together, we'll come up with something awesome."

"I have another idea," Justin said. "We've talked about how we're all related. We have Corwin and his wife as common ancestors."

Drew's eyes lit up like he could see where Justin's thoughts headed. "And Iulia told me Claire is descended directly from her on both sides, so either Corwin or Jacqueline was her descendant. If we can invoke that somehow?"

Turning over her hand, Claire stared at the locket face and its pulsing light. "Guys. I'm not a descendant."

Both Drew and Justin stared at her. Sophie seemed confused, the poor girl. Someone needed to explain this to her now, not later.

"I died," Claire said. "There was a lot of magicky stuff. Drew and the circumstances managed to shove Iulia out of her body and me into it. This body belonged to Iulia until a month ago. Technically, I'm the ancestor you're all descended from." She thought of her blood spraying in the stupid repeated ghost dominance battle. It had seemed important, and now she realized why.

"Which means, I think, that my blood is going to be pretty potent when it comes to attacking Iulia's magic and her ghost. Or soul. Or whatever she is."

The uncertainty of Iulia's condition reminded Claire of the uncertainty around her own. She still had only a vague memory from before her family died. Did that make her a ghost? A soul? A Phasm? How was a Phasm different from a ghost? She didn't know the answers to any of those questions.

They all still stared at her. "Unless that's crazy?"

"No," Drew said. "It's brilliant. Sophie, we need to think some more."

Justin stood with a nod. "Sounds like there's work to do, but none of it's about me. I'll see what I can do to find supplies for everyone."

Claire nodded and thought they had a chance. "I'll get to work on the basic sword and armor, and use my blood to make it."

CHAPTER 34

DREW

Sophie had to go back to the library. No one wanted her mom to notice her absence. Drew returned her and the books, then thought about visiting any number of places. He wanted to believe parts of Vancouver had been spared. His teachers and classmates deserved to live. They'd all been nice to him and Claire.

Wanting to see the destruction in daylight, he shifted to the top of the tallest building in Vancouver that he could think of. He landed on a giant pile of rubble. Not even an office building with more than a dozen floors had survived.

Mist hovered over the ground, thick and...moving. Ghosts bubbled from the debris. In the distance, he saw a defined figure surrounded by empty space, wading through the mist. With every step he took, mist faded.

His own mist keeping ghosts near him at bay, Drew watched. Dwight kept moving, dissipating mist with his back to Drew.

"He's... Is he? No, that can't be." Kay gasped in something like horror. "He's not taking control of them."

"No, he's not."

Drew noticed fraying on the edges of his mist and decided to leave. He didn't have any special skills or tools for combating ghosts. That needed to change. All of them would have to be able to fight Dwight and Iulia.

His mist cleared in Claire's demesne. He stood in the woods, alone.

"I'm not panicking," Drew said. He leaned against a tree and stared at another one.

"Neither am I," Kay said. "We're just taking a few moments to collect our respective wits before telling everyone about the horror we just witnessed. That's all."

"Master!" Mutt bounded into sight and wagged his tail. He spat a stick at Drew's feet. "Let's play fetch, Master! The sticks here taste like chicken. But I'm not chewing them. Claire said not to chew them or she won't make any more. I'm not chewing them, Master. I'm a good dog."

Kay giggled, the sound edged with hysteria.

Feeling the same way, Drew stared at his dog servant. He picked up the stick and flung it into the distance. Mutt vibrated with joy and darted after the stick.

"Why do we even keep him?" Drew mused. The dog had never beaten an enemy or successfully fought anything. He almost always ran. A regular dog had more courage than two Mutts put together.

"He's a good dog." Kay's giggles gained strength.

Drew stared at the space where Mutt had disappeared and tried to comprehend what they'd seen and what it meant. He needed to tell Claire and Justin. They needed to know. How could he say it out loud, though? They needed solutions, not bigger problems.

He couldn't see a solution. "We're all going to die."

"Probably."

Mutt bounded into sight again, carrying the stick. Wild, unrestrained happiness gleamed in his eyes. He spat the stick at Drew's feet and bounced, his tail wagging harder than before. "Do it again, Master!"

Picking up the stick again, he stared at it. His brain refused to comprehend the scope of a downed tree branch that tasted like chicken. "I'm not a coward," he told the stick.

"No, Master, you're not. You're very brave." Mutt ducked his head and lowered his tail. "I'm a coward, Master. I don't have powers like you. There's nothing I can do against a ghost or a witch, or other scary things. I stay behind because I don't want to fail you, Master."

Drew blinked. His gaze drifted to Mutt. Marie didn't have any fighting skills either, but Justin still loved her and protected her. Maybe they needed Mutt to stay at home and do stupid crap like this.

Kay stopped giggling. "You have a point. When life hands you ghosts, make lemonade."

Dismissing Kay's mismatched metaphor, Drew patted his hand with the stick. "You're a good dog, Mutt. I need to do things, though, so maybe see if Grandpa Jack wants to throw the stick next?"

"Yes, Master!"

He threw the stick and straightened. Finding Claire took no more effort than wanting to find her. Fifteen steps through the trees, he stumbled into a clearing with her handing a new sword to Justin. Unlike the previous silvery blade, this one gleamed with golden red, like the locket in her hand. At once, he wondered and didn't want to know how much of her own blood she'd used.

Justin hefted the blade and slashed it through the air. Rondy stepped forward with his own ghostly blade, and they sparred. The two blades clanged, producing a light, airy tone unlike anything Drew had heard before.

"Wow," Kay said. "That's some craftsmanship. Craftwomanship. Whatever. I'm really glad she's on our team, that's what I'm saying."

"Yeah." Drew hurried to her side. "We have another problem."

Claire nodded while watching Justin and Rondy. "Of course we do. Did Sophie's mom curse you?"

"No, nothing like that. I stopped in Vancouver. On it, really. On top of the rubble. The whole city is gone. I mean, everything. I don't even know where that much mud and rock came from. It seems absurd."

Kay poked him in the brain. "You're getting distracted. Tell her the horrifying part so we can all panic together."

"Right. The point is, there are ghosts rising from the rubble, and I saw Dwight."

"Well, yeah. If Iulia is part of him, and she's collecting a ghost army —"

"No. That's not what they're doing." Drew pressed his hands to his cheeks, mustering the courage to explain. He had no idea why speaking the words terrified him. Something about using his voice for this made it more concrete.

"Okay." Claire covered his hands with hers and met his gaze, her brow furrowed with concern. "What are they doing?"

The warmth of her hands helped. "They're devouring the ghosts. Eating them for power. We're not going to face an army of thousands of ghosts. We're going to face one with the power of thousands of ghosts." He gasped for breath, as if saying it had exhausted him.

"Oh. Damn. That's even worse." She seemed calm. Calculating.

Kay exploded with horrified exasperation. "How can she hear that and not panic?"

"Yes." Drew gulped, not sure how to make her understand. "It's worse. A lot worse. So much worse. That's a lot of power concentrated into one package. We can't counter it."

"Can't?" She raised her brow. "You mean it's hard and scary. Should we give up because it's hard and scary? Is that what you want? To hide in here until they give up and wander away? I'm sure they'll only do good things in other places. Hey, I'll bet they won't kill too many Knights and other people while they rampage. I mean, this is just about us, right?"

Her fierce determination cut through his terror. "No, that's not what I meant."

"Yes it is. But it's okay." She brushed her lips across his. "You're allowed to be scared."

Permission, coming from Claire, made a difference. The dam holding his fear in check broke. "I'm terrified," he whispered. Shivering gripped his spine, and he couldn't look her in the eye anymore. Suddenly, he understood why this hit him so hard.

Vancouver. All those people died for no reason. He knew some of them. But so many people—thousands of human beings lay under the rubble. Fear only covered half of what he felt.

He mourned the city that had become his home. Places he knew no longer existed. Teachers and students he knew no longer lived. The great candle over his city had been snuffed.

Until he'd seen it, the destruction and death hadn't felt real. It'd been distant, at arm's length. Then he stood on the rubble and watched Dwight and Iulia sacrifice everyone to an insatiable lust for power and revenge. The scope crushed him inside. A natural disaster would've been tragic and horrible. Knowing it had been unleashed on purpose made this so much worse.

She wrapped her arms around him and squeezed. "It's okay. We're not going back out today." Her warmth enveloped him. "Even if that means Dwight and Iulia get more and more powerful. We can't beat them how they were before, so we can't stop them from eating all those ghosts. We're going to take some time, think, and prepare as much as we can."

"What if they win?"

"Then we die and none of this matters to us anymore."

His eyes watered with tears ready to spill for Vancouver. "I don't want to die."

"Yeah, it sucks. I'd rather not do it again." She pulled away enough to push aside his sleeve and close her hand over his locket brand.

He felt her heartbeat, slow and even. The steady rhythm pressed on him, a comforting blanket like Mutt on his feet and Claire curled beside him.

She kissed his cheek and leaned her head against his shoulder. "We're not going to worry about it right now. We're going to have something to eat. Play with the girls and Mutt. Forget about all the reasons we have this oasis and enjoy it. Tomorrow, we work. And we're not going to face Iulia until we feel ready. Maybe it'll take a few days, and that's okay."

"I'm not quitting," Kay said. His voice shook, and Drew knew he felt the breadth of evil at work.

"Nobody is quitting," Drew said. They only needed to breathe.

CHAPTER 35

CLAIRE

Drew seemed so shaken that Claire wanted to give him privacy. She took a cue from Stace's hut and grew trees around them. They needed a place to sleep anyway, so she merged the trunks and warped them until they formed a round, windowless cabin. The floor became a soft, springy carpet of thick moss and clover. Leaves formed pillows stuffed with feathers.

She nudged Drew inside the cabin. He followed like a lost puppy. They sank onto the bed together, and she shut the door. Veins and heart-shaped leaves of an ivy-like plant crept across the ceiling and upper portion of the walls. At her command, they glowed with dim yellow light pulsing in time with her heartbeat.

Everyone probably deserved this level of seclusion. While Drew curled against her, she raised several more cabins. Later, she'd take requests and modify them to suit.

Lifting his head, Drew offered his glasses to her. She grew a shelf and set them on it. When she lowered her arm, Drew looked at her like he didn't know what to do. She touched his face, brushing her thumb across his cheek. The situation had upset him enough for tears.

He closed his eyes and sighed.

She pulled him close and kissed him.

Though he ran a hand along her side, he broke off the kiss before it lasted longer than a few heartbeats and touched his forehead to hers. "Do you remember the group home with the rocking horse?"

Whatever he needed, she was willing to give. If that meant telling stories and remembering, she could do that for him. "The one with the little dog that had fits whenever someone wore red?"

"Yeah." One corner of his mouth twitched upward. "That's the one."

That house had been the second place they lived together. "You'd just had your thirteenth birthday, and my twelfth was in two months. We realized my birthday was the same day that your parents died."

"Have I ever told you how much I like having something else to think about on August sixteenth every year?"

"No, but I figured as much."

He touched his nose to hers and kissed her again. "If I were a jerk, I'd say something about not wanting to die without...you know. But I'm not sure I ever want to mess around much with Kay in my head. He keeps pointing out how to do things better."

She laughed. "Shut up, Kay."

"Like that ever works." He sniffled and shook his head. "Ignoring him for this will take practice."

"No rush."

All the reasons Justin had given in his request for them to wait still made sense to Claire. She didn't want to start a family now. Maybe not ever. Iulia's children had caused more than their fair share of problems for the world. Occupying Iulia's body made Claire feel a sliver of responsibility for them.

He shifted his weight and wriggled until they faced each other, lying on their sides, holding each other and sharing warmth. "In the morning, I'll bring Sophie back and we'll work on trying to enchant weapons and armor."

Touching his face again, she traced the line of his jaw. "Are you going to tell me what happened to that stone I set off a volcano to get?"

"Oh. That." He sighed. "The node merged it into my aura while I was trying to break that cord trap and forge the stone into a focus. I'm not sure exactly what happened, but the node woke up as part of it. On the bright side, I can't lose it, and I'm connected to the node no matter where I go."

"Connected." Claire quirked an eyebrow at him. "I doubt the node did something for nothing?"

He kissed the tip of her nose. "What's one more mistress in the grand scheme of things?"

"Probably one more than you want."

"Probably. But better two than dead, right?" He huffed what sounded like a forced laugh.

She frowned. "I'm not your mistress."

"The brand on my arm says otherwise."

"That doesn't make me your mistress. It makes me..." She didn't know what word to use. From a certain perspective, she did control Drew, Justin, Rondy, and all the dragons. Without her demesne, they might all be dead now. She shivered at the thought of facing Justin's ghost. Someday, that would happen.

He kissed her again. "My mistress. Which is fine with me. I can't think of anyone I'd rather have my soul bound to forever."

"But that makes it sound like... Like you're my property. Or my dog. Like Mutt."

"Woof." He grinned.

She wanted to enjoy the fact he could crack a joke after being so upset ten minutes ago. The idea of Drew as her pet bothered her too much. "Knock it off. I'm serious."

"I know." He let go of her and rolled onto his back with a heavy sigh. "Would you like to see Vancouver?"

The abrupt change of subject gave Claire conversational whiplash. "What?"

"Do you want to see what Iulia did?" He covered his face. "Because I saw it, and I can't stop thinking that Justin could've forgotten about me, and then I'd be dead. Or he might've taken too long. Or he might've left a few minutes earlier and not realized the danger to us. I keep wondering what it would feel like, to be crushed by tons of rock and ice.

"What did it feel like for all those people who made all those ghosts? Was it so fast they didn't notice? Did some wind up in a bubble, protected by a tree or a boulder, thinking they might survive, only to run out of air? Did anyone have to watch their little kid's smashed body slide past before being broken? Or their—"

Claire touched a finger to his lips. Now she understood. She draped her body over his and held on. Her forehead rested against his neck. He smelled of ash and dirt. "You're going to hurt yourself imagining all that."

"I can't make it stop."

She didn't want to take away a part of Drew, especially not this part, but she needed to distract him. They could mourn after handling Iulia and Dwight. Until then, he needed rest and had work to do.

"We sat on the rocking horse together once. Do you remember that?" Claire didn't wait for a response. Of course he remembered it. "You hurt your knee in gym class that day. Playing soccer. Some boy slammed into you and shoved you to the ground harder than he needed to. I hit him in the shoulder. We fought while you held your knee.

"The teacher sent all three of us to the office, and no one listened when you said your knee hurt. The principal told us all off for fighting. He didn't care who started it or why. No one did. The nurse tried to check us all over while we wrote lines. I will not fight over sports. One hundred times. The principal shooed her away because we all deserved to suffer for being brats.

"When we got off the bus, you leaned on me to walk home. After dinner, I forgot you needed help to walk. We all rushed to the living room to watch TV. I claimed the rocking horse."

She paused, trying to remember why she liked the rocking horse so much. The foster father kept it in good shape. That husband and wife, as she recalled, had been good people. If only they'd been willing to adopt kids, she could've been happy enough there. Instead, they took kids for three to six months while waiting for another spot with a family.

The next home she'd gone to had been horrible. She pushed away those memories. Maybe they made her stronger, but she didn't need to relive them.

"By the time you reached the room, there was nowhere to sit but the floor. You tried. I watched you. It hurt your knee too much. So I got up and helped you to the rocking horse. Then I sat on your lap because I wanted to sit on that stupid horse. The foster father gave us a look, but he didn't do anything."

Drew let his arms fall. One landed on her back. "Not until I wrapped my arms around your waist and leaned my head on your shoulder. Then he grumbled and wheezed and made you move. I went to bed instead because I didn't want to take away your rocking horse."

"Can't have a girl sitting on a boy's lap." She used a gruff imitation of the foster father's voice. "Social services might walk in anytime and see that and think the worst."

"I didn't even know what that meant," Drew said. "The worst, he said. The worst what?"

Claire rubbed her nose on his chin. His two days of coppery stubble scratched her skin. "They worried a lot about the worst."

"But never gave us bratwurst."

She snorted. "That's a joke worthy of Ki in a good mood."

He grinned. "That seems like an insult, but I'll take it as a compliment. Because I can."

"Take it however you want." She squeezed him, hoping she'd given him enough of a memory to ease his grief. The thought that she should feel the grief too whispered on the edges of her mind, but she didn't. The deaths felt like nothing more than vague, undefined numbers. Even the idea of an expanse of debris didn't seem final and concrete, and she'd seen it.

The man in the car didn't bother her either. She figured his ghost had been too annoying, over and over, to let her feel his death. His daughter had been with her for only a short time. With luck, the kid's mom had come to claim her. Or someone like a better version of Aunt Stace.

Despite the weightlessness of all those deaths, she still had a burning pit of anger for Iulia.

"We'll avenge them, Drew. All of them. That's our job."

"I'd rather have the job of preventing it in the first place."

"Me too. We'll work on that after. Policing ghosts, keep tabs on witches, and all that."

Drew nodded and slid a finger across her forehead to shift a stray lock of hair. "Because there will be an after for us."

"Damn straight there will. I said so."

"Yes, Mistress." He kissed her.

Claire dimmed the lights.

CHAPTER 36

DREW

Justin's new sword lay on the ground at Drew's and Sophie's feet in Claire's demesne. Somewhere else, Claire worked on armor and more weapons. Justin had decided to spend as much of the day as possible with his family. Drew didn't blame him.

Avery had, at Justin's request, offered everyone the use of his apartment's bathroom for the short term, but they still needed to find a better solution. Drew thought if they brought in enough water, Claire could set up a water treatment system. Claire needed more information to do it. They'd work on it after dealing with Iulia. At least they knew they had Avery onboard. He'd find a way to get out of his job for the battle.

"The theory here is pretty simple," Sophie said. "The practice, though, I have no idea."

"Explain the theory," Drew said. "Please."

"To enchant an object, you fold magic into it, shaping it with your will to produce the desired effect. The same way you can choose between accelerating a plant's growth or blasting pests, you can choose what the weapon does. I've never tried folding magic, though. My mom says I don't have enough power for that."

Not for the first time, Drew wondered how much Sophie's lack of power came from her mom telling her about it. "But you understand the concept, right? I don't have a clue what folding magic even means."

"I doubt it has anything to do with folding laundry," Kay said, "but you don't know how to do that either."

"Sure. It's like this." Sophie plucked a blade of grass and wound it around her finger. A thin, wispy thread issued from her fingertip, wrapping around the grass. "You keep doing this until the whole thing is encased in a cocoon, then reach in and turn it inside out. According to Anne, if you're doing something big, you wind up in a metaphysical space, doing weird, crazy things."

Kay snorted. "How shocking. I guess it's another trip down memory lane for us. Let's not shred your aura this time."

Drew covered his mouth and stifled a laugh. "This'll be fun, then." He pushed his fingers under his glasses and rubbed his eyes. "I don't suppose there's anything you can do to help?"

"Oh." Sophie bit her lip and dropped the blade of grass. Her thread dissipated. "I don't think I have enough power to wrap a whole sword in one shot. You can't break the thread once you start or the whole thing falls apart."

"I have a wild idea," Kay said. "Your witch power came from her originally, so maybe she can connect to your aura and act like a guide."

"But how do I ask that?" Drew frowned at Sophie.

"Use words, you dumb sap. Girls aren't aliens. Neither are witches. You're not even trying to get under this one's skirt."

Drew blushed. "Uh, sure. Right. Um, Sophie, does anyone in your coven ever link auras?"

She squinted at him like she'd never heard anything so preposterous. "Link auras? Why would you do that?"

"To combine the abilities of two or more witches and accomplish something hard?"

"No. We don't do that. You can't do that. That's not how witchcraft works." For some reason, she seemed offended by the idea.

Drew stared at her, not sure how to interpret her flat, defensive denial. "Then what's the point of covens?"

She crossed her legs and arms and turned aside. "The same as any other club for people who have the same sort of skill or whatever."

"I'm not buying it," Kay said. "Five bucks says they specifically exclude her from that because she's 'not powerful enough' and she knows it, and it pisses her off. Knights know better than to believe witches form covens to share recipes for frog-eye soup and talk about witch or lady problems."

"Sophie." Drew touched her shoulder. He chose to be grateful he didn't have to hide Sophie from Claire anymore. Otherwise, she'd pick a moment like this to show up and get upset. "I know no one in your coven lets you do anything. That's why you helped me that first time. They don't think you're capable, and that's their mistake. I believe you can do anything if you put your mind to it, and I know they've taught you more than I know."

She heaved a sigh. "They never want me to do anything. I think my mom regrets forcing my ability open. She'd rather I couldn't do anything than being as weak as I am."

"What about you? Do you regret it?"

"You're getting the hang of this talking to girls thing. I'm proud of you, boy."

"No," Sophie snapped. She covered her face. "Yes." Then she shook her head. "I don't know."

Drew understood. He'd struggled with how to feel about the power forced on him. "How about if you and I have a coven? Just the two of us. We figure stuff out, do whatever we need, and back up all these Knights? Actually, that's what I'm already doing anyway. I guess I'm really just asking you to help me."

As she turned toward him again, tension drained from her whole body. "You'd want a low-power waste of a witch like me?" She spat the words with so much bitterness that Drew flinched.

He took her hand in both of his. Anger flared in his belly. Some of his foster parents and a lot of kids had called him names over the years. They'd belittled him for the holes in his clothes, being skinny, wearing glasses, red hair, freckles, being an orphan, and more. Claire had been the first person after his parents died to accept him, one hundred percent.

Either Sophie didn't have someone like that, or she'd learned not to trust anyone who said nice things. Both options sucked.

"If you tell Claire or Justin who called you that, either will punch them in the face for you. I would, but I'd hurt my hand."

She wiped her cheek. He hadn't noticed her tears until then. Her face didn't turn blotchy like Claire's. "Thanks."

"I don't care how much power you have or don't have, Sophie. I have plenty, and it's not doing me any good because I don't know how to use it. Let me be your battery. You use your knowledge with my power."

"I don't know."

Kay growled. "Someone is responsible for this girl being this timid, and I'd like to beat 'em to a pulp. You know what rhymes with witches?"

Drew squeezed Sophie's hand. She needed a friend. Not a superficial twit who liked her for being pretty or nice, but a real friend. Someone who cared and she could trust. Someone she could rage at. Someone who expected more from her because they knew she could handle it.

He could be that for someone besides Claire. When he told Claire about this, she'd offer the same thing.

They'd be a force to reckon with.

"I believe in you," he said, meaning it. "Not just enough to enchant this sword and whatever else we need, but as a person and as a witch. I believe that, if you want to, you can stand with us when we face Iulia. With your help, I believe we have a much better chance against her than without it."

Tears slid down Sophie's cheeks. She clamped her lips together in what looked like a monumental effort not to sob. Sniffling and wiping her cheek, she nodded.

"Okay. Let's do this. Tell me what to do, and I'll do it."

"I'm all for this," Kay said, "but I'd just like to note that I'm not sure how I feel about the likelihood of two different women able to hear me."

Drew stifled a smirk.

Sophie closed her eyes and took a deep breath. Drew watched her sky blue aura shift from a subtle heartbeat pulse to a more pronounced flaring. Thin tendrils flicked out and back. A sensation like feathers brushed against his skin.

Shivers wriggled down Drew's spine.

"Don't resist or push back," Sophie said. "This is supposed to be like shaking hands. Casual contact."

Though he still held her hand, the tendrils reached for him. They faded at the edge of his aura, as if she didn't have enough power to push them that far.

"She's going to give up," Kay said. "Reach for her. Bridge the distance."

"I don't know how," Drew said.

"Like I do. Best I got is picture yourself reaching out to touch her shoulder again, only don't use your hand. Use your mind."

The least useful instructions ever ran through Drew's head. He saw Sophie's shoulders drooping and knew Kay was right. Any moment, she'd give up. Too many people had convinced her she couldn't do anything.

He focused on one flailing tendril from her aura and pictured himself reaching for it. Sophie gasped. Nothing visible happened, but he felt and didn't quite hear a click. The sensation reminded him of popping a dislocated joint into place, except without the pain. In fact, it felt good. Right. Like he'd found a missing piece of himself and filled a hole with it.

Sophie gasped again. "Oh my God."

Compared to him, Sophie had no power at all. She offered a trickle of a stream into his vast ocean. But while he sat, marveling at the difference, Sophie picked up the sword and spun shining silk around it. The thick thread drained his power as it wrapped the sword from pommel to tip.

Drew had no idea how to do what she did. Even watching her use his own power, he still didn't understand. Figuring out how to do this would've taken days, weeks, maybe months. She wove so fast, with such deft fingers.

"I'm in love," Kay murmured.

Sophie paused like she'd heard his voice. Without a word, she continued until she'd wrapped the sword in a shining cocoon of sky-blue silver. With the thread still attached, she took a deep breath and plunged her hand into the cocoon.

Between one heartbeat and the next, the world spun. Drew stood with Kay and Sophie on a smooth, silvery surface gleaming with golden red. In every direction other than down, bands of sky-blue silver rippled. As with the other times he and Kay had been separate entities, Kay wore jeans and a T-shirt, and looked like a younger version of Kurt.

"Oh good," Drew said. "We're inside the weaving. That's great."

Kay held up his fists. "Do we have to smash something?"

Sophie squeaked. "Oh my God, who are you?"

"Kay, Sophie. Sophie, Kay. Now that we're all friends, what do we do?"

"I..." Sophie gulped. "I didn't realize you'd, you know, separate? And you don't seem surprised?"

"We've done a few crazy metaphysical things before," Kay said with a nonchalant shrug.

Drew laid a hand on Sophie's shoulder and pressed. "Sophie, we need you to focus. We have no idea what to do."

"Oh. Right." Sophie shook herself and scanned her surroundings. "I think we need to bind the bands to the sword. Everything about witchcraft is nurturing and growing, so—"

"No, it's not," Kay said. "We can crush things and shoot lightning bolts, remember?"

Sophie frowned. "I think the lightning bolts is because you're also a ghost. Possessed. Whatever. The combination is what gives you lightning bolts. The crushing bugs is because bugs, and that fits what I know."

"Shut up, Kay." Drew smacked Kay in the shoulder. "This is her thing, let her do it."

"I can beat you in here."

Drew grinned. "But you won't."

Kay raised a finger in mock threat. "But I could."

"Boys!" Sophie huffed in disgust. "One of us needs to get up there and coax the threads down while another of us pulls something out of the sword. Then we have them meet in the middle. No smashing, though. Nurturing. Growing."

With a shrug and an easy smile, Kay dropped any pretense of threat. "Sophie made the threads, and Claire made the sword. Dumbass here is bound to Claire, so he should handle the sword. I'll get you up to the threads. If you'll allow a knucklehead like me to touch you."

Amused by Kay's attempt at chivalry, Drew crouched and knocked on the ground. The ground rang with a rich, clear bell tone. "I think I can figure this out."

"I don't really see another option, so sure." Sophie patted Drew's shoulder. "Nurturing and growing, not smashing."

"Got it." He ignored the pair, not interested in how Kay handled his part. Or, for that matter, Sophie.

He pressed his palm to the surface. Claire's pulse thrummed in his chest and through his arm, meeting the sword and resonating with it. The metal showed no sign of yielding, but it recognized him.

"Nurturing and growing," he muttered.

When Claire wanted to connect with him, she touched the locket face to his matching brand. Drew rolled up his sleeve and contorted until the inside of his elbow touched the metal. The heartbeat thumped in his ears and flickered his vision. Then the metal melted, turning to a thick liquid, and his elbow slid into it.

"And connecting, apparently." He pushed both arms into the

metal. The sensation reminded him of holding Claire. Making fists to grab the liquid forced it out of his grip. When he opened his hands again, the liquid flowed over his skin.

"I guess grabbing isn't nurturing or growing." Thinking about how the liquid felt, he took a deep breath and pushed his whole body into the metal. The metal pressed around him. He knew he only had a short time before he ran out of breath, so he focused on what they needed.

Drew sensed that he moved, though he couldn't see anything. The metal opened, holding him by the arm with the brand and supporting his back. He sucked in air and opened his eyes. Sophie and Kay drifted toward him, riding a thick vine of sky-blue silver. The vine sprouted tiny leaves as it grew.

The vine reached him. He held a hand out for Sophie, figuring contact wouldn't hurt. She laced her fingers with his. Kay wrapped his hand around Drew's wrist.

Kay smirked at him. "I like this method of using magic better than smashing things and getting beat up."

"I'm okay with it too," Drew said.

Sophie giggled.

The liquid metal flowed around Drew, and the vine wrapped around it.

Drew blinked in bright light and realized they'd left the sword. Sophie sat beside him, and Kay rested in his head again. The sword lay across his and Sophie's knees. Sky-blue swirled with the golden-red, giving the blade a mesmerizing pattern, shifting in time with Claire's heartbeat.

"That was amazing," Drew said.

Claire stepped into view from behind a tree, carrying a pile of green things. "That looks cool. Here's Justin's armor, my armor, and my dagger.

I'll make you some armor, and you'll need some kind of weapon, plus both for Avery, and I'd like to see if we can bring Rondy." She set the three existing pieces at Drew and Sophie's feet.

"I guess we'll be at this all day?" Sophie said.

"Sounds like it." Drew's hands felt clammy. He rubbed them on his jeans.

"That feeling means we need to take a few to recharge," Kay said.

Drew nodded. "Sophie needs armor and a shield or something. She's coming with us."

"Sure thing." Claire ruffled his hair and walked away with a wave. "Plenty of memory to go around."

He watched her leave with a smile and waited while power flowed from the Portland node.

CHAPTER 37

CLAIRE

Three swords, one dagger, one staff, one round shield, and six very different suits of armor lay on the grass, all prepped and ready to face Iulia. Claire, Justin, and Rondy surveyed the assortment at Drew and Sophie's feet.

Sophie and Drew seemed more comfortable together, which would make Sophie's presence in the battle easier to work with. If the two witches stuck together, Claire didn't feel like she'd have to worry about either of them. Drew could take care of himself, and Sophie seemed capable enough to stay useful while hiding behind him and the shield.

"Give me a few minutes and I'll take you home," Drew said. He sat with his head hanging and shoulders drooping.

Though the pair had done a lot of work, Sophie seemed fine. Claire had a thought to ask about that but figured the explanation would either be ridiculously simple or way over her head. She'd bring it up later.

Justin picked up a sword. "We need to test all this before facing Iulia with it."

"How?" Rondy asked. "Iulia is a rather singular creature."

Sophie hefted the shield and didn't seem strained by its weight. "Also, when? Drew's not in any shape to test anything tonight. Tomorrow is Christmas Eve. Then Christmas. The day after Christmas, my family heads to Salem for the rest of winter break."

"Claire, Avery, and I will head Saint Francis and test the gear there," Justin said. "I don't know what Iulia did there, but it's clear that's her handiwork. If any of this works against that mess, all of it should. We can round up everyone and go deal with Iulia tomorrow evening. That'll make a nice Christmas present."

"Wait." Claire held up a hand. "Ki said that if I waited until Christmas, he'd tell me who set me up to make the volcano erupt. It wasn't Iulia. That means we can take out her helper, the one who forged that journal. Which should make Iulia and Dwight easier to tackle, shouldn't it? They might even know something that would help."

"Considering your previous encounter," Rondy said, "that seems worth waiting for."

Justin nodded. "Sounds like a plan, but it does mean we're not going to be home for Christmas. I doubt Marie will like that much. Or Avery, for that matter."

"It's really about priorities, isn't it?" Drew raised his head and straightened his back. "The longer we wait, the longer Iulia and Dwight have to gather power and cause more mayhem. If we let them have too long, they might get a bright idea to figure out how to make Mount Hood blow, or start fires in Portland, or something else."

Claire nodded. "They want our bodies. They're not going to stop killing people until they get what they want. Who knows what they'll do if they succeed."

"Maybe we can be home in time for dinner," Justin said.

"Just like Thanksgiving," Claire said.

Justin snorted. "Let's not bring that up. Or repeat it. Everybody get some rest and recharge as needed. Sophie, Drew will let you know tomorrow night if the test succeeds. In that case, expect him to pick you up on Christmas morning. We'll figure out a time later. I'll break the news to the family." He turned and left the clearing with a wave.

Claire appreciated him being the bearer of bad news. Marie had told her they considered Christmas the most important family holiday of the year. In the past six years, Claire had lost interest in it as anything other than a day with better than usual food. She'd been looking forward to the family fuss.

Rondy also withdrew, leaving the three teenagers together.

"I know you don't think I can—"

Claire held up a hand to stop Sophie. "Drew trusts you. I trust you. Just, however bad you think it's going to be, multiply that by a billion and you'll be close. Iulia isn't *a* witch, she's pretty much *the* witch. Being dead hasn't slowed her down much. We've only defeated her so far by getting lucky. This time, she's prepped and ready, and we're going to meet her on her terms because that's the only option we have."

Sophie covered her mouth. "That sounds worse than I thought."

Claire clamped her mouth shut before she said something stupid, like calling Sophie cute.

"I'm ready to take you home." Drew stood. "Claire, I'm going to stop at a ley line for a faster recharge, then I'll be back. I might also have to interact with Sophie's mom. That'll...make everything take longer."

Nodding, Claire stepped closer to Drew. She planted a quick kiss on his mouth. "You should let me know if she's the witch working for

Iulia. That'd save us a lot of time."

"I kind of doubt it, but I'll see what I can do." Mist rose between them.

Claire headed toward the rest of the family. She'd ignored the girls for a day. Two days? Too long.

She heard Marie before seeing her and wished she'd taken a different path.

"I'm not mad, Jay. I just— First Thanksgiving, and now Christmas. You're dealing with things that I don't understand, and that makes this so much worse. We all almost died in that lahar, and now you're running off to do something else that might get you killed. I don't know what to say to the girls. They can tell when I'm upset. They can tell when Claire's upset. They can tell when you're leaving to do something genuinely dangerous."

Claire skirted around them, suspecting the sudden lack of talking meant Justin had kissed his wife. Now that she thought of them as her parents, she didn't want to watch that stuff.

She focused on finding the girls. Her demesne knew where they played in a stream with Grandpa Jack. Despite knowing he couldn't eat anything he caught, he'd taken to fishing. For the girls' benefit, Claire had taken to stocking all the water sources with colorful fish too stupid to avoid the hooks for long.

As she rounded a thick fir tree, she stopped. In her path stood the stag. He'd sought her out. The noble creature, autonomous like Rondy, had made a habit of surprising her.

The stag bleated at her. She caught a feeling of frustration in the noise.

"Yeah, I wish I could understand you too. Then I could give you what you want."

He closed the distance between them and lowered his head. For a moment, she thought the stag bowed to her, then he touched her locket palm with his wet nose.

She obliged, petting his head. The green-tinted fur felt softer than she expected. He closed his eyes and bleated again, this time the sound less frustrated and more content. Along with it, she thought she caught hints of deeper meaning.

This stag, created by her for a specific purpose, and sentient beyond her expectations, had something it needed to communicate to her. She had no idea how to enable it.

No, she had one idea. Running her hands over his coat, she examined the parts under his ears and down his back. She checked under his mouth and down his neck, pushing hair aside to see his skin. The stag stood still while she explored each of his front legs and his chest, then his back. She stopped short of frisking his tail and behind, not sure she wanted to discover anything there, but did look over his hind legs.

Shaking her head, she didn't know what to do without having found the heart-shaped collection of whorls and dots that let her hear Kay inside Drew's head.

"Sorry. I'll try to think of something else, I guess. I just don't have any other ideas. And right now, I should spend some time with my sisters." She patted him on the back and went to find the girls. They'd make everything seem brighter.

CHAPTER 38

DREW

Instead of taking Sophie home, Drew shifted them to the nearby elementary school. They stood in the shelter of an overhang, on concrete clear of ash.

"I thought you were taking me home," Sophie said.

He pointed. "It's right through there. But we have to break this connection thing first. I didn't figure we should show up inside your house or on the front porch like this."

"Oh." Her face fell, showing she wanted to break it as much as he did—not at all. "Do we have to? Isn't it easier to just leave it?"

Wind stirred the ash, bringing a biting chill. Sophie shuffled closer and huddled with him. He wrapped his arms around her, holding her against the cold. Contact, he noted, even with clothing between their skin, made him more comfortable.

"I think we should leave it," Kay said.

Drew agreed but knew better. "I think your mom will notice."

"Probably." Sophie sighed. "I guess it's for the best. It didn't take long to merge anyway."

"No, it didn't." Now that he knew how to do it, he thought he could connect them in a heartbeat.

They stood in silence, doing nothing, for what felt like a long time. Guilt settled on Drew's shoulders. If Claire saw this, he didn't know what she'd do. Probably punch him in the face again. On a certain level, he deserved it. Holding Sophie with their auras merged felt more intimate than kissing Claire on a bed in the dark.

"This is hard," he said.

"It is."

"To hell with your mom," Kay said. "Come back with us."

Sophie giggled. "Kay, you're being silly." She pulled away.

Drew let go and stuffed his hands in his coat pockets. "Yeah. Silly." He took a deep breath and flexed his power to release her. He needed to talk to Claire about this. She needed to understand. They had no way to break the binding between them, and he didn't want to. A merged aura, forced magical closeness, couldn't compete with six years of solid friendship based on trust and respect.

He also didn't want anyone to get hurt.

The connection broke with an audible snap. The piled ash blew upward and swirled without a breeze. From the grimace on Sophie's face, she felt the same as he did—like he'd cut off an arm he didn't know he had until this morning. All his instincts demanded he forge the connection again.

If he touched Sophie, he'd fail at resisting that urge.

She took a step toward him. He shuffled back and looked away. They both stopped.

"I'll be back on Christmas," Drew said.

"Right." Sophie hugged herself and withdrew. "I'll have to sneak out. Come to my bedroom."

She squeaked. Drew looked up. Sophie had backed into her mom. Mrs. Harris wore a pink, knee-length jacket, and had her blonde hair up in a ponytail. She scowled. Her navy aura flared with enough prickly energy to rival Sophie five times over. Drew gulped.

"If you dare show up in her bedroom," Mrs. Harris said, "I'll string you up in my garden as a scarecrow."

"Mom!" Sophie's cheeks flared bright pink, and she covered her face with both hands.

"It's not like that," Drew sputtered. He felt heat rising in his own cheeks.

Mrs. Harris crossed her arms and stepped in front of Sophie. "You stay away from my daughter, you monster."

"I know I'm usually all for cowardly retreat in the face of witchcraft," Kay said. "But this is probably the best opportunity we're going to have to find out if she's on Iulia's side or just an angry witch. So put some backbone into it, boy. Stand up to her. You and me together, combined with our link to the node, is more than she can handle."

Drew hoped Kay was right. Instead of spinning mist and disappearing, he took a deep breath and played a part. "I don't really see how you have any say over whether I date your daughter or not."

Mrs. Harris bared her teeth and looked down her nose at him. "You're not going to talk to me like that."

Kay harrumphed. "Try a gross subject change. Bring up the journal."

With no better ideas, Drew followed Kay's suggestion. "Why did you give her that forged copy of Iulia's journal? Was it so you could get me killed? Is that how you handle problems?"

"Nice," Kay said.

Mrs. Harris furrowed her brow. "What?" She turned to Sophie. "What's he talking about? Who's Iulia?"

Lowering her hands, Sophie blinked at him. "One of our ancestors. You gave me her journal in that stack. Only it wasn't her journal. It was a forged copy with some maps in it. Where did you get it? This was the thin, black one. In bad shape but still readable."

"I didn't give you anything like that," Mrs. Harris said. To Drew's relief, she unclenched and perched her hands on her hips. "I gave you journals from Jacqueline, her daughter, her son's wife, and a few of the women in their children's generation. None of them had a name even close to Iulia."

"Then you're not the witch Iulia is using," Drew said. At this point, he thought he could reason with Mrs. Harris instead of bluffing her. "Someone else slipped that journal into the stack in the hopes it would find its way to me. Where did you get the rest?"

"The coven. They're freely available to anyone in the group." She pointed at him. "Which you're not invited to join."

For one moment, Drew had thought he could explain the whole situation to Mrs. Harris, and maybe get some extra support from the coven. That moment passed. He shrugged. "I don't need a coven."

"Then you're dumber than you look," Mrs. Harris snapped. She pointed at Sophie. "You're grounded."

Sophie stared at her. "For what? Going out with a boy?"

Mrs. Harris stabbed her finger at Drew. "That is not a boy. That's an abomination, and I forbid you to have any further contact with it." She took Sophie by the ear. Her aura flickered yellow as she drowned Sophie with power.

Grimacing in frustration and annoyance, Sophie turned and jogged toward her house.

"If you ever try to see my daughter again, I'll do much, much worse to you." Mrs. Harris turned on her heel and marched away.

"You'll try," Drew grumbled. He watched them with a scowl.

Kay huffed. "I'd like to beat the crap out of her."

"Yeah." He scuffed his boot in the ash. "I guess I'm going to have to break her out tomorrow."

"That'll be fun."

Drew snorted. He needed a walk before doing anything else so he didn't throw his anger at anyone who didn't deserve it. As he crossed the school, he thought over Mrs. Harris's ignorance about Iulia. Someone else in the coven knew about her, but they had no way to figure out who. For all he knew, more than one witch had signed on with her.

"You know, it occurs to me that I have no idea how we're going to find Iulia. She's not going to be at that bridge with Dwight again."

"She wants to fight Claire and Justin. I doubt she'll make herself hard to find."

"No, but we don't even know where to start looking. And I don't want to rely on Ki and the witch he'll point us at. There's got to be a more reliable way to find her. After eating all those ghosts, she's got a huge amount of power. That can't hide, can it?"

"I dunno. The node is hidden unless you go into those stupid tunnels."

Drew stopped and considered that point. "The node. You know, Iulia's been laying down some high-power traps. I wonder if she's able to tap the ley lines? And if she is, I wonder if the node can identify her? Power calls to power, right?"

"By that logic, we should be able to find Iulia on our own, but I'm not sure how to do it, so let's check with the node. Besides, better to keep it happy than ignore it."

Using the mist, Drew shifted them two steps outside the underground room housing the node. Kay sighed with pleasure in his head. Drew reached for the power and wrapped it around himself.

The node wrapped her arms around his neck from behind and caressed his chest. "Snared in my web again."

"I needed to recharge."

She held her mouth beside his ear, the cacophony of her voice whispering so loud he thought his brain might bleed. "You've been a busy bee. I sense tools of war."

"There's a threat to your city. We're going to fight it."

"Why?"

"Because we don't want to die."

The node covered his neck, applying enough pressure to assure Drew that she could crush him if she wanted to. Images flashed through his head too fast for him to recognize them. He got the impression that when Kay had offered her service, he'd also inadvertently granted access to his memories.

Unless the node could do this to anyone.

"I see the connections," the node murmur-shouted. "Humans. You fight for them. Some more than others. Love. I know this thing. Witches. You. Kay-entity. Interesting. Portland's destruction would not hurt me unless the land is broken with water, but the imbalance of this Iulia-Dwight-entity will cause great harm if allowed to continue."

"Oh good," Kay said.

Drew squeaked, the pressure on his neck too great to form true words.

"Your service is to be my agent for so long as you live."

Kay coughed. "I beg your pardon, ma'am. That's straining the boundaries of service."

"Accept my binding or I will kill you and find another."

Kay paused for a moment. "Okay, we accept. But the binding to Claire is older than yours."

"I acknowledge this. You are also her agent. When our interests conflict, you will negotiate."

Drew had too many powerful women in his life. He nodded. The pressure on his neck decreased. "Can you help us find the Iulia-Dwight-entity?"

The node raised a third hand and spun it around his head, leaving a golden trail. It wrapped around his eyes and sank into them. A thousand pinpricks of agony seared the right side of his face, from his hairline to his jaw.

"Your eyes will lead the way."

She released him. He stumbled forward, out of the node. Fire burned in his chest, and his eyes hurt. Spun mist took him to Claire's demesne. Despite all the power coursing through him, he sagged and leaned against a tree, too exhausted for words. He shuffled to bed and collapsed.

CHAPTER 39

CLAIRE

The next morning, Claire let Drew sleep when she got up. After sitting through a cold breakfast seething with tension, she and Justin escaped to Avery's apartment. The detective stood in his kitchen, wearing navy sweatpants and a gray T-shirt emblazoned with the police department logo. He glanced up from a frying pan of eggs, grunted, and ignored them. The aroma of coffee and bacon filled the air.

Avery's hair stuck at odd angles. He hadn't shaved in at least three days, leaving him with a scruffy beard streaked with gray. Compared to his usual tidiness and suit, he seemed tired and worn. He seemed more human and less authority figure for it.

"We're going to test new weapons and armor at the church," Justin said. He also had a few days of beard, which made him look like a Viking on his way to raid something.

Again, Avery grunted.

"We'd appreciate it if you came along," Claire said. "You know, in case this stuff doesn't work as well as we hope it will and you need to drag

Justin's sorry butt out of danger again."

"That's not how I would've put it," Justin said with a roll of his eyes.

Claire flashed him a bright smile.

Avery chuckled. "I'm not really awake yet. I finally got to sleep last night after bolstering Traffic since the eruption. Staying awake for forty hours straight is rough at my age."

"Sorry, Grandpa," Claire said. "I guess we can manage this without you."

He threw a wadded paper towel at her, which she caught. "Coffee. Breakfast. Shower. Fight ghosts. In that order. Go or wait. Your choice." Avery slid his eggs onto a plate already holding bacon, a peeled orange, and toast. He picked up a steaming mug and shuffled two steps to the plastic table in his kitchen.

Claire sat on the couch. Justin explained the plan.

"You want me to skip Christmas with my family to save the world." Avery sipped his coffee.

"Don't they hate you?" Claire asked. She remembered discovering that Brian, a bully who'd picked on her, had an abusive father. Now she sat in that guy's living room, asking for his help. It had been caused by her own father's Phasm, so it was never Avery's fault, but that didn't make everything all better for his wife and sons.

"Not as much as they did a month ago. Partly because I've been showing up when I said I would."

"I'm hoping we can keep it short," Justin said. "How long could a battle against Iulia really take?"

"I'm not going to dignify that with a response. If you intend to wait for me, make yourself comfortable."

Justin sat beside Claire. They waited while Avery drank his coffee, ate his breakfast, and took a shower. Claire thought about her upcoming meeting with Ki. If he wanted another favor for telling her who'd played him, she needed to be ready to explain what they intended to do and the danger they all faced.

An hour later, Avery emerged wearing his new suit, shoes, and trenchcoat, with his new sword belted at his side. The shower had transformed him back into the authority figure Claire knew.

They followed him out of the building and piled into his car. Claire had let Enion sleep, and Justin didn't want to drag Tariel across when Avery had a car.

No one spoke for the ride. Claire didn't sense any tension in the air. She also didn't think Avery liked being in this situation. Neither did she, of course. She'd told Sophie she trusted her, but that didn't mean she believed the magic stuff had worked.

The car stopped in front of the door to the back half of the church. Claire stepped out of the car and didn't see any reason to worry. Justin had talked about the walls bleeding. This place seemed normal, covered in ash like everything else. No music tempted her, and nothing reached for her.

She moved so the car could shut its door and pointed at the building. "Are you sure this is the right place?"

"Yes," Avery and Justin said. The car revved its engine.

"Okay then." Glad to avoid the church, Claire led the way to the dining hall. She climbed the steps to reach the front door, taking care to avoid kicking up the ash. The door opened at her touch, as if it had been waiting for her.

The moment she stepped over the threshold, the hairs on the back of her neck rose, and she shivered at a sharp chill. Something else occupied this space, and she felt it. She thought she heard a faint echo of a woman laughing, and it sounded like Iulia.

Malevolence hung thick in the air.

Avery stepped around her with his sword drawn. Also holding his sword, Justin nudged her forward. She gripped her dagger and held it out, not sure how to destroy the feeling this place gave her.

The door creaked. Claire turned to watch it drift shut. When it closed, it clanged with a note of finality.

"It's in the walls," she whispered.

Avery watched the ceiling, looking ready to stab it. "No, it's just an unusual ghost infestation."

"Maybe it was a few days ago." Claire lowered into a crouch and laid her locket palm on the industrial carpet. Something hard scraped across it. She snapped her hand back and jumped onto a bench. "This building is an entity now. Can't you feel it?"

"I can feel cold, and I can hear cackling," Justin said. "That doesn't make it an entity."

Claire wanted to leave, but she stood firm. Fleeing wouldn't solve this problem. "Stab the floor," she said.

Avery and Justin glanced at each other. Both men shrugged. Justin shifted his grip and pointed his blade at the floor. As he raised his sword to plunge it downward, a misty arm surged from the floor and punched him in the back. Justin staggered forward and caught himself on a bench.

"That hurt less than last time, so that's good."

Warm, salty blood sprayed from the windows as if someone had turned on spigots. Foggy arms punched from the ceiling and the floor at the same time. Avery spun, evading two blows at the same time, and slashed his sword through a third. Claire ducked and ran toward the back of the room, not sure why that seemed like a better idea than running for the door.

She slashed at an arm and leaped onto a table. As she jumped to another table, an arm shot from the floor and knocked her aside. Justin shouted her name. Her head hit a bench and she blinked up at the ceiling. Mist writhed across the surface above.

Arms clamped around her. She kept a tight grip on her dagger, hacking at everything she could reach while her brain regrouped.

In a way, the arms welcomed her. Claire couldn't put her finger on the full sensation, but it reminded her Justin's dad efforts. They invited her to let go, stop fighting, and join them. Voices whispered in her ears, urging her to relax.

Claire stopped fighting. She lay still, listening.

"These work pretty well," Avery said.

"Claire! Where are you?"

"So much work," fifty voices whispered. They echoed, and they didn't. "So much struggle. Let go. We'll take care of you."

Mist closed over her, holding her in a cool embrace. That felt wrong. A good hug didn't chill her body. Justin gave her his cloak if she felt cold. Drew rubbed her arms. Marie offered her a blanket. No one who cared about her wanted her cold. Except these voices.

They cared. Didn't they?

"We'll catch you when you fall."

"I don't want to fall," Claire murmured.

"It won't hurt."

"What if it does?"

"It won't."

"Claire!" Justin's voice came from a distance, muffled like when he called through her bedroom door.

She didn't have a bedroom door anymore. The volcano...

"Come to us."

They sounded so friendly and welcoming. Even though she wanted warmth, the chill leeched away feeling. Her arms seemed lighter already, and so did her legs. She couldn't even feel her toes anymore. What did she need toes for anyway? Or fingers. Fingers didn't do anything important.

"Join us."

One hand throbbed. She tried to raise her arm to see, but it felt weightless and leaden at the same time. The skin crawled.

Justin called for her again, his voice fluttering on the edge of her hearing. Why did he keep calling for her?

Hands touched her cheeks, freezing her skin. A woman leaned close. Her misty face seemed familiar.

"You want to be a good girl, don't you, Claire?" Iulia said.

She hadn't wanted anyone to call her a good girl for years. Not since that one foster mother patted her on the head and called her one, then did the same thing to the dog. After that, she wanted something different, something real. Something she got from Justin.

Justin was the only father she could remember. He gave her warmth, acceptance, and guidance. Not cold. She didn't need cold. Cold killed.

Growling at Iulia, she threw her effort into a struggle against whatever held her down.

Iulia snatched away her hands and hissed, retreating like she'd been burned.

Claire screamed at the mist in wordless frustration. A blade sliced through the fog and stuck into the floor. Her blood flowed inside that steel. Unable to lift her arm, she flopped her body toward it. She shoved her hand at the sharp edge, and kept shoving until it slashed off her thumb.

Her blood, red and shiny, sizzled as it spritzed into the mist. The mist faded. Feeling flooded into her arm. Sharp pain stung her toes. She picked up her thumb and stuck it to her hand.

"Thank goodness, Claire. I thought we'd lost you." Justin loomed over her, one hand still on his sword. He touched her face with his gloved hand.

She surged up and wrapped her arms around him. "Did you kill the building?"

"I think so. It's not bleeding anymore, and the fog is gone." Justin held her close.

She checked over his shoulder and saw Avery standing on a table, yanking his sword out of the ceiling.

"The damage to the building is minimal," Avery said. "They'll have to replace a few ceiling tiles. The ductwork might need some patching. At least I didn't hit a water pipe. I doubt they'll bother fixing the carpet, if they even notice the holes. The foundation should be fine."

Claire pulled away from Justin, and he let her go. "It was Iulia. She was in all of it."

"I'm not surprised." Justin lifted her hand and watched as the thumb healed in place.

"Dad." Claire dreaded the thing she thought she needed to say. Neither Justin nor Avery had been affected like she had, and she knew why. Even if she didn't like it, she knew. "I'm...I'm not really...alive? I'm a spirit of some kind, occupying this body? That's why churches feel weird?"

His mouth quirked into what would've been a smile if it held any happiness, and he didn't meet her gaze. She had her answer.

Avery sheathed his sword and didn't look away. "It's a challenge to state anything with certainty, but that does seem to be the case. If it's any consolation, I agree with Drew that you're a full soul and not merely an echo or shade."

"Does that make me..." She couldn't decide what to ask or how to word anything.

"No one knows the answers to questions like that," Justin said. He held her chin and looked at her. "And it doesn't matter. You're part of my family. I'm not turning you out because you're different. You're still who we adopted, and that's what's important."

She hugged him again and definitely didn't cry.

CHAPTER 40

DREW

Soft light glowed in the cabin when Drew woke. He lay alone on the bed. Still in his clothes from the night before, he yawned and rubbed his face. The right side stung. Claire hadn't hung a mirror anywhere that he knew, so he'd have to trek to water to see if the node had done anything visible.

Putting on his glasses, he shuffled outside. Bright light blinded him. He needed to ask Claire to turn down the intensity of the sun. Clouds never blocked it in her demesne, which made daytime unsettling in comparison to the near-constant gloom of Portland and Vancouver.

He heard little girls giggling through the trees and veered in the opposite direction. They liked making him the villain in their weird games —Unicorn Princess Knight, or something like it. His role tended to involve letting them throw things at him. Claire enjoyed playing with them more than he did. Maybe in a few years, he'd find them more entertaining. To think Justin was only a year older than him when Lisa was born.

"Good morning, Drew," Grandma Tammy said.

She stood at the sink of the large kitchen Claire had constructed for them, washing dishes. Warm wood, granite, and chrome formed all the surfaces. The room had three walls, with the fourth side open. So far, the chrome fridge worked well enough, as did the stove and oven.

Claire had put some effort into trying to build a water treatment facility, but it still needed work. She'd said something about needing time and a filter. He'd promised to look up some stuff in the library about it.

Drew stopped at the kitchen table, a thick slab of wood with eight chairs around it. "Morning," he mumbled.

Grandma Tammy looked up, then she frowned at him and gestured to indicate the side of her face. "What happened to you?"

He touched his right cheek and winced at the sting. "Nothing special. Does it look bad?"

Her brow lifted. She wiped her hands on a towel, then took his chin in her hand and scrutinized the right side of his face. "It looks… roses, actually. Kind of abstract, but definitely a tattoo of roses. Did you get into a fight with a gardener?"

"No. The node under Portland. It won."

Tammy let go and handed him a bowl for cereal.

"Great," Kay grumbled. "She slapped her brand on your face. Just what we need. Yes, officer, I saw him. He had a giant tattoo of roses covering half his face. At least Claire's family sentinel had the good sense to brand the inside of your elbow."

Drew stifled a laugh. He didn't think cops mattered much at this point. No prison could hold him, and he could heal gunshots. Having Avery on their side meant even less to worry about.

"That sounds like a problem," Tammy said. "Is it a problem?"

"Not really. More like a benefit with strings attached."

"If you say so. I don't know how you're going to explain that at school."

Filling his bowl with cereal, Drew sighed. "I guess that depends on whether I go back to school or not."

"Why wouldn't you? You're only a semester away from graduating."

He added milk and took his breakfast to the table. "What's the point? I'm not going to college anymore. A high school diploma won't help me fight ghosts or mutant bugs, or volcanoes, for that matter."

"That's one of the dumbest things I've ever heard you say," Kay spat.

Tammy stood across the table from him and planted her fists on her hips. "Now you listen to me, young man."

Blinking, he met her gaze with no idea what she intended to say that could change his mind. He'd already considered school worthless after getting stuck with Kay.

"You worked hard for a lot of years to get that diploma. I know that because you told me so yourself. You're one semester away from that. One semester. You're telling me you can't suck it up for six months and finish something you started?" She jabbed a finger at him. "Real men keep their word. Real men don't give up because it seems pointless or hard. You do that work, you finish high school, and you hold your head up high, knowing you followed through."

"Hot dang, boy," Kay said. "This lady knows what's what. You listen to her."

Drew scowled into his cereal. With Kay against him, he didn't have much choice. But it still seemed like a waste of time and effort.

"And if all that doesn't matter to you because your head is too far up your ass to know sense, then do it to be an example for Missy and Lisa. They look up to you more than you think. Do it because even if you have magic and whatever else, you're still going to need money to feed yourself and Claire. You know as well as I do that you're not going to steal because you're a decent person."

"Yes, ma'am," he mumbled into a spoonful of cereal. Somehow, he thought he could use magic to come up with food, but he didn't see a point to arguing with her. Like she said, he only had one semester.

"Good. I don't want to hear any more of this nonsense about not finishing school. I'm not going to tolerate that from either you or Claire. Marie didn't finish high school, and now all she can do is crap work for part of the year. Justin did, but he's got different problems with regular jobs."

"It worked!" Claire bounded into the kitchen and thumped into Drew from behind. She wrapped her arms around his neck and kissed his left cheek.

Drew spilled cereal on the table and splattered milk on his face. Grandma Tammy threw a hand towel at him.

"We killed the freaky ghost stuff with Avery's help. The weapons and armor work. You were—" She slid into the chair on his right side and stared at his face. "What—"

"The node. It's not a big deal. Sophie's mom isn't Iulia's witch. It's probably someone in the coven, but we're going to need Ki to tell us who. Also, I should be able to find Iulia now." He had no idea how the node's gift worked, but he saw no need to elaborate on that point.

"Good to know." She touched the side of his face.

He winced. "It's still tender."

"No wonder you slept so hard. Does it come with any real perks, or just downsides?"

"Don't look at me," Kay said. "Not touching this conversation."

"If we can find Iulia while she's on the west side of the city, I think I'll have more power at my disposal than on the east side." He paused, and wanted to leave it there, but knew he needed to at least say something about Sophie. "Um, so, there's a thing I need to tell you."

"Shoot." Claire raked a hand through his hair and tucked a curl behind his ear.

"The thing I did with Sophie yesterday. There was a metaphysical part, and...it's hard to explain because I don't really understand. Not exactly, anyway. The point is, when we do that thing, it makes us both more capable and powerful, but it also..." He stuck his spoon into his cereal and swished it back and forth.

"Makes you inclined to be touchy-feely?" When he stared at her, she snorted. "You really think I didn't notice?" She kissed his nose. "It's cool. I get it. Magic is like that. Finish your breakfast. We're going to see how well you can whack things with a staff for the rest of the day."

"Oh. Good." Tension eased from his shoulders. He hadn't realized how tight they'd gotten.

Claire stood and smiled at him. Sunlight glowed around her. Drew wondered if she really cared as little as she claimed about Sophie and his behavior toward her. Maybe. Maybe not. Time would tell.

He took her hand and held it to his cheek. "I love you."

Her smile dimmed. "We'll be okay."

His belly clenched. Iulia would find a way. She always seemed to. If Iulia took her body back, Drew would have to kill her this time. That would mean looking into her eyes and not hesitating.

Nodding, he let go. "Yeah." He ate his cereal.

CHAPTER 41

CLAIRE

Christmas Eve passed in a blur of weapon practice, playing games with little girls, and dodging questions. Aside from Missy and Lisa, half the people in her demesne wanted to talk about the fight with Iulia and the other half wanted to avoid that discussion. The girls kept dinner from becoming a torture session, then Claire and Drew escaped to their cabin.

Neither wanted to talk, both struggled to fall asleep. Claire hadn't felt this unsettled on a Christmas Eve since...ever. She didn't remember caring about this day. Maybe she had in the part before her memories covered. In her head, she decided to call that The Before. The Before had happened, but she knew nothing concrete about it.

Eventually, they fell asleep. Early in the morning, Missy and Lisa woke everyone to make sure they knew it was Christmas. After a hearty breakfast of eggs, sausages, pastries, and fruit, Claire, Drew, and Justin left with Tariel and Enion. They parted ways—Justin headed to meet with Avery, and Claire and Drew visited Nine Cans.

The bar was closed. Ki sat on the customer side, brooding over a glass of red wine. He'd left an empty tumbler on the bar at the next stool over. Drew stayed by the door with Enion in his hand. Claire approached the bar and took the stool beside Ki.

Ki reached behind the bar and used a nozzle to fill the tumbler with clear soda. "Merry Christmas," he said, his voice flat and empty.

"I didn't think you'd celebrate it." Claire considered the hour too early for soda, but she sipped it anyway out of politeness. He'd gone to the trouble to pour it for her, after all.

"I don't. I hate almost everything about this holiday."

"Almost?"

"The lights are nice."

"Can't argue with that."

Swirling his wine, Ki shook his head. "I should've known better."

Claire shrugged. She thought the same thing about herself. "You wanted to believe." She didn't know if he felt guilty about all the deaths or she would've tried to assuage that.

He sipped his wine and took a long time to respond. "I assume you came for her identity?"

"Yes, please."

"What will you do with this knowledge?"

Claire glanced at Drew, who nodded as if offering his approval. "Stop her."

"If you bring me her head, I'll repay you with a favor."

"Uh." Claire blanched. "I don't plan on cutting off anyone's head. I think she's controlled, and I mean to end that control. She'll get to live with the knowledge that she murdered thousands of people because she wasn't strong enough to resist."

Ki shrugged. "I suppose that's fitting. Not satisfying to me, but fitting."

"It's the best kind of justice I have to offer."

"Just desserts."

"If you'd like, I can come back after we take care of the giant ghost destroying everything and bring you into my demesne for dinner. Grandma Tammy is baking a pie."

He sighed. "That's a sweet offer. Don't waste your time on me."

She touched his arm. "I don't see it as a waste."

Patting her hand, he sighed again. "You're so young. I'm not physically able to leave, Claire. The seals binding me and my kind have, in addition to stealing our access to power, bound us to certain geographic locations. I can't leave what is now Portland's Chinatown. Lou can't leave her mountain. Klick is stuck on his mountain too. No one can move around. We're all stuck. And I miss Raven." He sipped his wine. "I miss her a great deal."

"Ki Oscar Teah," Drew said. "Ki Oh—" He huffed in amusement. "Coyote, the trickster. Why did I never put that together before?"

Ki snorted. "Probably because you're always either trying to avoid getting killed or trying not to think about your particular predicament."

"Is everyone else who visits here a bound god?" Drew asked.

Claire stared at Ki, not sure she understood the full ramifications of this revelation. Did he just tell her that Lou was actually Loowit, the goddess who'd been turned into Mount St. Helens? And that Klickitat, the native name for Mount Hood, belonged to another god?

What had she thrown into the mountain?

Instead of answering Drew, Ki leaned closer to Claire. "She's older than you, maybe in her fifties. Gray-streaked brown hair. Wears tie-dyed dresses. Which doesn't narrow it down much in Portland. But I know she's a witch and answers to Stace."

Claire blinked at him. "Are you kidding?"

"No. Go deal with her." Ki shooed her out. "Minors aren't supposed to be inside bars. Not that you're actually a minor anymore. He is, though."

Too stunned to form a retort, Claire stood and returned to Drew. He seemed as stupefied as she did. When she reached him, mist surrounded them. Then they stood outside Stace's cute little cottage. They stared at it for several heartbeats.

"I don't understand," Drew said. "How did neither of us notice?"

"The same way we didn't notice anything with Anne when Kurt's Phasm was controlling her?"

He opened his mouth, then shut it. "Fair point."

She imagined fighting Stace. The prospect made her squirm. Anne had used magic to make her dizzy and nauseous, then controlled her body. "How do you want to approach this? With Anne, we never figured out how to free her. We killed Kurt's Phasm."

"I...huh. Kay suggests knocking her out and tying her up."

"If she's possessed, that won't help. I guess I should also stab her? Justin said a small cut works."

They stared at the cottage again.

Drew shrugged. "Knock on the front door? Act innocent?"

Claire quirked an eyebrow at him. He wore his new jeans and hoodie, and held a straight, polished length of wood as tall as himself. She wore her green bodysuit with her dagger belted at her waist. "We're armed and armored against magic."

"She might not notice. We don't look that different from usual."

"She's probably noticed we're here by now, though." Claire took his hand and approached the front door. She half-expected the door to open before she knocked, but it didn't.

Drew squeezed her hand.

The door opened.

Stace squinted at them. "Drew, what are you doing here? On Christmas?" Her hair hung flat and lifeless. She wore a thick, quilted nightdress with a floral print and fluffy pink socks.

Claire always expected evil to appear more...flamboyant. Dark. Evil. And then it showed up wearing a grandma dress and fuzzy slippers.

"Merry Christmas, Aunt Stace!" Drew stepped close and hugged her. "I got you something, but the house was destroyed in the lahar across Vancouver, and I couldn't afford to replace it. Sorry!"

Claire had to work not to let her jaw fall open. She figured Kay came up with that for him, or maybe Drew improvised off Kay's less spectacular idea. "Yeah," Claire said. "Sorry."

"Oh, my goodness, Drew, that's the worst thing I've ever heard." Stace beckoned for them to come inside.

As Claire stepped inside, she thought about that one visit to Anne's had gone. All welcoming smiles one minute, then magic in the face. She shut the door for Stace and followed Drew as Stace led them inside.

"I wasn't expecting any company," she said, sounding flustered.

"No problem," Claire said, smiling with the most fake holiday cheer she'd ever shown. She set her hands on her hips to keep one close to her dagger. Any moment, a magical battle could explode in her face.

"That's okay, Aunt Stace," Drew said, showing as much fake cheer as Claire. His voice rang hollow, and his eyes gleamed with danger. "We won't stay long. Just wanted to make sure you know we're thinking about you. Now that we know where you live." He gestured for Stace to sit.

"And, you know, remember you."

Stace's smile dropped. "Oh dear."

Claire punched her in the face. Stace's head snapped to the side, and she stumbled backward. Drew lunged to catch her. His hands crackled with sparks made of mist. Stace's body spasmed.

Drew lowered Stace to the floor. "That was easier than I expected."

"I thought she was going to have serious battle skills, like Anne." Claire dropped to a knee beside Stace, who lay unconscious on the floor, and checked her pulse. She seemed fine. "Maybe Iulia only used her to make the volcano thing."

Enion raised his head from his perch around Claire's neck. He sniffed the air. "Leeloo?"

"Enion!" A tiny dragon jumped into sight on a bookshelf. Leeloo looked the same as all the other dragons—sleek, silver, and adorable. "Hurt slave. Bad Enion!"

"Whoa, Leeloo. Settle down." Claire leaped to intercept Leeloo before the dragon could expand and fill the room. She grabbed Leeloo.

Leeloo shrieked and blew a tiny puff of fire at Claire.

"Ow, quit it."

Claire tapped Leeloo's head. Leeloo bit her finger. Enion ran down Claire's arm and pounced on Leeloo.

Unwilling to get between the two dragons, Claire dropped them. They hit the floor and wrestled with tiny, angry chirps of accusation. Discounting the claws, fangs, and fire, they reminded Claire of Missy and Lisa squabbling over a page of stickers. She figured the size of the space kept them in their small forms, which she decided to appreciate.

Leaving them to their battle, she whirled to find Drew holding a groggy Stace to the floor with thick bands of mist.

"Stab her," Drew said with a scowl. "Just in case."

The look on his face bothered Claire. She frowned. "Drew, she didn't abandon you." Despite that, she crouched beside Stace with her dagger. "I'm angry that no one from either of my parents' families came for me, but that's not Stace's fault."

"Just do it."

Claire pushed up Stace's sleeve and sliced a shallow cut across her forearm. Blood welled. She saw nothing misty.

"She's not possessed," Claire said.

"Then Iulia did something to her mind. Keep her pinned down. I'm going in."

"What? What are you talking about?" Claire snatched his arm, ready to wrestle him to the floor if necessary. "We can just leave her tied up. She won't cause any more trouble while we deal with Iulia. She doesn't know how to fight."

Drew growled in the back of his throat. "We don't know that. We have to be sure. I'll make sure."

Leaning across Stace, Claire jerked him close. He lacked the strength to resist her, though she could tell he tried. With the tip of her nose less than an inch from his, she stared him down.

"Hurting her won't heal anything inside you."

"You don't understand."

"Say that again," she growled. "Look me in the eye and say that again."

Drew glared at her for two long heartbeats. Then he slumped his shoulders and sighed. Touching his forehead to hers, he closed his eyes. "I just want to be sure."

She knew better than to let him shrug it off and keep going. "Sure of what?"

He leaned away. She let go and watched him. Despite the way he'd sagged, she saw the stubborn set of his jaw. No matter what she said, he wouldn't let this go. But he'd explain it before she let him do anything else.

Looking at his hands in his lap, he shrugged. "I need to do this."

"Why? We can just leave her tied up with her own socks. She'll be fine after we destroy Iulia. You don't need to do anything more. We probably didn't even need to come here."

For what felt like a long time, he sat in a dejected heap. His mouth twitched several times.

The dragons stopped making noise. Claire figured Leeloo had given up and Enion could tell he shouldn't interrupt.

Drew finally raised his head. "What if we fail? What if she's not the only one in the coven? What if Iulia's hooks let her pull power or expertise? There are so many things we don't know. I understand why we need to face Iulia as soon as possible, but that doesn't mean we're ready."

Taking his hand, Claire gave him a half-smile. "I just didn't want you to do it angry. Go ahead. I'll watch over you."

CHAPTER 42

DREW

Without Claire, Drew knew he'd do stupid things. Stupider things. Worse things, too. Until she stopped him, he'd intended to rip Stace's mind apart. That would've made him a murderer. For the crime of wiping a memory to save her own butt.

"My Emmy made me a better man," Kay said. "Hot damn, she was a doll in her day."

Drew shook his head at Kay and touched the fingertips of one hand to Stace's face. He avoided the bruise already forming under her eye.

Kay harrumphed. "This is all witch crap, so don't expect much from me."

"I never expect much from you, Kay."

Claire snorted as she reached under the bookshelf for the dragons.

"Ha ha. Very funny. Don't screw up, boy. Both our asses on the line here."

Rather than responding, Drew took hold of Stace's aura. He had no idea how to do what he wanted, but that had never stopped him before.

Sophie would've been helpful, but he didn't want her to know about this. "Growing and nurturing," he murmured. "Intent."

Their auras clicked together. The sensation held much less satisfaction than when he'd merged with Sophie's aura. Compared to that, this reminded him of putting two pieces together in a jigsaw puzzle. Nothing about this connection compelled him closer to Stace. He'd have no trouble letting go when he finished.

Stace had a lot more power than Sophie. He thought she might match him in plain witch power. Thanks to Kay and the node, he could beat her anyway. With more practice and experimentation, he wondered if any witch could defeat him.

Claire could defeat him. Anytime, anywhere, from any distance, she could stop him. He suspected the node could do the same.

He used his connection to examine Stace's aura, looking for oddities. Having never seen it before she'd been taken by Iulia, he wondered if she normally had coppery brown. Iulia had encased Dwight in copper armor, which seemed suggestive of a link between the two. Especially since he knew Iulia had a clear aura.

The process felt like digging his fingers through loose dirt warmed by the sun. Without having to move his hands or Stace's physical body, he sifted through every inch of her aura and found nothing. Thinking the process probably required knowledge he lacked, he decided to give up. Then he swiped his hand through the metaphysical dirt and noticed a cooler layer underneath.

Auras had two layers, one inner and one outer. He'd connected to the outer layer with Stace. Maybe he'd connected to Sophie's inner layer, and maybe he'd done that because his witch stuff had come from her.

Being a witch needed a manual.

The coven probably had one.

At this point, even if he could convince Mrs. Harris to let him into the coven, he didn't want to join. They didn't give Sophie enough credit or respect. He didn't think they'd treat him any better. At least one of them would treat him worse.

Running his fingers through the cooler layer of dirt, he found something hard and sharp. He unearthed a hook about the size of a quarter, made of pure, clear energy. The hook hung in Stace's aura with nothing attached.

"If you take that out," Kay said, "Iulia's going to notice."

Drew flicked the hook to see how it reacted.

The hook sparked and doubled in size.

"Yeah, that's not good. Claire? I found Iulia's tampering, but I'm not sure if I should leave it or try to break it."

A dragon chirped with all the anger of a territorial bird. Something muffled the dragon.

"Why wouldn't you?" Claire's voice reached him from a distance and with an echo, as if it traveled through a long tube to reach him.

"Iulia will notice?" Drew pulled on the dirt and inspected the hook from the opposite angle. "Also, it seems to have a defense mechanism."

"Oh. Good point."

Another dragon chirped.

"Be quiet, Leeloo," Claire snapped. "Do you have any idea how to remove it?"

"Not really. I could probably blast it, but I'm not sure if that'll make things worse."

"I see three main options. One, you can futz with it and either make things worse or solve the problem. Two, we can grab Sophie and see if the two of you can fix it or make it worse. Three, we drop her off with Anne and ask her to fix it while we go collect everyone and attack Iulia. If you're not sure about what to do, I feel like that last option is best."

"I'm going to agree with her on that last option," Kay said.

Drew wanted to solve the problem. Taking Stace elsewhere felt like failing. He wrapped his fingers around the hook. The hook sprouted blades, slicing his fingers. With a yelp, he snatched away his hand and broke the connection.

"I'm in," he said. He checked his fingers as he spun mist around them, and found his skin intact. He'd get Anne to check him for Iulia tampering too.

Fifteen minutes later, having explained as little as possible, they left Stace with an annoyed Anne. At least she seemed to know what to do.

Drew took them from Anne's living room to Sophie's bedroom. At least, he tried to shift them into Sophie's bedroom.

Mist blocked their view as normal.

Kay squawked. "Don't panic!"

Drew gulped.

Both dragons shrieked.

The mist cleared.

They stood in the alcove with the overhang at the school where Drew had taken Sophie and encountered Mrs. Harris. Claire held one dragon in each hand, and they huddled against her chest.

"Hot dang," Kay said. "She's done something to the house. I wasn't expecting that. We can break through with some effort, I think, but maybe you should just send Claire to the front door."

"Of course this can't be easy," Drew muttered. "If Mrs. Harris sees me, she's going to flip out. Claire, can you go get Sophie, please?"

CHAPTER 43

CLAIRE

Sophie's mother answered the door. She wore a bright green sweater with red leggings and tiny Christmas tree dangly earrings. Voices in another room sounded happy.

Mrs. Harris looked down her nose at Claire and sniffed. "Your boyfriend isn't here." Her lip curled like she smelled something awful. "What are you wearing?"

"Clothing." How someone as pleasant as Sophie could have such a bitchy mom escaped Claire. Maybe Sophie's dad was cool. She hoped Enion and Leeloo stayed still. Her dragon hung around her neck as usual because Mrs. Harris had seen him before. Leeloo clung to Claire's dagger hilt.

"I'm not looking for Drew. I'm looking for Sophie."

"It's Christmas."

"Yeah." Claire shrugged. "And? Does that mean I'm not allowed to visit for some reason?"

Mrs. Harris peered past Claire, probably looking for Drew. "You should be with your own family."

"My family is dead. I guess that's why I don't know about these unspoken rules of holiday etiquette."

"I'm sorry." Mrs. Harris didn't sound sorry. "Sophie isn't available today. You can come back tomorrow."

"Sure thing." Claire turned her back on the woman. She knew she should keep trying, but she'd had enough of the lady's attitude. "Just remember I offered to do this the easy way and you picked the hard way."

As she stepped off the front porch, Mrs. Harris said, "What's that supposed to mean?"

"I hope you can afford home repairs." She plucked Enion from her neck and dropped him.

Enion flashed big. Claire stepped onto his back. Mrs. Harris screamed. The dragon leaped high enough to reach the garage roof and landed on it.

Wishing she had a full-length sword, Claire slammed her dagger into Sophie's window. The blade slid through a layer of magic thick enough to choke a horse, then hit the glass and stabbed through it.

Mrs. Harris made choking noises. Claire cut an X through the window. Enion breathed fire at it, then he shoved the window in with his front claws.

In her bedroom, dressed for adventure in jeans and a sweater, Sophie stared with her eyes wide and gasped. "What....what did you do?"

Claire smirked. "This is a jailbreak. We'll sort things out with your parents later. For now, we need your help to defeat the wicked witch-ghost of the west." She offered Sophie a hand to climb through the gaping hole in the wall.

Sophie took Claire's help and climbed onto the roof.

From the driveway, Mrs. Harris pointed at them. "Young lady, I forbid you to go anywhere!"

"Time to help, Leeloo." Claire patted the other dragon.

Leeloo flashed large and squatted for Sophie to sit on her back. "Leeloo good dragon!"

Sophie put a hand on Leeloo's back, her gaze stuck on her mother. "I...I don't know..."

"If you leave now," Mrs. Harris growled, "don't bother coming back."

Claire leaned toward Sophie. "She's bluffing. Besides, if we don't take down Iulia, there won't be a home to come back to."

Nodding, Sophie slid onto Leeloo's back. She opened her mouth to say something but didn't manage any words before the two dragons launched into the air.

"Not too fast, Enion! Sophie'll freeze to death."

"Leeloo is good dragon," Enion purred.

Leeloo tittered. "Enion good dragon too."

"Yep." Claire patted Enion's neck. "You're both good dragons. You can flirt later."

The two dragons landed on the school grounds, where Drew spun mist and took them to Claire's demesne.

"Oh my god, what did I do?" Sophie slid off Leeloo's back, wrung her hands, and paced.

Claire ignored the angst to command her demesne to bring her the armor and shield they'd made for Sophie. She watched Drew take a step toward Sophie, then take the step back, hold up his hands to reach for her, then make fists and cross his arms.

"Seriously?" Claire rolled her eyes. She intercepted Sophie and held out her hand. A tree branch deposited Sophie's armor there. "Look, Sophie."

Sophie stopped and stared at the armor. She'd requested jeans with a reinforced, shell-pink jacket. Then a different branch handed Claire the round shield. Sophie seemed at a loss for words.

"Focus," Claire said. She shoved the armor and shield at Sophie's chest. "You'll have plenty of time to freak out later. Right now? We need you to change into this stuff, link up with Drew, and get into the right headspace to fight the biggest, baddest ghost ever."

Sophie blinked at her. "You just cut a hole into my bedroom."

"I tried to come in through the front door, but your mom was uncooperative, and we don't have all the time in the world. I know this stuff doesn't seem urgent, but it's only a matter of time now before Iulia figures out we discovered she was using Stace. And things won't get better from there."

"Stace?"

Claire pressed the gear against Sophie's chest and draped an arm around her shoulders. At her command, a nearby tree stretched to the sides, forming a screen so Sophie could change her clothes. When Sophie didn't take the gear, Claire set it on the grass and helped the girl remove her sweater.

"Mom told me to stay, and I left." Sophie barely moved, but she didn't resist as Claire tugged the sweater off her arms.

"Yep. And she didn't do anything but shout at you. That's kind of funny, isn't it? I mean, she's a witch with a fair amount of power. Sure, she barricaded you inside the house and warded it so Drew couldn't get in. But once I cut through her warding, she didn't do anything but panic." Like her daughter, but Claire didn't say that part out loud. "Kind of puts her power into perspective, doesn't it?"

She helped Sophie step out of her shoes, then undid the fly and button for her jeans. "Your mom would be useless against Iulia is what it tells me. All that power, all those witches, and the only things they know how to do are pretty tame. I guess that's why they hate Knights so much."

"What?" Sophie stepped out of her jeans and pulled on the new ones. "We don't hate Knights."

Claire laughed. "Man, they don't tell you anything."

"Corwin was a Knight and he married Jacqueline, a witch, I know that much."

"You know what I noticed about that?" Claire held the jacket for Sophie. "Corwin died young. In his mid-twenties. They didn't live together very long."

Sophie's eyes widened again. She pointed.

When she turned, Claire saw the stag. He stood in a shaft of golden sunlight.

"Sorry," she told the stag. "We don't have time to figure you out right now."

The stag bleated.

"Why does it sound like a goat?" Sophie asked. "It's regal and noble. It should sound like that."

"I don't know. It just does." Claire waited for Sophie to zip up her jacket, but she didn't. She sighed. "If I could wave my hand and give it a human voice, I would, because it's got something to say."

"You can wave your hand and make everything else here do what you want."

"No, I can't." Claire considered bringing up Rondy, but she didn't want to get into that either. "The stag is autonomous. It was an accident."

The stag approached and bleated again.

Sophie touched his head. "He's so soft."

Lowering his head, the stag caught the light with the sharp points of his antlers.

Claire rolled her eyes. "Show off."

"Hey, that's weird." Sophie pointed at the antlers. "They form a heart shape from this angle. Also, there's all these marks all over them. I think I've seen this sort of mark before."

The light faded. Claire peered at the antlers and saw large-scale whorls and dots etched into the horns. She held up her hand and compared them.

"That makes sense," she said. "I mean, I made him."

Something moved too fast for Claire to track. Then an antler point stabbed through the locket face. At first, she felt a sharp stab of pressure. Another second later, it hurt.

"Finally," a man said. "I knew something had to work." His voice reminded Claire of Justin, but not quite. He had the same timbre and tone, but a bit of an Old West twang with a crisp edge. "I'll have you know I died fighting a witch, like my uncle before me. A different witch, of course."

Claire yanked her hand off the antler point. Healing kept her from bleeding much, and now she knew that stabbing the locket face wouldn't kill her. Or kill her body. Whatever.

"What?" Sophie frowned at the stag.

Drew rounded the screen. "Who's there? I don't recognize that voice."

"Corwin. I'm Corwin Evans. The stag, I was in the locket for a long time, and now I'm in a stag. Life is a funny thing. Who knew Jackie's desire to prevent me from becoming a corrupted Phasm would cause so much trouble."

"Wait." Claire didn't want to deal with this right now. She didn't care about anything but the fact of Iulia running free. Except she didn't understand. This confusion would distract her too much. She'd think about it the whole time and miss something important. Like an enchanted baseball bat aimed at her head.

"My dad made me the locket. To save my life."

"No, he *gave* you the locket to save your life. Your father, while a worthy Knight, had no ability to save your life on his own. Jackie made that locket. My will, bound inside it, kept you alive. He loved you too much for me to deny him, even though it meant a great deal of potential for my own demise. Apparently, though, I get to live again. As a stag, of all things. I think my sprite would've found that amusing."

Claire stared at the stag, then her hand. The locket had, until she made the stag, contained the soul of her great-great-great-grandfather, plus or minus one generation. This knowledge didn't help them stop Iulia. If it had been the soul of Iulia's son or something, that might've mattered.

"Okay. Whatever. We have to go save the world. We can all have a nice big family chat when we get back. Or we'll all be dead, in which case, who knows what happens to you."

"I'd prefer if none of you die in this battle, thank you," Corwin said. "As such, I have advice. When fighting witches, which I had to do more times in my life than I preferred, always pay attention to your surroundings. Their power comes from life, which means they can do all kinds of things you don't expect, especially to the landscape. I expect you have some experience fighting ghosts, but the most important thing is to ignore whatever they say, because they always want to knock you off balance with the things they remember."

"That sounds about right," Drew said.

"You, young man," Corwin said, turning to fix Drew with a stern stare, "have gotten yourself into deep waters. In more ways than one. Keep your head on straight. These ladies are counting on you to hold up your part of the fight. Don't let them down."

Drew gulped and nodded. "Yessir."

"Ladies," Corwin said, giving the impression he intended to also scold them. "Go kick some ass. I'd come help if I could."

Claire grinned. Corwin seemed like a decent guy. She wondered if his early death had made keeping the family together more challenging for Jackie.

"I won't wish you luck," Corwin said. "Instead, I'll pray for your victory." He bowed his head and turned to bound into the forest.

"That explains a lot," Claire said. "Or maybe it just makes more questions. Whatever. Let's go collect some Knights and pick a fight."

CHAPTER 44

DREW

As planned, Drew took them to St. Francis to wait for Justin and Avery. They brought Enion, Rhubark, and Rondy. No one knew if Rondy could leave the demesne, so Drew tried to bring him. The elder Knight ghost stood on the sidewalk, his body made of mist and emitting a golden glow around his shiny, green-tinted plate armor.

He'd attempted to include Corwin, just to see if he could. No such luck. They didn't trust Leeloo against Iulia, and left the rest of the dragons behind to make sure she didn't do anything crazy.

The city still had no sunshine, with weak light filtering through the dark cloud overhead. The street glowed with pools of yellow from the streetlights. Drew thought the darkness above swirled, but no one else seemed to notice. At least no ash fell today.

"I've never been to Portland," Rondy said. He scuffed his metal boot on the ash-covered concrete. "It's...darker and dirtier than I expected."

Claire snorted.

"Oh, he's a laugh riot," Kay said.

Drew smirked and saw Rondy grin. "Iulia is south and east of us." As he turned to look in that direction, he caught sight of Avery's car, followed by Tariel, both bringing their Knights up the street. Avery didn't bother getting out of his car. Tariel stopped beside the group.

"Are we as ready as we're going to get?" Justin sat on the horse with his back straight and his cloak tossed over one shoulder. Since he hadn't shaved in a few days, he reminded Drew even more of an action hero than ever.

"Almost." Drew offered a hand to Sophie.

She glanced at Claire as if afraid of an incoming punch to the face. Claire gestured for them to get on with it. Drew clicked his aura with Sophie's. As before, the connection touched him more than the one he'd forged with Stace. That first time hadn't been a fluke or inexperience. Their auras meshed. He felt complete.

Thank goodness he hadn't tried to consume her power.

Sophie squeezed his hand.

"Okay. Now we're ready." Drew spun mist and let the node guide him.

The mist cleared with the group in front of a familiar house. Nothing seemed amiss in front of Anne's home. Leafless trees swayed and creaked in a stiff, chill wind. Ash eddies flitted through the air.

Claire patted his shoulder. "Are you sure about this?"

He shrugged. "This is where the node thinks she is. I don't know what that means. Maybe it's tracking Stace?"

"If that's the case, maybe we can use Stace to find her." Justin climbed off Tariel's back and strode to the front door. He rang the bell.

Drew wanted to object to the frontal approach, but there was no point. Knights surrounded him. He had no chance of convincing all four of them to scout the house and backyard first.

The door opened. Faint buzzing echoed in Drew's ears, and his skin crawled. He wanted to rush into the building and run from it at the same time. Beside him, Claire hugged herself. Rondy pulled his sword and scowled at the building.

"I don't know what that is," Kay grumbled, "but I don't like it."

"It's Iulia," Drew murmured. "She's affecting ghosts."

"I hate her so hard," Claire said.

No one appeared in the doorway. Justin peered through the door. Avery joined him and touched his shoulder, getting Justin to step back.

"I shouldn't have come." Rondy sheathed his sword with a collection of forced movements. "I'm a threat to you all."

"She's calling," Claire whispered.

Kay groaned.

White haze clouded Drew's vision. He pushed down his glasses, thinking they'd fogged, but nothing changed.

"Resist," Sophie hissed.

Inside his head, Kay howled like a wolf baying at the moon. "Go into the house." His voice sounded coarse and strained. "Do it now or I'll force you into the corner."

Sophie gripped the front of his jacket and forced him to look at her instead of the house. "Listen to me, Kay. We're not going into that house. If you try anything against Drew, you'll have to deal with me."

The house exploded. Drew and Sophie turned in time to see Justin and Avery flying through the air, chased by broken wood and bits of insulation. The ceiling blew upward and the walls flew outward. Claire stood with her arms outstretched, offering an open invitation to the pain.

Rondy dropped to one knee and crossed himself. The two tiny dragons cowered at Claire's feet.

Drew tackled Claire to the ground. Sophie came with him. Grass grew so fast he heard it crackling with life.

"What are you doing?" Drew shouted at Claire.

"Hoping to clear my mind."

Pain tended to do that, he supposed. Drew lifted his head and pushed grass aside to see Anne and Stace standing on the bare foundation of Anne's house. Yellow energy crackled in Anne's hands, and copper glowed around Anne.

Behind them, Dwight brandished two copper baseball bats. He stood nine feet tall, with bulging muscles thicker than Drew's waist and solid copper covering his entire body from head to toe. Every inch of him vibrated with Iulia's pure, clear power. The house might've blown apart because he sneezed or stomped his foot.

"This isn't what I expected," Drew murmured.

"Yeah," Claire said. She sounded distracted.

Justin and Avery scraped themselves off the ground. Avery's car revved its engine. Tariel pawed the ground with a low, dangerous whinny.

Sophie wove Drew's power in complicated webs, forging a barrier around the three of them and Rondy. The dragons flashed large and leaped out of the protected area.

Drew's head felt like Kay punched his skull from the inside. "Get up, boy!" Kay shouted. "Get your ass over there or I'll get it over there for you."

"We're not doing that, Kay." Drew said. He didn't know how to keep all the ghosts in his life from following Iulia's compulsion to join her. Having Kay swing through his brain like a wrecking ball didn't help. One thing came to mind as warmth trickled from his nose.

Drew shucked his jacket, exposed his elbow, and pressed Claire's locket to his brand. Her heartbeat, erratic and too fast, filled his being.

Kay wrapped himself around Drew's consciousness, throttling him and making his head throb.

"You're bleeding from your ears," Sophie said.

He didn't care. "Listen to me, Claire. We need you. We're all bound to you, one way or another, and Iulia is trying to dominate us by radiating a compulsion. I don't understand any of this, but we need you to resist and take control. Control us, Claire. Be my mistress. I meant it as a joke before. I mean for real now. This battle is between you and Iulia, and you're fighting over me and everyone else. This is all up to you."

"Why is everything always so damned hard?" Claire ground her teeth. She met Drew's gaze with a glare. "Drew is mine. Kay, sit down and shut up."

Something slapped Drew's head from the inside. He groaned. Sophie squeaked. Kay yelped.

"What the—" Kay sounded more like himself.

While Kay expressed confusion with a litany of cursing, Claire wriggled out of Drew's grasp to accost Rondy. Drew held his head. Sophie wiped blood from his cheek.

"What should I do?" Sophie whispered.

"Whatever you can to help kick Iulia's damned ass," Kay growled.

"Seconded." Drew planted the end of his staff on the ground and used it to stand. He pushed the grass aside and saw Justin on his hands and knees, throwing up at Anne's feet. Avery faced animated trees with Tariel's help. Stace seemed to control the trees.

Dwight watched everything with a lazy, arrogant smirk.

As little as Drew wanted to harm Anne, he judged her the bigger threat for the moment. They needed Justin.

"Let's go." Rondy clapped Drew on the arm. He and Claire rushed Dwight.

Sophie bolstered the grass to help the pair converge on Dwight without having to climb the steps, dodge debris, or worry about the floor caving under their feet.

Drew held out his hand and blasted Anne with a crackling bolt of blue lightning. The bolt knocked her off her feet and sent her flying into a tree. She hit with a thud and fell to the ground, smoke rising from her hair. Justin stopped barfing and staggered to his feet.

Dwight's smirk twisted into a snarl. Claire and Rondy reached him. Metal clanged against metal as Dwight caught both their weapons with his bats. He'd learned more about fighting since they last met.

"Fight Stace for control of the trees," Drew muttered to Sophie. He didn't dare attack Stace. If he tried, he knew he wouldn't hold back, not like with Anne.

"Do you have any idea how hard it is to fight off that infernal woman?" Kay growled. "She doesn't get to stake a claim on us."

"No, she doesn't." Drew pushed with his will, shoving against Dwight. Dwight slid backward an inch, then Iulia's power blocked him. He saw the force ripple from Dwight and through Claire and Rondy with no effect on them. Clear, burning magical energy punched through his silver-blue wave, dispersing it with ease.

Iulia's magic manifested as a wall of force that slammed into him and knocked him off his feet. He hit the ground. Searing pain split his fingers. He lifted his hand to see his blood spraying into the air.

The hook.

He'd thought it meant nothing. Sophie hadn't noticed anything in his aura. Claire hadn't felt anything strange. Anne hadn't seen anything.

His blood drifted upward and winked like tiny stars.

"I'm getting us out of here!" Kay shouted.

CHAPTER 45

CLAIRE

Dwight swung his bats. Rondy caught one swing with his sword. Claire ducked under the other swing and threw her body at Dwight, hoping to use his size against him. She hit his leg and stabbed his thigh. His armor cracked, but not enough.

Nearby, dragon fire blazed, setting trees alight.

Dwight shoved Rondy backward and brought both bats down, aiming for Claire's head. Justin caught the blows with his sword, knocking them aside.

"You're not going to win this time." Justin slashed across Dwight's chest. His blade cut through the armor, exposing Dwight's T-shirt.

Claire rolled in a somersault to get behind Dwight. She didn't want to stay between Justin and his father, and the more angles of attack they used, the better. Besides, her dagger worked best when jammed into someone's back.

"Ungrateful brat," Dwight spat. "You'll give me my due." He cracked one bat against Justin's shoulder. The other hit Rondy's sword.

Justin staggered to the side. Rondy kicked Dwight's knee. Dwight stumbled a step. Claire slammed her dagger into his back. The blade cracked his armor again.

As Claire wrenched her dagger free to hit him again, Dwight's armor bulged with a lump at the small of his back. Dwight didn't seem to notice. He kept whacking at Justin and Rondy with his bat.

Her own face sneered at her as a reflection in copper. Confused and horrified, Claire watched two hands thrust toward her. Lightning crackled between them.

Iulia cackled. The lightning pulsed like it would leap from Iulia's hands. Claire cringed, expecting pain. Light flashed, and the lightning flowed in a different direction. It sizzled through the air, between Justin and Rondy and touching neither.

The lighting plunged into a cloud of swirling mist where Drew had been. Iulia receded, the mist vanished, and Claire couldn't see Drew or Sophie anymore.

Claire knew, without a doubt, that Iulia had entered her demesne. Bright, sharp pain on top of her head cracked her skull open and knocked her to the ground. Someone shouted her name.

In her demesne, her injuries healed faster. In her demesne, a group of ordinary people, all of them her family, had no defense from Iulia but Drew and Sophie.

She called Enion and let the locket take them home. Justin, Rondy, and Avery would have to handle Dwight.

Between one eyeblink and the next, the scenery changed to her forest. Enion helped her sit up with a large claw on her back. Her head healed.

"What the hell?" Drew said. He sounded close.

"Interesting," Iulia said.

Thunder boomed. Drew groaned. Sophie shrieked.

Claire scrambled to her feet and ran for the noise. This place belonged to her. Iulia didn't get to come to her demesne and break things. Missy and Lisa wouldn't be drawn into this fight. Neither would Marie or Grandma and Grandpa.

She sprinted with her dagger in hand. Enion ran beside her. Claire swatted trees aside until she had a direct line of sight to Iulia.

Iulia stood in full color as a being made of mist with acute definition. Unlike the last time Claire had seen her, she wore a loose, sleeveless red dress with a white lace veil over her dark hair. She stood with her back to Claire, her arms outstretched toward Drew and Sophie. Lightning arced between her hands and a brilliant, white-hot ball of light halfway between her and Drew.

Sophie mirrored her pose. Drew stood with her, his body an echo of hers from behind and his hands over hers. Together, they met Iulia's jagged energy with sleek, smooth lines of sky-blue tinted silver.

At Claire's command, grass formed a springboard for her. She bounced off it. Enion leaped with her. They crashed into Iulia from behind. Lightning scored the ground and blasted trees.

"Nice of you to join us, Claire." Iulia kicked to free herself.

Claire punched her in the shoulder. Iulia dispersed around Claire's fist to re-form on her feet. She peeled in half to avoid a blast of fire from Enion.

Not sure she understood what she saw, Claire stared as Iulia split into pieces and came together to evade Enion's claws. She sidestepped another blast of lightning from Drew and Sophie. Drew swung his staff. Iulia slid around it.

"I look forward to taking control of this charming demesne from you," Iulia said.

In the distance, Claire saw Marie scooping Missy into her arms and taking her to hide. The sight snapped her out of her shock.

"You can't do that," Claire snarled. She hopped to her feet. "This is my demesne."

Iulia laughed as she dodged another blow from Drew's staff. "Not for long."

"What do I do?" Sophie whispered.

"Give up and get out," Iulia said. She raised a hand and blasted Sophie with pure force while also parting to evade Claire's dagger, slipping out of the path of Enion's fire, and hopping over Drew's sweeping staff.

Force slammed Sophie to the ground and kept her there. She groaned and squirmed to no effect.

Claire had no idea how Iulia managed to do so many different things at once. How did she even pay attention to four enemies, let alone keep them all busy?

Still holding down Sophie, Iulia caught Drew's staff. "I'll take that." She whipped it out of Drew's inexperienced hands and clubbed him with it. Drew staggered to the side. Claire slashed through the air, missing Iulia again.

Instead of continuing to use the staff, Iulia tossed it aside. She reached for Drew and lifted him without touching him.

"This feels familiar, doesn't it?" She squeezed her hand. Drew pawed at his neck and struggled to breathe. Sky-blue flared around his neck as he did everything he could to keep her from crushing his neck. "I see you have a great deal more power now, which is admirable, but I've learned from my mistakes."

Claire stopped trying to cut Iulia. They needed another option. Something Iulia wouldn't see coming. A diversion.

"Let them go and I'll give your body back!"

"No!" Drew gasped.

Claire flung her dagger aside and held out an arm to stop Enion. "Let them both go and I give up."

Without letting up on either Drew or Sophie, Iulia laughed. "I don't believe you. Little girl, I watched you sacrifice your life so Justin could kill Caius. I watched you sacrifice yourself so Drew could kill me. I don't think you understand the meaning of the word 'surrender,' which makes this a ploy."

"Maybe." Claire crossed her arms to make her hands stop shaking. She didn't know how far she'd have to go with a bluff to convince Iulia to drop her guard. "On the other hand, maybe I'm willing to let this body fall to the ground and die just so you can't have it."

Iulia turned, her eyes narrowed. "I don't believe that either."

"Hey, it's a new world, right? Without a seal getting in the way, I'll be fine as just a soul." The words tumbled out of her mouth with so much bravado Claire thought she might have to follow through. She already knew she could fake being human well enough to pass. Not having a real body would suck, but if it helped them destroy Iulia, she could deal. Like Iulia said, she'd let herself die for less.

Drew's struggles weakened. Tendrils of smoke rose from Sophie's body. The power of thousands of ghosts battered them, and they couldn't last much longer.

"And after I get my body back, all of you hunt me and kill me? I don't think I'm going to let that happen. Like I said, I've learned from my mistakes."

"Suit yourself. I'm just going back to the other side, where I'm going to drop your body someplace. You'll never find it in time. See ya."

Claire left her demesne to the sound of Iulia's horrified shriek. She stepped into the plaza around Skidmore Fountain and waited. Either Iulia would come to face her, or Drew and Sophie would die. She liked her odds, though. Iulia wanted her body a lot more than she wanted anything else.

She tested her hold on Iulia's body, wondering if she really could leave it of her own free will. Holding up her hand, she stared at the locket. When Caius had bound it to her, he'd made it part of her heart. Now it lived in her hand. Corwin had stabbed the locket, so she knew that wouldn't kill her. Cutting off her hand sounded awful. She had cut herself with the dagger, so she knew it wouldn't harm her worse than making her bleed.

When she'd stood in front of St. Francis, she'd felt a pull more powerful than anything she'd ever encountered elsewhere. She knew it had been the attraction all ghosts feel for churches. Maybe the mixed sensations had come from her being more than an ordinary ghost. As a soul, maybe she had the power to resist, or couldn't find rest there.

Claire needed her dragon. She focused on his line of silver and yanked it hard enough to snap the line taut.

Enion appeared and fell to the cobblestones with a squawk. He held her dagger in his jaws because she had the best dragon ever.

Before he recovered, she took the blade and climbed onto his back. "Take me to Saint Francis. I have an idea."

CHAPTER 46

DREW

Iulia's rage-filled scream hurt Drew's ears. Compared to the pressure on his neck, of course, it was nothing. He knew he didn't intend to let Iulia kill them, and he suspected he needed to stall her so Claire could set up whatever brilliant idea she had. Or come up with one. He didn't believe for one moment that she'd let Iulia's body die so she had to wander as a ghost for the rest of eternity.

Iulia tossed Drew aside and spun. The huge column of force holding Sophie down stopped.

Sophie groaned.

Drew sat up and gasped for air. He thought to ask stupid questions, to distract Iulia from whatever she planned to do next. When he opened his mouth, he made a hoarse croaking noise.

"That'll heal," Kay said. "Give it time."

Iulia ran to the spot where Claire disappeared and stood with her back to them. She spread her arms and looked at the sky. Nothing happened.

Four dragons in their large size charged toward Iulia. Drew had the feeling Leeloo led and the other three dragons pursued. Enion had probably given orders for them to keep her restrained.

"Leeloo!" Iulia set her hands on her hips. "What are you doing here? I gave you a job to do!"

Leeloo slowed and stopped, tilting her head to the side. The other three dragons piled on her. After a moment of confused staring from twenty feet away, Leeloo launched into a storm of chatter. Her dragon escorts didn't stop her.

"I don't care," Iulia snapped. "I'll control them all when we succeed against these children. They'll do what you want, not what Enion wants. Now come over here and help me find a way out of this wretched place."

Leeloo chirped at her.

"Don't be stupid," Iulia snapped.

Letting her head droop, Leeloo submitted to the other dragons.

Drew thought he recognized Rhubark releasing Leeloo and stepping forward, except Rhubark had stayed behind to help with Dwight. The dragons all looked so similar, and this one held himself with a particular gravitas. Tomako? Maybe. He'd ask Claire later.

Iulia rolled her eyes, waved a hand, and flung a blast of power at him. Tomako ducked and rolled. He breathed fire at her. The flames licked around Iulia's edges without harming here.

"Oh, please. As if I wouldn't protect myself against dragon fire. Go play with your friends. I'll deal with all of you later."

Beyond her, Drew saw Corwin. He stood in a shaft of golden light, sparkling motes swirling and glittering against his antlers.

"Iulia. You will not leave until I allow it." He sounded stately and grand, like a king issuing a proclamation.

"Is that so?" Iulia pointed at Corwin and blasted him with more raw power than Drew had ever seen outside of the Portland node.

Corwin lowered his head and caught the blast with his antlers. The force shoved him backward by an inch.

"Jeepers," Kay said. "He's buying you time, dumbass. Get up and use it."

Drew scrambled to his hands and knees. He crawled to Sophie's side and helped her sit. "We have to help him," he whispered. The pain in his throat receded. "Claire needs time."

Sophie brushed her hair out of her face with both hands. "She can beat us."

"Yeah. But not while also dealing with him. Attack her."

Shaking her head and covering her face, Sophie leaned toward him. "I don't know how to attack anything. Nurturing and growing. That's what I can do."

Drew gulped. When Claire needed to stall someone, she put her body in their way. Sophie couldn't do that, and neither could he.

"Don't be a moron," Kay said. "Of course you can. The problem is that Iulia is a ghost. She doesn't have a physical form. Golly, I wonder what affects things without a physical form? Could it be all those weapons we spent so much time forging? Hey, look, she chucked your staff over there."

The staff lay in the grass a few dozen steps from Drew and Sophie. Tomako picked it up in his claws, his gaze fixed on Drew.

"Sophie, can you protect me while I try to whack her with a stick?"

She lifted her hands and blinked at him. "Maybe?"

"Dammit, girl!" Kay snapped. "No wonder no one thinks you can do anything. *You* don't think you can do anything. Get up and get it done."

Drew knew the feeling of incompetence. Claire had helped him overcome it. This time, he had to help Sophie overcome it. He scrambled to his feet and ran for the staff.

"I've never—"

Kay huffed. "I don't care! Do you think she's going to just let us all go with a la di da once she gets her body back? Iulia is a ruthless bitch, and she's not going to stop until we're all dead and she gets what she wants. Get on your feet, girl. I, for one, have no intention of dying today."

With or without Sophie's help, Drew charged Iulia. Tomako charged with him. Even with a dragon beside him, pure terror throbbed in Drew's veins. At least if he died, he'd go down with a friend. Then he remembered Iulia could do worse than killing him.

"You see that? Drew already knows the stakes. He's been here before."

Drew didn't let his chilling thoughts stop him. He reached Iulia with Tomako. But like Kay said, she didn't have a physical presence. Drew's staff slammed into her, but his body ran through her. Frigid cold threatened to rip away his breath and freeze his fingertips to brittle ice.

Tomako roared in defiance and leaped clear.

Iulia shrieked and fell forward. Her fountain of power flared and hit the ground. Claire's demesne resisted it, showing no sign of damage from the attack. Sophie grunted. A thin layer of silvery blue settled around Drew. Though he still stood partway in Iulia's ghost, the chill faded from his body.

"Attagirl," Kay said.

Drew scored another solid impact across Iulia's back.

"Move aside!"

Stumbling out of the way, Drew watched Corwin gallop at Iulia. He lowered his head, aiming his antlers at her. Iulia recoiled, her misty form leaving the ground. Drew swung his staff to prevent her escape.

As the staff hit, Iulia exploded with power. Drew held his staff in front of him. The silvery blue field surrounding him writhed and flickered. Sophie groaned. Strength drained from Drew's body.

Tomako stood behind him, providing his girth to resist the force.

"You're not powerful enough," Iulia growled.

Though she'd dumped more power than Drew could comprehend, she pumped out more and more. Devouring all those ghosts had given her an incredible, mind-boggling reservoir.

All four claws braced in the dirt, Tomako slid backward with Drew. Glancing aside, Drew saw Corwin losing ground too.

"Iulia!" Drew didn't know what else to do except ask her stupid questions. "Why did you forge a copy of your journal? Didn't you realize we'd figure that out?"

She laughed. "You didn't figure it out until much, much too late, little boy."

"Where's the real one?"

"You'll never find it."

"But then how will I craft a seal to replace yours?"

The power increased enough to shove Drew several steps. "You? You're just a boy. You need a pathetic, powerless little girl to do anything more complicated than pulling up your pants."

If he wanted to listen to insults, he could ask Kay. Worse, he didn't think they could do anything to her except deflect what she threw. "Corwin, let her go. It's time."

Iulia squawked and disappeared. The power evaporated. In its absence, Drew fell forward. Tomako caught him. Sophie collapsed. Corwin raised his head.

"I'm okay," Sophie said between gasps for breath.

"I'm not sure I agree with letting her out, but we clearly weren't winning." Corwin walked with Drew to Sophie's side. "I don't know what else we could've done here."

Tomako dipped his head in a bow, then rejoined the cluster of dragons.

Drew waved to the dragons, eager to keep them friendly. "Yeah. That was kind of my thought. Like, we needed an extra two witches, or a Knight or five. Or both."

"That...that... *woman*." Sophie took Drew's help to sit and screwed her face into an angry grimace. "I don't like Iulia at all."

"She certainly is a handful," Corwin said. "I wonder what Claire will do? Iulia has to be defeated. There's no option for failure against her."

Drew sighed and shook his head. "No, there isn't. I can find Claire pretty quick, at least. I don't know if Iulia can."

"Assume she can," Corwin said.

"Right." Drew helped Sophie stand. "We still come back to the question of how to destroy her. Even if we have all our Knights, plus Sophie, Kay, and me, I still don't see how we can defeat her."

Corwin shook his head. "Then don't. Find another way. You two should get going. Claire needs you."

Somehow, they had to destroy Iulia without defeating her. Sure. No problem. Maybe they could regale her with song and dance or challenge her to a chess match.

Drew hoped Claire had a brilliant idea that didn't involve slitting her own throat, because he had nothing.

334

CHAPTER 47

JUSTIN

Claire's disappearance worried Justin, but he had other problems. The copper armor healed itself. The metal prevented both him and Rondy from cutting into the ghost itself, then the damned stuff refilled the gaps before either of them could take advantage and stab the ghost inside.

At least Claire's new armor helped them absorb the blows better. Rondy's plate armor deflected well enough, and Justin's chainmail cushioned the impacts.

Fire burned the trees on Anne's property, thanks to the dragons. No, one dragon. Claire had taken Enion with her. He hoped she'd gone to do something constructive for the situation. Drew and Sophie had also left.

"I thought he didn't have fight training," Rondy said as he ducked under a swing.

Dwight laughed. "Like that matters. You're both useless. All your allies left. They must know how pointless this fight is. Give up already. You always do, in the end."

Justin clenched his jaws at he watched his father's ghost. The ass had made himself big enough for Justin to feel like an eight-year-old. He remembered the old man smacking the back of his head while he ate cereal. He'd hit the bowl and splatter cereal and milk all over the table and himself, which had given Dwight an excuse to get his favorite belt. Not that he'd ever needed an excuse.

The memory of that damned belt buckle made Justin scowl. "I'm not a kid anymore," he spat. "You don't scare me."

"Don't lie to me, boy." Dwight stomped his foot, causing the house foundation to jump.

Rondy and Justin fell to the ground. A dragon roared. Avery shouted something Justin didn't understand. Dwight slammed the ends of both bats into Rondy's armor. Justin rolled to his feet.

Kurt had done worse while teaching him to fight.

Kurt wouldn't save him this time.

No one would save him.

He slashed at Dwight's knee. A bat hit him in the chest and forced him back long enough for the copper to heal itself. This fight needed something. Justin caught a flash of white in the firelight. Tariel couldn't find a way to help or she would've been in the thick of this since it started.

Riding a horse would give him some elevation. He could look down at Dwight instead of the other way around.

Justin sprinted toward his horse. "Tariel!"

She turned and lowered her hindquarters. Without breaking his stride, he leaped onto her back and heaved himself into the saddle.

"Do you have a plan?" Tariel asked.

"Yes." Justin patted her neck. "Just like always."

"So this is a detailed plan with contingencies." She faced Dwight and pawed the ground with a defiant snort.

Under the circumstances, he didn't begrudge her the sarcasm. "Back up. Give yourself some room."

"And leave Rondy by himself?"

They watched Dwight use both bats to slam Rondy across the yard. Without Justin there to provide a distraction, the elder Knight hadn't stood a chance.

"He's not here for Rondy."

"Right." Tariel backed into the street. "Shall we get some speed?"

"What could possibly go wrong?" Justin pointed his sword at his father's ghost and used his free hand to beckon Dwight forward. "Come and get me, asshole."

"And here I thought you'd laid all your issues with him to rest." Tariel reared in challenge, pivoted, and darted up the street.

"All but this one where he showed up as a ghost and now wants to wear my body like a suit. Like any loving father would."

"Such ego," Tariel said.

"He'd probably take Avery's body instead if he had the chance, but Avery is so old."

"Yes, mid-forties is horrifyingly old."

"He's almost twice my age."

Behind them, Dwight roared. The trees shook. Streetlights exploded in showers of sparks.

Justin remembered running from Dwight and hiding in the basement. Later, the beating had been worse than if he'd stood and taken it.

"He's confused about how to express affection," Tariel said as she slowed to a stop and turned to face him.

"Yes, that's it. I'm sure of it. He just wants to tell me how much he loves me. How could I possibly have misinterpreted him for so long?" Justin snorted and raised his sword.

The man he faced had made his childhood hell. Dwight had probably been beaten by his own father. Maybe his mother had been cold or distant, but Justin didn't care.

The why wouldn't bring back Justin's mother.

He'd escaped and learned from better men, and this piece of crap wouldn't hurt anyone else, ever again.

"Run him down. Put him on the ground and don't let him up."

"With pleasure." Tariel lurched into a charge.

Justin held Tariel's reins and reveled in the glory of bearing down on his demon. Tariel's hooves rang on the asphalt, chiming like righteous thunder.

He saw Dwight holding his belt, caressing the buckle, relishing another chance to beat him. He saw his mother, lying on the floor, bleeding from her mouth and eye. He saw his own blood on the wall.

Racing to destroy Dwight's ghost, rage boiled out of his mouth in a battle cry.

Dwight braced for the impact, his bats held ready.

Tariel crashed into the coppery giant. Justin held his sword as it slammed into Dwight's armor. Dwight's eyes widened as Tariel propelled herself forward and knocked him over. She kicked his chest on the way down. He hit the ground and lost his grip on both bats. Tariel stomped his chest again.

Justin leaped off her back, sword pointed down, and slammed the blade through the armor with all his weight.

The armor crumbled. Pieces hit the street. Tariel stomped Dwight.

"Die again," Tariel snarled.

Ready for all this to end, Justin heaved his body against the sword again, shoving it through Dwight's body until it hit asphalt.

Dwight gurgled and spasmed. "She promised." His voice faded.

Justin yanked out the sword and sliced across his father's body. He watched the mist fray and discorporate.

"Good riddance."

CHAPTER 48

CLAIRE

Claire hesitated with her hand on the door at the church. As before, St. Francis felt welcoming and foreboding at the same time. Ethereal music beckoned, urging her to fling herself inside.

Enion stood behind her, keeping watch for Iulia. "Place feels funny."

"Yeah. I need to go inside, but I don't want to."

"Leave. Get carrots."

"It's the only way I can think of to defeat Iulia."

Enion sighed. "No more ghosts. Too much fight."

"Yeah. That's what I want." Maybe, Claire thought, when Drew got his hands on Iulia's real journal, they'd make a new seal. Or maybe the world needed ghosts. They'd have to think about it and talk it over with other people. Ki might have a worthwhile opinion, and he'd appreciate being asked instead of having constraints placed on him without his consent.

Enion hissed. "Iulia."

"Don't be hasty, Claire."

Claire turned to see Iulia at the bottom of the steps, with her hands raised as if she thought she could talk Claire into surrendering. Her dress fluttered with a breeze Claire didn't feel.

Enion breathed fire at Iulia. As she had in the demesne, Iulia split into parts to avoid it.

"Don't bother." Claire patted Enion's neck.

The dragon shut his mouth and glared at Iulia.

"I'm glad you can see reason." Iulia raised her hands and took a step closer.

Claire raised her dagger and regarded it. "You know, it's occurred to me that I can screw you completely by slitting my own throat. Actually, I guess it's your own throat."

"And then what?" Iulia stopped with her foot on the bottom step. "I can dominate you, and you know it. I have so much more power at my disposal than you do, it's laughable. Come, Claire. Abandon my body. You can stay a spirit if you want."

Could she drag Drew to her side the same way she'd done with Enion? She didn't know. Would Sophie come with him? If she didn't, would the distance between them cripple Drew?

At least she could feel that Drew still lived. He knew how to find her, so she only had to stall Iulia long enough to let him recover from whatever else Iulia might have done to him and arrive.

"You know what's funny? You claim you can dominate me, you have tons of power, and blah, blah, blah. But you haven't tried yet. I figure I'm probably at my most ghosty in my own demesne, but you didn't even make a move when I tackled you. It's almost like you're not as sure as you want me to believe."

"Oh, Claire." Iulia sighed, sounding aggrieved to have to consider such lowly matters. "There's so much you still don't know. If you were willing to learn, I could teach you. After all, I am your ancestor."

"Yes, you are. On both sides. Not that it matters much anymore. I mean, that body is gone." Claire shrugged and raised the knife to her neck. She tried to keep her grip loose so her hand wouldn't shake. "I've been thinking, though. That must've taken a lot of manipulation on Caius's part to make happen. I wonder if he expected my little brother to become some kind of ultimate Knight or something."

"He was never that smart." Iulia waved to dismiss the idea. "All blunt force with no finesse. Such subterfuge was beyond him, even over millennia."

"Sure. I get that. I met him, and he was kind of a jerk. Maybe not as bad as you want everyone to believe, but definitely not a good guy." Since Iulia seemed to play along, Claire pointed the dagger at her. "You, on the other hand? That's right up your alley."

Iulia raised her brow. "Are you suggesting I manipulated the bloodlines while I was crucified and tormented in the Ordeal?"

"No." Claire peered at her and took a leap of logic. "I'm suggesting you weren't crucified and tormented for two millennia like you appeared to be and claimed."

Iulia crossed her arms and fixed Claire with a steady, annoyed stare. "And what makes you think that?"

Claire had to think about it. She didn't know where that idea had come from. "Thinking back to when I found you, I have to say that you didn't seem very upset or traumatized. I mean, I could see becoming kind of numb to it, but you weren't numb. You were clear, coherent, and ready to kick Caius in the butt."

"The fact I'm strong enough—"

"Yeah, strong enough. You're really powerful. Like, a lot. I didn't quite grasp how much power you have until I saw you handle both Drew and Sophie at the same time. Now, maybe you were constrained by whatever you had to do to stay alive all this time without aging, because without your body, you've really been able to accomplish a lot. It's pretty amazing."

"You're so very clever," Iulia said. She took another step.

Claire backed against the door. If she could get Iulia inside, she knew something positive would happen. But where was Drew? She thought she'd stood with Iulia for a long time. He had to have recovered. "Drew has a theory that the trap you set at the school was supposed to hit me, and the one at Skidmore was supposed to hit him, but you accounted for the possibility we'd swap."

"He's a smart young man." Iulia's gaze flicked to Claire's locket hand.

With that hand, Iulia might control Drew and the dragons. Claire didn't think it would work that way, not this time. Corwin didn't live in the locket anymore, and Claire only animated this body. The locket had served its purpose, and now offered nothing more than a way to think about the connection between herself and Drew.

Looking at it that way, she considered whether or not she needed to touch the locket to his brand for any reason at all. Maybe she could reach Drew and Kay by wanting it enough.

Claire nodded. "Yes, he is. Why did you decide to get rid of Caius? What's the real reason? Since I know you didn't hate him as much as you claimed."

Iulia's eyes flashed with anger. "I absolutely despised him. He took me from my family, he cost me the chance for a daughter, and he claimed all the glory for everything the rest of us did. He didn't know the meaning of fidelity, didn't care about anyone but himself, and turned our sons into copies of himself. That egotistical, arrogant ass murdered my unicorn and tried to murder my dragon."

Claire still saw no sign of Drew. She knew she could count on him, but maybe not for this.

"He took everything from me, and I still propped him up on that thrice-damned pedestal of heroism for the glory of Rome." Iulia patted her chest with both hands. "Not once—*not even once!*—did he so much as thank me for everything I did for him."

"So you killed him."

Iulia lifted her chin. "I did no such thing. He died of some sort of wasting sickness at the age of one hundred and twenty-three. The second time, Justin killed him. I've never killed anyone. Unlike you, who killed me."

"Actually, Drew killed you. I wound up in here by accident." She gripped the door handle and yanked it open. The music increased in volume. From the way Iulia shivered, she heard it too.

Mist formed in the middle of the street. Drew had come, but Claire didn't need his help anymore.

She stepped backward, hoping Iulia failed to resist the lure of both her body and the siren call of the church. Her heel hit the threshold.

"So why destroy the seal? You created it, didn't you? What's the difference between Caius at the center and me at the center?"

Why did she ask? To distract Iulia? No, to stall. She didn't want to know what happened inside the church. If it meant her final rest, she wanted to delay that as long as possible. That made her a coward. To destroy Caius, she'd willingly sacrificed herself. It had sucked, but she'd done it.

Now she had to do it again. For Drew. For Justin. For Marie, Missy, Lisa, Tammy, Jack, Avery, and everyone else she knew. And for Sophie, who would make Drew happy enough if she could handle his quirks. It still sucked, but she'd still do it. Given a choice between failing to stop Iulia and dying, Claire chose dying. Again. Always.

Because she was a girl and a Knight.

Eyes wide with awe and fear, Iulia reached for her. She missed by a foot, her fingers clawing in empty space. "Claire," she whispered. "It's my body."

"Not anymore." Claire looked past her to Drew and tried to tell him without words that she loved him. She tried to give him permission to turn to Sophie for comfort.

She turned and ran inside the church, falling into the warm, melodious embrace.

Her vision blanked with white. She didn't hit the floor. Instead, she ran into someone.

He wore a park ranger uniform with a sword belted at his waist. Mark Terdan turned and faced her with a sad smile. "Hi, Pumpkin."

Claire knew her father's face. She'd seen him as a ghost and in that photograph. This meeting meant she died. Again. Frowning at him, she tried to figure out what to say. Nothing came to mind.

Mark brushed his knuckles down the side of her face. "You're so grown up. I worried you'd never make it, even with that locket."

Still unsure what to say, Claire held up her hand and let him see the locket.

"So clever. Walk with me." He reached for her hand.

"I don't remember you," she blurted.

"No, of course not. You're not really here, and you're not really there." Mark shook his head. "So much fear. Afraid of everything that comes with claiming that body for yourself. Afraid of dying. Afraid of letting down your new family. Afraid of what you've done. Afraid of failing."

Claire didn't understand. Except she did. Her body lay in a hole, its flesh blue and rubbery. The one she wore didn't belong to her. She'd stolen it. The owner wanted it back. Letting Iulia have it meant staying a spirit. Forever. This life she thought she had, she'd only borrowed.

"It's so simple, Pumpkin, but you still don't see it."

"I don't understand."

He sighed. "I don't suppose you do. You've danced on the edge of a choice without making it for about a month. Just keep moving, right? You're a Knight, and Knights plow forward at all costs." Setting his hand on her shoulder, he met her gaze. His eyes filled with silver tears. "Either it's Iulia's body or it's your body. Choose. Decide. Don't just bobble along with whatever happens.

"If you let Iulia take her body, your friends can kill her inside the church, and her ghost will be done. If you don't let Iulia take your body, you can stab her inside the church and her ghost will be done. This choice isn't about saving the world or defeating Iulia, or however else you want to frame it. This is about you, and only you."

"I don't know," Claire murmured. She liked living. It had a lot of drawbacks, though. Maybe Drew needed her gone so he could have his bacon and eat it too. Wandering as a spirit forever sounded great, until she considered that everyone she cared about would die, and she'd still wander as a spirit.

Like Ki. He had no choice but to walk the earth as a god with no power forever. Claire had a choice.

Mark squeezed her shoulder. "There's no wrong answer to this question, Pumpkin."

"I don't want to answer, though." She rubbed her face. "It doesn't seem fair. No one else gets to choose."

"That depends on how you look at it. A lot of people make choices every day that decide their fate. Go to college or not. Listen to someone or not. Wait for the light to change before crossing the street or not. Your choice just happens to be clearly about life and death."

In other words, Claire thought, shut up and pick one.

Sixteen forever or unfamiliar scars? Floating through walls or touching and being touched? Lying to the world or the pain of flesh?

The moment before she'd turned and run into the church, she'd seen Drew. She knew her choice.

CHAPTER 49

DREW

The moment he arrived with Sophie, Drew knew to keep his mouth shut. Claire stood at the open door of the church and had Iulia talking, revealing things. He sensed she needed to know the at least some of the answers. Sophie took a step to approach Iulia from behind, but Drew held out an arm to stop her.

"God, that music. It's so beautiful." Kay said. "Get closer."

Whatever music Kay meant, Drew couldn't hear it.

Claire met his gaze for a brief moment. She turned and ran inside.

Iulia screamed and braced herself against the doorframe.

"No!" Drew rushed up the stairs. He needed to get through that door.

Enion flashed tiny and darted inside.

Silvery blue flickered into life around Drew's body. Whispers called to him, driving him to the door. He needed to know what they said.

Beyond Iulia, blocking the door, he saw Claire sprawled on the floor between the pews. She didn't move. He needed to reach her.

"She's gone," Kay whispered.

Drew jabbed Iulia's back with his staff. She lost her grip and floated inside.

Kay rushed Drew, shoving him aside and taking control. Too stunned and focused on Claire to resist, Drew landed in a crumpled heap inside his own head.

"Ha! She's gone! This body is *mine*!" Kay turned his back on the church and ran down the steps.

"Kay, we had a deal!" Drew couldn't think. He never expected this.

"I had a deal with *Claire*. She's dead and gone. You do what I want now."

Enion wailed, his tiny voice keening like he had when Claire died the first time.

"We have to stop Iulia," Drew said, desperate to keep Kay from leaving. He didn't believe Claire died again. She couldn't have. Not like this. And if she had, then he didn't think he could get her back this time. Not from a church. Ghosts and souls found their final rest churches, not like a regular death.

"Who cares about Iulia? I don't have to stay around—"

A fir branch slammed into Kay's face. The impact knocked him to the ground. He slid down three steps. Sophie kicked him between the legs.

Drew cringed, grateful he couldn't feel it.

"Don't you dare," Sophie growled. Her blonde hair floated loose, giving her a golden halo.

"Hey, doll," Kay whimpered. He straightened as Drew's body healed. "Let's you and me beat it and find a—"

Sophie kicked his head. "I thought you were nice! But you're just like Iulia. You want something, so you take it. And here I liked you. I actually liked you! I would've tried to help you find a way to stick around on your own."

Kay turned away from her, giving Drew a view inside the church.

Iulia floated toward Claire's body. Her ghost didn't touch the floor. She moved slowly, like she had to swim against a current.

Sophie couldn't fight Kay and Iulia at the same time. Drew didn't know if Iulia needed fighting, but her mist didn't seem to dissipate inside the church. He guessed she had too much power, and someone needed to do something.

Claire's dagger was still in her hand. Every time Claire had tried to stab Iulia, she'd dodged it. Which meant it could probably hurt her. Someone had to get in there and use it against her.

Drew didn't know what would happen to him and Kay inside that church. Did it matter who had control of his body at the time? Did he care? Without Claire, what did he have? The prospect of going through that a second time hurt too much to bear.

"Sophie, throw us into the church!"

"Whoa," Kay said, raising Drew's arms. "Let's not go and do anything crazy."

"Do it, Sophie! Please."

Sophie raised her arms. The trees shivered. Kay rolled to his feet. Branches snared him. Mist rose as Kay tried to escape.

"You can't run from me," Sophie snapped. "We're linked."

Fog clouded Drew's vision. He thought they sailed through the air. Searing agony jolted across him. Shards of broken glass flowed through his veins. Kay hit the wall in the narthex and landed on the floor in a heap. His scream drowned the creaking of the wooden floor under his weight.

"What's going on?" a man shouted.

"That music," Kay whispered.

Drew heard himself screaming. He felt his flesh ripped apart. Mist streamed from his body. Kay bubbled out of his skin like poison drawn from a wound.

Without Kay, Drew couldn't heal. He couldn't crush bugs or move through mist. Drew minus Kay equaled ordinary—someone who couldn't help Claire, couldn't stand by her side and help her fight her battles.

Despite this latest takeover, Kay had grown on him. He'd gotten used to the snark and flapper slang inside his head. Losing Kay hurt more than he expected. They'd become friends, or so he'd thought.

"So beautiful."

Something inside him tore, like Kay had held himself in Drew's body with millions of tiny hooks and the force pulling him ripped them out.

He tasted blood. Warm liquid oozed down his cheeks and dribbled from his nose. His scream faded, and his throat pulsed with a ragged ache.

Kay left him. His voice stopped. He sank into the floor as he drifted toward the altar.

Drew felt empty, shriveled, dead. His body collapsed, leaving him staring at the soles of Claire's boots. Iulia hung above her, color draining from her misty form, and reached for Claire's hand. Beyond them, a man in black held a cross as if he could repel Iulia with it.

Sophie rushed to Drew's side. How long had he screamed? An eon?

"Drew, you need to take from me. We're connected, remember?"

Why would he do that? He couldn't handle losing Claire. Not again. Not in a church, where her spirit would find rest. "Let go," he rasped.

"No!" Sophie touched his cheek with a fingertip. Tears welled in her eyes. "I didn't know. If I'd known, I wouldn't have thrown you. But I didn't know."

"Stop Iulia," he murmured. He couldn't feel his arms or his legs. His heart thumped in his chest, slow and sluggish. Gaze stuck on Claire, he waited to die.

Sobbing, Sophie raised her hand. Drew saw Iulia ripple like a wave passed through her.

Claire surged up and stabbed her dagger into Iulia's chest. She let go of the blade and rolled to her feet.

Iulia gurgled and pawed at the hilt. Pure, blinding white light spilled around the blade. The dagger fell to the floor with a clatter. Moans filled the air as amorphous blobs of misty white spilled from the hole and fell in a glowing rain. Sparkling mist pattered on the floor, sinking into the wood.

Drew blinked. Claire backed toward him. She lived. Whatever had happened, she'd survived it. He reached for Sophie with what power he had left and held on with all his might. For Claire. Sky blue painted the world inside the church.

Sophie gasped while Iulia bled trapped ghosts. Power rushed into Drew. With Sophie's aura patching his own, he found the strength to call upon his link to the node. Portland would demand a payment for that, but he didn't care. Seeing Claire hold out her hand and try to catch the falling motes made up for anything.

Iulia deflated. Her form melted, sinking into the floor with the rest. All their voices faded.

Claire crouched beside Drew with Enion already on her shoulder and clutching her neck with his tiny claws. "We won."

"How?"

She grinned. "The usual way. I died, everyone else kept fighting. Next time we save the world, I'd like to try not dying to accomplish it."

Sophie giggled and wiped her face.

Helping Drew sit up, Claire wrinkled her nose at him. "You're drenched in blood."

He looked down at his jacket and nodded. "I am." By reflex, he paused and waited for Kay to make a joke at his expense. The emptiness reminded him of losing his parents. He slumped. "Kay is gone."

"He deserved something for that stunt," Sophie murmured, "but maybe not death."

Claire looked away, deeper into the church. He had no idea what she thought.

No more witty quips. No more teasing. No more weird slang. No more wisdom, or bad ideas, or knowledge. And no more living under the threat of losing control over his own body to a spirit he never wanted and could do nothing about.

"He's at rest." Claire smiled at him, her eyes showing she understood how conflicted he must feel about it. "And you're free." She wiped the locket hand across his cheek, smearing it with blood. "And also a witch, so don't think for a moment this gets you out of anything. You're coming with me the next time Justin makes me patrol or anything."

"What just happened here?" The priest approached them and offered Drew a white handkerchief. "Should I call an ambulance?"

"No, he's fine." Claire stood while Drew wiped his face.

Relief inside Drew warred with grief and anger, and all kinds of other things. He thought he might explode if he couldn't stop feeling all these things at once.

"Sorry to bring this to your church, Father," Claire said.

The priest looked from her to Drew to Sophie and back to Claire. "What, exactly, was this?"

"A mess I made that we've now cleaned up. C'mon, guys." Claire offered Drew and Sophie each a hand to stand. "We have to get back to the others. They might still be fighting that other ghost."

"I doubt it. Without Iulia, Dwight shouldn't be a match for those guys." Drew stood and braced himself against Claire while waiting for the world to stop spinning. The node didn't heal him, and neither did Sophie. He had to take care with himself. Like any other witch.

"Excuse us, Father," Claire said. "We have to go make sure we saved the whole world and not just part of it."

Drew laughed. He couldn't help it. The two girls helped him leave the church. They stopped on the sidewalk and seemed to wait for something.

"Are you going to take us to Anne's house?" Claire asked.

He shook his head, still too conflicted to figure out what to feel. "Kay is gone."

Claire raised an eyebrow at him. "So? You're still a witch."

"Witches can't do that," Sophie said.

"Can't? Or don't know how to?" Claire took the handkerchief from Drew and lifted his glasses so she could wipe under his eyes. "Drew, you watched Kay do that a thousand times. Try. If you can't, then fine, I'll get some more dragons and we'll fly. But at least try."

Now he knew how to feel—stupid. Doing nothing didn't work for anything, though. He took a deep breath, reached for power, and spun it around them.

Instead of mist, he formed a cocoon around them of sky blue streamers. Surprised something had happened, he thought of Anne's front yard and pulled. The streamers dissipated with them standing in front of the foundation of Anne's house.

He blinked in shock at the concrete slab where Anne's house once stood. Justin sat on the foundation with Anne, his arm draped across her shoulders, her leaning against him. Stace sat beside Anne with her head in her hands. Avery sat on the hood of his car, chatting with Rondy. Tariel and Rhubark stood watch over everyone.

"I did it."

"Yep." Claire kissed the tip of his nose. "Told ya." She waved and nodded for Drew and Sophie to join her as she approached Justin. Avery and Rondy followed her.

Drew hung back and took Sophie's hand. They didn't need to hear her explain what had happened at the church. Not the general idea, anyway. He wanted to know more about Claire's part, but that could wait.

He grinned at the question he could ask Sophie. "Do you want me to take you home?"

She sighed. "My mom threw me out of the house."

"Did she mean it?"

"I don't know. Claire did destroy my window. On Christmas. And she thinks I'm sleeping with you. And she's kind of tetchy about what you are."

Drew scuffed his hiking boot in the ash on the sidewalk. He almost didn't want to offer her a place to stay because he didn't know how to act around her. The three of them probably needed to have a long chat about relationship things. If Sophie had nowhere else to go, though, he couldn't turn her out.

"You can come home with us. Maybe staying away for a day or two will make her realize she shouldn't have said that."

"I don't have any stuff."

"Claire made armor and weapons out of her own blood and memories in her demesne, and you don't think she can come up with ordinary clothes?"

Sophie stared at him for a beat, then she burst into giggles.

Avery left the cluster at the slab and headed toward his car. "As much fun as this has all been, I need to get back to my family. My sons will be overjoyed at the amount of blood on my armor, even if they're disappointed I didn't get myself killed. Merry Christmas, everyone. Try not to cause any more disasters before New Year's."

A chorus of "Merry Christmas" chimed as he climbed into his car and drove away.

Watching Avery go made Drew think of secrets and witches, and where he'd offered to let Sophie stay. "I don't think we want your coven knowing about Claire's demesne."

Sophie covered her mouth. "Oh, goodness. No. They shouldn't hear about that. They're too..." She turned to watch Anne and Stace for a few moments without letting her thoughts show on her face. "Kay was right. They don't believe in me, so I don't believe in me. That coven is full of witches who think I'm useless. Taking up space. A mistake."

"You're not useless or a mistake." Drew wanted to slap Stace for all she'd done. He liked Anne, so he thought he might stick to saying rude things to her. "I think you're amazing, and if they can't see that, maybe it's time to stop letting them look."

After taking a deep breath, Sophie nodded. "Let's do that now." She marched to Anne.

Drew followed her.

As they closed the distance, they heard Justin say, "As long as you have a place to stay, that's what matters right now. We don't have any space for another person where we are."

"Putting you up is the least I can do after this fiasco," Stace said.

"I'm glad that's settled," Claire said.

Sophie approached Anne to stand in front of her. She bit her lip. "This isn't really a great time, I know. I'm doing it anyway." She traced a symbol in the air with her own flickering sky-blue energy. It faded too fast for Drew to get a good look at it. Something on Sophie's side of their connection broke. His power rushed in to fill the injury. Give and take. He could live with that kind of a relationship with Sophie.

"I hereby renounce my claim to membership in the Petal Society coven."

Anne grimaced. "In front of...?" She gestured to include Claire, Justin and Drew.

"Yes," Sophie said. She lifted her chin and crossed her arms. "In front of my friends, who are part of the magical community of Portland."

"Oh sweetie," Anne said with a sigh.

"This'll go over well," Stace muttered.

"You can tell my mom that I'll come back when I'm good and ready, and not one minute before." Sophie turned on her heel and marched to Rondy.

Drew watched her go and had to pretend he had an itch on his cheek to hide his grin. "We can go whenever you want," he told Justin and Claire.

As little as he wished misfortune on Anne, Drew appreciated the way he didn't have to see her house anymore. Too many unpleasant things had happened inside and outside it. With luck, she'd decide to sell the property and he'd never have to come back.

CHAPTER 50

CLAIRE

Claire stood in front of her Christmas tree bedecked with colored lights and tinsel. What her father had said in that between-place made a lot of sense now that she'd had an hour or two to think about it. The moment she'd stabbed Iulia, memories from her youth had flooded her. The church no longer lured her with music or promises of warmth and rest.

Taking someone else's body didn't mean she was alive. It meant she had a body. Only when she'd been forced to choose had she forged an anchor in this flesh. Her flesh. Her blood. No one else had a claim to it, and she finally considered this skin home.

Complete. Claire felt complete.

The tree, on the other hand, needed something. Her mother, she remembered, had four special ornaments, one for each member of the family—a horse, a pie, a heart, and a sword. Dad, Mom, Claire, and Tyler. This tree needed the same thing for a much bigger family.

She crafted a fuzzy white horse with silver hooves for Justin. Drew got a shaggy, brown dog. For Marie and the girls, she made a red heart, a furry unicorn, and a sword with a star at the tip. Grandpa Jack needed an easy chair, and Grandma Tammy got a gingerbread woman with a smile. A golden sword hung for Rondy. Claire didn't know Sophie well yet, so she made a pink sweater for her and figured she could always change it.

She scattered silver dragons across the tree, tossed on a diorama of a stable for Tariel, and added a complex, antler-reminiscent star at the top. The one stick placed on the boughs without a hook to dangle from, she intended for Mutt. In memory of Kay, she tucked a hat with roses beside it.

Though its owner probably wouldn't see it, she hung a black sedan on the tree. She liked uncorrupted Avery. He deserved a second chance, and she hoped his family gave him one.

Drew stepped to her side and slid his arm around her waist. "Looks good. Are you sure you want two Mutts?"

Claire kissed him on the cheek. She noticed a few dried flakes of blood at his hairline. Later, she'd make sure he caught them.

He reached out and touched the hat. "He would've liked that. It's a nice touch." Leaning back and forth, he checked the rest of the tree. "Where's yours?"

She shrugged. "I'm the tree."

"Then shouldn't we hang all the ornaments on you?"

Claire rolled her eyes at him. "Fine. I'll make one for me." She considered Enion, but she'd already made dragons for the dragons so they could see themselves without having to decode metaphors. Her mother had made her a heart, but Claire had picked that for Marie. Her adoptive mom held this whole group together more than Claire ever could.

"I dunno what to make."

Drew took her hand and lifted it so she saw him through the locket face. "Yeah, I can't imagine what anyone would see and think of you.

There's just nothing that comes to mind at all."

She snorted. Then she ran her fingertips over the design. "This is Iulia's mark."

"No, Iulia's mark was a circular version." He covered her hand with his. "This is what happens when someone takes Iulia's legacy and adds love."

Claire chuckled. "That's the cheesiest thing you've ever said."

Drew kissed the back of Claire's hand and grinned at her. "Am I wrong?"

"No." She squeezed his hand. Things had come full circle, in a way. For two millennia or so, the world had a respite from ghosts, and that had ended. Claire, who looked the same as the woman who put the seal into place, had destroyed it. Right or wrong, she'd undone all the work intended to make the world safer and better because the unintended consequences cost too much. In her opinion.

Once things settled more, and people relearned how to handle the new realities, she thought others would agree with her.

"There's something I need to say. To you." She couldn't ever find a good time to bring this up before, and now didn't seem great, but if she kept putting it off, it would never get done. "I shouldn't have beaten you up at Stace's house. I mean, it was partly because I know you can heal. Or could, anyway. Smacking you around didn't seem bad because of that, I mean. But it still was."

Drew smiled with relief. "You lead with your fist a lot more than you used to."

"Yeah." Maybe not choosing between the two worlds had detached her from both a tiny bit.

He kissed her fingers. "I don't heal like that anymore. I'm a normal person now."

"For some definitions of normal, sure." She grinned, but let it fade as soon as the moment passed. "What I'm saying is I'm sorry. There's no excuse for smacking you around, and I won't do it again."

"I love you too."

She leaned her head against his shoulder and stared at the tree. "She's really gone. We beat Iulia. Again."

Drew nodded. "Forever. So is Kay. Tomorrow, we'll wander through the city. Help people who need it. Decide which high school we want for next semester."

Claire didn't want to do one of those things, but it needed to get done. Otherwise, someone else would pick a school for them. Maybe Justin would choose a good one, or maybe he'd pick one where they already had rough memories.

She glanced behind them and saw the family. The fake sunlight glowing overhead felt lazy and indulgent, like a summer evening. Marie, Tammy, and Rondy fussed in the kitchen, preparing a Christmas dinner from what they had. Justin sat with Jack, talking and watching Sophie teach Missy and Lisa how to weave long blades of grass into bracelets. Mutt and Corwin lay on the ground together.

The dragons, she knew, frolicked in the nearby stream. None of her connections to anyone had broken, and her demesne remained. What did it all mean? That she had access to strange and unexpected things because of Iulia's blood, probably. She knew she wasn't a ghost anymore.

Raising one hand so Drew didn't have to let go, Claire picked a spot in the center of the tree and crafted a red-gold heart with whorls and dots, just like the one in her hand.

"Perfect," Drew said.

Though she wanted to kiss him, Claire erred on the side of everyone watching. Which brought another subject to mind. "What do you want to do about Sophie?"

"Do about her?"

"Yes. How should we cook your bacon?"

He laughed. "I don't know." Glancing at Sophie, he shrugged. "I think the three of us should sit down and have a really serious talk."

"That's fair. I like her, and I trust you, so we should be fine." Claire rubbed her nose against his. They'd come up with something. Together. As a family.

Speaking of family, she had something she needed to do, and like the apology, she knew she'd put it off again and again if she didn't just get it done. They had time.

"Can you take me someplace before dinner?"

"Anywhere you want."

Half an hour later, Claire and Drew walked into the small nursing home across the street from St. Francis, its location making Claire wonder if anything happened by coincidence.

The smell of impending death clung to the inside. At the entrance, Claire considered turning back and leaving this for later. Drew had put a lot of effort into finding it so fast, though. She plunged onward, asking the staff for directions until she found a small, barren room with an ancient, shriveled woman on the hospital-style bed, staring out the window at the darkness.

"Excuse me." Claire thought she had a vague, nightmarish memory of visiting this place as a small child. Maybe her parents had decided she couldn't handle it after that and never brought her back.

The woman turned her head and smiled. She suddenly seemed

twenty years younger, like she could get up and dance. "Hello, dear." Her voice crinkled like dry parchment.

"Virginia Terdan?" Claire took a few steps closer, leaving Drew in the doorway, and noticed the woman had only stubs for legs, maybe cut off at mid-thigh. One arm didn't have a hand. Her spotted skin seemed waxy and loose. All the anger she'd felt about this woman abandoning her evaporated. Virginia couldn't even take care of herself, let alone a little girl.

"Yes, though everyone calls me Ginny. And who are you?" She squinted at Claire. "My eyes aren't so good these days."

"Your granddaughter, Claire." She reached Ginny's side and smiled at her. "Mark was my dad."

"Oh!" Ginny's smile brightened even more. She moved her hand with a slight tremor and covered her mouth. "I thought you died in the fire. That's what they told me."

"No, I was at a friend's house that night. A sleepover." They'd both been adrift. Claire didn't know what to feel, but it brought tears to her eyes. "I didn't know you were here or I would've come sooner."

"Look at you, all grown up." She reached for Claire.

Claire took her hand. It felt thin, fragile, and weak. "I'm sixteen. A junior in high school. I found a family that adopted me, and they're good people."

"And who's that?" Ginny nodded to the doorway.

"My boyfriend, Drew."

Drew shuffled into the room and clasped her hand. "Pleased to meet you, ma'am."

She flicked her gaze up and down his body. "You both smell like magic. Did you know your grandfather was a Spirit Knight?"

Claire grinned. "No, but I know my dad was, so I'm not surprised.

Did we have any witches in the family?"

Ginny's eyes sparkled with mischief. "Let me tell you a story about my sisters," she said.

An hour later, with Ginny lively and telling incredible stories about the magical community in Portland of the 1960s and 70s, Drew nudged Claire.

"We really need to get home."

She wanted to stay and listen forever. "Oh. Right. Christmas dinner. I'll come back," she promised Ginny. "I know where you are now."

Ginny nodded like her whole day had brightened. "This has been the most unexpected Christmas present imaginable."

"Merry Christmas, Grandma Ginny." Claire stood and took Drew's hand.

He didn't bother waiting until they left the facility. In the middle of Ginny's room, Drew spun sky blue streamers in a cocoon. Ginny gasped with delight.

"There you are!" Grandma Tammy said. "Dinner's been ready for fifteen minutes, but we can hardly eat without the lady of the house. Come on."

They followed Tammy to the dinner table piled with food. Grandpa Jack sat at one end. Corwin took the other. Claire claimed a seat between Justin and Drew, across from Sophie. She breathed in the smell of ham, butter, and potatoes, not caring it had all come from boxes and cans. Missy stood on her chair until Claire made her booster seat. Though he couldn't eat, Rondy sat beside Corwin, with Mutt at his heel. Dragons in their tiny forms landed on the table and swarmed the vegetables.

"This Christmas," Grandpa Jack said as he stood and raised a glass, "we're grateful for something we usually take for granted. Our lives.

Without Claire having this incredible place I still don't really understand, and without Justin and his quick action, most of us would probably be dead." He nodded to them both. "Until we came here, I never really did understand how dire that job you do can be."

Claire's smile dimmed with a wish that she could have saved the whole city, and all the little towns between it and the mountain. She wished she'd looked inside the box, or somehow gotten Loowit to explain things, or convinced Ki to give her a different quest. Anything to have stopped the disaster that destroyed everything.

Like Drew said, they'd go out tomorrow. For him, the task meant being a decent person. She hoped her next journey would help her find atonement.

"Is Grandpa done talking yet?" Missy whispered, loud enough for everyone to hear.

Chuckles ran up and down the table.

Compared to her last Christmas, this one seemed like heaven. Claire wanted to express that somehow, so she raised her hand to get Grandpa Jack's attention. He nodded to her.

"I have a few things to say. I'll keep it short, Missy." As she stood, a blush flared on the little girl's cheeks. "A lot of crazy things have happened since I met Justin." For some reason, she wanted to gush about all of it.

The desire to be normal had disappeared. She wanted to talk about it all until her voice went hoarse.

Missy and Lisa, though, wouldn't understand any of it, and might get upset. Tonight, after the girls went to bed, she'd tell the adults about dying and being a ghost, about Iulia and her body, and about all the bindings between all of them. They deserved to know.

"The point is, I'm really grateful that you all took Drew and me in.

And I want to welcome Rondy to the family. He sacrificed too much to be here. And Sophie, who's smarter, braver, and more capable than anyone gives her credit for."

Rondy smiled. Sophie blushed.

Corwin tapped an antler point against a glass. "To family. May we ever be blessed with more love around our table than we expect." Claire could drink to that. Water. She could drink water to that. Clinking her glass against all those around her, she smiled and reveled in a sense of belonging she hadn't felt for a long time.

As she plopped mashed potatoes on her plate, Drew leaned close and murmured, "What happened inside that church?"

"I decided I wanted to live." The answer seemed at once flippant and grave. It felt right, though. True. "I'm not sure what I met, whether it was my dad or not. He told me I had to choose, so I did. I've got too much stuff left to do. Besides, us Knights are notoriously bad at giving up."

Drew chuckled and passed her the beans. "I hadn't noticed."

She kissed his cheek and knew they'd be fine. Portland needed them more than ever, but they'd pay attention and meet the challenges. With this much family by her side, this many people watching her back, she didn't fear anything anymore.

Other Books by Lee French

Spirit Knights

Girls Can't Be Knights

Backyard Dragons

Ethereal Entanglements

Ghost Is the New Normal

Boys Can't Be Witches

Maze Beset trilogy

Dragons In Pieces

Dragons In Chains

Dragons In Flight

Superheroes in Denim (compilation)

Fantasy in the Ilauris setting

Damsel In Distress

Shadow & Spice (short story)

Al-Kabar

Warden of Myveshar (coming Winter 2018)

WWW.AUTHORLEEFRENCH.COM

The Greatest Sin
(with Erik Kort)

The Fallen

Harbinger

Moon Shades

Illusive Echoes

A Curse of Memories

Darkside Seattle

Street Doc

Fixer

Mechanic

Hacker (coming Winter 2018)

Anthology Appearances
Into the Woods: a fantasy anthology

Merely This and Nothing More: Poe Goes Punk

Unnatural Dragons: a science fiction anthology

Artifact

What We've Unlearned: English Class Goes Punk

Hideous Progeny: Horror Goes Punk

Bridges (as editor)

Carnival (coming Fall 2018)

WWW.AUTHORLEEFRENCH.COM

ABOUT THE AUTHOR

Lee French lives in Olympia, WA, with two kids, two bicycles, and too much stuff. She is an avid gamer and a member of the Myth-Weavers online RPG community. In addition to spending too much time there, she also trains in taekwando, keeps a nice flower garden with one dragon and absolutely no lawn gnomes, works an excessive number of book events, and tries in vain every year to grow vegetables that don't get devoured by neighborhood wildlife.

She is an active member of the Science Fiction and Fantasy Writers of America and the Northwest Independent Writers Association, as well as serving the Olympia region as a NaNoWriMo Municipal Liaison.